UNDER the ANDES

The Adventure Has Begun

I expected I know not what result from Harry's hysterical rashness: confusion, pandemonium, instant death; but none of these followed.

I had reached his side and stood by him at the edge of the lake, where he had halted. Desiree Le Mire stopped short in the midst of the mad sweep of the Dance of the Sun.

For ten silent, tense seconds she looked down at us from the top of the lofty column, bending dangerously near its edge. Her form straightened and was stretched to its fullest height; her white, superb body was distinctly outlined against the black background of the upper cavern. Then she stepped backward slowly, without taking her eyes from us.

Suddenly as we gazed she appeared to sink within the column itself and in another instant disappeared from view.

We stood motionless, petrified; how long I know not. Then I turned and faced our own danger . . .

UNDER the ANDES
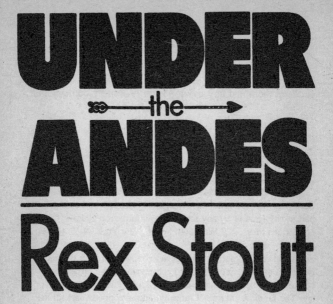

Rex Stout

PENZLER BOOKS · NEW YORK

A Division of Mysterious Press

PENZLER BOOKS EDITION

Under the Andes originally appeared in *The All-Story Magazine*, February 1914.

Penzler Books is a division of Mysterious Press.

Mysterious Press books are published in association with Warner Books, Inc.
666 Fifth Avenue
New York, N.Y. 10103

A Warner Communications Company

Printed in the United States of America

Originally published in hardcover by Penzler Books.
First Penzler Books Paperback Printing: November, 1986

10 9 8 7 6 5 4 3 2 1

INTRODUCTION

John McAleer

Rex Stout's writing career did not begin, as is commonly supposed, in 1929, with the publication of *How Like a God*. It began seventeen years earlier (in October 1912) when he published the short story "Excess Baggage" in *Short Stories* magazine. Rex was so elated at receiving a check for twenty-five dollars for this effort that he immediately wrote another six stories and submitted them to as many magazines. None was rejected. Knowing then that he had the potential to succeed as a writer, he set to work in earnest and, over the next four years, wrote two dozen additional short stories and four novels. These appeared in popular magazines of the day—*Lippincott's*, *Smart Set*, *Smith's Magazine*, *Black Cat*, *Short Stories*, and, most especially, *All-Story*, which bought the bulk of his output, including all four novels, *Her Forbidden Knight*, *A Prize for Princes*, *The Great Legend*, and that story which Sam Moskowitz, the ranking authority on scientific romances, says is "considered by the serious collector of old science fiction to be the best of his early work," a lost race novel, *Under the Andes*. Frank Munsey, the supreme potentate of the pulps, paid an unexpected compliment to *Under the Andes*. He published it, in its entirety—one hundred and thirty-nine pages—in *All-Story* (February 1914, XXVIII:2). Since Rex had conscientiously met the requirements of pulp publication and had produced chapter after chapter with cliff-hanger endings, there was no strategic advantage in publishing the entire story at one time. Apparently, it was adjudged too good to dismember.

By this time, Rex had become a favorite of Robert Hobart Davis, fiction editor of the Munsey publications and one of the great fiction editors of all time. Among those whom Davis nurtured were O. Henry, Irvin S. Cobb, Fannie Hurst, Damon Runyon, Faith Baldwin, and Mary Roberts Rinehart. And now, simultaneously, he was coaxing along the careers of Rex Stout and another young writer whose first novel also was published in October 1912—in *All-Story*. The writer was Edgar Rice Burroughs. The novel was *Tarzan of the Apes*. Rex did not think of Burroughs as a great writer, then or later, but he recognized that Burroughs had created, in Tarzan, a charismatic figure, a character with universal appeal. This, he saw, was a major achievement which eluded all but a handful of writers, and he longed for the day when his own creative imagination would call such a character into existence. Could it be that Nero Wolfe's jungle orchids are a vestige of his creator's early admiration for Tarzan? Better that than that the gargantuan Wolfe should be asked to swing through the treetops on vines.

With his pen, Rex could create millionaires like Paul Lamar, protagonist of *Under the Andes*, whose riches enable him to pursue his fancies without stint. But, at thirty, Rex himself never had experienced that kind of security. Quite otherwise, there were days when he lacked the money to pick up his clean shirts at the local laundry. After four years of concentrated effort he had attained some mastery over the craft of fiction. He could pursue a strong story line without overwhelming it with detail. He could write passable dialogue. He could individuate a character when it was someone he cared enough about. But the readers of the pulps were not looking for masterpieces, and even if they were, the circumstances of his life were such that he was not driven to write one. Paid at the rate of two and a half cents a word, he saw himself as nothing more than "a goddamn fiction factory." That fact so disgusted him that he racked up his quill, founded a school banking system, and set to work to earn the money he needed to address himself seriously to his art. Then, and only then, would he be able to make an important statement about life. It took him ten years to arrive at equivalency with Paul Lamar and another seven to gain equivalency with Burroughs by creating a character with universal appeal, but he did what he set out to do and then some. Tarzan, after all, is at most a nobleman of nature, both outwardly and inwardly simple, whereas Nero Wolfe is, in the words of Jacques Barzun, "a portrait of the Educated Man." But that is not all. Wolfe has at his side the inestimable Archie, who is, Barzun tells us, "one of the folk heroes in which the modern American temper can see itself transfigured." Both partake of the vitality of their creator. Small wonder that Philip José Farmer, in *Tarzan Alive* (1972), claimed that Tarzan's grandfather was the brother of Nero Wolfe's grandmother. Tarzan should be so lucky.

Under the Andes, a "scientific romance," is not only Rex Stout's one excursion into the lost race subgenre, it is, with the sole exception of "Pamfret and Peace," a short story published in 1913, in which a devil visits the world of the future (the year 1970!), his only experiment with fantasy fiction of any kind. Science fiction was repugnant to him. "The characters aren't real people," he complained. He would neither write it nor read it. Yet it was Rex's nature to do his conscientious best by anything that he attempted. "Peddling the preposterous in fiction," he concluded, "is by no means paltry per se. It depends on whether the reader feels himself gagging or whether he swallows it with pleasure." Having made his commitment to contribute to the lost race subgenre, Rex Stout held to his customary standards. The end result was a book that could be read with contentment and delight even by readers who, by long exposure to the subgenre, brought to the experience exacting standards and discriminating judgment. It must, therefore, come as no surprise to us that in 1972, in *Under the Moons of Mars*, Sam Moskowitz acclaimed *Under the Andes* as a novel that is "extraordinarily vigorous and well-written."

The question now most naturally arises, how did it happen that a splendid lost race novel, unstintingly crafted by a novelist whose subsequent efforts would earn him international respect and acclaim, remained all but forgotten for seventy years? Several things, none sufficient in itself but adequate if taken in aggregate, account for this neglect. In the first place, the copyright to *Under the Andes* did not belong to Rex Stout but to Frank Munsey and his successors. Rex could not expect to profit financially from its republication, of course, but even that fact would not have been crucial to him. He welcomed the income his writing brought him but was not avaricious. What mattered to him was not disappointing the expectations of his readers. To him everything he wrote between 1912 and 1916 was apprentice work. By the time he resumed writing again, after the seventeen year hiatus, he had, under the influence of Joseph Conrad (whose houseguest he had been in 1922), elevated his standards. He never reread what he had written earlier. Indeed, he kept no copies of the magazines in which his early work appeared or a record of what he had written and published then. He probably supposed it was uniformly wretched and best forgotten. It would have dismayed him to think that a readership loyal to Nero Wolfe and Archie Goodwin would, in anticipation of encountering more of the same, buy a book of his which would instead lure them into New York's Tenderloin district, as in *Her Forbidden Knight*; bear them off to the Trojan wars, as in *The Great Legend*; plunge them into Balkan intrigue (though this would bring them closer to the world from which Nero Wolfe emerged), as in *A Prize for Princes*; or sweep them into a fantastic confrontation with misshapen trolls in subterranean caverns in the Andes, as in *Under the Andes*. Rex Stout was not lacking in self-esteem but he was too reasonable to think he had such a hold on his readers that they would find value in everything he had written.

In the second place, those who did control the copyrights for Rex Stout's early works had, as well, the copyrights for thousands of other pieces of fiction. Moreover, in most instances they themselves lacked copies of the magazines in which this material appeared and, accordingly, had no way of assessing its merit and, therefore, of determining whether or not a market for it existed. Those few libraries that did have copies were reluctant to copy them. The pulp paper was fragile and fragmenting and even ordinary handling accelerated this process. I myself negotiated for six months with the Library of Congress in an unsuccessful attempt to get xerographic copies of the early stories for which I had gathered the pertinent bibliographical data. No matter that I specified the journal, the issue, the title, the pages. Even a personal appeal from Rex himself, on my behalf, availed nothing. As a further complication, two of the early stories had been written under a pen name, Evans Day. What claim could Rex Stout possibly have on these stories, I was asked. Why, they were the work of Evans Day. No point in insisting that Evans Day and Rex Stout were one and the same person. I was told, in terms that admitted no appeal, that the magazines I wanted were so imperiled by age that they had been removed from the shelves and stored away for safe-keeping. If I visited the Library of Congress in person I would not be allowed to examine them even if I had an eidetic memory and could mentally photograph them at a glance. Did the Library have plans to copy these stories before they were reduced to dust? No, it did not. It seemed as though Rex Stout's subterranean trolls were once again back in their caverns, buried from the sight of humanity, only these caverns were in Washington, D.C. and being maintained by the tax dollars of American citizens.

When I was sure all other avenues were closed to me, I reluctantly played my ace. My wife is a cousin of Thomas P. "Tip" O'Neill, Jr., Speaker of the House of Representatives.

I asked Tip to intervene. Before the week was out I had a call from the Librarian of Congress himself. I felt as awed as Archie Goodwin felt when "the big fish," J. Edgar Hoover, showed up on Wolfe's doorstep. But, unlike Wolfe, I was not scornful. "Congressman O'Neill," the caller informed me, "has always been very solicitous of the needs of the Library of Congress. Moreover, he has never before asked the Library for any favors. He is asking now for permission for you to receive copies of the material you need. Permission is granted."

I would have to pay the usual fee of twenty-five cents a page, of course, and, since several hundred pages would be copied for me, including *Under the Andes*, this was going to be a hefty investment. But I never doubted for a moment that it was worth it. I agreed at once and the Library acted so speedily to accommodate the wishes of Speaker O'Neill that I had the feeling that the xerographic copies were delivered to my house by special courier borne to Massachusetts, at supersonic speed, in a government jet. And Rex thought he had explored the outer reaches of the fantastic when he wrote *Under the Andes*! Little did he realize, in 1913, the adventures that lay ahead for the text itself in the world of the future.

To say that *Under the Andes* recounts the macabre adventures of three travelers—two American brothers, Paul and Harry Lamar, and a gorgeous international adventuress, Desirée Le Mire—who visit a lost world populated by troll-like descendants of Inca who went underground in the sixteenth century to escape Spanish tormentors, and to let matters rest there, is, of course, to be tantalizingly vague not only to the curious reader but to the inquiring investigator of novels belonging to the lost race subgenre. What were Stout's literary antecedents, he would like to know, and did he really know anything about the civilization of the Inca? Or did he recklessly and indiscriminately improvise, snatching his tale out of thin air?

We have a good idea of what Rex's literary sources were.

To begin with, simple men, uninstructed in the ways of science, had long subscribed to the belief that a mysterious race of men dwelt in the interior of the earth. That these subterranean people were dark, stunted, misshapen, and ugly was an assumption that logically followed. After all, shut away from sunlight and fresh air how could they be otherwise? In boyhood Rex made the acquaintance of George MacDonald's goblins in *The Princess and the Goblins*. In young manhood he was introduced to L. Frank Baum's Nome king and his hideous tribe. But his immediate source for his degenerate race of subhumans was obviously the race of Morlocks depicted in H.G. Wells's *Time Machine*, a tale which, as an avid reader of Wells, he knew well.

If Rex's memory of the Morlocks had at all dimmed it was undoubtedly refreshed by George Allan England's *Darkness and Dawn* which was published in another Munsey publication (later merged with *All-Story*), *Cavalier*, in 1912. George England had annexed Wells's creatures without shame.

Other lost race novels which Rex read, admired, and was influenced by were Sir Henry Rider Haggard's *King Solomon's Mines* (1885), Jules Verne's *Journey to the Center of the Earth* (1864), Arthur Conan Doyle's *The Lost World* (1912), and Ludwig Lewisohn's *Cave of the Glittering Lamps*, published in *All-Story* in 1911. The latter is an obvious source and may have been recommended to him as a possible model by Bob Davis, if, as is probable, Davis commissioned Rex to write a lost race novel, a type of tale popular with Munsey readers. Certainly, given Rex's temperament and his fine, analytical mind, he would not have been disposed, by natural inclination, to realize himself by writing stories in this subgenre. Indeed, he sought to circumvent that difficulty by introducing a core of sanity into his fantastic tale—the drama of Passion and Reason contending for dominance. With Paul Lamar as his persona, he aligned himself with Reason. Incidentally, while Rex did not know Ludwig Lewisohn when he scrutinized

Cave of the Glittering Lamps for helpful insights, the two men later, in Paris, became close friends, and there Lewisohn was the audience on which he tried out *How Like a God* as the pages came from his typewriter.

Sixty years after *Under the Andes* was published, Rex Stout liked to remember that, soon after its appearance, he had received a three page letter from a professor of anthropology at Rutgers University commending him for his knowledge of the Inca. Rex found this flattering since it was his recollection that he had read nothing on the subject. Since the Incas had an intricate and sophisticated civilization, Rex would have been justified in saying that knowledge of that civilization was a closed book to him. But much of that history was a closed book even to the Rutgers anthropologist because the thoroughness of the Spanish conquest obscured the records. What survives is inextricably blended with mythology.

We do know that the Inca empire at its height covered a region 2,000 miles long and 500 miles wide, some 350,000 square miles of territory in all. It was centered in present day Peru but extended into what is now Colombia, Ecuador, Chile, Argentina, and Bolivia. Inca civilization emerged about 1200 A.D. and, by the sixteenth century, held dominance over ten million people. The Incas used twenty foot stones in their masonry and laid out more than 1,100 miles of roads, some of these cut through solid rock. With woven osiers they built long suspension bridges over rivers. Their pottery was superb. Few secrets of today's textile industry were unknown to them. The government they evolved was a form of welfare state. Poverty among them was non-existent, but initiative was discouraged. Except for temple virgins, marriage was obligatory. Although they were sun worshippers, they acknowledged a great Creative god. He was, however, little worshipped. Unlike the Maya and Aztecs, they rarely engaged in human sacrifices. Anthropologists tell us also that the Inca had an unusual anatomical distinction, a bone in the back of their skulls that did not fuse with other bones as it did in men elsewhere. Rex Stout uses none of this information in *Under the Andes*. It would be presumptuous, however, to say he was unaware of it. Since it was no more pertinent to the lifestyle of the degenerate trolls he wrote about than the glory of Zenobia's Palmyra is to the straggling desert bands who today roam the sterile wastes where Palmyra once stood, to use it would have been gratuitous.

But Rex Stout did have accurate information about the Inca of which he made effective use. He spoke of his Inca as being the descendants of Manco-capac. Manco, indeed, was the first high priest of the Inca tribal god. Rex knew that the last Inca king was Atahualpa, imprisoned and murdered by the Spaniards in 1533. He knew of their great leader, Pacha-camac (1438-1471), the foremost man produced by aboriginal civilization in the Americas. His genius built the Inca empire. Rex knew of the enmity between the Inca and Hernando Pizarro, brother of the conqueror, Francisco Pizarro. Rex knew the Inca had been sun worshippers and took full advantage of the irony that found them, in the twentieth century, living in an environment where, for four hundred years, they never beheld the sun. He knew that Huanacauri was one of the most sacred spots in Peru. He showed detailed knowledge of the frame of quipu, the intricate system of knotted multi-colored cords—a rudimentary written language—through which the Inca sent messages and recorded transactions. If he choose to allow the Lamars to fear the prospect of being eaten by the Inca that is not to say that he was unaware that they did not practice cannibalism. After four hundred years of regressing who was to say that their descendants had not become cannibals? Besides, to raise that prospect was to raise the level of excitement, surely the storyteller's prerogative. Most intriguingly, Rex Stout obviously made a study of Inca mythology that was intimate enough to have enabled him to discover that the Inca believed their ancestors originally had emerged from certain caverns in the earth, in the hill of Tampu-tocco, at Poccari-tampu. How exquisitely ironic it is, therefore, that this lofty culture, which began with men who emerged from underground, vanishes when its members, put to rout by Spanish avarice, disappear back into the earth. Like James Fenimore Cooper's dystopian novel, *The Crater* (1847), *Under the Andes* can be read as a cautionary tale: This Inca world a microcosm depicting the destiny that awaits our civilization unless man establishes a relation with the universe based on reason and commonsense, the theme that would become Rex Stout's great, underlying concern in the Nero Wolfe saga.

In 1949, in "Grim Fairy Tales," Rex Stout wrote: "We enjoy reading about people who love and hate and covet—about gluttons and martyrs, misers and sadists, whores and saints, brave men and cowards. But also, demonstrably, we enjoy reading about a man who gloriously acts and decides, with no exception and no compunction, not as his emotions brutally command, but as his reason instructs." In *Under the Andes* Paul Lamar is that "man who gloriously acts and decides." But much of the time, Desirée Le Mire, the exotic dancer and international adventuress—"an entrancing mixture of Cleopatra, Sappho, Helen of Troy, and the devil"—a woman with a whim of iron, usurps his place in the spotlight. Desirée recalls many such women in history, as, for example, Adah Isaacs Menken (1835-1868), who, in 1863 was paid $100,000 in silver to dance, in flesh-colored tights, before an admiring throng of miners in Virginia City, Nevada. But Rex himself acknowledges that the woman he had primarily in mind when he wrote of Desirée, was Lola Montez (1818-1861), the Irish-born adventuress who danced her way into the hearts of men on four continents. In 1846 King Ludwig I of Bavaria became infatuated with Lola (*nee* Marie Gilbert), made her his mistress, and created her Countess of Landsfield. Soon Lola was the effective ruler of Bavaria and Ludwig was forced to abdicate. After four marriages, Lola spent her last days in New York, engaged in rescue work among women. This perhaps was fitting since, in the course of her busy lifetime, she had given employment to many, rescuing men from her. This sort of femme fatale intrigued Rex Stout. In a subsequent novel, *A Prize for Princes*, she turns up again, as Aline Solini who, anticipating the wiles of the wife of Nero Wolfe, tries to poison her Balkan spouse. Desirée does not go the poison route with Paul but, thwarted when he vanquishes passion with reason, does come within an ace of signing his death warrant. There may also be in Desirée a little of the Balzacian heroine who crossed the Andes disguised as a Spanish officer, dispensing deeds of derring-do en route.

At thirty-two, Paul Lamar is nearly the same age as Archie Goodwin, but he is sententious rather than witty, arrogant rather than ebullient, and lacks Archie's sense of fun. Like Rex Stout he has an analytical mind and is, as was Rex, an adept at chess. He is almost as well read as Nero Wolfe and nearly as woman-proof. "No woman," he says, with a straight face, "can possibly be amusing for more than a month at a time." This line alone causes us to wonder if, even after a seventy year delay, the world is ready for *Under the Andes* as a bound volume. If this passage is silently excised by some concerned editor before the book goes into print, I shall not be surprised.

Even while battling reeking monster fish and hordes of hirsute, spear-wielding trolls, Paul Lamar manages to make many apposite allusions to the works of Fielding, Cervantes, Byron, Balzac, Congreve, Voltaire, Kipling, and Aristotle, and to invoke, at appropriate times, the names of Amadis of Gaul, Francesco Colonna, and Albert Savarus. Harry, of course, who is the blind slave of passion, seems never to have read a book at all. He is the epitome of the man whose intellect is debauched by carnal desires. That fact provided Rex Stout with an added spot of fun at the close of the novel when he leaves the reader to wonder if Paul is quite as sane as he thinks he is, and Harry as imprudent as Paul believes him to be. Has the man of intellect, after all, by scrutinizing life in its every phase, cut himself off from the joys of existence?

The reader who expects to encounter, sooner or later, scenes of torrid passion in the caverns of the Inca will be disappointed in these expectations. Desirée, we are assured, has been the mistress of many men. We can infer that she sleeps with Harry Lamar since they travel across the United States and down into South America as husband and wife. We can even surmise that the Inca king who, if he is following the tradition of his forebears, has several wives, finds her an object of sexual desire, but details are not supplied. Rex Stout was writing a story in which Reason, not Passion, wins out. He believed that sex was acceptable in a story if it was essential to the story. He did not find it essential here. That was fortunate. The conventions of the day were against it and the Munsey readership would not have expected it.

A superficial reading suggests that *Under the Andes* belongs to the "slaughter-house school" of fiction, much in fashion in the era in which the novel was written. The dialogue between Reason and Passion which goes on throughout the book argues to the contrary, however. Let it be remarked, also, that Rex Stout showed true restraint in keeping within the conventions of the subgenre—the rapid pace of narration, the action scenes, the cliffhanger endings, all would have been expected by his readers and he never disappointed their anticipations. Paul Lamar himself remarks that the true artist "bows to his materials." In his own capacity to make such adjustments, by ostensibly adhering to the rules which governed the production of a lost race novel, Rex Stout already was exercising a talent that would see him utilizing later, to its full potential, the strictly defined terms by which Nero Wolfe, from the moment of his first appearance in *Fer-de-Lance*, governed the conduct of his life. While Rex, for the amusement of his sisters, does slip into his narrative a hypnotic, prehistoric reptile which evokes the image of their favorite stage personality, the popular hypnotist, Pauline, he shows exemplary restraint when he mentions Pike's Peak, in not pointing out that Zebulon Pike, who discovered Pike's Peak, was his kinsman, and yet greater restraint when, in describing Paul Lamar's seagoing yacht, he refrains from comparing it to a ship of comparable size, the presidential yacht *Mayflower* on which he had served for two years, during Theodore Roosevelt's presidency, as pay yeoman. The temptation to indulge in a long digression must have been enormous but Rex did not yield an inch. On the other hand, one unintentional bit of hilarity comes into the book when Desirée Le Mire, visiting the wilds of Colorado, enters what must have been little more than a glorified chuckwagon and grandly orders one of the favorite dishes of the future Nero Wolfe (the opening recipe, in fact, in the *Nero Wolfe Cookbook*), eggs *au beurre noir*. The short order cook cuts her down with one word—"Fried!"

Rex Stout's recollection was that he was paid $1,800 by *All-Story* for *Under the Andes*. Recently, though, two checks written by the Frank A. Munsey Company have come to light. The first, dated September 10, 1913, is for $320. On the back of the check the following statement appears: "By endorsement of this check the payee acknowledges payment in full for the following: one story entitled *Under the Andes* which the payee has sold with warranty of authorship and ownership, and with authority to copyright and all other rights whatsoever therein." This check was cashed on September 12, endorsed by Rex and, beneath his name, by his sister Ruth I[mogene]. Stout. That is not the whole story. On October 1, 1913, Rex received a further check from the Munsey Company, this one for $618. The same statement appears on the back of the check with this difference—instead of being described as "one story," *Under the Andes* is now described as "one serial." And after the title appears the parenthetical statement "additional payment." This check, endorsed by Rex and, once again, by Ruth, was cashed on October 3. If further payments were made, the checks have not reappeared. Why Ruth Stout cashed the checks is not known. Since at that time Rex and Ruth maintained a home for their parents and themselves, money may have been needed for household expenses. Incidentally, the actual writing of *Under the Andes* seems to have preceded payment by some months. A reporter who interviewed Rex in the spring of 1913, told *Topeka Daily Capital* readers on May 4, "At present he [Rex Stout] is at work upon a sixty thousand word serial, which is almost completed and has already been accepted by a New York magazine."

As matters developed, greater things were to come from *Under the Andes* than mere monetary recompense. Late in June, 1914, Bob Davis summoned Edgar Rice Burroughs to New York from Chicago, to discuss with him his future contributions to *All-Story*. At the Brevoort, Davis tactfully met over dinner with both Edgar and Rex. Burroughs latest production was a novel called *The Inner World* which was about Pellucidar, an underground world of his own devising. Originally it had been shorter, but at Davis's behest, Burroughs had expanded it, a fact which disposes us to believe that *Under the Andes* underwent a like metamorphosis for the same reason. That would account for the second check. *The Inner World*, inflated, now was about to appear in *All-Story* under the title by which it is still remembered—*At the Earth's Core*. In Rex's presence Davis urged Burrough's to follow up the book with a sequel. Burroughs met the offer warily. He commended the vitality of *Under the Andes* and congratulated Rex on his assured style. Sensing the exploratory implications of Burroughs remarks, Rex disclaimed all further ambitions to contribute to the lost race subgenre. It was, he indicated, about as likely that he would write a follow up to *Under the Andes* as it was that he would write a novel about a jungle ape man. This possible obstacle removed from his path, Burroughs needed only the news that *At the Earth's Core* had been responded to favorably by Munsey readers to produce a sequel. Over the years five more Pellucidar novels followed, the final one not appearing until 1963, thirteen years after the book of life had closed for Burroughs himself. That same year, Rex Stout, still vigorously writing at seventy-seven—having put some fifty years between himself and the lost race subgenre—published his twenty-sixth Nero Wolfe novel, *The Mother Hunt*, which concerns itself with nothing more preposterous than a few curious, handwoven, white horsehair buttons. Rex was having too much fun being ratiocinative to write otherwise.

In 1925, Britain's Henry Carew paid Rex Stout the compliment of further emulation. His novel, *The Vampire of the Andes*, recounted the desperate trials and struggles of Will Wootton who—you guessed it—visits an underground Inca civilization where men have been living for four hundred years. Thus *Under the Andes* had a sequel after all. When Rex learned of this a strong feeling welled up in his bosom—gratitude that he did not have to write it.

At the close of *Under the Andes* Harry Lamar threatens to make trouble if his brother Paul publishes an account of their adventures. Maybe that amounted to a curse and explains why *Under the Andes* has been out of print for seventy years. If so, we are pleased to report that the curse has been lifted. Read and enjoy, and may the road of your slumbers be troll-free.

John McAleer
Mount Independence
Lexington, Massachusetts
25 November 1984

UNDER THE ANDES

Chapter I.

THE SWEETHEART OF A KING.

The scene was not exactly new to me. Moved by the spirit of adventure, or by an access of *ennui* which overtakes me at times, I had several times visited the gaudy establishment of Mercer, on the fashionable side of Fifth Avenue in the Fifties. In either case I had found disappointment; where the stake is a matter of indifference there can be no excitement; and besides, I had been always in luck.

But on this occasion I had a real purpose before me, though not an important one, and I surrendered my hat and coat to the servant at the door with a feeling of satisfaction.

At the entrance to the main room I met Bob Garforth, leaving. There was a scowl on his face and his hand trembled as he held it forth to take mine.

"Harry is inside. What a rotten hole," said he, and passed on. I smiled at his remark—it was being whispered about that Garforth had lost a quarter of a million at Mercer's within the month—and passed inside.

Gaudy, I have said it was, and it needs no other word. Not in its elements, but in their arrangement.

The rugs and pictures and hangings testified to the taste of the man who had selected them; but they were abominably disposed, and there were too many of them.

The room, which was unusually large, held two or three leather divans, an English buffet, and many easy chairs. A smoking-table, covered, stood in one corner.

Groups of men were gathered about each of the three roulette wheels ranged along the farther side. Through a door to the left could be seen the poker tables, surrounded by grave or jocular faces. Above the low buzz of conversation there sounded the continual droning voices of the croupiers as they called the winning numbers, and an occasional exclamation from a "customer."

I made my way to the center wheel and stood at the rear of the crowd sursounding it.

The ball rolled; there was a straining of necks amid an intense silence; then, as the little pellet wavered and finally came to a rest in the hole number twenty-four a fervent oath of disappointment came from some one in front of me.

The next moment, rising on tiptoe to look over the intervening shoulders, I found myself looking into the white face of my younger brother Harry.

"Paul!" he exclaimed, turning quickly away.

I pushed my way through and stood at his side. There was no sound from the group of onlookers; it is not to be wondered at if they hesitated to offend Paul Lamar.

"My dear boy," said I, "I missed you at dinner. And though this may occupy your mind, it can scarcely fill your stomach. Haven't you had enough?"

Harry looked at me. His face was horribly pale and his eyes bloodshot; they could not meet mine.

"For Heaven's sake, Paul, let me alone," he said, hardly above a whisper. "I have lost ninety thousand."

In spite of myself I started. No wonder he was pale! And yet—

"That's nothing," I whispered back. "But you are making a show of yourself. Just now you were swearing like a sailor. See how your hand trembles! You were not made for this, Harry; it makes you forget that you're a gentleman. They are laughing at you. Come."

"But I say I have lost ninety thousand dollars," said the boy, and there was wildness in his eye. "Let me alone, Paul."

"I will repay you."

"No. Let me alone!"

"Harry!"

"I say no!"

His mouth was drawn tight and his eyes glared sullenly as those of a stubborn child. Clearly it was impossible to get him away without making a scene, which was unthinkable. For a moment I was at a complete loss; then the croupier's voice sounded suddenly in my ear:

"You are interrupting us, sir."

I silenced him with a glance and turned to my brother, having decided in an instant on the only possible course.

"Here, let me have your chair. I will get it back for you. Come!"

He looked at me for a moment in hesitation, then rose without a word and I took his place.

The thing was tiresome enough, but how could I have avoided it? The blood that rushes to the head of the gambler is certainly not food for the intellect; and, besides, I was forced by circumstances into an heroic attitude—and nothing is more distasteful to a man of sense. But I had a task before me; if a man lays bricks he should lay them well; and I do not deny that there was a stirring of my pulse as I sat down.

Is it possible for a mind to directly influence the movements of a little ivory ball? I do not say yes, but will you say no? I watched the ball with the eye of an eagle, but without straining; I played with the precision of a man with an unerring system, though my selections were really made quite at random; and I handled my bets with the sureness and swift dexterity with which a chess-master places his pawn or piece in position to demoralize his opponent.

This told on the nerves of the croupier. Twice I corrected a miscalculation of his, and before I had played an hour his hand was trembling with agitation.

And I won.

The details would be tiresome, but I won; and when, after six hours of play without an instant's rest, I rose exhausted from my chair and handed my brother the amount he had lost—I pocketed a few thousands for myself in addition. There were some who tried to detain me with congratulations and expressions of admiration, but I shook them off and led Harry outside to my car.

The chauffeur, poor devil, was completely stiff from the

long wait, and I ordered him into the tonneau and took the wheel myself.

Partly was this due to pity for the driver, partly to a desire to leave Harry to his own thoughts, which I knew must be somewhat turbulent. He was silent during the drive, which was not long, and I smiled to myself in the darkness of the early morning as I heard, now and then, an uncontrollable sigh break through his dry lips. Of thankfulness, perhaps.

I preceded him up the stoop and into the hall of the old house on lower Fifth Avenue, near Tenth Street, that had been the home of our grandfather and our father before us. There, in the dim light, I halted and turned, while Evans approached from the inner rooms, rubbing eyes heavy with sleep.

Good old Evans! Yet the faithfulness of such a servant has its disadvantages.

"Well?" said Harry in a thin, high voice.

The boy's nerves were stretched tightly; two words from me would have produced an explosion. So I clapped him on the shoulder and sent him off to bed. He went sulkily, without looking round, and his shoulders drooped like those of an old man; but I reflected that that would all be changed after a few hours of sleep.

"After all, he is a Lamar," I said to myself as I ordered Evans to bring wine and sandwiches to the library.

It was the middle of the following afternoon before Harry appeared down-stairs. He had slept eleven hours. I was seated in the library when I heard his voice in the hall:

"Breakfast! Breakfast for five at once!"

I smiled. That was Harry's style of wit.

After he had eaten his "breakfast for five" he came in to see me with the air of a man who was determined to have it out.

I myself was in no mood for talk; indeed, I scarcely ever am in such a mood, unless it be with a pretty woman or a great sinner. You may regard that sentence as tautological if you like; I sha'n't quarrel about it.

4

What I mean to say is that it was with a real effort I set myself to the distasteful task before me, rendered necessary by the responsibility of my position as elder brother and head of the family.

Harry began by observing with assumed indifference: "Well, and now there's the deuce to pay, I suppose."

"As his representative I am not a hard creditor," I smiled.

"I know, I know—" he began impetuously and stopped. I continued:

"My boy, there is always the deuce to pay. If not for one thing, then for another. So your observation would serve for any other time as well as now. The point is this: you are ten years younger than I, and you are under my care; and much as I dislike to talk, we must reach an understanding."

"Well?" said Harry, lighting a cigarette and seating himself on the arm of a chair.

"You have often thought," I continued, "that I have been trying to interfere with your freedom. But you are mistaken; I have merely been trying to preserve it—and I have succeeded."

"When our father and mother died you were fifteen years of age. You are now twenty-two; and I take some credit for the fact that those seven years have left no stain, however slight, on the name of Lamar."

"Do I deserve that?" cried Harry. "What have I done?"

"Nothing irremediable, but you must admit that now and then I have been at no small pains to—er—assist you. But there, I don't intend to speak of the past; and to tell the truth, I suspect that we are of one mind. You regard me as more or less of an incumbrance; you think your movements are hampered; you consider yourself to be treated as a child unjustly.

"Well, for my part, I find my duty —for such I consider it—grows more irksome every day. If I am in your way, you are no less in mine. To make it short, you are now twenty-two years old, you chafe at restraint, you think yourself abundantly able to manage your own affairs. Well—I have no objection."

Harry stared at me.

"You mean—" he began.

"Exactly."

"But, Paul—"

"There is no need to discuss it. For me, it is mostly selfishness."

But he wanted to talk, and I humored him. For two hours we sat, running the scale from business to sentiment, and I must confess that I was more than once surprised by a flash from Harry. Clearly he was developing, and for the first time I indulged a hope that he might prove himself fit for self-government.

At least I had given him the rope; it remained for time to discover whether or not he would avoid getting tangled up in it. When we had finished we understood each other better, I think, than we ever had before; and we parted with the best of feeling.

Three days later I sailed for Europe, leaving Harry in New York. It was my first trip across in eighteen months, and I aimed at pleasure. I spent a week in London and Munich, then, disgusted with the actions of some of my fellow countrymen with whom I had the misfortune to be acquainted, I turned my face south for Madrid.

There I had a friend.

A woman not beautiful, but eminently satisfying; not loose, but liberal, with a character and a heart. In more ways than one she was remarkable; she had an affection for me; indeed, some years previously I had been in a way to play *Albert Savaron* to her *Francesca Colonna,* an arrangement prevented only by my constitutional dislike for any prolonged or sustained effort in a world the slave of vanity and folly.

It was from the lips of this friend that I first heard the name of Desirée Le Mire.

It was late in the afternoon on the fashionable drive. Long, broad, and shady, though scarcely cool, it was here that we took our daily carriage exercise; anything more strenuous is regarded with horror by the ladies of Spain.

There was a shout, and a sudden hush; all carriages were halted and their occupants uncovered, for royalty was passing. The coach, a magnificent though cumbersome affair, passed slowly and gravely by. On the rear seat were the princess and her little English cousin, while opposite them sat the great duke himself.

By his side was a young man of five and twenty with a white face and weak chin, and glassy, meaningless eyes. I turned to my companion and asked in a low tone who he was. Her whispered answer caused me to start with surprise, and I turned to her with a question.

"But why is he in Madrid?"

"Oh, as to that," said my friend, smiling, "you must ask Desirée."

"And who is Desirée?"

"What! You do not know Desirée! Impossible!" she exclaimed.

"My dear," said I, "you must remember that for the past year and a half I have been buried in the land of pork and gold. The gossip there is neither of the poet nor the court. I am ignorant of everything."

"You would not have been so much longer," said my friend, "for Desirée is soon going to America. Who is she? No one knows. What is she? Well, she is all things to some men, and some things to all men. She is a courtezan among queens and a queen among courtezans.

"She dances and loves, and, I presume, eats and sleeps. For the past two years she has bewitched him"—she pointed down the drive to where the royal coach was disappearing in the distance—"and he has given her everything.

"It was for her that the Duke of Bellarmine built the magnificent chalet of which I was telling you on Lake Lucerne. You remember that Prince Dolansky shot himself 'for political reasons' in his Parisian palace? But for Desirée he would be alive to-day. She is a witch and a she-devil, and the most completely fascinating woman in the world."

7

I smiled.

"What a reputation! And you say she is going to America?"

"Yes. It is to be supposed that she has heard that every American is a king, and it is no wonder if she is tired of only one royal lover at a time. And listen, Paul—"

"Well?"

"You—you must not meet her. Oh, but you do not know her power!"

I laughed and pressed her hand, assuring her that I had no intention of allowing myself to be bewitched by a she-devil; but as our carriage turned and started back down the long drive toward the hotel I found myself haunted by the white face and staring eyes of the young man in the royal coach.

I stayed two weeks longer in Madrid. At the end of that time, finding myself completely bored (for no woman can possibly be amusing for more than a month at a time), I bade my friend *au revoir* and departed for the East. But I found myself just too late for an archeological expedition into the heart of Egypt, and after a tiresome week or so in Cairo and Constantinople I again turned my face toward the west.

At Rome I met an old friend, one Pierre Janvour, in the French diplomatic service, and since I had nothing better to do I accepted his urgent invitation to join him on a vacation trip to Paris.

But the joys of Paris are absurd to a man of thirty-two who has seen the world and tasted it and judged it. Still I found some amusement; Janvour had a pretty wife and a daughter eight years old, daintily beautiful, and I allowed myself to become soaked in domestic sentiment.

I really found myself on the point of envying him; Mme. Janvour was a most excellent housekeeper and manager. Little Eugénie and I would often walk together in the public gardens, and now and then her mother would join us; and, as I say, I found myself on the point of envying my friend Janvour.

This diversion would have ended soon in any event; but it was brought to an abrupt termination by a cablegram from my New York lawyers, asking me to return to America at once. Some rascality it was, on the part of the agent of my estate, which had alarmed them; the cablegram was bare of detail. At any rate, I could not afford to disregard it, and arranged passage on a liner sailing from Cherbourg the following day.

My hostess gave me a farewell dinner, which heightened my regret at being forced to leave, and little Eugénie seemed really grieved at my departure. It is pleasant to leave a welcome behind you; that is really the only necessary axiom of the traveler.

Janvour took me to the railroad station, and even offered to accompany me to Cherbourg; but I refused to tear him away from his little paradise.

We stood on the platform arguing the matter, when I suddenly became aware of that indistinct flutter and bustle seen in public places at some unusual happening or the unexpected arrival of a great personage.

I turned and saw that which was worthy of the interest it had excited.

In the first place, the daintiest little electric brougham in the world, fragile and delicate as a toy—a fairy's chariot. Then the fairy herself descended. She cannot be described in detail.

I caught a glimpse of glorious golden hair, softly massive; gray-blue eyes shot with lightning, restless, devouring, implacable, indescribably beautiful; a skin wondrously fine, with the purity of marble and the warmth of velvet; nose and mouth rather too large, but perfectly formed and breathing the fire and power of love. Really it was rather later that I saw all this; at the time there was but a confused impression of elegance and beauty and terrible power.

She passed from the brougham to her railway carriage supremely unconscious of the hundreds of eyes turned on her, and a general sigh of satisfaction and appreciation came from the throng as she disappeared within her compartment. I turned to Janvour.

"Who is she?"

"What?" he exclaimed in surprise. "But my dear Lamar, not to know her argues one a barbarian."

"Nevertheless, I do not know her."

"Well, you will have an opportunity. She is going to America, and, since she is on this train, she will, of course, take the same boat as yourself. But, my friend, beware!"

"But who is she?"

"Desirée Le Mire."

Chapter II.

BEGINNING THE DANCE.

It developed, luckily for me, that my lawyers had allowed themselves to become unduly excited over a trifle. A discrepancy had been discovered in my agent's accounts; it was clearly established that he had been speculating; but the fellow's excessive modesty and moderation had saved me from any serious inconvenience or loss.

Some twenty thousand or so was the amount, and I did not even put myself to the trouble of recovering it. I placed a friend of mine, a plodder and one of those chaps who are honest on account of lack of imagination, in the position thus vacated and sighed with mild relief.

My experiment with Harry had proved a complete success. Left to the management of his own affairs, he had shown a wisdom and restraint none the less welcome because unexpected. He was glad to see me, and I was no less glad to see him.

There was little new in town.

Bob Garforth, having gambled away his entire patrimony, had shot and killed himself on the street; Mrs. Ludworth had publicly defied gossip and smiled with favor on young Driscoll; the new director of the Metropolitan Museum had announced himself an enemy to tradition and a friend of progress; and Desirée Le Mire had consented to a two weeks' engagement at the Stuyvesant.

The French dancer was the favorite topic of discussion in all circles.

The newspapers were full of her and filled entire columns with lists of the kings, princes, and dukes who had been at her feet.

Bets were made on her nationality, the color of her eyes, the value of her pearls, the number of suicides she had caused—corresponding, in some sort, to the notches on the gun of a Western bad man. Gowns and hats were named for her by the enterprising department stores.

It was announced that her engagement at the Stuyvesant would open in ten days, and when the box-office opened for the advance sale every seat for every performance was sold within a few hours.

In the mean time the great Le Mire kept herself secluded in her hotel. She had appeared but once in the public dining-room, and on that occasion had nearly caused a riot, whereupon she had discreetly withdrawn. She remained unseen while the town shouted itself hoarse.

I had not mentioned her name to Harry, nor had I heard him speak of her, until one evening about two weeks after my return.

We were at dinner and had been discussing some commonplace subject, from which, by one of the freaks of association, the conversation veered and touched on classical dancing.

"The Russians are preeminent," said I, "because they possess both the inspiration—the fire—and the training. In no other nation or school are the two so perfectly joined. In the Turkish dancers there is perfect grace and freedom, but no life. In Desirée Le Mire, for example, there is indeed life; but she has not had the necessary training."

"What? Le Mire! Have you seen her?" cried Harry.

"Not on the stage," I answered; "but I crossed on the same ship with her, and she was kind enough to give me a great deal of her time. She seems to understand perfectly her own artistic limitations, and I am taking her word for it."

But Harry was no longer interested in the subject of dancing. I was besieged on the instant with a thousand questions.

Had I known Le Mire long? What was she like? Was it true that Prince Dolansky had shot himself in despair at losing her? Was she beautiful? How well did I know her? Would I take him to see her?

And within half an hour the last question was repeated so many times and with such insistence that I finally consented and left Harry delighted beyond words.

My own experience with Desirée Le Mire had been anything but exciting. The woman was interesting; there could be no doubt of that; but she possessed little attraction for me. Her charms, on close inspection, were really quite too evident.

I require subtlety in a woman, and so far as I could discover Le Mire knew not the meaning of the word. We had spent many hours during the trip across in pleasant companionship; she had done me the honor to tell me that she found my conversation amusing; and, after all, she was undeniably a pretty woman. She had invited me with evident sincerity to call on her in New York; but I had not as yet taken advantage of the invitation.

I did not then think, and I do not now believe, that I acted foolishly when I took Harry to see her. In any event, he would have seen her sooner or later, and since all temptations meet us at one time or another, it is best to have it out with them at as early a date as possible. At the time, indeed, I gave the subject no thought whatever; but if I had I should not have hesitated.

We took tea with her the following afternoon in her apartment, and I must confess that I myself was more than a little impressed when I entered. I realized then that on the ship nothing had been in her favor; she had been completely out of her element, and she was not a good sailor.

Here all was different. The stiffly ostentatious hotel rooms, by her own genius or that of her maid, had been transformed into something very nearly approaching perfection. I was amazed at the excellent taste displayed in her furniture and its arrangement, for it was clear that these were no hotel properties. Certainly a woman is at her best only when she is able to choose or create her own surroundings.

Harry was captivated, and I can scarcely blame him. But the poor lad betrayed himself so frankly! Though I suppose Le Mire was more or less accustomed to immediate surrender.

On that day, at least, she had reason to expect it. She satisfied the eye, which is saying a great deal and is the highest praise possible for a woman's beauty, when you consider the full strength of the word.

She was radiant, adorable, irresistible; I had to own that my first impression of her had been far too weak.

We talked for an hour. Harry had little to say as he sat devouring Le Mire with his eyes, and whenever she turned to him for an answer to a question or confirmation of an opinion he stammered and kept his composure with difficulty. Never, I suppose, did woman have clearer evidence of her power, nor sweeter, for Harry was by no means a fool to be carried away by the first pretty face that came in his way.

She simply overwhelmed him, and I repeat that I do not wonder at it, for my own pulse was not exactly steady. She asked us to dine with her.

I pleaded an engagement at the club and signed to Harry to do likewise; but he was completely gone and paid no attention to me. He accepted the invitation gratefully, with frank delight, and I left them together.

It was about ten o'clock when he came home that evening. I was seated in the library and, hearing him enter the hall, called to him.

What a face was his! His lips trembled with nervous feeling, his eyes glowed like the eyes of a madman. I half started from my chair in amazement.

"I have no time," said he in answer to my invitation to join me with a bottle. "I have a letter or two to write, and—and I must get some sleep."

"Did you just leave Le Mire?"

"Yes."

I looked at my watch.

"What under the sun did you find to talk about?"

"Oh, anything—nothing. I say, she's charming."

His essay at indifference was amusing.

"You find her so?"

"Rather."

14

"She seems to have taken a fancy to you."

Harry actually grew red.

"Hardly," he said; but there was hope in the word.

"She is hardly your kind, Harry. You know that. You aren't going in for this sort of thing?"

"This sort—I don't know what you mean."

"Yes, you do, Hal. You know exactly what I mean. To put the thing plainly, Le Mire is a dangerous woman—none more so in all the world; and, Harry boy, be sure you keep your head and watch your step."

He stood for a moment looking at me in silence with a half-angry frown, then opened his mouth as though to speak, and finally turned, without a word, and started for the door. There he turned again uncertainly, hesitating.

"I am to ride with Desirée in the morning," said he, and the next moment was gone.

"Desirée!"

He called her Desirée!

I think I smiled for an hour over that; and, though my reflections were not free from apprehension, I really felt but little anxiety. Not that I underrated Le Mire's fascination and power; to confess the truth, my ease of mind was the result of my own vanity. Le Mire had flattered me into the belief that she was my friend.

A week passed—a dull week, during which I saw little of Harry and Le Mire not at all. At the time, I remember, I was interested in some chemical experiments—I am a dabbler with the tubes—and went out but little. Then—this was on Friday—Harry sought me out in the laboratory to tell me he was going away. In answer to my question, "Where?" he said, "I don't know."

"How long will you be gone?"

"Oh, a week—perhaps a month."

I looked at him keenly, but said nothing. It would have done no good to force him into an equivocation by questions. Early the next morning he departed, with three trunks, and with no further word to me save a farewell. No sooner was he gone than I started for the telephone to call up Le Mire; but thought better of it and with a shrug of the shoulders returned to the laboratory.

It was the following Monday that was to see the first appearance of Le Mire at the Stuyvesant. I had not thought of going, but on Monday afternoon Billy Du Mont telephoned me that he had an extra ticket and would like to have me join him. I was really a little curious to see Le Mire perform and accepted.

We dined at the club and arrived at the theater rather late. The audience was brilliant; indeed, though I had been an ardent first-nighter for a year or two in my callow youth, I think I have never seen such a representation of fashion and genius in America, except at the opera.

Billy and I sat in the orchestra—about the twelfth row— and half the faces in sight were well known to me. Whether Le Mire could dance or not, she most assuredly was, or had, a good press-agent. We were soon to receive an exemplification of at least a portion of the reputation that had preceded her.

Many were the angry adjectives heaped on the head of the dancer on that memorable evening. Mrs. Frederick Marston, I remember, called her an insolent hussy; but then Mrs. Frederick Marston was never original. Others: rash, impudent, saucy, impertinent; in each instance accompanied by threats.

Indeed, it is little wonder if those people of fashion and wealth and position were indignant and sore. For they had dressed and dined hastily and come all the way down-town to see Le Mire; they waited for her for two hours and a half in stuffy theater seats, and Le Mire did not appear.

The announcement was finally made by the manager of the theater at a little before eleven o'clock. He could not understand, he said—the poor fellow was on the point of wringing his hands with agitation and despair—he could not understand why the dancer did not arrive.

She had rehearsed in the theater on the previous Thursday afternoon, and had then seemed to have every intention of fulfilling her engagement. No one connected with the theater had seen her since that time, but everything had gone smoothly; they had had no reason to fear such a *contretemps* as her nonappearance.

They had sent to her hotel; she was gone, bag and baggage. She had departed on Friday, leaving no word as to her destination. They had asked the police, the hotels, the railroads, the steamship companies—and could find no trace of her.

The manager only hoped—he hoped with all his heart—that his frank and unreserved explanation would appease his kind patrons and prevent their resentment; that they would understand—

I made my way out of the theater as rapidly as possible, with Billy Du Mont at my side, and started north on Broadway.

My companion was laughing unrestrainedly.

"What a joke!" he exclaimed. "And gad, what a woman! She comes in and turns the town upside down and then leaves it standing on its head. What wouldn't I give to know her!"

I nodded, but said nothing. At Forty-Second Street we turned east to Fifth Avenue, and a few minutes later were at the club. I took Du Mont to a secluded corner of the grill, and there, with a bottle of wine between us, I spoke.

"Billy," said I, "there's the deuce to pay. You're an old friend of mine, and you possess a share of discretion, and you've got to help me. Le Mire is gone. I must find her."

"Find Le Mire?" He stared at me in amazement. "What for?"

"Because my brother Harry is with her."

Then I explained in as few words as possible, and I ended, I think, with something like this:

"You know, Billy, there are very few things in the world I consider of any value. She can have the lad's money, and, if necessary, my own into the bargain. But the name of Lamar must remain clean; and I tell you there is more than a name in danger. Whoever that woman touches she kills. And Harry is only a boy."

Billy helped me, as I knew he would; nor did he insist on unnecessary details. I didn't need his assistance in the search, for I felt that I could accomplish that as well alone.

But it was certainly known that Harry had been calling on Le Mire at her hotel; conjectures were sure to be made, leading to the assertions of busy tongues; and it was the part of my friend to counteract and smother the inevitable gossip. This he promised to do; and I knew Billy. As for finding Harry, it was too late to do anything that night, and I went home and to bed.

The next morning I began by calling at her hotel. But though the manager of the theater had gotten no information from them, he had pumped them dry. They knew nothing.

I dared not go to the police, and probably they would have been unable to give me any assistance if I had sought it. The only other possible source of information I disliked to use; but after racking my brain for the better part of the day I decided that there was nothing else for it, and started on a round of the ticket offices of the railroads and steamship companies.

I had immediate success. My first call was at the office where Harry and I were accustomed to arrange our transportation. As I entered the head clerk—or whatever they call him—advanced to greet me with a smile.

"Yes," said he in response to my question; "Mr. Lamar got his tickets from me. Let's see—Thursday, wasn't it? No, Friday. That's right—Friday."

"Tickets!" I muttered to myself. And in my preoccupation I really neglected to listen to him. Then aloud: "Where were the—tickets for?"

"Denver."

"For Friday's train?"

"Yes. The Western Express."

That was all I wanted to know. I hurried home, procured a couple of hastily packed bags, and took the afternoon train for the West.

Chapter III.

A MODERN MARANA.

My journey westward was an eventful one; but this is not a "History of Tom Jones," and I shall refrain from detail. Denver I reached at last, after a week's stop-over in Kansas City. It was a delightful adventure—but it had nothing to do with the story.

I left the train at the Rocky Mountain city about the middle of the afternoon. And now, what to do? I think I am not a fool, but I certainly lack the training of a detective, and I felt perfectly rudderless and helpless as I ordered the taxi-driver to take me to the Alcazar Hotel.

I was by no means sure that Harry had come to Denver. He was traveling with a bundle of animated caprice, a creature who would have hauled him off the train at Rahway, New Jersey, if she had happened to take a fancy to the place. At the moment, I reflected, they might be driving along Michigan Boulevard, or attending a matinée at the Willis Wood, or sipping mint juleps at the Planters'.

Even if they were in Denver, how was I to find them? I keenly regretted the week I had lost. I was sure that Harry would avoid any chance of publicity and would probably shun the big hotels. And Denver is not a village.

It was the beauty of Le Mire that saved me. Indeed, I might have foreseen that; and I have but poorly portrayed the force of her unmatchable fascination unless you have realized that she was a woman who could pass nowhere without being seen; and, seen, remembered.

I made inquiries of the manager of the hotel, of course, but was brought up sharply when he asked me the names of my friends for whom I was asking. I got out of it somehow, some foolish evasion or other, and regarded my task as more difficult than ever.

That same evening I dined at the home of my cousin, Hovey Stafford, who had come West some years before on account of weak lungs, and stayed because he liked it. I met his wife that evening for the first time; she may be introduced with the observation that if she was his reason for remaining in the provinces, never did man have a better one.

We were on the veranda with our after-dinner cigars. I was congratulating Hovey on the felicity of his choice and jocularly sympathizing with his wife.

"Yes," said my cousin, with a sigh, "I never regretted it till last week. It will never be the same again."

Mrs. Hovey looked at him with supreme disdain.

"I suppose you mean Señora Ramal," said she scornfully.

Her husband, feigning the utmost woe, nodded mournfully; whereupon she began humming the air of the *Chanson du Colonel,* and was stopped by a smothering kiss.

"And who is the Señora Ramal?" I asked.

"The most beautiful woman in the world," said Mrs. Hovey.

This from a woman who was herself beautiful! Amazing! I suppose my face betrayed my thought.

"It isn't charity," she smiled. "Like John Holden, I have seen fire-balloons by the hundred, I have seen the moon, and—then I saw no more fire-balloons."

"But who is she?"

Hovey explained. "She is the wife of Señor Ramal. They came here some ten days ago, with letters to one or two of the best families, and that's all we know about them. The *señora* is an entrancing mixture of Cleopatra, Sappho, Helen of Troy, and the devil. She had the town by the ears in twenty-four hours, and you wouldn't wonder at it if you saw her."

Already I felt that I knew, but I wanted to make sure.

"Byron has described her," I suggested, "in *Childe Harold.*"

"Hardly," said Hovey. "No midnight beauty for hers, thank you. Her hair is the most perfect gold. Her eyes are green; her skin remarkably fair. What she may be is unknowable, but she certainly is not Spanish; and, odder still, the *señor* himself fits the name no better."

But I thought it needless to ask for a description of Harry; for I had no doubt of the identity of Señor Ramal and his wife. I pondered over the name, and suddenly realized that it was merely "Lamar" spelled backward!

The discovery removed the last remaining shadow of doubt.

I asked in a tone of assumed indifference for their hotel, expressing a desire to meet them—and was informed by Hovey that they had left Denver two days previously, nor did he know where they had gone.

Thus did I face another obstacle. But I was on the track; and the perfume of a woman's beauty is the strongest scent in the world as well as the sweetest. I thanked my cousin for a pleasant evening—though he did not know the extent of my debt to him—and declined his urgent invitation to have my luggage brought to his home.

On my way to the hotel I was struck by a sudden thought: Señor Ramal could not be my brother or my cousin would have recognized him! But I immediately reflected that the two had not seen each other for some ten years, at which time Harry had been a mere boy.

The following morning, with little difficulty, I ascertained the fact that the Ramals had departed—at least ostensibly—for Colorado Springs.

I followed. That same evening, when I registered at the Antlers Hotel, a few minutes before the dinner hour, I turned over two pages of the book, and there before me was the entry, "Señor and Señora Ramal, Paris." It was in Harry's handwriting.

After dinner—a most excellent dinner, with melons from La Junta and trout from the mountain streams—I descended on the hotel clerk with questions. He was most obliging—a sharp, pleasant fellow, with prominent ears and a Rocky Mountain twang.

"Señor and Señora Ramal? Most assuredly, sir. They have been here several days. No, they are not now in the hotel. They left this afternoon for Manitou, to take dinner there, and are going to make the night trip up the Peak."

An idea immediately suggested itself to me. They would, of course, return to the hotel in the morning. All I had to do was to sit down and wait for them; but that would have been dull sport. My idea was better.

I sought out the hotel's wardrobe—there is nothing the Antlers will not do for you—and clothed myself in khaki, leggings, and boots. Then I ordered a car and set out for Manitou, at the foot of the mountain.

By ten o'clock I was mounted on a donkey, headed for the top, after having been informed by a guide that "the man and the beautiful lady" had departed an hour previous.

Having made the ascent twice before, I needed no guide. So I decided; but I regretted the decision. Three times I lost the path; once I came perilously near descending on the village below—well, without hesitation. It was well after midnight when I passed the Half-way House, and I urged my donkey forward with a continual *rat-a-tat-tat* of well-directed kicks in the effort to make my goal.

You who have experienced the philosophical calm and superb indifference of the Pike's Peak donkey may imagine the vocabulary I used on this occasion—I dare not print it. Nor did his speed increase.

I was, in fact, a quarter of an hour late. I was still several hunderd yards from the summit when the sun's first rays shot through the thin atmosphere, creating colorful riot among the clouds below, and I stopped, holding my breath in awe.

There is no art nor poetry in that wonderful sight; it is glorious war. The sun charges forth in a vast flame of inconceivable brilliance; you can almost hear the shout of victory. He who made the universe is no artist; too often He forgets restraint, and blinds us.

I turned, almost regretting that I had come, for I had been put out of tune with my task. Then I mounted the donkey and slowly traversed the few remaining yards to the Peak.

There, seated in the dazzling sunshine on the edge of a

huge boulder near the eastern precipice, were the two I sought.

Le Mire's head was turned from me as she sat gazing silently at the tumbling, gorgeous mass of clouds that seemed almost to be resting on her lap; Harry was looking at her. And such a look!

There was no rival even in nature that could conquer Le Mire; never, I believe, did woman achieve a more notable victory than hers of that morning. I watched them for several minutes before I moved or spoke; and never once did Harry's eyes leave her face.

Then I advanced a step, calling his name; and they turned and caught sight of me.

"Paul!" cried Harry, leaping to his feet; then he stopped short and stared at me half defiantly, half curiously, moving close to Le Mire and placing his hand on her shoulder like a child clinging to a toy.

His companion had not moved, except to turn her head; but after the first swift shadow of surprise her face brightened with a smile of welcome, for all the world as though this were a morning call in her boudoir.

"Señor and Señora Ramal, I believe?" said I with a smile, crossing to them with an exaggerated bow.

I could see Harry cocking his ear to catch the tone of my first words, and when he heard their friendliness a grin overspread his face. He took his hand from Le Mire's shoulder and held it out to me.

"How did you come here? How did you find us?"

"You forgot to provide Le Mire with a veil," said I by way of answer.

Harry looked at me, then at his companion. "Of course," he agreed—"of course. By Jove! that was stupid of us."

Whereupon Le Mire laughed with such frank enjoyment of the boy's simplicity that I couldn't help but join her.

"And now," said Harry, "I suppose you want to know—"

"I want to know nothing—at present," I interrupted. "It's nearly six o'clock, and since ten last night I've been on top of the most perfectly imbecile donkey ever devised by nature. I want breakfast."

Velvet lids were upraised from Le Mire's eyes. "Here?" she queried.

I pointed to the place—extreme charity might give it the title of inn—where smoke was rising from a tin chimney.

Soon we were seated inside with a pot of steaming black coffee before us. Harry was bubbling over with gaiety and good will, evidently occasioned by my unexpected friendliness, while Le Mire sat for the most part silent. It was easy to see that she was more than a little disturbed by my arrival, which surprised me.

I gazed at her with real wonder and increasing admiration. It was six in the morning; she had had no sleep, and had just finished a most fatiguing journey of some eight hours; but I had never seen her so beautiful.

Our host approached, and I turned to him:

"What have you?"

There was pity in his glance.

"Aigs," said he, with an air of finality.

"Ah!" said La Mire. "I want them—let's see—*au beurre noire,* if you please."

The man looked at her and uttered the single word: "Fried."

"Fried?" said she doubtfully.

"Only fried," was the inexorable answer. "How many?"

Le Mire turned to me, and I explained. Then she turned again to the surly host with a smile that must have caused him to regret his gruffness.

"Well, then, fr-r-ied!" said she, rolling the "r" deliciously. "And you may bring me five, if you please."

It appeared that I was not the only hungry one. We ate leisurely and smoked more leisurely still, and started on our return journey a little before eight o'clock.

It was late in the afternoon when we arrived at the Antlers. The trip was accomplished without accident, but Le Mire was thoroughly exhausted and Harry was anything but fresh. That is the worst of mountain climbing: the exaltation at the summit hardly pays you for the reaction at the foot. We entered the broad portico with frank sighs of relief.

I said something about joining them at dinner and left for my own rooms.

At dinner that evening Harry was in high spirits and took great delight in everything that was said, both witty and dull, while Le Mire positively sparkled.

She made her impression; not a man in the well-filled room but sent his tribute of admiring glances as she sat seemingly unconscious of all but Harry and myself. That is always agreeable; a man owes something to the woman who carries a room for him.

I had intended to have a talk with Harry after dinner, but I postponed it; the morning would assuredly be better. There was dancing in the salon, but we were all too tired to take advantage of it; and after listening to one or two numbers, during which Le Mire was kept busy turning aside the importunities of would-be partners, we said good night and sought our beds.

It was late the next morning when the precious pair joined me in the garden, and when we went in for breakfast we found the dining-room quite empty. We did not enjoy it as on the morning previous; the cuisine was of the kind usually—and in this case justly—described as "superior," but we did not have the same edge on our appetite.

We were not very talkative; I myself was almost taciturn, having before me the necessity of coming to an understanding with Harry, a task which I was far from relishing. But there were certain things I must know.

"What do you say to a ride down the valley?" said Harry. "They have excellent horses here; I tried one of 'em the other day."

"I trust that they bear no resemblance to my donkey," said I with feeling.

"Ugh!" said Le Mire with a shudder. "Never shall I forget that ride. Besides," she added, turning to Harry, "this morning I would be in the way. Don't you know that your

25

brother has a thousand things to say to you? He wants to scold you; you must remember that you are a very bad boy."

And she sent me a glance half defiant, half indifferent, which plainly said: "If I fight you, I shall win; but I really care very little about it one way or the other."

After breakfast she went to her room—to have her hair dressed, she said—and I led Harry to a secluded corner of the magnificent grounds surrounding the hotel. During the walk we were both silent: Harry, I suppose, was wondering what I was going to say, while I was trying to make up my own mind.

"I suppose," he began abruptly, "you are going to tell me I have acted like a fool. Go ahead; the sooner it's over the better."

"Nothing of the sort," said I, glad that he had opened it. He stopped short, demanding to know what I meant.

"Of course," I continued, "Le Mire is a most amazing prize. Not exactly my style perhaps, but there are few men in the world who wouldn't envy you. I congratulate you.

"But there were two things I feared for several reasons— Le Mire's fascination, your own youth and impulsive recklessness, and the rather curious mode of your departure. I feared first and most that you would marry her; second, that you would achieve odium and publicity for our name."

Harry was regarding me with a smile which had in it very little of amusement; it held a tinge of bitterness.

"And so," he burst out suddenly, "you were afraid I would marry her! Well, I would. The last time I asked her"—again the smile—"was this morning."

"And—"

"She won't have me."

"Bah!" I concealed my surprise, for I had really not thought it possible that the lad could be such a fool. "What's her game, Harry?"

"Game the deuce! I tell you she won't have me."

"You have asked her?"

"A thousand times. I've begged her on my knees. Offered her—anything."

"And she refuses?"

"Positively."

"Refuses?"

"With thanks."

I stared at him for a moment in silence. Then I said: "Go and get her and bring her here. I'll find out what she wants," and sat down on a bench to wait. Harry departed for the hotel without a word.

In a few minutes he returned with Le Mire. I rose and proffered her a seat on the bench, which she accepted with a smile, and Harry sat down at her side. I stood in front of them.

"Le Mire," said I, and I believe I frowned, "my brother tells me that you have been offered the name of Lamar in marriage."

"I have thanked him for it," said she with a smile.

"And declined it."

"And—declined it," she agreed.

"Well," said I, "I am not a man of half measures, as you will soon see, Le Mire. Besides, I appreciate your power. On the day," I continued with slow precision—"on the day that you give me a contract to adhere to that refusal you may have my check for one million dollars."

She surprised me; I admit it. I had expected a burst of anger, with a touch of assumed hauteur; the surrender to follow, for I had made the stake high. But as I stood looking down at her, waiting for the flash of her eye, I was greeted by a burst of laughter—the frank laughter of genuine mirth. Then she spoke:

"Oh, you Americans! You are so funny! A million dollars! It is impossible that I should be angry after such a compliment. Besides, you are so funny! Do you not know Le Mire? Am I not a princess if I desire it—tomorrow—today? Bah! There is the world—is it not mine? Mrs. Lamar? Ugh! Pardon me, my friend, but it is an ugly name.

"You know my ancestors? De L'Enclos, Montalais, Maintenon, La Marana! They were happy—in their way—and they were great. I must do nothing unworthy of them. Set your mind at rest, Mr. Lamar; but, really, you should have known better—you who have seen the world and Le Mire in Paris! And now our amusement is perhaps ended? Now we must return to that awful New York? *Voilà!*"

Indeed I had not understood her. And how could I? There is only one such woman in a generation; sometimes none, for nature is sparing of her favorites. By pure luck she sat before me, this twentieth-century Marana, and I acknowledged her presence with a deep bow of apology and admiration.

"If you will forgive me, *madame,*" I said, "I will—not attempt to make reparation, for my words were not meant for you. Consider them unspoken. As for our amusement, why need it end? Surely, we can forget? I see plainly I am not a St. Evremond, but neither am I a fool. My brother pleases you—well, there he is. As for myself, I shall either stay to take care of you two children, or I shall return to New York, as you desire."

Le Mire looked at me uncertainly for a moment, then turned to Harry and with a fluttering gesture took his hand in her own and patted it gaily. Then she laughed the happy laugh of a child as she said:

"Then it is well! And, *monsieur,* you are less an American than I thought. By all means, stay—we shall be so jolly! Will we not, my little friend?"

Harry nodded, smiling at her. But there was a troubled look in his face.

Chapter IV.

ALLONS!

The events of the month that followed, though exciting enough, were of a similarity that would make their narration tedious, and I shall pass over them as speedily as possible.

We remained at Colorado Springs only two days after that morning in the garden. Le Mire, always in search of novelty, urged us away, and, since we really had nothing in view save the satisfaction of her whims, we consented. Salt Lake City was our next resting-place, but Le Mire tired of it in a day.

"I shall see the Pacific," she said to Harry and me, and we immediately set out for San Francisco.

Is it necessary for me to explain my attitude? But surely it explains itself. For one thing, I was disinclined to leave Harry in a position where he was so abundantly unable to take care of himself. For another, I take amusement wherever it offers itself, and I was most certainly not bored.

The vagaries and caprices of a beautiful woman are always interesting, and when you are allowed to study them at close range without being under the necessity of acting the part of a faithful lover they become doubly so.

Le Mire managed Harry with wonderful tact and finesse; I sat back and laughed at the performance, now and then applying a check when her riotous imagination seemed likely to run away with us.

At San Francisco she achieved a triumph, notorious to the point of embarrassment. Paul Lamar, of New York, had introduced himself into the highest circle of society, and in turn had introduced his friends, Señor and Señora Ramal. The *señora* captured the town in a single night at a reception and ball on Telegraph Hill.

The day following there were several dozens of cards left for her at our hotel; invitations arrived by the score. She

29

accepted two or three and made the fortune of two drawing-rooms; then suddenly tired of the sport and insulted a most estimable lady, our hostess, by certain remarks which inadvertently reached the ears of the lady's husband.

"You have done for yourself, Le Mire," I told her.

She answered me with a smile—straightway proceeded to issue invitations for an "entertainment" at our hotel. I had no idea what she meant to do; but gave the thing no thought, feeling certain that few, or none, of the invitations would be accepted—wherein I was badly mistaken, for not one was refused.

Well, Le Mire danced for them.

For myself it was barely interesting; I have passed the inner portals of the sacred temples of India, and the human body holds no surprises for me. But the good people of San Francisco were shocked, astonished, and entranced. Not a man in the room but was Le Mire's slave; even the women were forced to applaud. She became at once a goddess and an outcast.

The newspapers of the following morning were full of it, running the scale of eulogy, admiration, and wonder. And one of the articles, evidently written by a man who had been considerably farther east than San Francisco, ended with the following paragraph:

In short, it was sublime, and with every movement and every gesture there was a something hidden, a suggestion of a personality and mysterious charm that we have always heretofore considered the exclusive property of just one woman in the world. But Desirée Le Mire is not in San Francisco; though we declare that the performance of last evening was more than enough to rouse certain suspicions, especially in view of Le Mire's mysterious disappearance from New York.

I took the paper to Desirée in her room, and while she read the article stood gazing idly from a window. It was about eleven in the morning; Harry had gone for a walk, saying that he would return in half an hour to join us at breakfast.

"Well?" said Desirée when she had finished.

"But it is not well," I retorted, turning to face her. "I do not reproach you; you are being amused, and so, I confess, am I. But your name—that is, Le Mire—has been mentioned, and discovery is sure to follow. We must leave San Francisco at once."

"But I find it entertaining."

"Nevertheless, we must leave."

"But if I choose to stay?"

"No; for Harry would stay with you."

"Well, then—I won't go."

"Le Mire, you will go?"

She sent me a flashing glance, and for a moment I half expected an explosion. Then, seeming to think better of it, she smiled:

"But where? We can't go west without falling into the ocean, and I refuse to return. Where?"

"Then we'll take the ocean."

She looked up questioningly, and I continued:

"What would you say to a yacht—a hundred and twenty foot steamer, with a daredevil captain and the coziest little cabins in the world?"

"Bah!" Le Mire snapped her fingers to emphasize her incredulity. "It does not exist."

"But it does. Afloat and in commission, to be had for the asking and the necessary check. Dazzling white, in perfect order, a second Antoine for a chef, rooms furnished as you would your own villa. What do you say?"

"Really?" asked Le Mire with sparkling eyes.

"Really."

"Here—in San Francisco?"

"In the harbor. I saw her myself this morning."

"Then I say—*allons!* Ah, my friend, you are perfection! I want to see it. Now! May I? Come!"

I laughed at her ager enthusiasm as she sprang up from her chair.

"Le Mire, you are positively a baby. Something new to play with! Well, you shall have it. But you haven't had breakfast. We'll go out to see her this afternoon; in fact, I have already made an appointment with the owner."

"Ah! Indeed, you are perfection. And—how well you know me." She paused and seemed to be searching for words; then she said abruptly: "M. Lamar, I wish you to do me a favor."

"Anything, Le Mire, in or out of reason."

Again she hesitated; then:

"Do not call me Le Mire."

I laughed.

"But certainly, Señora Ramal. And what is the favor?"

"That."

"That—"

"Do not call me Le Mire—nor Señora Ramal."

"Well, but I must address you occasionally."

"Call me Desirée."

I looked at her with a smile.

"But I thought that that was reserved for your particular friends."

"So it is."

"Then, my dear *señora,* it would be impertinent of me."

"But if I request it?"

"I have said—anything in or out of reason. And, of course, I am one of the family."

"Is that the only reason?"

I began to understand her, and I answered her somewhat dryly: "My dear Desirée, there can be none other."

"Are you so—cold?"

"When I choose."

"Ah!" It was a sigh rather than an exclamation. "And yet, on the ship—do you remember? Look at me, M. Lamar. Am I not—am I so little worthy of a thought?"

Her lips were parted with tremulous feeling; her eyes glowed with a strange fire, and yet were tender. Indeed, she was "worthy of a thought"—dangerously so; I felt my pulse stir. It was necessary to assume a stoicism I was far from feeling, and I looked at her with a cynical smile and spoke in a voice as carefully deliberate as I could make it.

"Le Mire," I said, "I could love you, but I won't." And I turned and left her without another word.

Why? I haven't the slightest idea. It must have been my vanity. Some few men had conquered Le Mire; others had surrendered to her; certainly none had ever been able to resist her. There was a satisfaction in it. I walked about the lobby of the hotel till Harry returned, idiotically pleased with myself.

At the breakfast table I acquainted Harry with our plans for a cruise, and he was fully as eager about it as Le Mire had been. He wanted to weigh anchor that very afternoon. I explained that it was necessary to wait for funds from New York.

"How much?" said he. "I'm loaded."

"I've sent for a hundred thousand," said I.

"Are you going to buy her?" he demanded with astonishment.

Then we fell to a discussion of routes. Harry was for Hawaii; Le Mire for South America.

We tossed a coin.

"Heads," said Desirée, and so it fell.

I requested Le Mire to keep to the hotel as closely as possible for the days during which it was necessary for us to remain in San Francisco. She did so, but with an apparent effort.

I have never seen a creature so full of nervous energy and fire; only by severe restraint could she force herself to even a small degree of composure. Harry was with her nearly every minute, though what they found to talk about was beyond my comprehension. Neither was exactly bubbling over with ideas, and one cannot say "I love you" for twenty-four hours a day.

It was a cool, sunny day in the latter part of October when we weighed anchor and passed through the Golden

Gate. I had leased the yacht for a year, and had made alternative plans in case Le Mire should tire of the sport, which I thought extremely probable.

She and Harry were delighted with the yacht, which was not surprising, for she was as perfect a craft as I have seen. Sides white as sea-foam; everything above decks of shining brass, below mahogany, and as clean and shipshape as a Dutch kitchen. There were five rooms besides the captain's, and a reception-room, dining-room, and library. We had provisioned her well, and had a jewel of a cook.

Our first port was Santa Catalina. We dropped anchor there at about five o'clock in the afternoon of such a day as only southern California can boast of, and the dingey was lowered to take us ashore.

"What is there?" asked Le Mire, pointing to the shore as we stood leaning on the rail waiting for the crew to place the ladder.

I answered: "Tourists."

Le Mire shrugged her shoulders. "Tourists? Bah! *Merci, non. Allons!*"

I laughed and went forward to the captain to tell him that *madame* did not approve of Santa Catalina. In another minute the dingey was back on its davits, the anchor up, and we were under way. Poor captain! Within a week he became used to Le Mire's sudden whims.

At San Diego we went ashore. Le Mire took a fancy to some Indian blankets, and Harry bought them for her; but when she expressed an intention to take an Indian girl— about sixteen or seventeen years old—aboard the yacht as a "companion," I interposed a firm negative. And, after all, she nearly had her way.

For a month it was "just one port after another." Mazatlan, San Blas, Manzanillo, San Salvador, Panama City—at each of these we touched, and visited sometimes an hour, sometimes two or three days. Le Mire was loading the yacht with all sorts of curious relics. Ugly or beautiful, useful or worthless, genuine or faked, it mattered not to her; if a thing suited her fancy she wanted it—and got it.

At Guayaquil occurred the first collision of wills. It was our second evening in port. We were dining on the deck of the yacht, with half a dozen South American generals and admirals as guests.

Toward the end of the dinner Le Mire suddenly became silent and remained for some minutes lost in thought; then, suddenly, she turned to the bundle of gold lace at her side with a question:

"Where is Guayaquil?"

He stared at her in amazement.

"It is there, *señora,*" he said finally, pointing to the shore lined with twinkling lights.

"I know, I know," said Le Mire impatiently; "but where is it? In what country?"

The poor fellow, too surprised to be offended, stammered the name of his native land between gasps, while Harry and I had all we could do to keep from bursting into laughter.

"Ah," said Desirée in the tone of one who has made an important discovery, "I thought so. Ecuador. *Monsieur,* Quito is in Ecuador."

The general—or admiral, I forget which—acknowledged the correctness of her geography with a profound bow.

"But yes. I have often heard of Quito, *monsieur.* It is a very interesting place. I shall go to Quito."

There ensued immediately a babel. Each of our guests insisted on the honor of accompanying us inland, and the thing would most assuredly have ended in a bloody quarrel on the captain's polished deck, if I had not interposed in a firm tone:

"But, gentlemen, we are not going to Quito."

Le Mire looked at me—and such a look! Then she said in a tone of the utmost finality:

"I am going to Quito."

I shook my head, smiling at her, whereupon she became furious.

"M. Lamar," she burst forth, "I tell you I am going to Quito! In spite of your smile! Yes! Do you hear? I shall go!"

Without a word I took a coin from my pocket and held it

up. I had come to know Le Mire. She frowned for a moment in an evident attempt to maintain her anger, then an irresistible smile parted her lips and she clapped her hands gaily.

"Very well," she cried, "toss, *monsieur!* Heads!"

The coin fell tails, and we did not go to Quito, much to the disappointment of our guests. Le Mire forgot all about it in ten minutes.

Five days later we dropped anchor at Callao.

This historic old port delighted Le Mire at once. I had told her something of its story: its successive bombardments by the liberators from Chile, the Spanish squadron, buccaneering expeditions from Europe and the Chilean invaders; not to mention earthqakes and tidal waves. We moored alongside the stone pier by the lighthouse; the old clock at its top pointed to the hour of eight in the morning.

But as soon as Le Mire found out that Lima was but a few miles away, Callao no longer held any interest for her. We took an afternoon train and arrived at the capital in time for dinner.

There it was, in picturesque old Lima, that Le Mire topped her career. On our first afternoon we betook ourselves to the fashionable *paseo,* for it was a band day, and all Lima was out.

In five minutes every eye in the gay and fashionable crowd was turned on Le Mire. Then, as luck would have it, I met, quite by chance, a friend of mine who had come to the University of San Marcos some years before as a professor of climatology. He introduced us, with an air of importance, to several of the groups of fashion, and finally to the president himself. That night we slept as guests under the roof of a luxurious and charming country house at Miraflores.

Le Mire took the capital by storm. Her style of beauty was peculiarly fitted for their appreciation, for pallor is considered a mark of beauty among Lima ladies. But that could scarcely account for her unparalleled triumph. I have often wondered—was it the effect of a premonition?

The president himself sat by her at the opera. There were two duels attributed to her within a week; though how the deuce that was possible is beyond me.

On society day at the bull-ring the cues were given by Le Mire; her hand flung the rose to the matador, while the eight thousand excited spectators seemed uncertain whether they were applauding her or him. Lima was hers, and never have I seen a fortnight so crowded with incidents.

But Le Mire soon tired of it, as was to be expected. She greeted me one morning at the breakfast table:

"My friend Paul, let us go to Cerro de Pasco. They have silver—thousands and thousands of tons—and what you call them? Ornaments."

"And then the Andes?" I suggested.

"Why not?"

"But, my dear Desirée, what shall we do with the yacht?"

"Pooh! There is the captain. Come—shall I say please?"

So we went to Cerro de Pasco. I wrote to Captain Harris, telling him not to expect us for another month or so, and sending him sufficient funds to last till our return.

I verily believe that every one of note in Lima came to the railroad station to see us off.

Our compartment was a mass of flowers, which caused me to smile, for Le Mire, curiously enough, did not like them. When we had passed out of the city she threw them out of the window, laughing and making jokes at the expense of the donors. She was in the best of humor.

We arrived at Oroya late in the afternoon, and departed for Cerro de Pasco by rail on the following morning.

This ride of sixty-eight miles is unsurpassed in all the world. Snow-capped peaks, bottomless precipices, huge masses of boulders that seem ready to crush the train surround you on every side, and now and then are directly above or beneath you.

Le Mire was profoundly impressed; indeed, I had not supposed her to possess the sensibility she displayed; and as for me, I was most grateful to her for having suggested the trip. You who find yourselves too well-acquainted with the Rockies and the Alps and the Himalayas should try the Andes. There is a surprise waiting for you.

But for the story.

We found Cerro de Pasco, interesting as its situation is, far short of our expectations. It is a mining town, filled with laborers and speculators, noisy, dirty, and coarse. We had been there less than forty-eight hours when I declared to Harry and Le Mire my intention of returning at once.

"But the Andes!" said Le Mire. "Shall we not see them?"

"Well—there they are."

I pointed through the window of the hotel.

"Bah! And you call yourself a traveler? Look! The snow! My friend Paul, must I ask twice for a favor?"

Once again we tossed a coin.

Ah, if Le Mire had only seen the future! And yet—I often wonder—would she have turned her back? For the woman craved novelty and adventure, and the gameness of centuries was in her blood—well, she had her experience, which was shared only in part by Harry and myself.

Those snow-capped peaks! Little did we guess what they held for us. We were laughing, I remember, as we left behind us the edge of civilization represented by Cerro de Pasco.

We found it impossible to procure a complete outfit in the mining town, and were forced to despatch a messenger to Lima. He returned in two days with mules, saddles, saddle-bags, boots, leather leggings, knickerbockers, woolen ponchos, and scores of other articles which he assured us were absolutely necessary for any degree of comfort. By the time we were ready to start we had a good-sized pack-train on our hands.

The proprietor of the hotel found us an *arriero*, whom he declared to be the most competent and trustworthy guide in all the Andes—a long, loose-jointed fellow with an air of complete indifference habitually resting on his yellow, rather sinister-looking face. Le Mire did not like him, but I certainly preferred the hotel proprietor's experience and knowledge to her volatile fancy, and engaged the *arriero* on the spot.

Our outfit was complete, and everything in readiness, when Harry suddenly announced that he had decided not to go, nor to allow Le Mire to do so.

"I don't like it," he said in troubled tones. "I tell you, Paul, I don't like it. I've been talking to some of the miners and *arrieros,* and the thing is foolhardy and dangerous."

Then, seeing the expression on my face, he continued hastily: "Oh, not for myself. You know me; I'll do anything that any one else will do, and more, if I can. But Desirée! I tell you, if anything happened to her I—well—"

I cut him short:

"My dear boy, the idea is Desirée's own. And to talk of danger where she is concerned! She would laugh at you."

"She has," Harry confessed with a doubtful smile.

I clapped him roughly on the shoulder.

"Come, brace up! Our caravan awaits us—and see, the fairy, too. Are you ready, Desirée?"

She came toward us from the inner rooms of the hotel, smiling, radiant. I shall never forget the picture she presented. She wore white knickerbockers, a white jacket, tan-leather boots and leggings and a khaki hat.

Her golden hair, massed closely about her ears and upon her forehead, shimmered in the bright sun dazzlingly; her eyes sparkled; her little white teeth gleamed in a happy, joyous smile.

We lifted her to the back of her mule, then mounted our own. Suddenly a recollection shot through my brain with remarkable clearness, and I turned to Le Mire:

"Desirée, do you know the first time I ever saw you? It was in an electric brougham at the Gare du Nord. This is somewhat different, my lady."

"And infinitely more interesting," she answered. "Are you ready? See that stupid *arriero!* Ah! After all, he knew what he was about. Then, *messieurs—allons!*"

The *arriero,* receiving my nod uttered a peculiar whistle

through his teeth. The mules pricked up their ears, then with one common movement started forward.

"Adios! Adios, señora! Adios, señores!"

With the cry of our late host sounding in our ears we passed down the narrow little street of Cerro de Pasco on our way to the snow-capped peaks of the Andes.

Chapter V.

THE CAVE OF THE DEVIL.

You may remember that I made some remark concerning the difficulty of the ascent of Pike's Peak. Well, that is mere child's play—a morning constitutional compared to the paths we found ourselves compelled to follow in the great Cordillera.

Nor was it permitted us to become gradually accustomed to the danger; we had not been two hours out of Cerro de Pasco before we found ourselves creeping along a ledge so narrow there was scarcely room for the mules to place their hoofs together, over a precipice three thousand feet in the air—straight. And, added to this was the discomfort, amounting at times to positive pain, caused by the *soroche.*

Hardly ever did we find ground sufficiently broad for a breathing space, save when our *arriero* led us, almost by magic it seemed, to a camping place for the night. We would ascend the side of a narrow valley; on one hand roared a torrent some hundreds of feet below; on the other rose an uncompromising wall of rock. So narrow would be the track that as I sat astride my mule my outside leg would be hanging over the abyss.

But the grandeur, the novelty, and the variety of the scenery repaid us; and Le Mire loved the danger for its own sake. Time and again she swayed far out of her saddle until her body was literally suspended in the air above some frightful chasm, while she turned her head to laugh gaily at Harry and myself, who brought up the rear.

"But Desirée! If the girth should break!"

"Oh, but it won't."

"But if it should?"

"Tra-la-la! Come, catch me!"

And she would try to urge her mule into a trot—a futile effort, since the beast had a much higher regard for his skin than she had for hers; and the mule of the *arriero* was but a few feet ahead.

Thus we continued day after day, I can't say how many. There was a fascination about the thing that was irresistible. However high the peak we had ascended, another could be seen still higher, and that, too, must be scaled.

The infinite variety of the trail, its surprises, its new dangers, its apparent vanishings into thin air, only to be found, after an all but impossible curve, up the side of another cliff, coaxed us on and on; and when or where we would have been able to say, "thus far and no farther" is an undecided problem to this day.

About three o'clock one afternoon we camped in a small clearing at the end of a narrow valley. Our *arriero,* halting us at that early hour, had explained that there was no other camping ground within six hours' march, and no *hacienda* or *pueblo* within fifty miles. We received his explanation with the indifference of those to whom one day is like every other day, and amused ourselves by inspecting our surroundings while he prepared the evening meal and arranged the camp beds.

Back of us lay the trail by which we had approached—a narrow, sinuous ribbon clinging to the side of the huge cliffs like a snake fastened to a rock. On the left side, immediately above us, was a precipice some thousand feet in height; on the right a series of massive boulders, of quartzite and granite, misshapen and lowering.

There were three, I remember, placed side by side like three giant brothers; then two or three smaller ones in a row, and beyond these many others ranged in a mass unevenly, sometimes so close together that they appeared to be jostling one another out of the way.

For several days we had been in the region of perpetual snow; and soon we gathered about the fire which the *arriero* had kindled for our camp. Its warmth was grateful, despite our native woolen garments and heavy ponchos.

The wind whistled ominously; a weird, senseless sound that smote the ear with madness. The white of the snow and the dull gray of the rocks were totally unrelieved by any touch of green or play of water; a spot lonely as the human soul and terrifying as death.

Harry had gone to examine the hoofs of his mule, which had limped slightly during the afternoon; Le Mire and I sat side by side near the fire, gazing at the play of the flames. For some minutes we had been silent.

"In Paris, perhaps—" she began suddenly, then stopped short and became again silent.

But I was fast dropping into melancholy and wanted to hear her voice, and I said:

"Well? In Paris—"

She looked at me, her eyes curiously somber, but did not speak. I insisted:

"You were saying, Desirée, in Paris—"

She made a quick movement and laughed unpleasantly.

"Yes, my friend—but it is useless. I was thinking of you. 'Ah! A card! Mr. Paul Lamar. Show him in, Julie. But no, let him wait—I am not at home.' That, my friend, would be in Paris."

I stared at her.

"For Heaven's sake, Desirée, what nonsense is this?"

She disregarded my question as she continued:

"Yes, that is how it would be. Why do I talk thus? The mountains hypnotize me. The snow, the solitude—for I am alone. Your brother, what is he? And you, Paul, are scarcely aware of my existence.

"I had my opportunity with you, and I laughed it away. And as for the future—look! Do you see that waste of snow and ice, glittering, cold, pitiless? Ha! Well, that is my grave."

I tried to believe that she was merely amusing herself, but the glow in her eyes did not proceed from mirth. I followed her fixed gaze across the trackless waste and, shivering, demanded:

"What morbid fancy is this, Desirée? Come, it is scarcely pleasant."

She rose and crossed the yard or so of ground between us to my side. I felt her eyes above me, and try as I would I could not look up to meet them. Then she spoke, in a voice low but curiously distinct:

"Paul, I love you."

"My dear Desirée!"

"I love you."

At once I was myself, calm and smiling. I was convinced that she was acting, and I dislike to spoil a good scene. So I merely said:

"I am flattered, *señora*."

"Ah!"

She sighed, placing her hand on my shoulder.

"You laugh at me. You are wrong. Have I chosen this place for a flirtation? Before, I could not speak; now you must know. There have been many men in my life, Paul; some fools, some not so, but none like you. I have never said, 'I love you.' I say it now. Once you held my hand—you have never kissed me."

I rose to my feet, smiling, profoundly fatuous, and made as if to put my arm around her.

"A kiss? Is that all, Desirée? Well—"

But I had mistaken her tone and overreached. Not a muscle did she move, but I felt myself repulsed as by a barrier of steel. She remained standing perfectly still, searching me with a gaze that left me naked of levity and cynicism and the veneer of life; and finally she murmured in a voice sweet with pain:

"Must you kill me with words, Paul? I did not mean that—now. It is too late."

Then she turned swiftly and called to Harry, who came running over to her only to meet with some trivial request, and a minute later the *arriero* announced dinner.

I suppose that the incident had passed with her, as it had with me; little did I know how deeply I had wounded her. And when I discovered my mistake, some time later and under very different circumstances, it very nearly cost me my life, and Harry's into the bargain.

During the meal Le Mire was in the jolliest of moods apparently. She retold the tale of Balzac's heroine who crossed the Andes in the guise of a Spanish officer, performing wondrous exploits with her sword and creating havoc among the hearts of the fair ladies who took the dashing captain's sex for granted from his clothing.

The story was a source of intense amusement to Harry, who insisted on the recital of detail after detail, until Desirée allowed her memory to take a vacation and substitute pure imagination. Nor was the improvisation much inferior to the original.

It was still light when we finished dinner, a good three hours till bedtime. And since there was nothing better to do, I called to the *arriero* and asked him to conduct us on a tour of exploration among the mass of boulders, gray and stern, that loomed up on our right.

He nodded his head in his usual indifferent manner, and fifteen minutes later we started, on foot. The *arriero* led the way, with Harry at his heels, and Desirée and I brought up the rear.

Thrice I tried to enter into conversation with her; but each time she shook her head without turning round, and I gave it up. I was frankly puzzled by her words and conduct of an hour before; was it merely one of the trickeries of Le Mire or—

I was interested in the question as one is always interested in a riddle; but I tossd it from my mind, promising myself a solution on the morrow, and gave my attention to the vagaries of nature about me.

We were passing through a cleft between two massive rocks, some three or four hundred yards in length. Ahead of us, at the end of the passage, a like boulder fronted us.

Our footfalls echoed and reechoed from wall to wall; the only other sound was the eery moaning of the wind that reached our ears with a faintness which only served to increase its effect. Here and there were apertures large enough to admit the entrance of a horse and rider, and in many places the sides were crumbling.

I was reflecting, I remember, that the formation was

undoubtedly one of limestone, with here and there a layer or quartzite, when I was aroused by a shout from Harry.

I approached. Harry and Desirée, with Felipe, the *arriero*, had halted and were gazing upward at the wall of rock which barred the exit from the passage. Following their eyes, I saw lines carved on the rock, evidently a rude and clumsy attempt to reproduce the form of some animal.

The thing was some forty feet or so above us and difficult to see clearly.

"I say it's a llama," Harry was saying as I stopped at his side.

"My dear boy," returned Desirée, "don't you think I know a horse when I see one?"

"When you see one, of course," said Harry sarcastically. "But who ever saw a horse with a neck like that?"

As for me, I was really interested, and I turned to the *arriero* for information.

"Si, señor," said Felipe, *"Un caballo."*

"But who carved it?"

Felipe shrugged his shoulders.

"Is it new—Spanish?"

Another shrug. I became impatient.

"Have you no tongue?" I demanded. "Speak! If you don't know the author of that piece of equine art say so."

"I know, *señor*."

"You know?"

"Si, señor."

"Then, for Heaven's sake, tell us."

"His story?" pointing to the figure on the rock.

"Yes, idiot!"

Without a sign of interest, Felipe turned twice around, found a comfortable rock, sat down, rolled a cigarette, lighted it, and began. He spoke in Spanish dialect; I shall preserve the style as far as translation will permit.

"Many, many years ago, *señor*, Atahualpa, the Inca, son of Huayna-Capac, was imprisoned at Cajamarco. Four, five hundred years ago, it was. By the great Pizarro. And there was gold at Cuzco, to the south, and Atahualpa, for his ransom, ordered that this gold be brought to Pizarro.

"Messengers carried the order like the wind, so swift that in five days the priests of the sun carried their gold from the temples to save the life of Atahualpa."

Felipe paused, puffing at his cigarette, glanced at his audience, and continued:

"But Hernando Pizarro, brother of the great Pizarro, suspected a delay in the carriers of gold. From Pachacamac he came with twenty horsemen, sowing terror in the mountains, carrying eighty loads of gold. Across the Juaja River and past Lake Chinchaycocha they came, till they arrived at the city of Huánuco.

"There were temples and gold and priests and soldiers. But when the soldiers of the Inca saw the horses of the Spaniards and heard the guns, they became frightened and ran away like little children, carrying their gold. Never before had they seen white men, or guns, or horses.

"With them came many priests and women, to the snow of the mountains. And after many days of suffering they came to a cave, wherein they disappeared and no more were seen, nor could Hernando Pizarro and his twenty horsemen find them to procure their gold.

"And before they entered the cave they scaled a rock near its entrance and carved thereon the likeness of a horse to warn their Inca brethren of the Spaniards who had driven them from Huánuco. That is his story, *señor*."

"But who told you all this, Felipe?"

The *arriero* shrugged his shoulders and glanced about, as much as to say, "It is in the wind."

"But the cave?" cried Desirée. "Where is the cave?"

"It is there, *señora*," said Felipe, pointing through a passage to the right.

Then nothing would do for Desirée but to see the cave. The *arriero* informed her that it was difficult of access, but she turned the objection aside with contempt and commanded him to lead.

Harry, of course, was with her, and I followed somewhat

unwillingly; for, though Felipe's history was fairly accurate, I was inclined to regard his fable of the disappearing Incas as a wild tradition of the mountains.

He had spoken aright—the path to the cave was not an easy one. Here and there deep ravines caused us to make a wide détour or risk our necks on perilous steeps.

Finally we came to a small clearing, which resembled nothing so much as the bottom of a giant well, and in the center of one of the steep walls was an opening some thirty or forty feet square, black and rugged, and somehow terrifying.

It was the entrance to the cave.

There Felipe halted.

"Here, *señor*. Here entered the Incas of Huánuco with their gold."

He shivered as he spoke, and I fancied that his face grew pale.

"We shall explore it!" cried Desirée, advancing.

"But no, *senora!*" The *arriero* was positively trembling. "No! *Señor*, do not let her go within! Many times have my countrymen entered in search of the gold, and *americanos*, too, and never did they return. It is a cave of the devil, *señor*. He hides in the blackness and none who enter may escape him."

Desirée was laughing gaily.

"Then I shall visit the devil!" she exclaimed, and before either Harry or I could reach her she had sprung across the intervening space to the entrance and disappeared within.

With shouts of consternation from Felipe ringing in our ears, we leaped after her.

"Desirée!" cried Harry. "Come back, Desirée!"

There was no answer, but echoing back from the night before us came faint reverberations—could they be footsteps! What folly! For I had thought that she had merely intended to frighten poor Felipe, and now—

"Desirée!" Harry called again with all the strength of his lungs. "Desirée!"

Again there was no answer. Then we entered the cave

together. I remember that as we passed within I turned and saw Felipe staring with white face and eyes filled with terror.

A hundred feet and we were encompassed by the most intense darkness. I muttered: "This is folly; let us get a light," and tried to hold Harry back. But he pushed me aside and groped on, crying: "Desirée! Come back, Desirée!"

What could I do? I followed.

Suddenly a scream resounded through the cavern. Multiplied and echoed by the black walls, it was inhuman, shot with terror, profoundly horrible.

A tremor ran through me from head to foot; beside me I heard Harry gasp with a nameless fear. An instant later we dashed forward into the darkness.

How long we ran I could never tell; probably a few seconds, possibly as many minutes.

On we rushed, blindly, impelled not by reason, but by the memory of that terrible cry, side by side, gasping, fearful. And then—

A step into thin air—a mighty effort to recover a footing—a wild instant of despair and pawing helpless agony. Then blackness and oblivion.

Chapter VI.

CAPTURED.

The fall—was it ten feet or a thousand? I shall never know. Hurtling headlong through space, a man can scarcely be expected to keep his wits about him.

Actually, my only impression was of righteous indignation; my memory is that I cursed aloud, but Harry denies it.

But it could not have been for long, for when we struck the water at the bottom we were but slightly stunned by the impact. To this Harry has since agreed; he must have been as lucky as myself; for I took it headlong with a clean cleavage.

I rose to the top, sputtering, and flung out my arms in the attempt to swim—or, rather, to keep afloat—and was overjoyed to find my arms and legs answer to the call of the brain.

About me was blackest night and utter silence, save a low, unbroken murmur, unlike any other sound, hardly to be heard. It was in my effort to account for it that I first became aware of the fact that the water was a stream, and a moving one—moving with incredible swiftness, smooth and all but silent. As soon as I became convinced of this I gave up all attempt to swim, and satisfied myself with keeping my head above the surface and drifting with the current.

Then I thought of Harry, and called his name aloud many times. The reverberations throughout the cave were as the report of a thousand cannon; but there was no response.

The echoes became fainter and fainter and died away, and again all was silence and impenetrable night, while I battled with the strong suction of the unseen current, which was growing swifter and swifter, and felt my strength begin to leave me.

Terror, too, began to call to me as the long minutes passed endlessly by. I thought, "If I could only see!" and strained my eyes in the effort till I was forced to close them from the dizzy pain. The utter, complete darkness hid from

51

me all knowledge of what I passed or what awaited me beyond.

The water, carrying me swiftly onward with its silent, remorseless sweep, was cold and black; it pressed with tremendous power against me; now and then I was forced beneath the surface and fought my way back, gasping and all but exhausted.

I forgot Desirée and Harry; I lost all consciousness of where I was and what I was doing; the silent fury of the stream and the awful blackness maddened me; I plunged and struggled desperately, blindly, sobbing with rage. This could not have lasted much longer; I was very near the end.

Suddenly, with a thrill of joy, I realized that the speed of the current was decreasing. Then a reaction of despair seized me; I tried to strangle hope and resign myself to the worst. But soon there was no longer any doubt; the water carried me slower and slower.

I floated with little difficulty, wondering—could it be an approach to a smaller outlet which acted as a dam? Or was it merely a lessening of the incline of the bed of the stream? I cursed the darkness for my helplessness.

Finally the water became absolutely still, as I judged by the absence of pressure on my body, and I turned sharply at a right angle and began to swim. My weariness left me as by magic, and I struck out with bold and sweeping strokes; and by that lack of caution all but destroyed myself when my head suddenly struck against a wall of stone, unseen in the darkness.

I was stunned completely and sank; but the ducking revived me; and when I returned to the surface I swam a few careful strokes, searching for the wall. It was not there, and I had no idea of its direction. But I had now learned caution; and by swimming a few feet first one way, then another, and taking care not to go far in any one direction, I finally discovered it.

My hand easily reached the top, and, grasping the slippery surface with a grip made firm by despair, and concentrating every ounce of strength in one final effort, I drew myself out of the water and fell completely exhausted on the ground.

Under such circumstances time has no place in a man's calculations; he is satisfied to breathe. I believe that I lay barely conscious for several hours, but it may have been merely as many minutes. Then I felt life stir within me; I stretched my arms and legs and sat up. Gradually entered my mind the thought of Desirée and Harry and the Andes above and Felipe shuddering with terror as he flew from the cave of the devil.

First came Harry; but hope did not enter. It was inconceivable that he, too, should have escaped that fearful torrent; stupendous luck alone had saved me from being dashed senseless against the rocks and guided me to the ledge on which I rested.

Then he was gone! I had no thought of my own peril. I had gone through the world with but little regard for what it held; nothing had been sacred to me; no affection had been more than a day's caprice; I had merely sucked amusement from its bitter fruit.

But I loved Harry; I realized it with something like astonishment. He was dear to me; a keen, intense pain contracted my chest at the thought of having lost him; tears filled my eyes; and I raised up my voice and sang out wildly:

"Harry! Harry, lad! Harry!"

The cavern resounded. The call went from wall to wall, then back again, floating through black space with a curious tremor, and finally died away in some dim, unseen corridor. And then—then came an answering call!

Owing to the conflicting echoes of the cavern, the tone could not be recognized. But the word was unmistakable; it was "Paul."

I sprang to my feet with a shout, then stood listening. Out of the blackness surrounding me came the words, in Harry's voice, much lower, but distinct:

"Paul! Paul, where are you?"

"Thank Heaven!" I breathed; and I answered:

"Here, Harry boy, here."

"But where?"

"I don't know. On a ledge of rock at the edge of the water. Where are you?"

"Same place. Which side are you on?"

"The *right* side," I answered with heartfelt emphasis. "That is to say, the outside. If it weren't for this infernal darkness—Listen! How far away does my voice sound?"

But the innumerable echoes of the cavern walls made it impossible to judge of distance by sound. We tried it over and over; sometimes it seemed that we were only a few feet apart, sometimes a mile or more.

Then Harry spoke in a whisper, and his voice appeared to be directly in my ear. Never have I seen a night so completely black as that cavern; we had had several hours, presumably, for our eyes to adjust themselves to the phenomenon; but when I held my hand but six inches in front of my face I could not get even the faintest suggestion of its outline.

"This is useless," I declared finally. "We must experiment. Harry!"

"Yes."

"Turn to your left and proceed carefully along the edge. I'll turn to my right. Go easy, lad; feel your way."

I crawled on my hands and knees, no faster than a snail, feeling every inch of the ground. The surface was wet and slippery, and in places sloped at an angle that made me hang on for dear life to keep from shooting off into space.

Meantime I kept calling to Harry and he to me; but, on account of our painfully slow progress, it was half an hour or more before we discovered that the distance between us was being increased instead of lessened.

He let fly an oath at this, and his tone was dangerous; no wonder if the lad was half crazed! I steadied him as well as I could with word of encouragement, and instructed him to turn about and proceed to the right of his original position. I, also, turned to the left.

Our hope of meeting lay in the probability that the ledge

surrounded a circular body of water and was continuous. At some point, of course, was the entrance of the stream which had carried us, and at some other point there was almost certainly an outlet; but we trusted to luck to avoid these. Our chances were less than one in a thousand; but, failing that, some other means must be invented.

The simplest way would have been for me to take to the water and swim across to Harry, counting on his voice as a guide; but the conflicting echoes produced by the slightest sound rendered such an attempt dangerous.

I crept along that wet, slimy, treacherous surface, it seemed, for hours. I could see nothing—absolutely nothing; everything was black void; it was hard to appreciate reality in such a nightmare. On the one side, nameless dangers; on the other, the unseen, bottomless lake; enough, surely, to take a man's nerve. My fear for Harry killed anxiety on my own account. We kept continually calling:

"Harry!"

"Yes."

"Steady."

"Yes. I'm coming along. I say, we're closer, Paul."

I hesitated to agree with him, but finally there was no longer any doubt of it. His voice began to reach me almost in natural tones, which meant that we were near enough for the vibrations to carry without interference from the walls.

Nearer still it came; it was now only a matter of a few feet; Harry gave a cry of joy, and immediately afterward I heard his low gasp of terror and the sound of his wild scrambling to regain a foothold. In his excitement he had forgotten caution and had slipped to the edge of the water.

I dared not try to go his assistance; so I crouched perfectly still and called to him to throw himself flat on his face. How my eyes strained despairingly as I cursed the pitiless darkness! Then the scrambling ceased and the boy's voice sounded:

"All right, Paul! All right! Gad, I nearly went!"

A minute later I held his hand in mine. At that point the incline was at a sharp angle, and we lay flat on our backs.

For many minutes we lay silently gripping hands; Harry was trembling violently from nervous fatigue, and I myself was unable to speak.

What strength is there in companionship! Alone, either of us would probably have long before succumbed to the strain of our horrible situation; but we both took hope and courage from that hand-clasp.

Finally he spoke:

"In Heaven's name, where are we, Paul?"

"You know as much as I do, Harry. This cursed darkness makes it impossible even to guess at anything. According to Felipe, we are being entertained by the devil."

"But where are we? What happened? My head is dizzy—I don't know—"

I gripped his hand.

"And no wonder. 'Tis hardly an every-day occurrence to ride an underground river several miles under the Andes. Above us a mountain four miles high, beneath us a bottomless lake, round us darkness. Not a very cheerful prospect, Hal; but, thank Heaven, we take it together! It is a grave—ours and hers. I guess Desirée knew what she was talking about."

There came a cry from Harry's lips—a cry of painful memory:

"Desirée! I had forgotten, Desirée!"

"She is probably better off then we are," I assured him. I felt his gaze—I could not see it—and I continued:

"We may as well meet the thing squarely like men. Pull yourself together, Harry; as for Desirée, let us hope that she is dead. It's the best thing that could happen to her."

"Then we are—no, it isn't possible."

"Harry boy, we're buried alive! There! That's the worst of it. Anything better than that is velvet."

"But there must be a way out, Paul! And Desirée—Desirée—"

His voice faltered. I clapped him roughly on the shoulder.

"Keep your nerve. As for a way out—at the rate that

stream descends it must have carried us thousands of feet beneath the mountain. There is probably a mile of solid rock between us and the sunshine. You felt the strength of that current; you might as well try to swim up Niagara."

"But there must be an outlet at the other end."

"Yes, and most probably forty or fifty miles away—that's the distance to the western slope. Besides, how can we find it? And there may be none. The water is most probably gradually absorbed by the porous formation of the rocks, and that is what causes this lake."

"But why isn't it known? Felipe said that the cave had been explored. Why didn't they discover the stream?"

Well, it was better to talk of that than nothing; at least, it kept Harry from his childish cries for Desirée. So I explained that the precipice over which we had fallen was presumably of recent origin.

Geologically the Andes are yet in a chaotic and formative condition; huge slides of Silurian slates and diorite are of frequent occurrence. A ridge of one of these softer stones had most probably been encased in the surrounding granite for many centuries; then, loosened by water or by time, had crumbled and slid into the stream below.

"And," I finished, "we followed it."

"Then we may find another," said Harry hopefully.

I agreed that it was possible. Then he burst out:

"In the name of Heaven, don't be so cool! We can't get out till we try. Come! And who knows—we may find Desirée."

Then I decided it was best to tell him. Evidently the thought had not entered his mind, and it was best for him to realize the worst. I gripped his hand tighter as I said:

"Nothing so pleasant, Harry. Because we're going to starve to death."

"Starve to death?" he exclaimed. Then he added simply, with an oddly pathetic tone: "I hadn't thought of that."

After that we lay silent for many minutes in that awful darkness. Thoughts and memories came and went in my brain with incredible swiftness; pictures long forgotten presented themselves; an endless, jumbled panorama.

They say that a drowning man reviews his past life in the space of a few seconds; it took me a little more time, but the job was certainly a thorough one. Nor did I find it more interesting in retrospect than it had been in reality.

I closed my eyes to escape the darkness. It was maddening; easy enough then to comprehend the hysterics of the blind and sympathize with them. It finally reached a point where I was forced to grit my teeth to keep from breaking out into curses; I could lie still no longer, exhausted as I was, and Harry, too. I turned on him:

"Come on, Hal; let's move."

"Where?" he asked in a tone devoid of hope.

"Anywhere—away from this beastly water. We must dry out our clothing; no use dying like drowned rats. If I only had a match!"

We rose to our hands and knees and crawled painfully up the slippery incline. Soon we had reached dry ground and stood upright; then, struck by a sudden thought, I turned to Harry:

"Didn't you drink any of that water?"

He answered: "No."

"Well, let's try it. It may be or last drink, Hal; make it a good one."

We crept back down to the edge of the lake (I call it that in my ignorance of its real nature), and, settling myself as firmly as possible, I held Harry's hand while he lowered himself carefully into the water. He was unable to reach its surface with his mouth without letting go of my hand, and I shook off my poncho and used it as a line.

"How does it taste?" I asked.

"Fine!" was the response. "It must be clear as a bell. Lord, I didn't know I was so thirsty!"

I was not ignorant of the fact that there was an excellent chance of the water being unhealthful, possibly poisoned, what with the tertiary deposits of copper ores in the rock-basins; but the thought awakened hope rather than fear. There is a choice even in death.

But when I had pulled Harry up and descended myself I

soon found that there was no danger—or chance. The water had a touch of alkali, but nothing more.

Then we crept back up the wet ledge, and once more stood on dry ground.

The surface was perfectly level, and we set off at a brisk pace, hand in hand, directly away from the lake. But when, about a hundred yards off, we suddenly bumped our heads against a solid wall of rock, we decided to proceed with more caution.

The darkness was intensified, if anything. We turned to the right and groped along the wall, which was smooth as glass and higher than my best reach. It seemed to the touch to be slightly convex, but that may have been delusion.

We had proceeded in this manner some hundred yards or more, advancing cautiously, when we came to a break in the wall. A few feet farther the wall began again.

"It's a tunnel," said Harry.

I nodded, forgetting he could not see me. "Shall we take it?"

"Anything on a chance," he answered, and we entered the passage.

It was quite narrow—so narrow that we were forced to advance very slowly, feeling our way to avoid colliding with the walls. The ground was strewn with fragments of rock, and a hasty step meant an almost certain fall and a bruised shin. It was tedious work and incredibly fatiguing.

We had not rested a sufficient length of time to allow our bodies to recuperate from the struggle with the torrent; also, we began to feel the want of food. Harry was the first to falter, but I spurred him on. Then he stumbled and fell and lay still.

"Are you hurt?" I asked anxiously, bending over him.

"No," was the answer. "But I'm tired—tired to death—and I want to sleep."

I was tempted myself, but I brought him to his feet, from some impulse I know not what. For what was the use? One spot was as good as another. However, we struggled on.

Another hour and the passage broadened into a clearing.

At least so it seemed; the walls abruptly parted to the right and left. And still the impenetrable, maddening darkness and awful silence!

We gave it up; we could go no farther. A few useless minutes we wasted, searching for a soft spot to lie on—moss, reeds, anything. We found none, of course; but even the hard, unyielding rock was grateful to our exhausted bodies. We lay side by side, using our ponchos for pillows; our clothing at least was dry.

I do not know how long I slept, but it seemed to me that I had barely dozed off when I was awakened by something—what?

There was no sound to my strained ears. I sat up, gazing intently into the darkness, shuddering without apparent reason. Then I reflected that nothing is dangerous to a man who faces death, and I laughed aloud—then trembled at the sound of my own voice. Harry was in sound sleep beside me; his regular breathing told of its depth.

Again I lay down, but I could not sleep. Some instinct, long forgotten, quivered within me, telling me that we were no longer alone. And soon my ear justified it.

At first it was not a sound, but the mere shadow of one. It was rhythmic, low, beating like a pulse. What could it be? Again I sat up, listening and peering into the darkness. And this time I was not mistaken—there was a sound, rustling, sibilant.

Little by little it increased, or rather approached, until it sounded but a few feet from me on every side, sinister and menacing. It was the silent, suppressed breathing of something living—whether animal or man—creeping ever nearer.

Then was the darkness doubly horrible. I sat paralyzed with my utter helplessness, though fear, thank Heaven, did not strike me! I could hear no footstep; no sound of any kind but that low, rushing breathing; but it now was certain that whatever the thing was, it was not alone.

From every side I heard it—closer, closer—until finally I

felt the hot, fetid breath in my very face. My nerves quivered in disgust, not far from terror.

I sprang to my feet with a desperate cry to Harry and swung toward him.

There was no answering sound, no rush of feet, nothing; but I felt my throat gripped in monstrous, hairy fingers.

I tried to struggle, and immediately was crushed to the ground by the overpowering weight of a score of soft, ill-smelling bodies.

The grasp on my throat tightened; my arms relaxed, my brain reeled, and I knew no more.

Chapter VII.

THE FIGHT IN THE DARK.

I returned to consciousness with a sickening sensation of nausea and unreality. Only my brain was alive; my entire body was numb and as though paralyzed. Still darkness and silence, for all my senses told me I might have been still in the spot where I had fallen.

Then I tried to move my arms, and found that my hands and feet were firmly bound. I strained at the thongs, making some slight sound; and immediately I heard a whisper but a few feet away:

"Are you awake, Paul?"

I was still half dazed, but I recognized Harry's voice, and I answered simply: "Yes. Where are we?"

"The Lord knows! They carried us. You have been unconscious for hours."

"They carried us?"

"Yes. A thousand miles, I think, on their backs. What—what are they, Paul?"

"I don't know. Did you see them?"

"No. Too dark. They are strong as gorillas and covered with hair; I felt that much. They didn't make a sound all the time. No more than half as big as me, and yet one of them carried me as if I were a baby—and I weigh one hundred and seventy pounds."

"What are we bound with?"

"Don't know; it feels like leather; tough as rats. I've been working at it for two hours, but it won't give."

"Well, you know what that means. Dumb brutes don't tie a man up."

"But it's impossible."

"Nothing is impossible. But listen!"

There was a sound—the swift patter of feet; they were approaching. Then suddenly a form bent over me close; I could see nothing, but I felt a pressure against my body and an ill-smelling odor, indescribable, entered my nostrils. I felt a sawing movement at my wrists; the thongs pulled back and forth, and soon my hands were free. The form straightened away from me, there was a clatter on the ground near my head, and then silence.

There came an oath from Harry:

"Hang the brute! He's cut my wrist. Are your hands free, Paul?"

"Yes."

"Then bind this up; it's bleeding badly. What was that for?"

"I have an idea," I answered as I tore a strip from my shirt and bandaged the wound, which proved to be slight. Then I searched on the ground beside me, and found my surmise correct.

"Here you go, Hal! here's some grub. But what the deuce is it? By Jove, it's dried fish! Now, where in the name of—"

But we wasted no more time in talk, for we were half starved. The stuff was not bad; to us who had been fasting for something like thirty-six hours—for our idea of time was extremely hazy—it was a gorgeous banquet. And close by there was a basin full of water.

"Pretty decent sort of beggars, I say," came Harry's voice in the darkness. "But who are they?"

"Ask Felipe," I answered, for by this time I was well convinced of the nature and identity of our captors. "As I said, dumb brutes don't bind men with thongs, nor feed them on dried fish. Of course it's incredible, but a man must be prepared to believe anything."

"But, Paul! You mean—"

"Exactly. We are in the hands of the Incas of Huánuco—or rather their descendants."

"But that was four hundred years ago!"

"Your history is perfect, like Desirée's geography," said I dryly. "But what then? They have merely chosen to live under the world instead of on it; a rather wise decision, a cynic might say—not to mention the small circumstance that they are prisoners.

"My dear Hal, never allow yourself to be surprised at

anything; it is a weakness. Here we are in total darkness, buried in the Andes, surrounded by hairy, degenerate brutes that are probably allowing us to eat in order that we may be in condition to be eaten, with no possibility of ever again beholding the sunshine; and what is the thought that rises to the surface of my mind? Merely this: that I most earnestly desire and crave a Carbajal perfecto and a match."

"Paul, you say—eat—"

"Most probably they are cannibals. The Lord knows they must have some sort of mild amusement in this fearful hole. Of course, the idea is distasteful; before they cut us up they'll have to knock us down."

"That's a darned silly joke," said Harry with some heat.

"But it's sober truth, my boy. You know me; I never pose. There is nothing particularly revolting in the thought of being eaten; the disadvantage of it lies in the fact that one must die first. We all want to live; Heaven knows why. And we stand a chance.

"We know now that there is food to be had here and sufficient air. It is nearly certain that we won't get out, but that can come later. And what an experience! I know a dozen anthropologists that would give their degrees for it. I can feel myself getting enthusiastic about it."

"But what if they—they—"

"Say it. Eat us? We can fight. It will be strange if we can't outwit these vermin. And now silence; I'm going to begin. Listen hard—hard! The brutes are noiseless, but if they are near we can hear their breathing."

"But, Paul—"

"No more talk. Listen!"

We lay silent for many minutes, scarcely breathing. Not the slightest sound reached our ears through the profound darkness; utter, intense silence. Finally I reached over and touched Harry on the shoulder, and arose to my knees.

"Good enough! We're alone. We'll have to crawl for it. Keep close behind me; we don't want to get separated. The first thing is to find a sharp stone to cut through these thongs. Feel on the ground with your hands as we go."

It was not easy to rise at all, and still harder to make any progress, for our ankles were bound together most effectively; but we managed somehow to drag ourselves along. I was in front; suddenly I felt Harry pull at my coat, and turned.

"Just the thing, Paul. Sharp as a knife. Look!"

I groped for his hand in the darkness and took from it the object he held out to me—a small flat stone with a sharp-saw edge.

"All right; let me work on you first."

I bent down to the thongs which bound his ankles. I was convinced that they were not of leather, but they were tough as the thickest hide. Twice my overeagerness caused the tool to slip and tear the skin from my hand; then I went about it more carefully with a muttered oath. Another quarter of an hour and Harry was free.

"Gad, that feels good!" he exclaimed, rising to his feet. "Here, Paul; where's the stone?"

I handed it to him and he knelt down and began sawing away at my feet.

What followed happened so quickly that we were hardly aware that it had begun when it was already finished.

A quick, pattering rush of many feet warned us, but not in time. Hurtling, leaping bodies came at us headlong through the air and crushed us to the ground, buried beneath them, gasping for breath; there must have been scores of them. Resistance was impossible; we were overwhelmed.

I heard Harry give a despairing cry, and the scuffle followed; I myself was utterly helpless, for the thongs which bound my ankles had not been cut through. Not a sound came from our assailants save their heavy, labored breathing.

I remember that, even while they were sitting on my head and chest and body, I noted their silence with a sort of impersonal curiosity and wondered if they were, after all, human. Nor were they unnecessarily violent; they merely subdued us, rebound our wrists and ankles more tightly than before, and departed.

But—faugh! The unspeakable odor of their hairy bodies is in my nostrils yet.

"Are you hurt, Paul?"

"Not a bit, Harry lad. How do you like the perfume?"

"To the deuce with your perfume! But we're done for. What's the use? They've lived in this infernal hole so long they can see in the dark better than we can in the light."

Of course he was right, and I was a fool not to have thought of it before and practised caution. The knowledge was decidedly unpleasant. No doubt our every movement was being watched by a hundred pairs of eyes, while we lay helpless in the darkness, bound even more tightly than before.

"Look here," said Harry suddenly, "why can't we see their eyes? Why don't they shine."

"My dear boy," said I, "in this darkness you couldn't see the Kohinoor diamond if it were hanging on your nose, drawing-room travelers to the contrary notwithstanding. We have one advantage—they can't understand what we say, but they even up for it by not saying anything."

There was a short silence, then Harry's voice:

"Paul—"

"Well?"

"I wonder—do you think Desirée—" He hesitated, his voice faltering.

"I think the same as you do," said I.

"But I don't know—after all, there is a chance. Just a bare chance, isn't there?"

"You know as well as I do, Harry. The chances are a million to one that Desirée—thank Heaven—has escaped all this! And isn't that best! Would you have her here with us?"

"No—no. Only—"

"Lying here, bound hand and foot? She would make a dainty morsel for our friends."

"For the Lord's sake, Paul—"

"Well, let us forget her—for the present. Nor do we want to make a dainty morsel if we can help it. Come, brace up, Hal. It's up to us to turn a trick."

"Well?"

"I don't know why I didn't think of it before. I guess we were both too dazed to have good sense. What have you got strapped to your belt?"

"A gun," said Harry. "Of course I thought of that. But what good is it after that ducking? And I have only six cartridges."

"Nothing else?"

I could almost feel his silent gaze; then suddenly he cried out:

"A knife!"

"At last!" said I sarcastically. "And so have I. A six-inch, double-edged knife, sharp as a razor and pointed like a needle. They didn't have sense enough to search us, and we didn't have sense enough to realize it. I can feel mine under me now against the ground."

"But they'll see us."

"Not if we use a decent amount of caution. The trouble is, I can't reach my knife with my wrists bound. There's only one way. Lie perfectly still; let them think we've given it up. I'm going to try something."

I drew up my knees, twisted over on the hard rock, and lay flat on my belly. Then I drew up my hands and let my face rest on them, like a dog with his head on his paws. And then, keeping my body perfectly still, and with as little movement of the jaws as possible, I sought the tough thongs with my teeth.

That was a tedious job and a distasteful one. For many minutes I gnawed away at those thick cords like a dog on a bone. It was considerably later that I discovered what those cords were made of; thank Heaven, I was ignorant of it at the time! All I knew was that they were, to use one of Harry's phrases, "tough as rats."

I did not dare pull with my wrists, for fear they would fly

suddenly apart and betray me to the unseen watchers. It was necessary to cut clear through with my teeth, and more than once I was on the point of giving it up. There was a nauseating, rancid taste to the stuff, but I dared not even raise my head to expectorate.

Finally my teeth met; the cords were severed. I felt carefully about with my tongue to make sure there were no others; then, without moving my hands in the slightest degree, carefully raised my head.

It was then that I first noticed—not light, but a thinning out of the darkness. It was, of course, merely the adjustment of my eyes to the new conditions. I could make out no forms surrounding me, but, looking down, I could clearly distinguish the outline of my hands as they lay on the ground before me.

And, again looking up, I fancied that I could see, some twenty or thirty feet to the right, that the darkness again became suddenly dense and impenetrable.

"That must be a wall," I muttered, straining my eyes toward it.

"What's that?" asked Harry sharply.

Obedient to my instructions, the lad had lain perfectly motionless and silent for over an hour, for it must have taken me at least that long to gnaw through the cords.

"I said that must be a wall. Look, Harry, about thirty feet to the right. Doesn't it appear to you that way?"

"By Jove," he exclaimed after a moment of silence, "it's geting light! Look!"

I explained that, instead of "it's getting light," his eyes were merely becoming accustomed to the darkness.

"But what do you think of that? Is it a wall?"

After a moment's silence he answered: "Ye-es," and then more positively: "Yes. But what good does that do us?"

"That's what I am about to tell you. Listen! I've cut the cords on my wrists, and I'm going to get my knife—"

"How the deuce did you manage that?" Harry interrupted.

"With my teeth. I've been rather busy. I'm going to get my

knife—cautiously, so they won't suspect if they are watching us. We must lie close together on our sides, facing each other, so I can cut the thongs on your wrists without being seen. Then you are to get your knife—carefully. Do you understand?"

"Yes."

For the first time there was fight in Harry's voice; the curious, barely perceptible tremor of the man of courage.

"All right. Go easy."

We went about the thing slowly, turning but an inch at a time; a second mistake might prove fatal. We heard no sound of any kind, and ten minutes later we were lying flat on our backs side by side, keeping our hands hidden between our bodies, that the absence of the thongs might not be discovered. Each of us held in his right hand the hilt of a six inch knife. Cold steel is by no means the favorite weapon of an American, but there are times—

"Have you got your knife, Harry?"

"Yes."

"Good! Now listen close and act quick. When I give the word reach down and grasp the cords round your ankles in your left hand, then cut them through with one stroke. Then to your feet; grasp my jacket, and together to the wall—that's for our backs. And then—let 'em come!"

"All right, old man."

"Don't waste any time; they'll probably start for us the instant we sit up. Be sure you get your feet free at the first stroke; feel them well with your left hand first. Are you ready?"

"Yes." And his voice was now calm and perfectly steady.

"Then—one, two, three—go!"

We bent and cut and sprang to our feet, and dashed for the wall. There was a sound of rushing feet—our backs hugged the kindly rock—I heard Harry's shout, "Here they come!"—dim, rushing forms—fingers clutching at my throat.

I felt the blade of my knife sink into soft and yielding flesh, and a warm, thick liquid flow over my hand and arm.

Chapter VIII.

THE DANCE OF THE SUN.

It seemed to me then in the minutes that followed that there were thousands of black demons in that black hole. At the first rushing impact I shouted to Harry: "Keep your back to the wall," and for response I got a high, ringing laugh that breathed the joy of battle.

The thing was sickening. Harry is a natural fighting man; I am not. Without the wall at our backs we would have been overpowered in thirty seconds; as it was, we were forced to handle half a dozen of them at once, while the others surged in from behind. They had no weapons, but they had the advantage of being able to see us.

They clutched my throat, my arms, my legs, my body; there was no room to strike; I pushed the knife home. They fastened themselves to my legs and feet and tried to bring me down from beneath; once, in slashing at the head of one whose teeth were set in my calf, I cut myself on the knee. It was difficult to stand in the wet, slippery pool that formed at my feet.

Suddenly I heard a sound that I understood too well—the curious, rattling sound of a man who is trying to call out when he is being strangled.

"Harry!" I cried, and I fought like a wild man to get to him, with knife, feet, hands, teeth. I reached his coat, his arm; it was dangerous to strike so near him in the dark, but I felt him sinking to the ground.

Then I found the taut, straining fingers about his throat, and lunged forward with the knife—and the fingers relaxed.

Again we were fighting together side by side.

As their bodies fell in front of us we were pressed harder, for those behind climbed up on the corpses of their fellows and literally descended on our heads from the air. We could not have held out much longer; our breath was coming in quick, painful gasps; Harry stumbled on one of the prostrate brutes and fell; I tried to lift him and was unequal to the task.

It appeared to be the end.

Suddenly there rang throughout the cavern a sound as of a gigantic, deep-toned bell. The walls sent it back and forth with deafening echoes; it was as though the mountain had descended with one tremendous crash into its own bowels.

As though by magic, the assault ceased.

The effect was indescribable. We could see nothing; we merely became suddenly aware that there were no longer hands clutching at our throats or hairy bodies crushing us to the ground. It was as though the horde of unseen devils had melted into thin air. There were movements on the ground, for many of them had been wounded; a man cannot always reach the spot in the dark. This lasted for two or three minutes; they were evidently removing those who still had life in them, for the straining breath of men dragging or lifting burdens was plainly audible.

Gradually that, too, died away with the last reverberations of the mysterious sound that had saved us, and we found ourselves alone—or at least unmolested—for in the darkness we could see nothing, except the dim outlines of the prostrate forms at our feet.

The cavern was a shambles. The smell was that of a slaughter-house. I had had no idea of the desperateness of our defense until I essayed to scramble over the heap of bodies to dry ground; I shuddered and grew faint, and Harry was in no better case.

Worse, he had dropped his knife when we stumbled, and we were forced to grope round in that unspeakable mess for many minutes before we found it.

"Are you hurt, lad?" I asked when once we stood clear.

"Nothing bad, I think," he answered. "My throat is stiff, and two or three of the brutes got their teeth in me. In the name of Heaven, Paul, what are they? And what was that bell?"

These were foolish questions, and I told him so. My leg was bleeding badly where I had slashed myself, and I, too,

had felt their teeth. But, despite our utter weariness and
our wounds, we wanted nothing—not even rest—so badly
as we wanted to get away from that awful heap of flesh and
blood and the odor of it.

Besides, we did not know at what moment they might
return. So I spoke, and Harry agreed. I led the way; he
followed.

But which way to turn? We wanted water, both for our
dry and burning throats and for our wounds; and rest and
food. We thought little of safety. One way seemed as likely
as another, so we set out with our noses as guides.

A man encounters very few misfortunes in this world
which, later in life, he finds himself unable to laugh at;
well, for me that endless journey was one of the few.

Every step was torture. I had bandaged the cut on my leg
as well as possible, but it continued to bleed. But it was
imperative that we should find water, and we struggled on,
traversing narrow passages and immense caverns, always
in complete darkness, stumbling over unseen rocks and
encountering sharp corners of cross passages.

It lasted I know not how many hours. Neither of us would
have survived alone. Time and again Harry sank to the
ground and refused to rise until I perforce lifted him; once
we nearly came to blows. And I was guilty of the same
weakness.

But the despair of one inspired the other with fresh
strength and courage, and we struggled forward, slower
and slower. It was soul-destroying work. I believe that in
the last hour we made not more than half a mile. I know
now that for the greater part of the time we were merely
retracing our steps in a vicious circle!

It was well that it ended when it did, for we could not
have held out much longer. Harry was leading the way, for I
had found that that slight responsibility fortified him. We
no longer walked, we barely went forward, staggering and
reeling like drunken men.

Suddenly Harry stopped short, so suddenly that I ran

against him; and at the same time I felt a queer sensation—for I was too far gone to recognize it—about my feet.

Then Harry stooped over quickly, half knocking me down as he did so, and dropped to his knees; and the next instant gave an unstead cry of joy:

"Water! Man, it's water!"

How we drank and wallowed, and wallowed and drank! That water might have contained all the poisons in the world and we would have neither known nor cared. But it was cool, fresh, living—and it saved our lives.

We bathed our wounds and bandaged them with strips from our shirts. Then we arranged our clothing for cushions and pillows as well as possible, took another drink, and lay down to sleep.

We must have slept a great many hours. There was no way to judge of time, but when we awoke our joints were as stiff as though they had gotten rusty with the years. I was brought to consciousness by the sound of Harry's voice calling my name.

Somehow—for every movement was exquisite pain—we got to our feet and reached the water, having first removed our clothing. But we were now at that point where to drink merely aggravated our hunger. Harry was in a savage humor, and when I laughed at him he became furious.

"Have some sense. I tell you, I must eat! If it were not for your—"

"Go easy, Hal. Don't say anything you'll be sorry for. And I refuse to consider the sordid topic of food as one that may rightfully contain the elements of tragedy. We seem to be in the position of the king of vaudeville. If we had some ham we'd have some ham and eggs—if we had some eggs."

"You may joke, but I am not made of iron!" he cried.

"And what can we do but die?" I demanded. "Do you think there is any chance of our getting out of this? Take it like a man. Is it right for a man who has laughed at the world to begin to whine when it becomes necessary to leave it?

"You know I'm with you; I'll fight, and what I find I'll

take; in the mean time I prefer not to furnish amusement for the devil. There comes a time, I believe, when the stomach debases us against our wills. May I die before I see it."

"But what are we to do?"

"That's more like it. There's only one hope. We must smell out the pantry that holds the dried fish."

We talked no more, but set about bathing and dressing our wounds. Gad, how that cold water took them! I was forced to set my teeth deep into my lip to keep from crying out, and once or twice Harry gave an involuntary grunt of pain that would not be suppressed.

When we had finished we waded far to the right to take a last deep drink; then sought our clothing and prepared to start on our all but hopeless search. We had become fairly well limbered up by that time and set out with comparative ease.

We had gone perhaps a hundred yards, bearing off to the right, when Harry gave a sudden cry: "My knife is gone!" and stopped short. I clapped my hand to my own belt instinctively, and found it empty both of knife and gun! For a moment we stood in silence; then:

"Have you got yours?" he demanded.

When I told him no he let out an oath.

His gun was gone, also. We debated the matter, and decided that to attempt a search would be a useless waste of time; it was next to certain that the weapons had been lost in the water when we had first plunged in. And so, doubly handicapped by this new loss, we again set out.

There was but one encouragement allowed to us: we were no longer in total darkness. Gradually our eyes were becoming accustomed to the absence of light; and though we could by no means see clearly, nor even could properly be said to see at all, still we began to distinguish the outlines of walls several feet away; and, better than that, each of us could plainly mark the form and face of the other.

Once we stood close, less than a foot apart, for a test; and when Harry cried eagerly, "Thank Heaven, I can see your nose!" our strained feelings were relieved by a prolonged burst of genuine laughter.

There was little enough of it in the time that followed, for our sufferings now became a matter not of minutes or hours, but of days. The assault of time is the one that unnerves a man, especially when it is aided by gnawing pain and weariness and hunger; it saps the courage and destroys the heart and fires the brain.

We dragged ourselves somehow ever onward. We found water; the mountain was honeycombed with underground streams; but no food. More than once we were tempted to trust ourselves to one of those rushing torrents, but what reason we had left told us that our little remaining strength was unequal to the task of keeping our heads above the surface. And yet the thought was sweet—to allow ourselves to be peacefully swept into oblivion.

We lost all idea of time and direction, and finally hope itself deserted us. What force it was that propelled us forward must have been buried deep within the seat of animal instinct, for we lost all rational power. The thing became a nightmare, like the crazy wanderings of a lost soul.

Forward—forward—forward! It was a mania.

Then Harry was stricken with fever and became delirious. And I think it was that seeming misfortune that saved us, for it gave me a spring for action and endowed me with new life. As luck would have it, a stream of water was near, and I half carried and half dragged him to its edge.

I made a bed for him with my own clothing on the hard rock, and bathed him and made him drink, while all the time a string of delirious drivel poured forth from his hot, dry lips.

That lasted many hours, until finally he fell into a deep, calm sleep. But his body was without fuel, and I was convinced he would never awaken; yet I feared to touch him. Those were weary hours, squatting by his side with his hand gripped in my own, with the ever-increasing pangs of hunger and weariness turning my own body into a roaring furnace of pain.

Suddenly I felt a movement of his hand; and then came his voice, weak but perfectly distinct:

"Well, Paul, this is the end."

"Not yet, Harry boy; not yet."

I tried to put cheer and courage into my own voice, but with poor success.

"I—think—so. I say, Paul—I've just seen Desirée."

"All right, Hal."

"Oh, you don't need to talk like that; I'm not delirious now. I guess it must have been a dream. Do you remember that morning on the mountain—in Colorado—when you came on us suddenly at sunrise? Well, I saw her there—only you were with her instead of me. So, of course, she must be dead."

His logic was beyond me, but I pressed his hand to let him know that I understood.

"And now, old man, you might as well leave me. This is the end. You've been a good sport. We made a fight, didn't we? If only Desirée—but there! To Hades with women, I say!"

"Not that—don't be a poor loser, Hal. And you're not gone yet. When a man has enough fight in him to beat out an attack of fever he's very much alive."

But he would not have it so. I let him talk, and he rambled on, with scarcely an idea of what he was saying. The old days possessed his mind, and, to tell the truth, the sentiment found a welcome in my own bosom. I said to myself, "This is death."

And then, lifting my head to look down the dark passage that led away before us, I sprang to my feet with a shout and stood transfixed with astonishment. And the next instant there came a cry of wonder from Harry:

"A light! By all the gods, a light!"

So it was. The passage lay straight for perhaps three hundred yards. There it turned abruptly; and the corner thus formed was one blaze of flickering but brilliant light which flowed in from the hidden corridor.

It came and went, and played fitfully on the granite walls; still it remained. It was supernaturally brilliant; or so it seemed to us, who had lived in utter darkness for many days.

I turned to Harry, and the man who had just been ready to die was rising to his feet!

"Wait a minute—not so fast!" I said half angrily, springing to support him. "And, for Heaven's sake, don't make any noise! We're in no condition to fight now, and you know what that light means."

"But what is it?" demanded the boy excitedly. "Come on, man—let's go!"

To tell the truth, I felt as eager as he. For the first time I understood clearly why the Bible and ancient mythology made such a fuss about the lighting up of the world. Modern civilization is too far away from its great natural benefits to appreciate them properly.

And here was a curious instance of the force of habit—or, rather, instinct—in man. So long as Harry and I had remained in the dark passage and byways of the cavern we had proceeded almost entirely without caution, with scarcely a thought of being discovered.

But the first sight of light made us wary and careful and silent; and yet we knew perfectly well that the denizens of this underworld could see as well in the darkness as in the light—perhaps even better. So difficult is it to guide ourselves by the human faculty of pure reason.

Harry was so weak he was barely able to stand, even in the strength of this new excitement and hope, and we were forced to go very slowly; I supported him as well as I was able, being myself anything but an engine of power. But the turn in the passage was not far away, and we reached it in a quarter of an hour or less.

Before we made the turn we halted. Harry was breathing heavily even from so slight an exertion, and I could scarcely suppress a cry of amazement when, for the first time in many days, the light afforded me a view of his face.

It was drawn and white and sunken; the eyes seemed set deep in his skull as they blinked painfully; and the hair on his chin and lip and cheeks had grown to a length incredible in so short a space of time. I soon had reason to know that I probably presented no better an appearance, for he was staring at me as though I were some strange monster.

"Good Heavens, man, you look like a ghost!" he whispered.

I nodded; my arm was round his shoulder.

"Now, let's see what this light means. Be ready for anything, Harry—though Heaven knows we can find nothing worse than we've had. Here, put your arm on my shoulder. Take it easy."

We advanced to the corner together within the patch of light and turned to the right, directly facing its source.

It is impossible to convey even a faint idea of the wild and hugely fantastic sight that met our gaze. With us it was a single, vivid flash to the astonished brain. These are the details:

Before us was an immense cavern, circular in shape, with a diameter of some half a mile. It seemed to me then much larger; from where we stood it appeared to be at least two miles to the opposite side. There was no roof to be seen; it merely ascended into darkness, though the light carried a great distance.

All round the vast circumference, on terraced seats of rock, squatted row after row of the most completely hideous beings within possibility.

They were men; I suppose they must have the name. They were about four feet tall, with long, hairy arms and legs, bodies of a curious, bloated appearance, and eyes— the remainder of the face was entirely concealed by thick hair—eyes dull and vacant, of an incredibly large size; they had the appearance of ghouls, apes, monsters—anything but human beings.

They sat, thousands of them, crouched silently on their stone seats, gazing, motionless as blocks of wood.

The center of the cavern was a lake, taking up something more than half of its area. The water was black as night, and curiously smooth and silent. Its banks sloped by degrees for a hundred feet or so, but at its edge there was a perpendicular bank of rock fifteen or twenty feet in height.

Near the middle of the lake, ranged at an equal distance from its center and from each other, were three—what shall I call them?—islands, or columns. They were six or eight feet across at their top, which rose high above the water.

On top of each of these columns was a huge vat or urn, and from each of the urns arose a steady, gigantic column of fire. These it was that gave the light; and it was little wonder we had thought it brilliant, since the flames rose to a height of thirty feet or more in the air.

But that which left us speechless with profound amazement was not the endless rows of silent, grinning dwarfs, nor the black, motionless lake, nor the leaping tongues of flame. We forgot these when we followed the gaze of that terrifying audience and saw a sight that printed itself on my brain with a vividness which time can never erase. Closing my eyes, I see it even now, and I shudder.

Exactly in the center of the lake, in the midst of the columns of fire, was a fourth column, built of some strangely lustrous rock. Prisms of a formation new to me—innumerable thousands of them—caused its sides to sparkle and glisten like an immense tower of whitest diamonds, blinding the eye.

The effect was indescribable. The huge cavern was lined and dotted with the rays shot forth from their brilliant angles. The height of this column was double that of the others; it rose straight toward the unseen dome of the cavern to the height of a hundred feet.

It was cylindrical in shape, not more than ten feet in diameter. And on its top, high above the surface of the lake, surrounded by the mounting tongues of flame, whirled and swayed and bent the figure of a woman.

Her limbs and body, which were covered only by long, flowing strands of golden hair, shone and glistened strangely in the lurid, weird light. And of all the ten thousand reflections that shot at us from the length of the column not one was so brilliant, so blinding, as the wild glow of her eyes.

Her arms, upraised above her head, kept time with and served as a key to every movement of her white, supple body. She glided across, back and forth, now this way, now that, to the very edge of the dizzy height, with wild abandon, or slow, measured grace, or the rushing sweep of a panther.

The thing was beauty incarnate—the very idea of beauty itself realized and perfected. It was staggering, overwhelming. Have you ever stood before a great painting or a beautiful statue and felt a thrill—the thrill of perception—run through your body to the very tips of your fingers?

Well, imagine that thrill multiplied a thousandfold and you will understand the sensation that overpowered me as I beheld, in the midst of that dazzling blaze of light, the matchless Dance of the Sun.

For I recognized it at once. I had never seen it, but it had been minutely described to me—described by a beautiful and famous woman as I sat on the deck of a yacht steaming into the harbor of Callao.

She had promised me then that she would dance it for me some day—

I looked at Harry, who had remained standing beside me, gazing as I had gazed. His eyes were opened wide, staring at the swaying figure on the column in the most profound astonishment.

He took his hand from my shoulder and stood erect, alone; and I saw the light of recognition and hope and deepest joy slowly fill his eyes and spread over his face. Then I realized the danger, and I endeavored once more to put my arm round his shoulder; but he shook me off with hot impatience. He leaped forward with the quickness of lightning, eluding my frantic grasp, and dashed straight into the circle of blazing light!

I followed, but too late. At the edge of the lake he stopped, and, stretching forth his arms toward the dancer on the column, he cried out in a voice that made the cavern ring:

"Desirée! Desirée! Desirée!"

Chapter IX.

BEFORE THE COURT.

I expected I know not what result from Harry's hysterical rashness: confusion, pandemonium, instant death; but none of these followed.

I had reached his side and stood by him at the edge of the lake, where he had halted. Desirée Le Mire stopped short in the midst of the mad sweep of the Dance of the Sun.

For ten silent, tense seconds she looked down at us from the top of the lofty column, bending dangerously near its edge. Her form straightened and was stretched to its fullest height; her white, superb body was distinctly outlined against the black background of the upper cavern. Then she stepped backward slowly, without taking her eyes from us.

Suddenly as we gazed she appeared to sink within the column itself and in another instant disappeared from view.

We stood motionless, petrified; how long I know not. Then I turned and faced our own danger. It was time.

The Incas—for I was satisfied of the identity of the creatures—had left their seats of granite and advanced to the edge of the lake. Not a sound was heard—no command from voice or trumpet or reed; they moved as with one impulse and one brain.

We were utterly helpless, for they numbered thousands. And weak and starving as we were, a single pair of them would have been more than a match for us.

I looked at Harry; the reaction from his moment of superficial energy was already upon him. His body swayed slightly from side to side, and he would have fallen if I had not supported him with my arm. There we stood, waiting.

Then for the first time I saw the ruler of the scene. The Incas had stopped and stood motionless. Suddenly they dropped to their knees and extended their arms—I thought—toward us; but something in their attitude told me the truth. I wheeled sharply and saw the object of their adoration.

Built into the granite wall of the cavern, some thirty feet from the ground, was a deep alcove. At each side of the entrance was an urn resting on a ledge, similar to those on the columns, only smaller, from which issued a mounting flame.

On the floor of the alcove was a massive chair, or throne, which seemed to be itself of fire, so brilliant was the glow of the metal of which it was constructed. It could have been nothing but gold. And seated on this throne was an ugly, misshapen dwarf.

"God save the king!" I cried, with a hysterical laugh; and in the profound silence my voice rang from one side of the cavern to the other in racing echoes.

Immediately following my cry the figure on the throne arose; and as he did so the creatures round us fell flat on their faces on the ground. For several seconds the king surveyed them thus, without a sound or movement; then suddenly he stretched forth his hand in a gesture of dismissal. They rose as one man and with silent swiftness disappeared, seemingly melting away into the walls of rock. At the time the effect was amazing; later, when I discovered the innumerable lanes and passages which served as exits, it was not so difficult to understand.

We were apparently left alone, but not for long. From two stone stairways immediately in front of us, which evidently led to the alcove above, came forth a crowd of rushing forms. In an instant they were upon us; but if they expected resistance they were disappointed.

At the first impact we fell. And in another moment we had been raised in their long, hairy arms and were carried swiftly from the cavern. Scarcely five minutes had elapsed since we had first entered it.

They did not take us far. Down a broad passage directly away from the cavern, then a turn to the right, and again one to the left. There they dropped us, quite as though we were bundles of merchandise, without a word.

By this time I had fairly recovered my wits—small wonder if that amazing scene had stunned them—and I knew what I wanted. As the brute that had been carrying me turned to go I caught his arm. He hesitated, and I could feel his eyes on me, for we were again in darkness.

But he could see—I thanked Heaven for it—and I began a most expressive pantomime, stuffing my fingers in my mouth and gnawing at them energetically. This I alternated with the action of one drinking from a basin. I hadn't the slightest idea whether he understood me; he turned and disappeared without a sign—at least, without an audible one.

But the creature possessed intelligence, for I had barely had time to turn to Harry and ascertain that he was at least alive, when the patter of returning footsteps was heard. They approached; there was the clatter of stone on the ground beside us.

I stood eagerly; a platter, heaped, and a vessel, full! I think I cried out with joy.

"Come, Harry lad; eat!"

He was too weak to move; but when I tore some of the dried fish into fragments and fed it to him he devoured it ravenously. Then he asked for water, and I held the basin to his lips.

We ate as little as it is possible for men to eat who have fasted for many days, for the stuff had a sharp, concentrated taste that recommended moderation. And, besides, we were not certain of getting more.

I wrapped the remainder carefully in my poncho, leaving the platter empty, and lay down to rest, using the poncho for a pillow. I had enough, assuredly, to keep me awake, but there are bounds beyond which nature cannot go. I slept close by Harry's side, with my arm across his body, that any movement of his might awaken me.

When I awoke Harry was still asleep, and I did not disturb him. I myself must have slept many hours, for I felt considerably refreshed and very hungry. And thirsty; assuredly the provender of those hairy brutes would have been most excellent stuff for the free-lunch counter of a saloon.

I unwrapped the poncho; then, crawling on my hands and knees, searched about the ground. As I had expected, I found another full platter and basin. I had just set the latter down after taking a hearty drink when I heard Harry's voice.

"Paul."

"Here, lad."

"I was afraid you had gone. I've just had the most devilish dream about Desirée. She was doing some crazy dance on top of a mountain or something, and there was fire, and—Paul! Paul, was it a dream?"

"No, Hal; I saw it myself. But come, we'll talk later. Here's some dried fish for breakfast."

"Ah! That—that—now I remember! And she fell! I'm going—"

But I wanted no more fever or delirium, and I interrupted him sternly:

"Harry! Listen to me! Are you a baby or a man? Talk straight or shut up, and don't whine like a fool. If you have any courage, use it."

It was stiff medicine, but he needed it, and it worked. There was a silence, then his voice came, steady enough:

"You know me better than that, Paul. Only—if it were not for Desirée—but I'll swallow it. I think I've been sick, haven't I?"

Poor lad! I wanted to take his hand in mine and apologize. But that would have been bad for both of us, and I answered simply:

"Yes, a little fever. But you're all right now. And now you must eat and drink. Not much of a variety, but it's better than nothing."

I carried the platter and basin over to him, and sat down by his side, and we fell to together.

But he would talk of Desirée, and I humored him. There was little enough to say, but he pressed my hand hopefully and gratefully when I expressed my belief that her disappearance had been a trick of some sort and no matter for apprehension.

"We must find her, Paul."

"Yes."

"At once."

But there I objected.

"On the contrary, we must delay. Right now we are utterly helpless from our long fast. They would handle us like babies if it came to a fight. Try yourself; stand up."

He rose to his hands and knees, then sank back to the ground.

"You see. To move now would be folly. And of course they are watching us at this minute—every minute. We must wait."

His only answer was a groan of despair.

In some manner the weary hours passed by.

Harry lay silent, but not asleep; now and then he would ask me some question, but more to hear my voice than to get an answer. We heard or saw nothing of our captors, for all our senses told us we were quite alone, but our previous experience with them had taught us better than to believe it.

I found myself almost unconsciously reflecting on the character and nature of the tribe of dwarfs.

Was it possible that they were really the descendants of the Incas driven from Huánuco by Hernando Pizarro and his horsemen nearly four hundred years before? Even then I was satisfied of it, and I was soon to have that opinion confirmed by conclusive evidence.

Other questions presented themselves. Whey did they not speak? What fuel could they have found in the bowels of the Andes for their vats of fire? And how did sufficient air for ten thousand pairs of lungs find its way miles underground? Why, in the centuries that had passed, had none of them found his way to the world outside?

Some of these questions I answered for myself; others remained unsolved for many months, until I had opportunity to avail myself of knowledge more profound than my own. Easy enough to guess that the hidden deposits of the mountain had yielded oil which needed only a spark from a piece of flint to fire it; and any one who knows anything of the geological formation of the Andes will not wonder at their supply of air.

Nature is not yet ready for man in those wild regions. Huge upheavals and convulsions are of continual occurrence; underground streams are known which rise in the eastern Cordillera and emerge on the side of the Pacific slope. And air circulates through these passages as well as water.

Their silence remains inexplicable; but it was probably the result of the nature of their surroundings. I have spoken before of the innumerable echoes and reverberations that followed every sound of the voice above a whisper. At times it was literally deafening; and time may have made it so in reality.

The natural effect through many generations of this inconvenience or danger would be the stoppage of speech, leading possibly to a complete loss of the faculty. I am satisfied that they were incapable of vocalization, for even the women did not talk! But that is ahead of the story.

I occupied myself with these reflections, and found amusement in them; but it was impossible to lead Harry into a discussion. His mind was anything but scientific, anyway; and he was completely obsessed by fear for the safety of Desirée. And I wasn't sorry for it; it is better that a man should worry about some one else than about himself.

Our chance of rescuing her, or even of saving ourselves, appeared to me woefully slim. One fear at least was gone, for the descendants of Incas could scarcely be cannibals; but there are other fates equally final, if less distasteful. The fact that they had not even taken the trouble to bind us was an indication of the strictness of their watch.

The hours crept by. At regular intervals our food was replenished and we kept the platter empty, storing what we could not eat in our ponchos against a possible need.

It was always the same—dried fish of the consistency of

leather and a most aggressive taste. I tried to convey to one of our captors the idea that a change of diet would be agreeable, but either he did not understand me or didn't want to.

Gradually our strength returned, and with it hope. Harry began to be impatient, urging action. I was waiting for two things besides the return of strength; first, to lay in a supply of food that would be sufficient for many days in case we escaped, and second, to allow our eyes to accustom themselves better to the darkness.

Already we were able to see with a fair amount of clearness; we could easily distinguish the forms of those who came to bring us food and water when they were fifteen or twenty feet away. But the cavern in which we were confined must have been a large one, for we were unable to see a wall in any direction, and we did not venture to explore for fear our captors would be moved to bind us.

But Harry became so insistent that I finally consented to a scouting expedition. Caution seemed useless; if the darkness had eyes that beheld us, doubly so. We strapped our ponchos, heavy with their food, to our backs, and set out at random across the cavern.

We went slowly, straining our eyes ahead and from side to side. It was folly, of course, in the darkness—like trying to beat a gambler at his own game. But we moved on as noiselessly as possible.

Suddenly a wall loomed up before us not ten feet away. I gave a tug at Harry's arm, and he nodded. We approached the wall, then turned to the right and proceeded parallel with it, watching for a break that would mean the way to freedom.

I noticed a dark line that extended along the base of the wall, reaching up its side to a height of about two feet and seemingly melting away into the ground. At first I took it for a separate strata of rock, darker than that above. But there was a strange brokenness about its appearance that made me consider it more carefully.

It appeared to be composed of curious knots and protuberances. I stopped short, and, advancing a step or two toward the wall, gazed intently. Then I saw that the dark line was not a part of the wall at all; and then—well, then I laughed aloud in spite of myself. The thing was too ludicrous.

For that "dark line" along the bottom of the wall was a row of squatting Incas! There they sat, silent, motionless; even when my laugh rang out through the cavern they gave not the slightest sign that they either heard or saw. Yet it was certain that they had watched our every move.

There was nothing for it but retreat. With our knives we might have fought our way through; but we were unarmed, and we had felt one or two proofs of their strength.

Harry took it with more philosophy than I had expected. As for me, I had not yet finished my laugh. We sought our former resting-place, recognizing it by the platter and basin which we had emptied before our famous and daring attempt to escape.

Soon Harry began:

"I'll tell you what they are, Paul; they're frogs. Nothing but frogs. Did you see 'em? The little black devils! And Lord, how they smell!"

"That," I answered, "is the effect of—"

"To the deuce with your mineralogy or anthromorphism or whatever you call it. I don't care what makes 'em smell. I only know they do—as Kipling says of the oonts—'most awful vile.' And there the beggars sit, and here we sit!"

"If we could only see—" I began.

"And what good would that do us? Could we fight? No. They'd smother us in a minute. Say, wasn't there a king in that cave the other day?"

"Yes; on a golden throne. An ugly little devil—the ugliest of all."

"Sure; that why he's got the job. Did he say anything?"

"Not a word; merely stuck out his arm and out we went."

"Why the deuce don't they talk?"

I explained my theory at some length, with many and various scientific digressions. Harry listened politely.

"I don't know what you mean," said he when I had finished, "but I believe you. Anyway, it's all a stupendous joke. In the first place, we shouldn't be here at all. And, secondly, why should they want us to stay?"

"How should I know? Ask the king. And don't bother me; I'm going to sleep."

"You are not. I want to talk. Now, they must want us for something. They can't intend to eat us, because there isn't enough to go around. And there is Desirée. What the deuce was she doing up there without any clothes on? I say, Paul, we've got to find her."

"With pleasure. But, first, how are we going to get out of this?"

"I mean, when we get out."

Thus we rattled on, arriving nowhere. Harry's loquacity I understood; the poor lad meant to show me that he had resolved not to "whine." Yet his cheerfulness was but partly assumed, and it was most welcome. My own temper was getting sadly frayed about the edge.

We slept through another watch uneventfully, and when we woke found our platter of fish and basin of water beside us. I estimated that some seventy-two hours had then passed since we had been carried from the cavern; Harry said not less than a hundred.

However that may be, we had almost entirely recovered our strength. Indeed, Harry declared himself perfectly fit; but I still felt some discomfort, caused partly by the knife-wound on my knee, which had not entirely healed, and partly, I think, by the strangeness and monotony of our diet. Harry's palate was less particular.

On awaking, and after breaking our fast, we were both filled with an odd contentment. I really believe that we had abandoned hope, and that the basis of our listlessness was despair; and surely not without reason. For what chance had we to escape from the Incas, handicapped as we were by the darkness, and our want of weapons, and their overwhelming numbers?

And beyond that—if by some chance lucky we did escape—what remained? To wander about in the endless caves of darkness and starve to death. At the time I don't think I stated the case, even to myself, with such brutal frankness, but facts make their impression whether you invite them or not. But, as I say, we were filled with an odd contentment. Though despair may have possessed our hearts, it was certainly not allowed to infect our tongues.

Breakfast was hilarious. Harry sang an old drinking-song to the water-basin with touching sentiment; I gave him hearty applause and joined in the chorus. The cavern rang.

"The last time I sang that," said Harry as the last echoes died away, "was at the Midlothian. Bunk Stafford was there, and Billy Du Mont, and Fred Marston—I say, do you remember Freddie? And his East Side crocodiles?

"My, but weren't they daisies? And polo? They could play it in their sleep. And—what's this? Paul! Something's up! Here they come—Mr. and Mrs. Inca and all the children!"

I sprang hastily to my feet and stood by Harry's side. He was right.

Through the half darkness they came, hundreds of them, and, as always, in utter silence. Dimly we could see their forms huddled together round us on every side, leaving us in the center of a small circle in their midst.

"Now, what the deuce do they want?" I muttered. "Can't they let us eat in peace?"

Harry observed: "Wasn't I right? 'Most awful vile!'"

I think we both felt that we were joking in the face of death.

The forms surrounding us stood silent for perhaps ten seconds. Then four of their number stepped forward to us, and one made gestures with a hairy arm, pointing to our rear. We turned and saw a narrow lane lined on either side by our captors. Nothing was distinct; still we could see well enough to guess their meaning.

"It's up to us to march," said Harry.

I nodded.

"And step high, Hal; it may be our last one. If we only had our knives! But there are thousands of 'em."

"But if it comes to the worst—"

"Then—I'm with you. Forward!"

We started, and as we did so one of the four who had approached darted from behind and led the way. Not a hand had touched us, and this appeared to me a good sign, without knowing exactly why.

"They seem to have forgotten their manners," Harry observed. "The approved method is to knock us down and carry us. I shall speak to the king about it."

We had just reached the wall of the cavern and entered a passage leading from it, when there came a sound, sonorous and ear-destroying, from the farther end. We had heard it once before; it was the same that had ended our desperate fight some days before. Then it had saved our lives; to what did it summon us now?

The passage was not a long one. At its end we turned to the right, following our guide. Once I looked back and saw behind us the crowd that had surrounded us in the cave. There was no way but obedience.

We had advanced perhaps a hundred, possibly two hundred yards along the second passage when our guide suddenly halted. We stood beside him.

He turned sharply to the left, and, beckoning to us to follow, began to descend a narrow stairway which led directly from the passage. It was steep, and the darkness allowed a glimpse only of black walls and the terrace immediately beneath our feet; so we went slowly. I counted the steps; there were ninety-six.

At the bottom we turned again to the right. Just as we turned I heard Harry's voice, quite low:

"There are only a dozen following us, Paul. Now—"

But I shook my head. It would have been mere folly, for, even if we had succeeded in breaking through, we could never have made our way back up the steps. This I told Harry; he admitted reluctantly that I was right.

We now found ourselves in a lane so low and narrow that it was necessary for us to stoop and proceed in single file. Our progress was slow; the guide was continually turning to beckon us on with gestures of impatience.

At length he halted and stood facing us. The guard that followed gathered close in the rear, the guide made a curious upward movement with his arm, and when we stood motionless repeated it several times.

"I suppose he wants us to fly," said Harry with so genuine a tone of sarcasm that I gave an involuntary smile.

The guide's meaning was soon evident. It took some seconds for my eye to penetrate the darkness, and then I saw a spiral stair ascending perpendicularly, apparently carved from the solid rock. Harry must have perceived it at the same moment, for he turned to me with a short laugh:

"Going up? Not for me, thank you. The beggar means for us to go alone."

For a moment I hesitated, glancing round uncertainly at the dusky forms that were ever pressing closer upon us. We were assuredly between the devil and the deep sea.

Then I said, shrugging my shoulders: "It's no good pulling, Harry. Come on; take a chance. You said it—going up!"

I placed my foot on the first step of the spiral stair.

Harry followed without comment. Up we went together, but slowly. The stair was fearfully steep and narrow, and more than once I barely escaped a fall.

Suddenly I became aware that light was descending on us from above. With every step upward it became brighter, until finally it was as though a noonday sun shone in upon us.

There came an exclamation from Harry, and we ascended faster. I remember that I counted a hundred and sixty steps—and then, as a glimmering of the truth shot through my brain into certainty, I counted no more.

Harry was crowding me from below, and we took the last few steps almost at a run. Then the end, and we stumbled out into a blaze of light and surveyed the surrounding scene with stupefaction and wonder.

It was not new to us; we had seen it before, but from a different angle.

We were on the top of the column in the center of the lake; on the spot where Desirée had whirled in the dance of the sun.

Chapter X.

THE VERDICT.

For many seconds we stood bewildered, too dazed to speak or move. The light dazzled our eyes; we seemed surrounded by an impenetrable wall of flame. There was no sensation of heat, owing, no doubt, to the immense height of the cavern and our comparatively distant removal from the flames, which mounted upward in narrow tongues.

Then the details began to strike me.

I have said the scene was the same as that we had previously beheld. Round the walls of the immense circular cavern squatted innumerable rows of the Incas on terraced seats.

Below, at a dizzy distance, was the smooth surface of the lake, black and gloomy save where the reflections from the blazing urns pierced its depths. And directly facing us, set in the wall of the cavern, was the alcove containing the throne of gold.

And on the throne was seated—not the diminutive, misshapen king, but Desirée Le Mire!

She sat motionless, gazing directly at us. Her long gold hair streamed over her shoulders in magnificent waves; a stiffly flowing garment of some unknown texture covered her limbs and the lower part of her body; her shoulders and breasts and arms were bare, and shone with a dazzling whiteness.

Beside her was a smaller seat, also of gold, and on this crouched the form of an Inca—the king. About them, at a respectful distance, were ranged attendants and guards—a hundred or more, for the alcove was of an impressive size. The light from the four urns shone in upon it with such brightness that I could clearly distinguish the whites of Desirée's eyes.

All this I saw in a single flash, and I turned to Harry:

"Not a word, on your life! This is Desirée's game; trust her to play it."

"But what the deuce is she doing there?"

I shrugged my shoulders.

"She seems to have found another king. You know her fondness for royalty."

"Paul, for Heaven's sake—"

"All right, Hal. But we're safe enough, I think. Most probably our introduction to court. This is what they call 'the dizzy heights of prominence.' Now keep your eyes open—something is going to happen."

There was a movement in the alcove. Four of the attendants came forward, carrying a curious framework apparently composed of reeds and leather, light and flexible, from the top bar of which hung suspended several rope-like ribbons, of various lengths and colors and tied in curious knots. They placed it on the ground before the double throne, at the feet of Desirée.

All doubt was then removed from my mind concerning the identity of our captors and their king. For these bundles of knotted cords of different sizes and colors I recognized at once.

They were the famous Inca *quipos*—the material for their remarkable mnemonic system of communication and historical record. At last we were to receive a message from the Child of the Sun.

But of what nature? Every cord and knot and color had its meaning—but what? I searched every avenue of memory to assist me; for I had latterly confined my studies exclusively to Eastern archeology, and what I had known of the two great autochthonous civilizations of the American Continent was packed in some dim and little used corner of my brain. But success came, with an extreme effort.

I recollected first the different disposition of the *quipos* for different purposes—historical, sacred, narrative, *et cetera*. Then the particulars came to me, and immediately I recognized the formula of the *quipos* before the throne. They were arranged for adjudication—for the rendering of a verdict.

Harry and I were prisoners before the bar of the *quipos!* I turned to him, but there was not time for talk. The king had risen and stretched out his hand.

Immediately the vast assemblage rose from their stone seats and fell flat on their faces. It was then that I noticed, for the first time, an oval or elliptical plate of shining gold set in the wall of the cavern just above the outer edge of the alcove.

This, of course, was the representation of Pachacamac, the "unknown god" in the Inca religion. Well, I would as soon worship a plate of gold as that little black dwarf.

For perhaps a minute the king stood with outstretched arm and the Incas remained motionless on their faces. Then he resumed his seat and they rose. And then the trial began.

The king turned on his throne and laid his hand on Desirée's arm; we could see her draw away from his touch with an involuntary shudder. But this apparent antipathy bothered his kingship not at all; it was probably a most agreeable sensation to feel her soft, white flesh under his black, hairy hand, and he kept it there, while with the other arm he made a series of sweeping gestures which I understood at once, but which had no meaning for Desirée. By her hand he meant the *quipos* to speak.

We had a friend in court, but she was dumb, and I must give her voice. There was no time to be lost; I stepped to the edge of the column and spoke in a voice loud enough to carry across the cavern—which was not difficult in the universal silence.

"He means that you are to judge us by the *quipos*. The meaning is this—yellow, slavery; white, mercy; purple, reward; black, death. The lengths of the cords and the number of knots indicate the degree of punishment or reward. Attached to the frame you will find a knife. With that detach the cord of judgment and lay it at the feet of the king."

Again silence; and not one of the vast throng, nor the king himself, appeared to pay the slightest attention to my voice. The king continued his gestures to Desirée.

She rose and walked to the frame of *quipos* and took in her hand the knife which she found there suspended by a cord. There she hesitated, with the knife poised in the air, while her eyes sought mine—and found them.

I felt a tug at my arm, but I had no time for Harry then. I was looking at Desirée, and what I saw caused a cold shudder to flutter through my body. Not of fear; it was the utter surprise of the thing—its incredible horror. To die by the hands of those hairy brutes was not hard, but Desirée to be the judge!

For she meant death for us; I read it in her eyes. One of the old stale proverbs of the stale old world was to have another justification. I repeat that I was astounded, taken completely by surprise; and yet I had known something of "the fury of a woman scorned."

It was as though our eyes shot out to meet each other in an embrace of death. She saw that I understood and she smiled—what a smile! It was triumphant, and yet sad; a vengeance, and a farewell. She put forth her hand.

It wavered among the *quipos* as though uncertainly, then closed firmly on the black cord of death.

A thought flashed through my mind with the speed of lightning. I raised my voice and sang out:

"Desirée!"

She hesitated; the hand which held the knife fell to her side and again her eyes sought mine.

"What of Harry?" I called. "Take two—the white for him, the black for me."

She shook her head and again raised the knife; and I played my last card.

"Bah! Who are you? For you are not Le Mire!" I weighted my voice with contempt. "Le Mire is a child of fortune, but not of hell!"

At last she spoke.

"I play a fair hand, *monsieur!*" she cried, and her voice trembled.

"With marked cards!" I exclaimed scornfully. "The advantage is yours, *madame;* may you find pleasure in it."

There was a silence, while our eyes met. I thought I had lost. Le Mire stood motionless. Not a sound came from the audience. I felt Harry pulling at my arm, but shook myself free, without taking my eyes from Le Mire's face.

Suddenly she spoke:

"You are right, my friend Paul. I take no advantage. Leave it to Fortune. Have you a coin?"

I had won my chance. That was all—a chance—but that was better than nothing. I took a silver peseta from my pocket—by luck it had not been lost—and held it in the air above my head.

"Heads!" cried Desirée.

I let the coin fall. It rolled half-way across the top of the column and stopped at the very edge. I crossed and stooped over it. It lay heads up!

Harry was behind me; as I straightened up I saw his white, set face and eyes of horror. He, too, had seen the verdict; but he was moved not by that, but by the thought of Desirée, for Harry was not a man to flinch at sight of death.

I stood straight, and my voice was calm. It cost me an effort to clear it of bitterness and reproach. I could not avoid the reflection that but for Desirée we would never have seen the cave of the devil and the Children of the Sun; but I said simply and clearly:

"You win, *madame.*"

Desirée stared at me in the most profound surprise. I understood her, and I laughed scornfully aloud, and held my head high; and I think a voice never held so complete a disdain as did mine as I called to her:

"I am one who plays fair, even with death, Le Mire. The coin fell heads—you win your black cord fairly."

She made no sign that she had heard; she was raising the knife. Suddenly she stopped, again her hand fell, and she said:

"You say the purple for reward, Paul?"

I nodded—I could not speak. Her hand touched the white cord and passed on; the yellow, and again passed on. Then there was a flash of the knife—another—and she approached the king and laid at his feet the purple cord.

Then, without a glance toward us, she resumed her seat on the golden throne.

A lump rose to my throat and tears to my eyes. Which was very foolish, for the thing had been completely theatrical. It was merely a tribute from one of nature's gamblers to the man who "played fair, even with death"; nevertheless, there was feeling in it, and the eternal mercy of woman.

For all that was visible to the eye the verdict made not the slightest impression on the rows of silent Incas. Not a movement was seen; they might have been carved from the stone on which they were seated.

Their black, hairy bodies, squat and thick, threw back the light from the flaming torches as though even those universal rays could not penetrate such grossness.

Suddenly they rose—the king had moved. He picked the purple cord from the ground, and, after passing his hand over it three times, handed it to an attendant who approached.

Then he stretched out his hand, and the Incas, who had remained standing, turned about and began to disappear. As before, the cavern was emptied in an incredibly short space of time; in two minutes we were alone with those in the alcove.

There was a sound behind us. We turned and saw a great slab of stone slowly slide to one side in the floor, leaving an aperture some three feet square. Evidently it had been closed behind us when we had ascended; we had had no time to notice it then. In this hole presently appeared the head and shoulders of our guide, who beckoned to us to follow and then disappeared below.

I started to obey, but turned to wait for Harry, who was gazing at Desirée. His back was toward me and I could not see his face; his eyes must have held an appeal, for I saw Desirée's lips part in a smile and heard her call:

"You will see me!"

Then he joined me, and we began the descent together.

I found myself wondering how these half-civilized brutes had possibly managed to conceive the idea of the spiral stair. It was known to neither the Aztecs nor the Incas, in America; nor to any of the primitive European or Asiatic civilizations. But they had found a place where nothing else would do—and they made it. Another of the innumerable offspring of Mother Necessity.

I took time to note its construction. It was rude enough, but a good job for all that. It was not exactly circular; there were many angles, evidently following the softer strata in the rock; they had bowed to their material—the way of the artist.

Even the height of the steps was irregular; some were scarcely more than three inches, while others were twelve or fourteen. You may know we descended slowly and with care, especially when we had reached the point where no light came from above to aid us. We found our guide waiting for us at the bottom, alone.

We followed him down the low and narrow passage through which we had previously come. But when we reached the steps which led up to the passage above and to the cave where we had formerly been confined, he ignored them and turned to the right. We hesitated.

"He's alone," said Harry. "Shall we chuck the beggar?"

"We shall not, for that very reason," I answered. "It means that we are guests instead of captives, and far be it from us to outrage the laws of hospitality. But seriously, the safest thing we can do is to follow him."

The passage in which we now found ourselves was evidently no work of nature. Even in the semidarkness the mark of man's hand was apparent. And the ceiling was low; another proof, for dwarfs do not build for the accommodation of giants. But I had some faint idea of the pitiful inadequacy of their tools, and I found myself reflecting on the stupendous courage of the men who had undertaken such a task, even allowing for the fact that four hundred years had been allowed them for its completion.

Soon we reached a veritable maze of these passages. We must have taken a dozen or more turns, first to the right, then to the left. I had been marking our way on my memory as well as possible, but I soon gave up the attempt as hopeless.

Several times our guide turned so quickly that we could scarcely follow him. When we signified by gestures our desire to go slower he seemed surprised; of course, he expected us to see in the dark as well as he.

Then a dim light appeared, growing brighter as we advanced. Soon I saw that it came through an opening in the wall to our left, which we were approaching. Before the opening the guide halted, motioning us to enter.

We did so, and found ourselves in an apartment no less than royal.

Several blazing urns attached to the walls furnished the light, wavering but brilliant. There were tables and rude seats, fashioned from the same prismatic stones which covered the column in the lake, and from their surfaces a thousand points of color shone dazzlingly.

At one side was a long slab of granite covered with the skins of some animal, dry, thick, and soft. The walls themselves were of the hardest granite, studded to a height of four or five feet with tiny, innumerable spots of gold.

Harry crossed to the middle of the apartment and stood gazing curiously about him. I turned to the door and looked down the outer passage in both directions—our guide had disappeared.

"We appear to be friends of the family," said Harry with a grin.

"Thanks to Desirée, yes."

"Thanks to the devil! What did she mean—what could she mean? Was it one of her jokes? For I can't believe that she would—would—"

"Have sent us to death? Well—who knows? Yes, it may have been one of her jokes," I lied.

For, of course, Harry knew nothing of the cause of

Desirée's desire for revenge on me, and it would have served no good purpose to tell him.

We talked for an hour or more, examining our apartment meanwhile with considerable curiosity.

The gold excited our wonder; had it come from Huánuco four hundred years ago, or had they found it here in the mountain?

I examined the little blocks of metal or gems with which the tables and seats were inlaid, but could make nothing of them. They resembled a carbon formation sometimes found in quartzite, but were many times more brilliant than anything I had ever seen, excepting precious stones.

The hides which covered the granite couch were also unknown to me; they were of an amazing thickness and incredibly soft.

We were amusing ourselves with an attempt to pry one of the bits of gold from the wall when we heard a sound behind us.

We turned and saw Desirée.

She stood in the entrance, smiling at us as though we had been caught in her boudoir examining the articles on her dressing-table. She was clothed as she had been on the throne; a rope girdle held her single garment, and her hair fell across her shoulders, reaching to her knees. Her arms and shoulders appeared marvelously white, but they may have been by way of contrast.

Harry sprang across to her with a single bound. In another moment his arms were round her; she barely submitted to the embrace, but she gave him her lips, then drew herself away and crossed to me, extending her hands in a sort of wavering doubt.

But that was no time for hostilities, and I took the hands in my own and bent over them till my lips touched the soft fingers.

"A visit from the queen!" I said with a smile. "This is an honor, your majesty."

"A doubtful one," said Desirée. "First of all, my friend, I

want to congratulate you on your *savoir faire. Par Bleu,* that was the part of a man!"

"But you!" cried Harry. "What the deuce did you mean by pretending to play the black? I tell you, that was a shabby trick. Most unpleasant moment you gave us."

Desirée sent me a quick glance; she was plainly surprised to find Harry in ignorance of what had passed between us that evening in the camp on the mountain. Wherein she was scarcely to be blamed, for her surprise came from a deep knowledge of the ways of men.

"I am beginning to know you, Paul," she said, looking into my eyes.

"Now what's up?" demanded Harry, looking from her to me and back again. "For Heaven's sake, don't talk riddles. What does that mean?"

But Desirée silenced him with a gesture, placng her fingers playfully on his lips. They were seated side by side on the granite couch; I stood in front of them, and there flitted across my memory a picture of that morning scene in the grounds of the Antlers at Colorado Springs, when Desirée and I had had our first battle.

We talked; or, rather, Harry and Desirée talked, and I listened. First he insisted on a recital of her experiences since her reckless dash into the "cave of the devil," and she was most obliging, even eager, for she had had no one to talk to for many days, and she was a woman. She found in Harry a perfect audience.

Her experience had been much the same as our own. She, too, had fallen down the unseen precipice into the torrent beneath.

She asserted that she had been carried along by its force scarcely more than a quarter of an hour, and had been violently thrown upon a ledge of rock. It was evident that this must have been long before the stream reached the lake where Harry and I had found each other, for we had been in the water hardly short of an hour.

She had been found on the ledge by our hairy friends, who had carried her on their backs for many hours. I remembered the sensations of Harry and myself, who were men, and together, and gave a shudder of sympathy as Desirée described her own horror and fear, and her one attempt to escape.

Still the brutes had shown her no great violence, evidently recognizing the preciousness of their burden. They had carried her as gently as possible, but had absolutely refused to allow her to walk. At regular intervals they gave her an opportunity to rest, and food and water.

"Dried fish?" I asked hopefully.

Desirée nodded, with a most expressive grimace, and Harry burst into laughter.

Then of the elevation to her evident authority. Brought before the king, she had inspired the most profound wonder and curiosity. Easy, indeed, to understand how the whiteness of her skin and the beauty of her form and face had awakened the keenest admiration in the breast of that black and hairy monarch. He had shown her the most perfect respect; and she had played up to the role of goddess by displaying to the utmost her indifferent contempt for royalty and its favors.

Here her remarks grew general and evasive, and when pressed with questions she refused details. She declared that nothing had happened; she had been fed and fawned upon, nor been annoyed by any violence or unwelcome attentions.

"That is really too bad," said I, with a smile. "I was, then, mistaken when I said 'your majesty'?"

"Faugh!" said Desirée. "That is hardly witty. For a time I was amused, but I am becoming bored. And yet—"

"Well?"

"I—don't—know. They are mine, if you know what I mean. *Eh, bien,* since you ask me—for I see the question in your eye, friend Paul—I am content. If the world is behind me forever, so be it. Yes, they are unattractive to the eye, but they have power. And they worship me."

"Desirée!" cried Harry in astonishment; and I was myself a little startled.

"Why not?" she demanded. "They are men. And besides, it is impossible for us to return. With all your cleverness, M. Paul, can you find the sunlight? To remain is a necessity; we must make the best of it; and I repeat that I am satisfied."

"That's bally rot," said Harry, turning on her hotly. "Satisfied? You are nothing of the sort. I'll tell you one thing—Paul and I are going to find our way out of this, and you are coming with us."

For reply Desirée laughed at him—a laugh that plainly said, "I am my own mind, and obey no other." It is one of the most familiar cards of the woman of beauty, and the most effective. It conquered Harry.

He gazed at her for a long moment in silence, while his eyes filled with an expression which one man should never show to another man. It is the betrayal of the masculine sex and the triumph of the feminine.

Suddenly he threw himself on his knees before her and took her hands in his own. She attempted to withdraw them; he clasped her about the waist.

"Do you not love me, Desirée?" he cried, and his lips sought hers.

They met; Desirée ceased to struggle.

At that moment I heard a sound—the faintest sound—behind me.

I turned.

The king of the Incas was standing within the doorway, surveying the lovers with beadlike, sparkling eyes.

Chapter XI.

A ROYAL VISITOR.

If it had not been for the manifest danger, I could have laughed aloud at what I read in the eyes of the king. Was it not supremely ridiculous for Desirée Le Mire, who had been sought after by the great and the wealthy and the powerful of all Europe, to be regarded with desire by that ugly dwarf? And it was there, unmistakably.

I sang out a sharp warning, but it was unnecessary; Desirée had already caught sight of the royal visitor. She pushed Harry from her bodily. He sprang to his feet in angry surprise; then, enlightened by the confusion in her face, turned quickly and swore as he, too, saw the intruder.

How critical the situation was I did not know, despite Desirée's assertions. His eyes were human and easily read; they held jealousy; and when power is jealous there is danger.

But Desirée proved herself equal to the occasion. She remained seated on the granite couch for a long minute without moving; confusion left her eyes as she gazed at us apparently with the utmost composure; but I who knew her could see that her brain was working with the rapidity of lightning. Then her glance passed to the figure at the doorway, and with a gesture commanding and truly royal in its simplicity, she held her hand forth, palm down, to the Inca king.

Like an obedient trained monkey he trotted across the intervening space, grasped her soft white hand in his monstrous paw, and touched his lips to her fingers.

That was all, but it spoke volumes to one who could divine the springs of action. I remember that at the time there shot through my mind a story I had heard concerning Desirée in Paris. The Duke of Bellarmine, then her protector, had one evening entered her splendid apartment on the Rue Jonteur—furnished, of course, by himself—and had found his divinity entertaining one Jules Chavot, a

young and beautiful poet. Whereupon he had launched
forth into the most bitter reproaches and scornful denunci-
ations.

"*Monsieur,*" Desirée had said, with the look of a queen
outraged, when he had finished, "you are annoying. Little
Chavot amuses me. You are aware that I never refuse
myself anything which I consider necessary to my amusement, and just now I find you very dull."

And the noble duke, conquered by that glance of fire and
those terrible words, had retired with humble apologies,
after receiving a gracious permission to call on the following day!

In short, Desirée was irresistible; the subjection of the
Inca king was but another of her triumphs, and not the
most remarkable.

And then I looked at Harry, and was aware of a new
danger. He was glaring at the Inca with eyes which told
their own story of the fire within, and which were waiting
only for suspicion to become certainty. I called to him:

"Harry! Hold fast!"

He glanced at me, gave a short laugh, and nodded.

Then came Desirée's voice, in a low tone of warning:
"On your knees!"

Her meaning was clear; it was to us she spoke. The king
had turned from her and was regarding us steadily with
eyes so nearly closed that their meaning was impenetrable.
Harry and I glanced at each other and remained standing.
Then Desirée's voice again:

"Harry! If you love me!"

It was the appeal to a child; but love is young. Immediately Harry dropped to his knees, facing the king; and
I followed him, wondering at myself. To this day I do not
know what the compelling force was that pulled me down.
Was it another instance of the power of Desirée?

For perhaps a minute we remained motionless on our
knees while the king stood gazing at us, it seemed to me
with an air of doubt. Then slowly, and with a gait that
smacked of majesty despite his ungainly appearance and

diminutive stature, he stalked across to the doorway and disappeared in the corridor without.

Harry and I looked at each other, kneeling like two heathen idols, and burst into unrestrained laughter. But with it was mixed a portion of anger, and I turned to Desirée.

"In the name of Heaven, was that necessary?"

"You do it very prettily," said she, with a smile.

"That is well, but I don't care to repeat it. Harry, for the sake of my dignity, employ a little discretion. And what do you suppose the beggar will do about it?"

"Nothing," said Desirée, shrugging her shoulders. "Only he must be pacified. I must go. I wonder if you know you are lodged in the royal apartments? His majesty's room—he has but one—is in the corridor to the left of this.

"Mine is on the right—and he is probably stamping the place to pieces at this moment." She left the granite couch and advanced half way to the door. "*Au revoir, messieurs.* Till later— I shall come to see you."

The next moment she was gone.

Harry and I, left alone, had enough to think and talk about, but there was ten minutes of silence before we spoke. I sat on one of the stone seats, wondering what the result would be—if any—of the king's visit and his discovery.

Harry paced up and down the length of the apartment with lowered head. Presently he spoke abruptly:

"Paul, I want to know exactly what you think of our chances for getting out of this."

"Why—" I hesitated. "Harry, I don't know."

"But you've thought about it, and you know something about these things. What do you think?"

"Well, I think they are slim."

"What are they?"

"Nothing less than miracles. There are just two. First— and I've spoken of this before—we might find an underground stream that would carry us to the western slope."

"That is impossible—at least, for Desirée. And the second?"

"Nature herself. She plays queer tricks in the Andes. She might turn the mountain upside down, in which case we would find ourselves on top. Seriously, the formation here is such that almost anything is possible. Upheavals of vast masses of rock are of ordinary occurrence. A passage might be opened in that way to one of the lower peaks.

"We are surrounded by layers of limestone, granite, and quartzite, which are of marked difference both in the quality of hardness and in their ability to withstand the attacks of time. When one finds itself unable to support the other, something happens."

"But it might not happen for a hundred years."

"Or never," I agreed.

Again silence. Harry stood gazing at one of the flaming urns, buried in thought—easy to guess of what nature. I did not think fit to disturb him, till presently he spoke again.

"What do you suppose that ugly devil will do about—what he saw in here?"

I smiled. "Nothing."

"But if he should? We are helpless."

"Trust Desirée. It's true that she can't even talk to him, but she'll manage him somehow. You saw what happened just now."

"But the creature is no better than a dumb brute. He is capable of anything. I tell you, we ought to get her away from here."

"To starve?"

"And we're none too safe ourselves. As for starving, we could carry enough of their darned fish to last a year. And one thing is sure: we won't get back to New York lying round here waiting for something to turn up—even a mountain."

"What do you want to do?"

"Clear out. Get Desirée away from that ugly brute. If we only had our knives!"

"Where would we go?"

In that question was the whole matter. To escape with Desirée was possible—but then what? We knew by experience what it meant to wander hopelessly about in the darkness of those desolate caverns, without food, and depending on Providence for water. Neither of us cared to repeat that trial, especially with the added difficulty of a woman to care for. But what to do?

We decided to wait for the future, and in the mean time lay in a supply of provisions, and, if possible, devise some sort of weapons.

It is worth remarking here that the Incas, so far as we had seen, used no weapons whatever. This was most probably the result of their total isolation and consequent freedom from foreign hostility.

In the matter of food we were soon to receive an aggreeable surprise. It was about an hour after Desirée had left us that the royal steward—I give him the title on my own responsibility—arrived, with pots and pans on a huge tray.

In the first place, the pots and pans were of solid gold. Harry stared in amazement as they were placed in brilliant array on one of the stone tables; and when we essayed to lift the empty tray from another table on which it had been placed we understood why the steward had found it necessary to bring four assistants along as cup-bearers.

There was a king's ransom on that table, in sober truth, for there could be no doubt but that this was part of the gold which had been carried from Huánuco when it had been demanded by Pizarro as payment for the life of Atahualpa.

But better even than the service was that which it contained. It may not have been such as would enhance the reputation of a French *chef,* but to us then it seemed that the culinary art could go no farther.

There was a large platter; Harry lifted its cover in an ecstasy of hope; but the next instant his face fell ludicrously.

"Our old friend, Mr. Dried Fish," he announced sadly, and gave it up.

Then I tried my luck, and with better success.

First I uncovered a dish of stew, steaming hot! To be sure, it was fish, but it was hot. Then a curious, brittle kind of bread; I call it that, though on trial it appeared to be made from the roe of some kind of fish. Also there was some excellent fish-soup, also hot, and quite delicious.

Four hundred years of development had taught the royal *chefs* to prepare fish in so many different ways that we almost failed to recognize them as of the same family.

"Couldn't be better," said Harry, helping himself liberally to the stew. "We can eat this, and cache the dried stuff. We'll have enough for an army in a week."

"As for me, I saw before me the raw material for our weapons. When we had emptied the golden platter that held our "bread," I secreted it under the cover of the granite couch. When the serving-men called to remove the dishes they apparently did not notice its absence. So far, success.

Some hours later Desirée paid us a second call. She appeared to be in the gayest of spirits, and I eyed her curiously from a seat in the corner as she and Harry sat side by side, chatting for all the world as though they had been in her own Paris drawing-room.

Was it possible that she was really satisfied, as she had said? What imaginable food could these black dwarfs find to appease her tremendous vanity? Or was she merely living the motto of the French philosopher?

Harry was demanding that he be allowed to visit her apartment; this she refused, saying that if he were found there by the king nothing could avert a catastrophe. Harry's brow grew black; I could see his effort to choke back his anger. Then Desirée led him away from the topic, and soon they were both again laughing merrily.

Some forty-eight hours passed; in that perpetual blackness there was no such thing as day. We saw no one save Desirée and the serving men. Once a messenger appeared carrying a bundle of *quipos;* I was able to decipher their meaning sufficiently to understand that we were invited to to some religious ceremony in the great cavern. But I thought it injudicious to allow a meeting between Harry and the king, and returned a polite refusal.

It may be of interest to some to know the method, which was extremely simple, as in ordinary communications the *quipos* are easy to read. I removed two knots from the white cord—the sign of affirmative—and placed two additional ones on the black cord—the sign of negative. Then on the yellow cord—the sign of the Child of the Sun and submission to him—I tied two more knots to show that our refusal meant no lack of respect to their deity.

Which, by the way, was not a little curious.

Here were the descendants of the subjects of Manco-Capac, himself a son of the orb of day, still holding to their worship of the sun, though they had not seen its light for four centuries. Deserted by their god, they did not abandon him; an example from which the followers of another and more "civilized" religion might learn something of the potency of faith.

But to the story.

As I say, I was anxious to avoid a meeting between Harry and the king, and subsequent events proved my wisdom. Harry was acting in a manner quite amazing; it was impossible for me to mention the king even in jest without him flying into a violent temper.

As I look back now I am not surprised; for our harrowing experiences and the hopelessness of our situation and the wilfulness of Desirée were enough, Heaven knows, to jerk his nerves; but at the time I regarded his actions as those of a thoughtless fool, and told him so, thinking to divert his anger to myself. He took no notice of me.

We were left entirely to ourselves. At regular intervals our food was brought to us, and within a week we had accumulated a large supply of the dried fish against necessity, besides my collection of six golden platters, of which more later.

Once in about twenty-four hours two Incas, who appeared to be our personal attendants—for we were actually able to recognize them after half a dozen visits—arrived to perform the offices of chambermaid and valet. The floor of the apartment was scrubbed, the urns refilled with oil, and the skin cover of the granite couch was changed. It seemed that another belief—in cleanliness—had refused to be dislodged from the Inca breast.

When I managed, by dint of violent and expressive gestures, to convey to our valet the idea that we desired a bath, he led us down the corridor some two hundred feet to a stream of cool running water. We took advantage of the opportunity to scrub our clothing, which was sadly in need of the operation.

I had early made an examination of the urns which furnished our light. They were of gold and perfect in form, which convinced me that they had been brought by the fugitives from Huánuco, as, indeed, the *quipos* also, and several other articles we found, including our golden table service.

The urns were filled with an oil which I was unable to recognize. There was no wick, but round the rim or lip of each was set a broad ring carved of stone, which made the opening at the top only about two inches in diameter. Through this the flame arose to a height of about two feet.

Of smoke there was none, or very little, a circumstance which was inexplicable, as there seemed to be no possibility of the generation of gas within so small space. But the oil itself was strange to me, and its properties may be charged to nature.

As I say, I had collected six of the golden platters, one at a time. Together they weighed about twenty pounds—for they were small and rather thin—which was near the amount required for my purpose. I explained the thing to Harry, and we set to work.

We first procured a vessel of granite from the attendant on some pretext or other—this for melting the gold. Then we pried a slab of limestone from a corner of one of the seats; luckily for us it was very soft, having been selected by the Incas for the purpose of inserting in its face the crystal prisms. Then we procured a dozen or more of the prisms themselves, and, using them as chisels, and small blocks of granite as hammers, set to work at the block of limestone.

It was slow work, but we finally succeeded in hollowing out a groove in its surface about eighteen inches long and two inches deep. That was our mold.

Then to melt the golden platters. We took four of the urns, placing them in a group on the floor, and just at the tip of the flames placed the granite vessel, supported by four blocks of stone which we pried loose from one of the seats. In the vessel we placed the golden platters.

But we found, after several hours, that we did not have sufficient heat—or rather that the vessel was too thick to transmit it. And again we set to work with our improvised chisels and hammers, to shave off its sides and bottom. That was more difficult and required many hours for completion.

Finally, with the profane portion of our vocabularies completely exhausted and rendered meaningless by repetition, and with bruised and bleeding hands, we again arranged our furnace and sat down to wait. We had waited until the dishes from our dinner had been removed, and we were fairly certain to be alone for several hours.

Finally the gold was melted, stubbornly but surely. We took the thick hide cover from the couch and, one on each side, lifted the vessel of liquid metal and filled our mold. In an hour it was hardened into a bar the shape of a half-cylinder. We removed it and poured in the remainder of the gold.

It would appear that the gain was hardly worth the pains, and I admit it. But at the least I had kept Harry occupied with something besides his amatory troubles, and at the best we had two heavy, easily handled bars of metal that would prove most effective weapons against foes who had none whatever.

We had just removed the traces of our work as completely as possible and secreted the clubs of yellow metal in a corner of the apartment when the sound of pattering footsteps came from the corridor.

Harry gave me a quick glance; I moved between him and the door. But it was Desirée.

She entered the room hurriedly and crossed to the farther side, then turned to face the door. Her cheeks were glowing brightly, her eyes flashed fire, and her breast heaved with unwonted agitation. Before either she or I had time to speak Harry had sprung to her side and grasped her arm.

"What has he done now?" he demanded in a tone scarcely audible in its intensity.

"I—don't—know," said Desirée without removing her eyes from the door. "Let me go, Harry; let me sit down. Paul! Ah! I was afraid."

"For us?" I asked.

"Yes—partly. The brute! But then, he is human, and that is his way. And you—I was right—you should have gone to the Cave of the Sun when he required your presence."

"But it was merely an invitation. Cannot one refuse an invitation?" I protested.

"But, my dear Paul, the creature is royal—his invitations are commands."

"Well, we were busy, and we've already seen the Cave of the Sun."

"Still it was an error, and I think you will pay for it. There have been unusual preparations under way for many hours. The king has been in my apartment, and messengers and guards have been arriving constantly, each with his little bundle of *quipos,* as you call them."

"Did you see the *quipos?*"

"Yes."

"Did any of them contain a red cord, suspended alone, with a single knot at either end?"

"Yes, all of them," said Desirée without an instant's hesitation.

"That means Harry and me," I observed. "But the message! Can you remember any of them?"

She tried, but without success. Which will not surprise any one who has ever seen the collection at the museum at Lima.

Then Harry broke in:

"Something else has happened, Desirée. No bunch of cords tied in silly knots ever made you look as you did just now. What was it?"

"Nothing—nothing, Harry."

"I say yes! And I want to know! And if it's what I think it is we're going to clear out of here now!"

"As though we could!"

"We can! We have enough provisions to last for weeks. And see here," he ran to the corner where he had hidden the golden clubs and returned with them in his hands, "with these we could make our way through them all. Tell me!"

There was a strange smile on Desirée's lips.

"And so you would fight for me, Harry?" she said half-wistfully, half—I know not what. Then she continued in a tone low but quite distinct: "Well, it is too late. I am the king's."

She lied—I saw it in her eyes. Perhaps she meant to save Harry from his folly, to quiet him by the knowledge that he need not fight for what was no longer his own; but she was mistaken in her man.

Harry did not stop to read her eyes—he heard her words. He took two slow steps backward, then stood quite still, while his face grew deadly white and his eyes were fastened on hers with a look that made me turn my own away. His soul looked out from them—how he loved the woman—and I could not bear it!

Nor, after a moment, could Desirée. She took a step forward, extending her arms to him and cried out:

"Harry! No! It was a lie, Harry! Don't—don't!"

And they gazed at each other, and I at Desirée, and thus we were unaware that a fourth person had entered the room, until he had crossed its full length and stood before me. It was the Inca king.

119

I took no time for thought, but jumped straight for Harry and threw my arms round him, dragging him back half-way across the room. Taken completely by surprise, he did not struggle. I noticed that he still held in his hands the bars of gold he had shown to Desirée.

The king regarded us for a second with a scowl, then turned to her.

She stood erect, with flashing eyes. The king approached; she held out her hand to him with an indescribable gesture of dignity.

For a moment he looked at her, then his lips curled in an ugly snarl, and, dashing her hand aside, he leaped forward in swift fury and grasped her white throat with his fingers.

There was a strangled scream from Desirée, a frantic cry from Harry—and the next instant he had torn himself free from my arms, dropping the bars of gold at my feet.

A single bound and he was across the room; a single blow with his fist and the king of the Incas dropped senseless to the floor.

Chapter XII.

AT THE DOOR.

Desirée shrank back against the wall, covering her face with her hands. Harry stood above the prostrate figure of the king, panting and furious.

As for me, I gave no thought to what had been done—the imminent peril of the situation possessed my mind and stung my brain to action.

I ran to the figure on the floor and bent over him. There was no movement—his eyes were closed. Calling to Harry to watch the corridor without, I quickly tore my woolen jacket into strips—my fingers seemed to be made of steel— and bound the wrists and ankles of the Inca firmly, trussing him up behind.

Then with another strip I gagged him, thinking it best to err on the side of prudence. In another moment I had dragged him to the corner of the room behind the granite couch and covered him with its hide-cover.

Then I turned to Harry:

"Is the coast clear?"

"Yes," he answered from the doorway.

"Then here—quick, man! Get the clubs and the grub. Desirée—come! There's not a second to lose."

"But, Paul—" she began; then, seeing the utter folly of any other course than instant flight, she sprang to Harry's side to assist him with the bundles of provisions.

There was more than we could carry. Harry and I each took a bundle under our left arm, carrying the clubs in the other hand. Desirée attempted to take two bundles, but they were too heavy for her, and she was forced to drop one.

With a last hasty glance at the motionless heap in the corner we started, Harry leading and myself in the rear, with Desirée between us.

But it was not to be so easy. We were nearly to the door when there came a grating, rumbling sound from above, and a huge block of granite dropped squarely across the doorway with a crash that made the ground tremble beneath our feet.

Stupefied, we realized in a flash that the cunning of the Incas had proved too much for us. Harry and I ran forward, but only to invite despair; the doorway was completely covered by the massive rock, an impenetrable curtain of stone weighing many tons, and on neither side was there an opening more than an inch wide. We were imprisoned beyond all hope of escape.

We stood stunned; Desirée even made no sound, but gazed at the blocked doorway in a sort of stupid wonder. It was one of those sudden and overwhelming catastrophes that deprive us for a moment of all power to reason or even to realize.

Then Harry said quietly:

"Well, the game's up."

And Desirée turned to me with the calm observation:

"They must have been watching us. We were fools not to have known it."

"Impossible!" Harry asserted; but I agreed with Desirée; and though I could see no opening or crevice of any sort in the walls or ceiling, I was convinced that even then the eyes of the Incas were upon us.

Our situation was indeed desperate. With our every movement spied upon, surrounded by four solid walls of stone, and beyond them ten thousand savage brutes waiting to tear us to pieces—what wildest fancy could indulge in hope?

Then, glancing up, my eye was arrested by the heap under the cover in the corner. There, in the person of the Inca king, lay our only advantage. But how could we use it?

Desirée's voice came in the calm tones of despair:

"We are lost."

Harry crossed to her and took her in his arms.

"I thank Heaven," he said, "that you are with us." Then he turned to me: "I believe it is for the best, Paul. There never was a chance for us; we may as well say it now. And it is better to die here, together, than—the other way."

I smiled at his philosophy, knowing its source. It came not from his own head, but from Desirée arms. But it was truth.

We sat silent. The thing was beyond discussion; too elemental to need speech for its explanation or understanding. I believe it was not despair that kept back our words, but merely the dumb realization that where all hope is gone words are useless—worse, a mockery.

Finally I crossed the room and removed the cover from the body of the Child of the Sun. He had recovered consciousness; his little wicked eyes gleamed up at me with an expression that would have been terrifying in the intensity of its malignant hatred if he had not been utterly helpless. I turned to Harry:

"What are we going to do with him?"

"By Jove, I had forgotten!" exclaimed the lad. "Paul, perhaps if we could communicate with them—" He stopped, glancing at the closed doorway; then added: "But it's impossible."

"I believe it is possible," I contradicted. "If the Incas were able to lower that stone at any moment you may be sure they are prepared to raise it. How, Heaven only knows; but the fact is certain. Do you think they would have condemned their precious king to starvation?"

"Then the king can save us!"

"And how?"

"Our lives for his. We'll give him nothing to eat, and if, as you say, they have some way of watching us, they'll be forced to negotiate. You can talk with the *quipos*, and tell them that unless they give us our freedom and let us go in safety they'll have a dead king. From the way they seem to worship him they'd come through in a minute."

"Oh, they'd promise, all right," I agreed; "but how could we hold them to it?"

"Well, a promise is a promise. And it's our only chance."

"No, Harry; to trust them would be folly. The minute we stepped through that doorway they would be on us—the whole beggarly, smelly lot of them."

"Then there is no chance—none whatever?" put in Desirée.

"None. We may as well admit the worst. And the worst is best for us now. Really, we are in luck; we die in our own way and at our own time. But there is one difficulty."

Then, in answer to their glances of inquiry, I added significantly: "We have no weapons. We cannot allow ourselves to starve—the end must come before that, for as soon as they saw us weakening we would be at their mercy."

There was comprehension and horror in Desirée's eyes, but she looked at me with a brave attempt to smile as she took from her hair something which gleamed and shone in the light from the flaming urns. It was a tiny steel blade with a handle of pearl studded with diamonds.

I had seen it before many times—a present, Desirée had told me, from the young man I had seen in the royal coach on that day in Madrid when I had first heard the name of Le Mire.

"Will that do?" she asked calmly, holding it out to me with a firm hand.

Brave Le Mire! I took the dagger and placed it in my pocket, and, looking at Harry, exchanged with him a nod of understanding. No words were necessary.

"But I must confess I am a coward," said Desirée. "When the time comes I—I could not bear to see—to wait—"

I looked at her and said simply: "You shall be first," and she gave me a smile of thanks that spoke of a heart that would not fail when the final moment arrived. And in my admiration of her high courage I forgot the horror of the task that must be mine.

It was a relief to have admitted the worst and discussed it calmly; there is no torment like suspense, and ours was at an end. A load was lifted from our hearts, and a quiet sympathy created between us, sincere as death itself. And it was in our power to choose for ourselves the final moment—we were yet masters of our fates.

All action seems useless when hope is dead, but certain

things needed to be done, and Harry and I bestirred ourselves. We extinguished the flame in all the urns but one to save the oil, not caring to depart in darkness.

Our supply of water, we found, was quite sufficient to last for several days, if used sparingly; for we intended to support life so long as we had the fuel. Then responsibility ceases; man has a right to hasten that which fortune has made inevitable.

The hours passed by.

We talked very little; at times Desirée and Harry conversed in subdued tones which I did not overhear; I was engaged with my own thoughts. And they were not unpleasant; if, looking death in the face, a man can preserve his philosophy unchanged, he had made the only success in life that is worth while.

We ate and drank, but gave neither water nor food to our fellow prisoner. Not because I really expected to force negotiations with the Incas—but the thing was possible and was worth a trial. I knew them well enough to appraise correctly the value of any safe-conduct they might give us.

I was a little surprised to find in Desirée no levity, the vulgar prop for courage based on ignorance. There was a tenderness in her manner, especially toward Harry, that spoke of something deeper and awoke in my own breast a deeper respect for her. The world had not known Desirée Le Mire—it had merely been fascinated and amused by her.

Many hours had passed in this tomblike apathy. Two or three times I had advised Desirée to lie down to rest and, if possible, to sleep. She had refused, but I became insistent, and Harry added his voice to my own. Then, to please us, she consented; we arranged the cover on the granite couch and made her as comfortable as possible.

In five minutes she was fast asleep. Harry stood a few feet away from the couch, looking down at her. I spoke to him, in a low tone:

"And you must rest too, Hal. One of us must remain on watch; I'll take it first and call you when I feel drowsy. It may be a needless precaution, but I don't care to wake up and find myself in the condition of our friend yonder."

He wanted to take the first watch himself, but I insisted, and he arranged our ponchos on the ground, and soon he too was sleeping easily and profoundly. I looked from him to Desirée with a smile, and reflection that Socrates himself could not have met misfortune with more sublime composure.

It was possible that the stone curtain across the doorway could be raised noiselessly, and that made it necessary to keep my eyes fastened on it almost continuously. This became irksome; besides, twice I awoke to the fact that my thoughts had carried me so far away from my surroundings that the stone could have been raised to the roof and I would not have noticed it.

So, using my jacket for a cushion, I seated myself on the ground in the threshold, leaning my back against the stone, and gave myself up to meditation.

I had sat thus for three hours or more, and was thinking of calling Harry to relieve me, when I felt a movement at my back. I turned quickly and saw that the stone was moving upward.

Slowly it rose, by little frequent jerks, not more than an eighth of an inch at a time. In fifteen minutes it was only about four inches from the ground. There was no sound save a faint grating noise from above.

I stood several feet away, holding one of the golden clubs in my hand, thinking it unnecessary to rouse Harry until the space was wide enough to cause apprehension. Or rather, because I had no fear of an assault—I was convinced that our ruse had succeeded, and that they were about to communicate with us by means of the *quipos*.

The stone was raised a little over a foot, then became stationary. I waited, expecting to see a bundle of *quipos* thrust through the opening, but they did not appear.

Instead, five golden vessels were pushed across the ground until they were inside, clear of the stone; I could see the black, hairy hands and arms, which were immediately withdrawn.

Then the granite curtain fell with a crash that caused me to start with its suddenness and awakened both Harry and Desirée.

Two of the vessels contained water, two oil, and the other dried fish. Harry, who had sprung to his feet excitedly, grumbled in disgust.

"At least, they might have sent us some soup. But what's their idea?"

"It means that Desirée was right," I observed. "They have some way of watching us. And, seeing that we refused to provide their beloved monarch with provender, they have sent him an allowance from the pantry."

Harry grinned.

"Will he get it?"

"Hardly," said I with emphasis. "We'll make 'em treat with us if it's only to observe their diplomacy. There'll be a message from them within twenty-four hours. You'll see."

"Anyway, we know now that they can raise that stone whenever they feel like it. But in the name of Archimedes, how?"

He advanced to the doorway and examined the block of granite curiously, but there was no clue to its weight or thickness from the inside. I explained that there were several ways by which the thing could be raised, but that the most probable one was by means of a rolling pulley, which required merely some rounded stones and a flat surface above, with ropes of hide for stays.

It had been several hours since we had last eaten, and we decided to at once convey to the spies without our intentions concerning our prisoner. So we regaled ourselves with dried fish and water, taking care not to approach the king, who had rolled over on his side and lay facing us, looking for all the world, in the dim light, like a black dog crouched on the floor.

Harry relieved me at my post against the door, and I lay down to sleep. Desirée had seated herself beside him, and the low tones of their voices came to me as I lay on the couch (which Desirée had insisted I should occupy) in an indistinct, musical murmur. This for perhaps ten minutes; then I slept.

That became our routine. During the many weary hours that followed there was never a moment when one of us was not seated with his back against the stone across the doorway; we dared not trust our eyes. Usually Harry and Desirée watched together, and, when I relieved them, slept side by side on the couch.

Sometimes, when we were all awake, Desirée was left on guard alone; but Harry and I were never both asleep at the same time.

An estimate of the time we spent thus would be the wildest guess, for time was heavy and passed on leaden feet. But I should say we had been imprisoned for something like four days, possibly five, when the monotony came to an abrupt end.

I had come off watch, and Harry and Desirée had taken my place. Before I lay down I had taken some water to the prisoner, for we had some time before admitted the necessity of giving him drink. But of food he had had none.

Harry told me afterward that I had slept for two or three hours, but it seemed to me rather as many minutes, when I was awakened by the sound of his voice calling my name. Glancing at the doorway, I sprang to my feet.

The stone was slowly rising from the floor; already there was a space of a foot or more. Desirée and Harry stood facing it in silence.

"You have seen nothing?" I asked, joining them.

"Nothing," said Harry. "Here, take one of these clubs. Something's up."

"Of course—the stone," I observed facetiously, yawning. "Probably nothing more important than a bundle of *quipos*. Lord, I'm sleepy!"

Still the stone moved upward, very slowly. It reached a height of two feet, yet did not halt.

"This is no *quipos*," said Harry, "or if it is, they must be going to send us in a whole library. Six inches would have been enough for that."

I nodded, keeping my eyes on the ever-widening space at our feet.

"This means business, Hal. Stand ready with your club. Desirée, go to the further corner, behind that seat."

She refused; I insisted; she stamped her foot in anger.

"Do you think I'm a child, to run and hide?" she demanded obstinately.

I wasted no time in argument.

"You will go," I said sternly, "or I shall carry you and tie you. This is not play. We must have room and know that you are safe."

To my surprise, she made no reply, but quietly obeyed. Then, struck by a sudden thought, I crossed to where she stood behind a stone seat in the corner.

"Here," I said in a low tone, taking the little jeweled dagger from my pocket and holding it out to her, "in case—"

"I understand," she said simply, and her hand closed over the hilt.

By that time the stone was half-way to the top of the doorway, leaving a space over three feet high, and was still rising. I stood on one side and Harry on the other, not caring to expose ourselves immediately in front.

Suddenly he left his post and ran to one of the stone seats and began prying at the blocks of granite. I saw at once his intention and our mistake; we should have long before barricaded the door on the inside. But was too late now; I knew from experience the difficulty of loosening those firmly wedged blocks, and I called out:

"No good, Hal. We were fools not to have thought of it before, but there is no time for it now. Come back; I couldn't stop 'em alone."

Nevertheless, he continued his exertions, and succeeded in getting one of the blocks partially free; but by that time the doorway was almost completely uncovered, and he saw the folly of attempting further.

He resumed his post on the right of the door—I was on the left.

The stone appeared to be going faster. It reached the top—passed it—and quickly swung in toward the wall and disappeared, probably to rest on a ledge above.

We stood waiting, tense and alert. The open doorway gaped on the black, empty corridor, into which the light from our single urn shone dimly. We could see or hear nothing, no indication that any one was in the passage, but we dared not look out in that darkness. The suspense was trying enough; Harry ripped out an impatient oath and made a movement as though to step in the entrance, but I waved him back.

Then came the avalanche, with a suddenness and fury that nigh overwhelmed us.

Crouching, rushing forms filled the doorway from both directions and leaped savagely at us. After so many weary days of dull inaction and helpless, hopeless apathy, a mad joy fired my brain and thrilled my heart as I raised my club on high and struck a blow for freedom and life.

That blow crushed the skull of one whose fingers were at my throat, and he dropped like a log at my feet; but his place was already filled. Again I swung the club; another swayed, toppling against the doorway and leaning there with the blood streaming from his broken head, quite dead, but held erect by the pressure of his fellows from behind.

If the doorway had been but a foot wider we would have been overwhelmed almost instantly. As it was, but three or four could get to us at once, and they found the gold which their ancestors had carried from the temples of Huánuco waiting for them. My arm seemed to have the strength of a hundred arms; it swung the heavy club as though it had been a feather, and with deadly accuracy.

Harry fought like a demon. I think I did all that a man could do, but he did more, and withal more coolly. I brought down my club on heads, shoulders, chests, and rarely failed to get my man.

But the impact of Harry's blows was like the popping of a

Maxim. I saw him reach over and grasp the throat of one who had his teeth set in my shoulder, and, holding him straight before him with his arm extended, break his neck with one blow. Again, his club descended on one black skull with a glancing blow and shot off to the head of another with the force of a sledge-hammer.

At the time I did not know that I saw these things; it was all one writhing, struggling, bloody horror; but afterward the eyes of memory showed them to me.

Still they came. My arm rose and fell seemingly without order from the brain; I was not conscious that it moved. It seemed to me that ever since the beginning of time I had stood in that butcher's doorway and brought down that bar of gold on thick, black skulls and distorted, grinning faces. But they would not disappear. One fell; another took his place; and another, and another, and another.

The bodies of those who fell were dragged away from underneath. I did not see it, but it must have been so, or soon we would have raised our own barricade for defense— a barricade of flesh. And there was none.

I began to weaken, and Harry saw it, for he gasped out: "Steady—Paul. Take it—easy. They can't—last—forever."

His blows were redoubled in fury as he moved closer to me, taking more than his share of the attack, so that I almost had time to breathe.

But we could not have held out much longer. My brain was whirling madly and a weight of a thousand tons seemed dragging me remorselessly, inevitably to the ground. I kept my feet through the force of some crazy instinct, for will and reason were gone.

And then, for an instant, Harry's eyes met mine, and I read in them what neither of us could say, nor would. With the fury of despair we struck out together in one last effort.

Whether the Incas saw in that effort a renewed strength that spoke of immortality, or whether it happened just at that moment that the pressure from behind was removed, no longer forcing them to their death, I do not know. It may have been that, like some better men, they had merely had enough.

From whatever cause, the attack ceased almost with the suddenness with which it had begun; they fell back from the doorway; Harry lunged forward with raised club, and the forms melted away into the darkness of the corridor.

Harry turned and looked at me as I stood swaying from side to side in the doorway. Neither of us could speak. Together we staggered back across the room, but I had not gone more than half way when my legs bent under me and I sank to the floor. Dimly I saw Harry's face above me, as though through a veil—then another face that came close to my own—and a voice:

"Paul! My love! They have killed him!"

Soft white arms were about my neck, and a velvet cheek was pressed against my own.

"Desirée!" I gasped. "Don't! Harry! No, they have not killed me—"

Then Harry's voice:

"That's all right, old fellow. I know—I have known she loves you. This is no time to talk of that. Listen, Paul—what you were going to do for Desirée—if you can—they will be back at any moment—"

That thought kindled my brain; I raised myself onto my elbow.

"I haven't the strength," I said, hardly knowing how I spoke. "You must do it, Harry; you must. And quick, lad! The dagger! Desirée—the dagger!"

What followed came to me as in a dream; my eyes were dim with the exhaustion that had overcome my body. Desirée's face disappeared from before my face—then a silence—then the sound of her voice as though from a distance:

"Harry—come! I can't find it! I dropped it when I ran across—it must be here—on the floor—"

And then another sound came that I knew only too well—the sound of rushing, pattering feet.

I think I tried to rise to my own feet. I heard Harry's

voice crying in a frenzy: "Quick—here they come! Desirée, where is it?"

There was a ringing cry of despair from Desirée, a swinging oath from Harry, and the next instant I found myself pinned to the floor by the weight of a score of bodies.

Chapter XIII.

INTO THE WHIRLPOOL.

I hardly know what happened after that. I was barely conscious that there was movement round me, and that my wrists and ankles were being tightly bound. Harry told me afterward that he made one last desperate stand, and was halted by a cry from Desirée, imploring him to employ the club in the intended office of the dagger.

He wheeled about and raised it to strike; then his arm dropped, unable to obey for the brutal horror of it. In another instant he and Desirée, too, had been overpowered and carried to the floor by the savage rush.

This he told me as we lay side by side in a dark cavern, whither we had been carried by the victorious Incas. I had expected instant death; the fact that our lives had been spared could have but one meaning, I thought: to the revenge of death was to be added the vindictiveness of torture.

We knew nothing of Desirée's fate. Harry had not seen her since he had been crushed to the floor by that last assault. And instead of fearing for her life, we were convinced that a still more horrible doom was to be hers, and hoped only that she would find the means to avoid it by the only possible course.

I have said that we again found ourselves in darkness, but it was much less profound than it had been before. We could distinctly see the four walls of the cavern in which we lay; it was about twelve feet by twenty, and the ceiling was very low. The ground was damp and cold, and we had neither ponchos nor jackets to protect us.

A description of our state of mind as we lay exhausted, wounded, and bound so tightly that any movement was impossible, would seem to betray a weakness. Perhaps it was so; but we prayed for the end—Harry with curses and oaths, myself in silence. There is a time when misery becomes so acute that a man wants only deliverance and gives no thought to the means.

That was reaction, and gradually it lessened. And when, after we had lain unconscious for many hours (we can hardly be said to have slept) they came to bathe our wounds and bruises and bring us food and drink, the water was actually grateful to our hot, suffering flesh, and we ate almost with relish. But before they left they again bound our wrists firmly behind us, and tightened the cords on our ankles.

If they meditated punishment they certainly seemed to be in no hurry about it. The hours passed endlessly by. We were cared for as tenderly as though we had been wounded comrades instead of vanquished foes, and though we were allowed to remain on the damp, hard rock of the cavern, we gradually recovered from the effects of that gruesome struggle in the doorway, and our suffering bodies began to feel comparative comfort.

"What the deuce are they waiting for?" Harry growled, after one of their visits with food and water. "Why don't they end it?"

"Most likely because a well man can appreciate torture better than a sick one," I answered, not having seen fit to speak of it before. "You may be sure we'll get all that's coming to us."

"But what will they do?"

"Heaven knows. They are capable of anything. We'll get the worst."

There was a silence; then Harry said slowly, hesitating: "Paul—do you think—Desirée—"

"I don't think—I dare not think about her," I interrupted. "And it is our fault; we failed her. I should have put her beyond their reach, as I promised. I have reproached myself bitterly, Hal; you need add nothing."

"Do you think I would? Only—there is something else. About what she said to you. I knew that, you know."

I was silent; he continued:

"I knew it long ago. Do you think I am blind? And I want

136

to say this while I have a chance—it was uncommon good of you. To take it the way you did, I mean."

His simplicity made me uncomfortable, and I made no answer. Indeed, the thing was beyond discussion; it was merely a bare fact which, when once stated, left nothing to be said. So I refused to humor Harry's evident desire to thrash out the topic, and abruptly changed the subject.

We must have lain bound in that cavern little short of a week. Our wounds and bruises were completely healed, save one gash on Harry's side where he had been hurled against the sharp edge of one of the stone seats as he had been borne to the floor. But it was not painful, and was nearly closed. And we could feel the return of strength even through the stiffness caused by the inactivity of our muscles.

We had given up wondering at the delay by the time it came to an end. When they finally came and cut our bonds and led us from the cavern we felt nothing keener than a mere curiosity as to what awaited us at the end of our journey. For myself, there was a distinct sensation of thankfulness that uncertainty was to end.

They took no chances with us, but paid us the compliment of a truly royal escort—at least, in number. There could not have been less than two hundred of them in front, behind, and on either side, as we left the cavern and proceeded along a narrow, winding passage to the left.

Once, as we started, we stretched our arms high and stood on tiptoe to relieve the stiffness of our joints; and immediately found ourselves clutched on every side by a score of hands.

"Gad! We seem to have made an impression!" Harry grinned. On the way down the passage we marched with the Prussian goose-step, and felt the blood quickening to life in our legs and arms.

We had proceeded in this manner for some ten minutes when we rounded a corner which I recognized at once by the peculiar circular formation of the walls. We were on our way to the great cavern—the cavern where we had first seen Desirée, and where later she had won the toss for our lives and then preserved them.

Another minute and we had reached the steps leading to the tunnel under the lake. Here our guards seemed in doubt as to just what to do; those in front halted and stood hesitant, and it seemed to me that as they gazed below down the stone stair their eyes held a certain shrinking terror. Then one came up from behind and with a commanding gesture ordered them to descend, and they obeyed.

Harry and I still found ourselves surrounded by a full company; there were fifty or sixty ahead of us and at least twice that number behind. The idea of a successful struggle was so patently impossible that I believe it never entered our minds.

There was further delay at the bottom of the stairs, for, as I have said before, the tunnel was extremely narrow and it was barely possible to walk two abreast. None of them turned back, but Harry and I could scarcely restrain a laugh at the sight of those immediately in front of us treading on the toes of their fellows to keep out of our way. With all their savage brutality I believe they possessed little real bravery.

Five minutes more and we had reached the end of the tunnel and found ourselves at the foot of the spiral stairway. The passage was so blocked by those ahead that we were unable to approach it; they flattened their squatty bodies against the wall and we were forced to squeeze our way past them.

There we stood, barely able to make out their black forms against the blacker wall, when the one who appeared to be the leader approached and motioned to us to ascend. We hesitated, feeling instinctively that this was our last chance to make a stand, weighing our fate.

That was a dark moment, but though I did not know it, Providence was with us. For, happening to glance downward, beneath the spiral stair—for there was no ground immediately beneath it—I saw a faint glimmer and a movement as though of a dim light in the black, yawning space at my feet. (You must understand that we were now inside the base of the column in the center of the great cavern.)

Moved either by curiosity or a command of Providence, I stooped and peered intently downward, and saw that the movement was the almost imperceptible reflection of a stray ray of light from above on the surface of water. At the time I merely wondered idly if the water came from the same source as that in the lake outside, not thinking it sufficiently important to mention to Harry.

Then a question came from him:

"No good, Paul. They are a hundred to one, and we are empty-handed. Do we go?"

"There is nothing else to do," I answered, and I placed my foot on the first step of the spiral stair.

Behind us came the guide, with a dozen others at his heels.

The ascent seemed even longer and more arduous than before, for then we had been propelled by keen curiosity. Twice I stumbled in the darkness, and would have fallen if it had not been for Harry's supporting hand behind me. But finally we reached the top and stepped out into the glare of the great cavern. I saw the stone slab close to behind us, noiselessly, and wondered if I should ever see it open again.

We looked about us, and as our eyes sought the alcove in the wall opposite, we gave a simultaneous start of surprise, and from Harry's lips came a cry, half of gladness, half of wonder. For, seated on the golden throne, exactly as before, was Desirée. By her side was seated the Inca king; round them, guards and attendants.

We gazed at her in astonishment, but she did not look at us; even at that distance we could see that her eyes were lowered to the ground. Harry called her name—there was no answer. Again he called, and I caught him by the arm.

"Don't, Hal! She can't possibly do us any good, and you may do her harm. If she doesn't answer, it is because she has a reason."

He was silent, but not convinced, and would probably have argued the matter if our attention had not been arrested by a movement in the alcove.

The king rose and extended an arm, and the Incas who filled the seats surrounding the cavern fell flat on their faces.

"We don't seem to have thinned them out any," I observed. "I believe there are actually more than before. Where do they all come from?"

"The Lords knows!"

"And, by the way, it is now apparent why they waited so long to attend to us. The king naturally wanted to be present at the entertainment, and he had to take time to recover from his little fasting operation. —But now, what in the name of—my word, the thing is to be done in all propriety! Look!"

The king had dropped his arm, and the Incas were again sitting as Nature had intended they should sit, instead of on their noses. And four attendants had approached the throne, bearing a frame of *quipos*.

"So we are to have a fair trial," Harry observed.

"With the king for judge."

"And a hundred dead rats as evidence."

"Right; they can't get even with us, anyway; there are only two of us. And as far as the other is concerned, I have an idea."

The king had left his throne and approached the outer edge of the alcove, until he stood almost directly under the oval plate of gold representing Pachacamac or the unknown god.

To this he knelt and made a succession of weird, uncouth gestures that suggested a lunatic or a traveling hypnotist. Evidently the good Pachacamac approved whatever suggestions the royal priest communicated, for he rose to his feet with a solemn grin and strutted majestically to the rear, facing the frame of *quipos*.

It was evident that he no longer had faith in Desirée's interpretation of the divine will of the great Pachacamac. It is a royal privilege to be able to judge your own enemies.

The hand of the Child of the Sun passed slowly up and down the frame of *quipos,* betraying a commendable reluctance. It touched the yellow cord and passed on; grasped the white and dropped it.

"The old hypocrite!" exclaimed Harry in disgust. "Does he imagine he is playing with us?"

Then there was an imperceptible movement, rather felt than seen, throughout the vast assemblage, and Desirée sank back on her throne of gold with a shudder as the king severed with the knife the black cord of death and laid it on the ground at her feet.

I looked at Harry; his face became slightly pale, but his eyes met mine firmly, speaking of a fortitude unconquerable. Then we again riveted our gaze on the alcove opposite.

An attendant approached from the rear and stood before the golden throne, while the king motioned to Desirée to take up the black cord. For a moment she did not understand him, then she drew back, shaking her head firmly.

The king did not wait to argue the matter, but stooped himself and picked up the cord and handed it to the attendant, who received it with a great show of respect and retired to the rear, where a commotion was created by its appearance.

The judgment was passed, but what was to be the nature of the execution? That uncertainty and the weirdness of the scene gave to the thing an air of unreality that shut out the tragic and admitted only the grotesque.

I have many times in my life felt nearer to death than when I stood on the top of that lofty column, surrounded by the thousands of squatting dwarfs, whose black bodies reflected dully the mounting light from the flaming urns.

I cannot say what we expected, for we knew not what to expect. Many conjectures entered my mind, but none of them approached the fact. But, thinking that our guide might now return at any moment to lead us below, and not caring to be surprised by an attack from behind on that narrow precipice, I moved across to the rear, where I could keep my eyes on the alcove opposite, and at the same time watch the stone slab which closed the opening to the spiral stairway. A word to Harry and he joined me.

"Perhaps we can open it from above," he suggested.

"Not likely," I answered, "and, anyway, what's the use?"

He knelt down and tugged at it, but there was no edge on which to obtain a purchase. The thing was immovable.

Five minutes passed, during which there was no movement, either in the audience on the stone seats or in the alcove. But there was an indefinable air of expectancy on the faces of the king and those surrounding him, and I kept a sharp eye on the stone slab.

Another five minutes and still nothing happened. Harry called across to Desirée, or rather began to call, for I stopped him with a jerk. It was impossible for her to aid us, and her situation was already sufficiently perilous.

Then, becoming impatient, I decided to try to move the stone slab myself. Kneeling down, I placed the palms of my hands firmly against its surface and pressed with all my weight.

And then I knew. Complete comprehension flashed through my brain on the instant. I sprang to my feet, and my thought must have shown on my face, for Harry looked at me in surprise, demanding:

"What is it? What is it, Paul?"

And I answered calmly:

"We're caught, Hal. Like rats in a trap. Oh, the black devils! Listen! We have no time to lose. Bend over and touch the palm of your hand to the ground."

He did so, plainly puzzled. Then he drew his hand hastily away, exclaiming: "It's hot!"

"Yes." I spoke quickly. "Our boots kept us from feeling it before, and the stone doesn't throw out enough heat to feel it in the air. They've built a fire under us in the column. The stone is thick and heats slowly."

"But what—that means—"

"It means one of two things. In a few minutes this floor will be baking hot. Then we either fry on their stone griddle

142

or drown in the lake. You see the distance below—only a man crazed by suffering or one incredibly brave would take that leap. This is their little entertainment—they expect us to dance for them."

"But the lake! If we could take it clean—"

I saw that the lake was our only chance, if there could be said to be any in so desperate a situation. To be sure, there seemed to be no possibility of escaping, even if we took the water without injury. On every side its bank was lined with the watching Incas, and the bank itself was so steep that to ascend it would have required wings.

The heat began to be felt even through the soles of our heavy boots; involuntarily I lifted one foot, then the other. I saw the Child of the Sun in the alcove lean forward with an appreciative grin. Another minute—

I jerked my wits together—never did my brain answer with better speed. And then I remembered that flash of water I had seen under the spiral stairway at the base of the column. I had thought at the time that it might be connected with the lake itself. If that were so—

I turned to Harry and conveyed my idea to him in as few words as possible as we walked up and down, side by side. It was impossible longer to stand still—the stone was so hot that the bare hand could not be held against it for an instant. I saw that he did not comprehend what I said about the water in the column, but he did understand my instructions, and that was all that was necessary.

We ran to the edge of the column nearest the alcove.

Removing our woolen knickerbockers—for better ease in the water—we placed them on the hot stone, and on top of them our boots, which we had also removed. Thus our feet were protected as we stood on the extreme edge of the column, taking a deep breath for strength and nerve.

I saw the thousands of black savages—who had been cheated of their dance—crane their necks forward eagerly.

I saw the king gesture excitedly to an attendant, who turned and flew from the alcove.

I saw Desirée spring up from the golden throne and run

to the edge of the alcove, crying to us in a tone of despair. But I did not hear her words, for I myself was calling:

"Take it clean, Hal. Ready—go!"

The next instant we were flying headlong through the air toward the surface of the lake a hundred feet below.

Men have told me since that I never made that dive, or that I greatly overestimated the distance, and I admit that as I look back at it now it appears incredible. Well, they are welcome to their opinion, but I would not advise them to try to argue the matter with Harry.

The impact with the water all but completely stunned me; as I struck the surface it seemed that a thousand cannons had exploded in my ears. Down, down I went—lucky for us that the lake was apparently bottomless!

I seemed to have gone as far below the water as I had been above it before I was able to twist myself about and meet it with my belly. Then, striking out with every ounce of strength in me, I made for the surface as rapidly as possible. I had started with my lungs full of air, but that headlong plunge had emptied them.

I made the surface at last and looked round for Harry, calling his name. For perhaps thirty seconds I called in vain, then there came an unanswering shout off to the left. The urns were far above us now, and the light on the surface of the lake was very dim, but soon I made out Harry's head. He was swimming easily toward me, apparently unhurt.

"All right, Hal?"

"Right. And you?"

"Sound as a whistle. Now make for the column."

At the instant that we turned to swim toward the column I became aware of a strong current in the water carrying us off to the right. It was inexplicable, but there was no time then for speculation, and we struck out with bold, sweeping strokes.

The Incas had left the stone seats and advanced to the water's edge. I could see their black, sinister faces, thousands of them, peering intently at us through the dim light, but they made no sound.

Once I cast a glance over my shoulder and saw Desirée standing at the edge of the alcove with her clenched fists pressed to her throat. Beside her stood the Child of the Sun. Harry, too, saw her and sent her a shout of farewell, but there was no answer.

We were now less than thirty feet from the column. Its jeweled sides sparkled and shone before us; looking up, our eyes were dazzled. Something struck the water near me. I glanced to the right and saw what moved me to hasten my stroke and call to Harry to do likewise.

The black devils were increasing the fun by hurling stones at us from the bank—apparently with the kind approval of Pachacamac.

As we neared the column the current which tended to carry us to the right became stronger, but still we seemed not to be approaching the bank. What could it mean? The struggle against it was fast taking our strength.

Looking up, I saw that we had swung round to the other side of the column—it was between us and the alcove. Then I understood. We were in a whirlpool, ever increasing in force, which was carrying us swiftly in a circle from left to right and approaching the column.

I called a swift warning to Harry, who was some ten feet to my left, and he answered that he understood. The stones from the bank were falling thick about us now; one struck me on the shoulder, turning me half round.

The current became swifter—so swift that we were almost helpless against it and were carried around and around the column, which was but a few feet away. And always complete silence.

Nearer and nearer we were carried, till, thrusting out my arm, the tips of my fingers brushed against the side of the column. The water whirled with the rapidity of a mill-stream; ten more seconds and our brains would have been dashed against the unyielding stone. It was now but half an arm's length away. I kept thrusting out my arm in a wild endeavor to avoid it.

Suddenly my outstretched hand found a purchase in a

break in the wall, but the force of the water tore it loose and swept me away. But when I reached the same spot again I thrust out both hands, and, finding the edge, held on desperately. The next instant Harry's body was swept against mine, doubling the strain on my fingers.

"The column!" I gasped. "Inside—through the wall—opening—I am holding—"

He understood, and the next moment he, too, had grasped the edge. Together we pulled ourselves, little by little, toward the opening; for our strength was nearly spent, and the force of the maelstrom was nigh irresistible.

It was as I had thought. The base of the column consisted merely of two massive pillars, some twelve feet in length and circular in shape. The water rushed in through each of the two openings thus left, and inside of the column was the center of the whirlpool, sucking the water from both sides. The water I had seen; I had not counted on the whirlpool.

We had pulled ourselves round till our bodies rested against the edge of the opening, clinging to either side. Inside all was blackness, but we could judge of the fury of the maelstrom by the force of the current outside. Stones hurled by the Incas were striking against the sides of the column and in the water near us.

We were being hunted from life like dogs, and a hot, unreasoning anger surged through my brain—anger at the grinning savages on the bank, at the whirling black water, at Harry, at myself.

Whichever way we looked was death, and none worth choosing.

"I can't hold—much longer," Harry gasped. "What's the use—old man—Paul—come—I'm going—"

He disappeared into the black, furious whirlpool with that word. The next instant my own fingers were torn from their hold by a sudden jerk of the water, and I followed.

Chapter XIV.

A FISHING PARTY.

Water, when whirling rapidly, has a keen distaste for any foreign object; but when once the surface breaks, that very repulsion seems to multiply the indescribable fury with which it endeavors to bury the object beneath its center.

Once in the whirlpool, I was carried in a swift circle round its surface for what seemed an age, and I think could not have been less than eight or ten seconds in reality. Then suddenly I was turned completely over, my limbs seemed to be torn from my body, there was a deafening roar in my ears, and a crushing weight pressed against me from every side.

Any effort of any kind was worse than useless, as well as impossible; indeed, I could hardly have been said to be conscious, except for the fact that I retained sufficient volition to avoid breathing or swallowing the water.

The pressure against my body was terrific; I wondered vaguely why life had not departed, since—as I supposed—there was not a whole bone left in my body. My head was bursting with dizziness and pain; my breast was a furnace of torture.

Suddenly the pressure lessened and the whirling movement gradually ceased, but still the current carried me on. I struck out wildly with both arms—in an effort, I suppose, to grasp the proverbial straw.

I found no straw, but something better—space. Instinct led the fight to reach it with my head to get air, but the swiftness of the current carried me again beneath the surface. My arms seemed powerless; I was unable to direct them.

I hardly know what happened after that. A feeling of most intense suffocation in my chest; a relaxation of all my muscles; a sensation of light in my smarting eyes; a gentle pressure from the water beneath, like the rising gait of a saddle-horse; and suddenly, without knowing why or when

147

or how, I found myself lying on hard ground, gasping, choking, sputtering, not far from death, but nearer to life than I had thought ever to be again.

I lay for several minutes unable to move; then my brain awoke and called for life. I twisted over on my face, and moved my arms out and in with the motion of a swimmer; the most exquisite pains shot through my chest and abdomen. My head weighed tons.

Water ran from my nose and mouth in gurgling streams. The roaring, scarcely abated, pounded in my ears. I was telling myself over and over with a most intense earnestness: "But if I were really dead I shouldn't be able to move." It appears that the first sense to leave a drowning man, and the last to return, is the sense of humor.

In another ten minutes, having rid my lungs of the water that had filled them, I felt no pain and but little fatigue. My head was dizzy, and there was still a feeling of oppression on my chest; but otherwise I was little the worse for wear. I twisted carefully over on my side and took note of my surroundings.

I lay on a narrow ledge of rock at the entrance to a huge cavern. Not two feet below rushed the stream which had carried me; it came down through an opening in the wall at a sharp angle with tremendous velocity, and must have hurled me like a cork from its foaming surface. Below, it emptied into a lake which nearly filled the cavern, some hundreds of yards in diameter. Rough boulders and narrow ledges surrounded it on every side.

This I saw in time, but the first thing that caught my eye was no work of nature. Fastened to the wall on the opposite side of the cavern, casting a dim, flickering light throughout its vast space, were two golden, flaming urns.

It was not fear, but a sort of nausea, that assailed me as I realized that I was still in the domain of the Incas.

The ledge on which I lay was exposed to view from nearly every point of the cavern, and the sight of those urns caused me to make a swift decision to leave it without delay. It was wet and slippery and not over three feet in width; I rose to my feet cautiously, having no appetite for another ducking.

At a distance of several feet lay another ledge, broad and level, at the farther end of which rose a massive boulder. I cleared the gap with a leap, barely made my footing, and passed behind the boulder through a crevice just wide enough to admit my body.

Then through a narrow lane onto another ledge, and from that I found my way into a dark recess which gave assurance at least of temporary safety. The sides of the cavern were a veritable maze of boulders, sloping ledges, and narrow crevices. Nature here scarcely seemed to have known what to do with herself.

I seated myself on a bit of projecting limestone, still wet and shivering. I had no boots nor trousers; my feet were bruised and swollen, and my flannel shirt and woolen underwear were but scanty protection against the chill air, damp as they were. Also, I seemed to feel a cold draft circling about me, and was convinced of the fact by the flickering flames in the golden urns.

Desolate, indeed, for I gave Harry up as lost. The thought generated no particular feeling in me; death, by force of contrast, may even appear agreeable; and I told myself that Harry had been favored of the gods.

And there I sat in the half-darkness, shrinking from a danger of whose existence I was not certain, clinging miserably to the little that was left of what the world of sunshine had known as Paul Lamar, gentleman, scientist, and connoisseur of life; *sans* philosophy, *sans* hope, and— *sans-culotte*.

But the senses remain; and suddenly I became aware of a movement in the water of the lake. It was as though an immense trout had leaped and split the surface. This was repeated several times, and was followed by a rhythmic sound like the regular splash of many oars. Then silence.

I peered intently forth from my corner in the recess, but could see nothing, and finally gave it up.

As the minutes passed by my discomfort increased and

stiffness began to take my joints. I realized the necessity of motion, but lacked the will, and sat in a sort of dumb, miserable apathy. This, I should say, for an hour; then I saw something that roused me.

I had before noticed that on the side of the cavern almost directly opposite me, under the flaming urns, there was a ledge some ten or twelve feet broad and easily a hundred in length. It met the surface of the lake at an easy, gradual slope. In the rear, exactly between the two urns, could be seen the dark mouth of a passage, evidently leading directly away from the cavern.

Out of this passage there suddenly appeared the forms of two Incas. In the hand of each was what appeared to be a long spear—I had evidently been mistaken in my presumption of their ignorance of weapons.

They walked to one end of the long ledge and dragged out into the light an object with a flat surface some six feet square. This they launched on the surface of the lake; then embarked on it, placing their spears by their sides and taking up, instead, two broad, short oars. With these they began to paddle their perilous craft toward the center of the lake with short, careful strokes.

About a hundred feet from the shore they ceased paddling and exchanged the oars for their spears, and stood motionless and silent, waiting, apparently, for nothing.

I, also, remained motionless, watching them in dull curiosity. There was little danger of being seen; for, aside from the darkness of my corner, which probably would have been no hindrance to them, a projecting ledge partly screened my body from view.

The wait was not a long one, and when it ended things happened with so startling a suddenness that I scarcely grasped the details.

There was a loud splash in the water like that I had heard before, a swift ripple on the surface of the lake, and simultaneously the two Indians lunged with their spears, which flew to their mark with deadly accuracy. I had not before noticed the thongs, one end of which was fastened to the shaft of the spear and the other about the waist of the savage.

There followed a battle royal. Whatever the thing was that had felt the spears, it certainly lost no time in showing its resentment. It thrashed the water into furious waves until I momentarily expectedthe raft to be swamped.

One Inca stood on the farther edge of the craft desperately plying an oar; the other tugged lustily at the spear-thongs. I could see a black, twisting form leap from the water directly toward the raft, and the oarsman barely drew from under before it fell. It struck the corner of the raft, which tipped perilously.

That appeared to have been a final effort, for there the battle ended. The oarsman made quickly for the shore, paddling with remarkable dexterity and swiftness, while the other stood braced, holding firmly to the spear-thongs. Another minute and they had leaped upon the ledge, drawing the raft after them, and, by tugging together on the lines, had landed their victim of the deep.

It appeared to be a large black fish of a shape I had never before seen. But it claimed little of my attention; my eye was on the two spears which had been drawn from the still quivering body and which now lay on the ground well away from the water's edge, while the two Incas were dragging their catch toward the mouth of the passage leading from the cavern.

I wanted those spears. I did not stop to ask myself what I intended to do with them; if I had I would probably have been hard put to it for an answer. But I wanted them, and I sat in my dark corner gazing at them with greedy eyes.

The Incas had disappeared in the passage.

Finally I rose and began to search for an exit from the recess in which I had hidden myself. At first there appeared to be none, but at length I found a small crevice between two boulders in the rear. Into this I squeezed my body with some difficulty.

The rock pressed tightly against me on both sides, and the sharp corners bruised my body, but I wormed my way through for a distance of fifteen or twenty feet. Then the crevice opened abruptly, and I found myself on a broad ledge ending apparently in space. I advanced cautiously to its edge, but intervening boulders shut off the light, and I could see no ground below.

Throwing prudence to the winds, I let myself over the outermost corner, hung for a moment by my hands, and dropped. My feet touched ground almost instantly—the supposedly perilous fall amounted to something like twelve inches.

I turned round, feeling a little foolish, and saw that from where I stood the ledge and part of the lake were in full view. I could see the spears still lying where they had been thrown down.

But as I looked the two Incas emerged from the passage. They picked up the spears, walked to the raft, and again launched it and paddled toward the center of the lake.

I thought, "Here is my chance; I must make that ledge before they return," and I started forward so precipitately that I ran head on into a massive boulder and got badly stunned for my pains. Half dazed, I went on, groping my way through the semidarkness.

The trail was one to try a llama. I climbed boulders and leaped across chasms and clung to narrow, slippery edges with my finger-nails. Several times I narrowly escaped dumping myself into the lake, and half the time I was in plain view of the Incas on the raft.

My hands and feet were bruised and bleeding, and I had bumped into walls and boulders so often that I was surprised when I took a step without getting a blow. I wanted those spears.

I found myself finally within a few yards of my destination. A narrow crevice led from where I stood directly to the ledge from which the Incas had embarked. It was now necessary to wait till they returned to the shore, and I drew back into the darkness of a near-by corner and stood motionless.

They were still on the raft in the middle of the lake,

waiting, spear in hand. I watched them in furious impatience, on the border of mania.

Suddenly I saw a dark, crouching form outlined against a boulder not ten feet away from where I stood. The form was human, but in some way unlike the Incas I had seen. I could not see its face, but the alertness suggested by its attitude made me certain that I had been discovered.

Vaguely I felt myself surrounded on every side; I seemed to feel eyes gazing unseen from every direction, but I could not force myself to search the darkness; my heart rose to my throat and choked me, and I stood absolutely powerless to make a sound or movement, gazing in a sort of dumb fascination at that silent, crouching figure.

Suddenly it crouched lower still against the black background of the boulder.

"Another second and he will be at my throat," I thought—but I stood still, unable to move.

But the figure did not spring. Instead, it suddenly straightened up to almost twice the height of an Inca, and I caught a glimpse of a white face and ragged, clinging garments.

"Harry!" I whispered. I wonder yet that it was not a shout.

"Thank God!" came his voice, also in a whisper; and in another moment he had reached my side.

A hurried word or two—there was no time for more—and I pointed to the Incas on the raft, saying: "We want those spears."

"I was after them," he grinned. "What shall we do?"

"There's no use taking them while the Incas are away," I replied, "because they would soon return and find them gone. Surely we can handle two of them."

As I spoke there came a sound from the lake—a sudden loud splash followed by a commotion in the water. I looked around the corner of the boulder and saw that the spears again found their mark.

"Come," I whispered, and began to pick my way toward the ledge.

Harry followed close at my heels. It was easier here, and we soon found ourselves close to the shore of the lake, with a smooth stretch of rock between us and the fisherman's landing-place. The urns, whose light was quite sufficient here, were about fifty feet to the right and rear.

The Incas had made their kill and were paddling for the shore. As they came near, Harry and I sank back against the boulder, which extended to the boundary of the ledge. Soon the raft was beached and pulled well away from the water, and the fish—I was amazed at its size—followed.

They drew forth the spears and laid them on the ground, as they had done formerly; and, laying hold on the immense fish, still floundering ponderously about, began to drag it toward the mouth of the passage.

"Now," whispered Harry, and as he stood close at my side I could feel his body draw together for the spring.

I laid a hand on his arm.

"Not yet. Others may be waiting for them in the passage. Wait till they return."

In a few minutes they reappeared in the light of the flaming urns. I waited till they had advanced half-way to the water's edge, some thirty feet away. Then I whispered to Harry: "You for the left, me for the right," and released my hold on his arm, and the next instant we were bounding furiously across the ledge.

Taken by surprise, the Incas offered no resistance whatever. The momentum of our assault carried them to the ground; their heads struck the hard granite with fearful force and they lay stunned.

Harry, kneeling over them, looked up at me with a question in his eyes.

"The lake," said I, for it was no time for squeamishness.

Our friend the king thought us dead, and we wanted no witnesses that we had returned to life. We laid hold of the unconscious bodies, dragged them to the edge of the lake, and pushed them in. The shock of the cold water brought one of them to life, and he started to swim, and we—well, we did what had to be done.

We had our spears. I examined them curiously.

The head appeared to be of copper and the shaft was a long, thin rod of the same material. But when I tried it against a stone and saw its hardness I found that it was much less soft, and consequently more effective, than copper would have been. That those underground savages had succeeded in combining metals was incredible, but there was the evidence; and, besides, it may have been a trick of nature herself.

The point was some six inches long and very sharp. It was set on the shaft in a wedge, and bound with thin, tough strips of hide. Altogether, a weapon not to be laughed at.

We carried the spears, the raft, and the oars behind a large boulder to the left of the ledge with considerable difficulty. The two latter not because we expected them to be of any service, but in order not to leave any trace of our presence, for if any searchers came and found nothing they could know nothing.

We expected them to arrive at any moment, and we waited for hours. We had about given up watching from our vantage point behind the boulder when two Incas appeared at the mouth of the passage. But they brought only oil to fill the urns, and after performing this duty departed, without a glance at the lake or any exhibition of surprise at the absence of their fellows.

Every now and then there was a commotion in some part of the lake, and we could occasionally see a black, glistening body leap into the air and fall again into the water.

"I'm hungry," Harry announced suddenly. "I wonder if we couldn't turn the trick on that raft ourselves?"

The same thought had occurred to me, but Harry's impulsiveness had made me fearful of expressing it. I hesitated.

"We've got to do something," he continued.

I suggested that it might be best to wait another hour or two.

"And why? Now is as good a time as any. If we intend to find Desirée—"

"In the name of Heaven, how can we?" I interrupted.

"You don't mean to say you don't intend to try?" he exclaimed

"Hal, I don't know. In the first place, it's impossible. And where could we take her and what could we do—in short, what's the use? Why the deuce should we prolong the thing any further?

"In the world I refused to struggle because nothing tempted me; in this infernal hole I have fought when there was nothing to fight for. If civilization held no prize worth an effort, why should I exert myself to preserve the life of a rat? Faugh! It's sickening! I wondered why I wanted those spears. Now I know. I have an idea I'm going to be coward enough to use one—or enough of a philosopher."

"Paul, that isn't like you."

"On the contrary, it is consistent with my whole life. I have never been overly keen about it. To end it in a hole like this—well, that isn't exactly what I expected; but it is all one—after. Understand me, Hal; I don't want to desert you; haven't I stuck? And I would still if there were the slightest possible chance. Where can we go? What can we do?"

There was a long silence; then Harry's voice came calmly:

"I can stay in the game. You call yourself a philosopher. I won't quarrel about it, but the world would call you a quitter. Whichever it is, it's not for me. I stay in the game. I'm going to find Desirée if I can, and, by the Lord, some day I'm going to cock my feet up on the fender at the Midlothian and make 'em open their mouths and call me a liar!"

"A worthy ambition."

"My own. And, Paul, you can't—you're not a quitter."

"Personally, yes. If I were here alone, Hal"—I picked up one of the spears and passed my palm over its sharp point—"I would quit cold. But not—not with you. I can't share your enthusiasm, but I'll go fifty-fifty on the rest of it, including the fender—when we see it."

"That's the talk, old man. I knew you would."

"But understand me. I expect nothing. It's all rot. If by any wild chance we should pull out in the end I'll admit you were right. But I eat under compulsion, and I fight for you. You're the leader unless you ask my advice."

"And I begin right now," said Harry with a grin. "First, to get Desirée. What about it?"

We discussed plans all the way from the impossible to the miraculous and arrived nowhere. One thing only we decided—that before we tried to find our way back to the great cavern and the royal apartments we would lay in a supply of food and cache it among the boulders and ledges where we then were. For if ever a place were designed for a successful defense by two men against thousands it was that one. And we had the spears.

Still no one had appeared in the cavern, and we decided to wait no longer. We carried the raft back to the ledge. It was fairly light, being made of hide stretched tightly across stringers of bone, but was exceedingly clumsy. Once Harry fell, and the thing nearly toppled over into the lake with him on top of it; but I caught his arm just in time.

Another trip for the oars and spears, and everything was ready. We launched the raft awkwardly, nearly shipping it beneath; but finally got it afloat with ourselves aboard. We had fastened the loose ends of the spear-thongs about our waists.

I think that raft was the craziest thing that ever touched water. It was a most excellent diver, but was in profound ignorance of the first principle of the art of floating.

After a quarter of an hour of experimentation we found that by standing exactly in a certain position, one on each side and paddling with one hand, it was possible to keep fairly level. If either of us shifted his foot a fraction of an inch the thing ducked like a stone.

We finally got out a hundred feet or so and ceased paddling. Then, exchanging our oars for the spears, we waited.

The surface of the lake was perfectly still, save for a

barely perceptible ripple, caused no doubt by the under-current which was fed by the stream at the opposite side. The urns were so far away that the light was very dim; no better than half darkness. The silence was broken by the sound of the rushing stream.

Suddenly the raft swayed gently; there was a parting of the water not a foot away toward the front, and then—well, the ensuing events happened so quickly that their order is uncertain.

A black form arose from the water with a leap like lightning and landed squarely on the raft, which proceeded to perform its favorite dive. It would have done so with much less persuasion, for the fish was a monster—it appeared to me at that moment to be twenty feet long.

On the instant, as the raft capsized, Harry and I lunged with our spears, tumbling forward and landing on each other and on top of the fish. I felt my spear sinking into the soft fish almost without resistance.

The raft slipped from under, and we found ourselves floundering in the water.

I have said the spear-thongs were fastened about our waists. Otherwise, we would have let the fish go; but we could hardly allow him to take us along. That is, we didn't want to allow it; but we soon found that we had nothing to say in the matter. Before we had time to set ourselves to stroke we were begin towed as though we had been corks toward the opposite shore.

But it was soon over, handicapped as he was by four feet of spears in his body. We felt the pull lessen and twisted ourselves about, and in another minute had caught the water with a steady dog-stroke and were holding our own.

Soon we made headway, but it was killing work.

"He weighs a thousand tons," panted Harry, and I nodded.

Pulling and puffing side by side, we gradually neared the center of the lake, passed it, and approached the ledge. We were well-nigh exhausted when we finally touched bottom and were able to stand erect.

Hauling the fish onto the ledge, we no longer wondered at his strength. He could not have been an ounce under four hundred pounds, and was fully seven feet long. One of the spears ran through the gills; the other was in his middle, just below the backbone. We got them out with some difficulty and rolled him up high and dry.

We straightened to return for the spears which we had left at the edge of the water.

"He's got a hide like an elephant," said Harry. "What can we skin him with?"

But I did not answer.

I was gazing straight ahead at the mouth of the passage where stood two Incas, spear in hand, returning my gaze stolidly.

Chapter XV.

THE RESCUE.

I was quick to act, but the Incas were quicker still. I turned to run for our spears, and was halted by a cry of warning from Harry, who had wheeled like a flash at my quick movement. I turned barely in time to see the Incas draw back their powerful arms, then lunge forward, the spears shooting from their hands.

I leaped aside; something struck my leg; I stooped swiftly and grasped the spear-thong before there was time for the Inca to recover and jerk it out of my reach. The other end was fastened about his waist; I had him, and giving an instant for a glance at Harry, saw that he had adopted the same tactics as myself.

Seeing that escape was impossible, they dashed straight at us.

It wasn't much of a fight. One came at me with his head lowered like a charging bull; I sidestepped easily and floored him with a single blow. He scrambled to his feet, but by that time I had recovered the spear and had it ready for him.

I waited until he was quite close, then let him have it full in the chest. The fool literally ran himself through, hurling himself on the sharp point in a brutal frenzy. He lay on his back, quite still, with the spear-head buried in his chest and the shaft sticking straight up in the air.

I turned to Harry, and in spite of myself smiled at what I saw. He stood with his right arm upraised, holding his spear ready. His left foot was placed well and gracefully forward, and his body bent to one side like the classic javelin-thrower. And ten feet in front of him the other Inca had fallen flat on his face on the ground with arms extended in mute supplication for quarter.

"What shall I do?" asked Harry. "Let him have it?"

"Can you?"

"The fact is, no. Look at the poor beggar—scared silly. But we can't let him go."

It was really a question. Mercy and murder were alike impossible. We finally compromised by binding his wrists and ankles and trussing him up behind, using a portion of one of the spear-thongs for the purpose, and gagging him. Then we carried him behind a large boulder some distance from the ledge and tucked him away in a dark corner.

"And when we get back—if we ever do—we can turn him loose," said Harry.

"In that case I wouldn't give much for his chances of a happy existence," I observed.

We wasted no time after that, for we wanted no more interruptions. Some fifteen precious minutes we lost trying to withdraw the spear I had buried in the body of the Inca, but the thing had become wedged between two ribs and refused to come out. Finally we gave it up and threw the corpse in the lake.

We then removed the oars and spears and raft—which had floated so near to the ledge that we had no difficulty in recovering it—to our hiding-place, and last we tackled our fish.

It was a task for half a dozen men, but we dared not remain on the ledge to skin him and cut him up. After an hour of exertion and toil that left us completely exhausted, we managed to get him behind a large boulder to the left of the ledge, but it was impossible to carry him to the place we had selected, which could be reached only by passing through a narrow crevice.

The only knives we had were the points of the spears, but they served after a fashion, and in another hour we had him skinned and pretty well separated. He was meaty and sweet. We discovered that with the first opportunity, for we were hungry as wolves. Nor did we waste much time bewailing our lack of a fire, for we had lived so long on dried stuff that the opposite extreme was rather pleasant than otherwise.

We tore him into strips as neatly as possible, stowing

them away beneath a ledge, a spot kept cool by the water but a foot below.

"That'll be good for a month," said Harry. "And there's more where that came from. And now—"

I understood, and I answered simply: "I'm ready."

We had but few preparations to make. The solidest parts of the fish which we had laid aside we now strapped together with one of the extra spear-thongs and slung them on our backs. We secreted the oars and raft and the extra spear as snugly as possible.

Then, having filled ourselves with raw fish and a last hearty drink from the lake, we each took a spear and started on a search wilder than any ever undertaken by Amadis of Gaul or Don Quixote himself. Even the Bachelor of Salamanca, in his saddest plight, did not present so outrageous an appearance to the eye as we. We wore more clothing than the Incas, which is the most that can be said for us.

We were unable to even guess at the direction we should take; but that was settled for us when we found that there were but two exits from the cavern. One led through the boulders and crevices to a passage full of twists and turns and strewn with rocks, almost impassable; the other was that through which the Incas had entered. We chose the latter.

Fifty feet from the cavern we found ourselves in darkness. I stopped short.

"Harry, this is impossible. We cannot mark our way."

"But what can we do?"

"Carry one of those urns."

"Likely! They'd spot us before we even got started."

"Well—let them."

"No. You're in for the finish. I know that. I want to find Desirée. And we'll find her. After that, if nothing else is left, I'll be with you."

"But I don't want a thousand of those brutes falling on us in the dark. If they would end it I wouldn't care."

"Keep your spear ready."

I had given him my promise, so I pushed on at his side. I had no stomach for it. In a fight I can avoid disgracing myself, because it is necessary; but why seek it when there is nothing to be gained? Thus I reflected, but I pushed on at Harry's side.

As he had said, I was in for the finish. What I feared was to be taken again by the Incas unseen in the darkness. But that fear was soon removed when I found that we could see easily some thirty or forty feet ahead—enough for a warning in case of attack.

Our flannel shirts and woolen undergarments hung from us in rags and tatters. Our feet were bare and bruised and swollen. Our faces were covered with a thick, matted growth of hair. Placed side by side with the Incas it is a question which of us would have been judged the most terrifying spectacles by an impartial observer.

I don't think either of us realized the extreme foolhardiness of that expedition. The passage was open and unobstructed, and since it appeared to be the only way to their fishing-ground, was certain to be well traveled. The alarm once given, there was no possible chance for us.

We sought the royal apartments. Those we knew to be on a level some forty or fifty feet below the surface of the great cavern, at the foot of the flight of steps which led to the tunnel to the base of the column. I had counted ninety-six of those steps, and allowing an average height of six inches, they represented a distance of forty-eight feet.

How far the whirlpool and the stream which it fed had carried us downward we did not know, but we estimated it at one hundred feet. That calculation left us still fifty feet below the level of the royal apartments.

But we soon found that in this we were mistaken. We had advanced for perhaps a quarter of an hour without incident when the passage came to an abrupt end. To the right was an irregular, twisting lane that disappeared around a corner almost before it started; to the left a wide and straight passage, sloping gently upward. We took the latter.

We had followed this for about a hundred yards when we

saw a light ahead. Caution was useless; the passage was straight and unbroken and only luck could save us from discovery. We pushed on, and soon stood directly within the light which came from an apartment adjoining the passage. It was not that which we sought, however, and we gave it barely a glance before we turned to the right down a cross passage, finding ourselves again in darkness.

Soon another light appeared. We approached. It came from a doorway leading into an apartment some twenty feet square. It was empty, and we entered.

There were two flaming urns fastened to the wall above a granite couch. Stone seats were placed here and there about the room. The walls were studded with spots of gold to a height of four or five feet.

We stopped short, gazing about us.

"It looks like—" Harry whispered, and then exclaimed: "It is! See, here is where we took the blocks from this seat!"

So it was. We were in the room where we had imprisoned the Inca king and where we ourselves had been imprisoned with Desirée.

"She said her room was to the right of this," whispered Harry excitedly. "What luck! If only—"

He left the sentence unfinished, but I understood his fear. And with me there was even no doubt; I had little hope of finding Desirée, and was sorry, for Harry's sake, that we had been so far successful.

Again we sought the passage. A little farther on it was crossed by another, running at right angles in both directions. But to the right there was nothing but darkness, and we turned to the left, where, some distance ahead, we could see a light evidently proceeding from a doorway similar to the one we had just left.

We went rapidly, but our feet made scarcely any sound on the granite floor. Still we were incautious, and it was purely by luck that I glanced ahead and discovered that which made me jerk Harry violently back and flatten myself against the wall.

"What is it?" he whispered.

In silence I pointed with my finger to where two Incas stood in the passage ahead of us, just without the patch of light from the doorway, which they were facing. They made no movement; we were as yet undiscovered. They were about a hundred feet away from where we stood.

"Then she's here!" whispered Harry. "They are on guard."

I nodded; I had had the same thought.

There was no time to lose; at any moment that they should chance to glance in our direction they were certain to see us. I whispered hastily and briefly to Harry. He nodded.

The next instant we were advancing slowly and noiselessly, hugging the wall. We carried our spears ready, though we did not mean to use them, for a miss would have meant an alarm.

"If she is alone!" I was saying within myself, almost a prayer, when suddenly one of the Incas turned, facing us squarely, and gave a start of surprise. We leaped forward.

Half a dozen bounds and we were upon them, before they had had time to realize their danger or move to escape it. With a ferocity taught us by the Incas themselves we gripped their throats and bore them to the floor.

No time then for the decencies; we had work to do, and we crushed and pounded their lives out against the stone floor. There had not been a sound. They quivered and lay still; and then, looking up at some slight sound in the doorway, we saw Desirée.

She stood in the doorway, regarding us with an expression of terror that I did not at first understand; then suddenly I realized that, having seen us disappear beneath the surface of the lake after our dive from the column, she had thought us dead.

"*Bon Dieu!*" she exclaimed in a hollow voice of horror. "This, too! Do you come, *messieurs?*"

"For you," I answered. "We are flesh and bone, Desirée, though in ill repair. We have come for you."

"Paul! Harry, is it really you?"

Belief crept into her eyes, but nothing more, and she stood gazing at us curiously. Harry had sprung to her side; she did not move as he embraced her.

"Are you alone?"

"Yes."

"Good. Here, Harry—quick! Help me. Stand aside, Desirée."

We carried the bodies of the two Incas within the room and deposited them in a corner. Then I ran and brought the spears, which we had dropped when we attacked the Incas. Desirée stood just within the doorway, seemingly half dazed.

"Come," I said; "there is no time to be lost. Come!"

"Where?" She did not move.

"With us. Isn't that enough? Do you want to stay here?"

She shuddered violently.

"You don't know—what has happened. I want to die. Where are you going to take me?"

"Desirée," Harry burst out, "for Heaven's sake, come! Must we carry you?"

He grasped her arm.

Then she moved and appeared to acquiesce. I started ahead; Harry brought up the rear, with an arm round Desirée's shoulders. She started once more to speak, but I wheeled sharply with a command for silence, and she obeyed.

We reached the turn in the corridor and passed to the right, moving as swiftly and noiselessly as possible. Ahead of us was the light from the doorway of the room in which we had formerly been imprisoned.

We had nearly reached it when I saw, some distance down the corridor, moving forms. The light was very dim, but there appeared to be a great many of them.

I turned, with a swift gesture to Harry and Desirée to follow, and dashed forward to the light and through the doorway into the room. Discovery was inevitable, I thought, in any event, but it was better to meet them at the door to the room than in the open passage. And we had our spears.

But by a rare stroke of luck we had not been seen. As we stood within the room on either side of the doorway, out of the line of view from the corridor, we heard the patter of many footsteps approaching.

They neared the doorway, and I glanced at Harry, pointing to his spear significantly. He gave me a nod of understanding. Let them come; we would not again fall into their hands alive.

The footsteps sounded just without the doorway; I stood tense and alert, with spear ready, expecting a rush momentarily. Then they passed, passed altogether, and receded down the corridor in the direction whence we had come. I wanted to glance out at their number, but dared not. We stood still till all was again perfectly silent.

Then Desirée spoke in a whisper:

"It is useless; we are lost. That was the king. He is going to my room. In ten seconds he will be there and find me gone."

There was only one thing to do, and I wasted no time in dicussing it. A swift command to Harry, and we dashed from the doorway and down the corridor to the left, each holding an arm of Desirée. But she needed little of our assistance; the presence of the Inca king seemed to have inspired her with a boundless terror, and she flew, rather than ran, between us.

We reached the bend in the passage, and just beyond it the light—the first one we had seen on our way in. I had our route marked on my memory with complete distinctness. Soon we found ourselves in the wide, sloping passage that carried us to the level below, and in another five seconds had reached its end and the beginning of the last stretch.

At the turn Harry stumbled and fell flat, dragging Desirée to her knees. I lifted her, and he sprang to his feet unhurt.

She was panting heavily. Harry had dropped his spear in the fall, and we wasted a precious minute searching for it in the darkness, finally finding it where it had slid, some twenty feet ahead. Again we dashed forward.

A light appeared ahead in the distance, dim but unmistakable—the light of the urns in the cavern for which we were headed. Suddenly Desirée faltered and would have fallen but for our supporting arms.

"Courage!" I breathed. "We are near the end."

She stopped short and sank to the ground.

"It is useless," she gasped. "I hurt my ankle when I fell. I can go no farther. Leave me!"

Harry and I with one impulse stooped over to pick her up, and as we did so she fainted away in our arms. We were then but a few hundred feet from our goal; the light from the urns could be plainly seen gleaming on the broad ledge by the lake.

Suddenly the sound of many footsteps came from behind. I turned quickly, but the passage was too dark. I could see nothing. The sound came closer and closer; there seemed to be many of them, advancing swiftly. I straightened and raised my spear.

Harry grasped my arm.

"Not yet!" he cried. "One more try; we can make it."

He thrust his spear into my hand, and in another instant had thrown Desirée's unconscious body over his shoulder and was staggering forward toward the cavern. I followed, while the sound of the footsteps behind grew louder and louder.

We neared the end of the passage; we reached it; we were on the ledge. Even with Desirée for a burden, Harry moved so swiftly that I found it difficult to keep up with him. The strength of a god was in him, which was but just, since he had his goddess in his arms.

On the ledge, near the edge of the water, stood two Incas. They turned at our approach and rushed at us. Unlucky for them, for Harry's example had fired my brain and put the strength of a giant in me.

To this day I don't know what followed—whether I used my spear or my fists or my head. I know only that I leaped at them in irresistible fury and left them stretched on the ground before they had reached Harry or halted him.

We crossed the ledge and made for the boulders to the left. The crevice which led to our hiding-place was too narrow for Harry and his burden. I sprang forward and grasped Desirée's shoulders; he held her ankles, and we got her through to the ledge beyond.

Then I leaped back through the crevice, and barely in time. As I looked out a black, rushing horde emerged from the passage and dashed across the ledge toward us. I stood at the entrance to the narrow crevice, spear in hand.

They appeared to have no sense of the fact that my position was impregnable, but dashed blindly at me. The crevice in which I stood, and which was the only way through to the ledge where Harry had taken Desirée, was not more than two feet wide. With unarmed savages for foes, one man could have held it against a million.

But they came and I met them. I stood within the crevice, some three or four feet from its end, and when one appeared in the opening I let him have the spear. Another rushed in and fell on top of the first.

As I say, they appeared to be deprived of the power to reason. In five minutes the mouth of the crevice was completely choked with bodies, some, who were merely wounded, struggling and squirming to extricate themselves from the bloody tangle.

I heard Harry's voice at my back:

"How about it? Want some help?"

"Not unless they find some gunpowder," I answered. "The idiots eat death as though it were candy. We're safe; they can never break through here."

"Are they still coming?"

"They can't; they've blocked the way with their smelly black carcasses. How is Desirée?"

"Better; she's awake. I've been bathing her ankle with cold water. She has a bad sprain; how the deuce she ever managed to hobble on it even two steps is beyond me."

"A sprain? Are you sure?"

"I think so; it's badly swollen. Maybe only a twist; a few hours will tell."

I heard him return to the ledge back of me; I dared not turn my head.

Thinking I heard a sound above, I looked up; but there was nothing to fear in that direction. The boulders which formed the sides of the crevice extended straight up to the roof of the cavern. We appeared, in fact, to be fortified against any attack.

With one exception—hunger. But there would be plenty of time to think of that; for the present we had our fish, which was sufficient for the three of us for a month, if we could keep it fresh that long. And the water was at our very feet.

The bodies wedged in the mouth of the crevice began to disappear, allowing the light from the urns to filter through; they were removing their dead. I could see the black forms swaying and pulling not five feet away. But I stood motionless, saving my spear and my strength for any who might try to force an entrance.

Soon the crevice was clear, and from where I stood I commanded a view of something like three-quarters of the ledge. It was one mass of black forms, packed tightly together, gazing at our retreat.

They looked particularly silly and helpless to me then, rendered powerless as they were by a little bit of rock. Brute force was all they had; and nature, being the biggest brute of all, laughed at them.

But I soon found that they were not devoid of resource. For perhaps fifteen minutes the scene remained unchanged; not one ventured to approach the crevice. Then there was a sudden movement and shifting in the mass; it split suddenly in the middle; they pressed off to either side, leaving an open lane between them leading directly toward me.

Down this lane suddenly dashed a dozen or more of the savages, with spears aloft in their brawny arms. I was taken by surprise and barely had time to cut and run for the ledge within.

As it was I did not entirely escape; the spears came whistling through the crevice, and one of them lodged in my leg just below the thigh.

I jerked it out with an oath and turned to meet the attack. I was now clear of the crevice, standing on the ledge inside, near Harry and Desirée. I called to them to go to one side, out of the range of the spears that might come through. Harry took Desirée in his arms and carried her to safety.

As I expected, the Incas came rushing through the crevice—that narrow lane where a man could barely push through without squeezing. The first got my spear full in the face—a blow rather than a thrust, for I had once or twice had difficulty in retrieving it when I had buried it deep.

As he fell I struck at the one behind. He grasped the spear with his hand, but I jerked it free and brought it down on his head, crushing him to the ground. It was mere butchery; they hadn't a chance in the world to get at me. Another fell, and the rest retreated. The crevice was again clear, save for the bodies of the three who had fallen.

I turned to where Harry and Desirée were seated on the further edge of the ledge. Her body rested against his; her head lay on his shoulder.

As I looked at them, smiling, her eyes suddenly opened wide and she sprang to her feet and started toward me.

"Paul! You are hurt! Harry, a bandage—quick; your shirt—anything!"

I looked down at the gash on my leg, which was bleeding somewhat freely.

"It's nothing," I declared; "a mere tear in the skin. But your ankle! I thought it was sprained?"

She had reached my side and bent over to examine my wound; but I raised her in my arms and held her before me.

"That," I said, "is nothing. Believe me, it isn't even painful. I shall bandage it myself; Harry will take my place here. But your foot?"

"That, too, is nothing," she answered with a half-smile. "I merely twisted it; it is nearly well already. See!"

She placed her weight on the injured foot, but could not suppress a faint grimace of pain.

Calling to Harry to watch the crevice, I took Desirée in my arms and carried her back to her seat.

"Now sit still," I commanded. "Soon we'll have dinner; in the mean time allow me to say that you are the bravest woman in the world, and the best sport. And some day we'll drink to that—from a bottle."

But facts have no respect for sentiment and fine speeches. The last words were taken from my very mouth by a ringing cry from Harry:

"Paul! By gad, they're coming at us from the water!"

Chapter XVI.

THE ESCAPE.

The ledge on which we rested was about forty feet square. Back of us was a confused mass of boulders and chasms, across which I had come when I first encircled the cavern and found Harry.

In front was the crevice, guarded by the two massive boulders. On the right the ledge met the solid wall of the cavern, and on the left was the lake itself, whose waters rippled gently at our very feet.

At sound of Harry's warning cry I ran to the water's edge and peered round the side of the boulder. He was right; but what I saw was not very alarming.

Two rafts had been launched from the enemy's camp. Each raft held three Incas—more would have sunk them. Two were paddling, while the third balanced himself in the center, brandishing a spear aloft.

Turning to Desirée, I called to her to move behind a projecting bit of rock. Then, leaving Harry to guard the crevice in case of a double attack, I took three of our four spears—one of which had made the wound in my leg—and stood at the water's edge awaiting the approach of the rafts.

They came slowly, and their appearance was certainly anything but terrifying.

"Not much of a navy," I called to Harry; and he answered, with a laugh: "Lucky for us! Look at our coast defense!"

One of the rafts was considerably ahead of the other, and in another minute it had approached within fifty feet of the ledge. The Inca in the center stood with legs spread apart and his spear poised above his head; I made no movement, thinking that on such precarious footing he would have difficulty to hurl the thing at all. Wherein I underrated his skill, and it nearly cost me dear.

Suddenly, with hardly a movement of his body, his arm snapped forward. I ducked to one side instinctively and heard the spear whistle past my ear with the speed of a bullet, so close that the butt of the shaft struck the side of my head a glancing blow and toppled me over.

I sprang quickly to my feet, and barely in time, for I saw the Inca stoop over, pick up another spear from the raft, and draw it back above his head. At the same moment the second raft drew up alongside, and as I fell to the ground flat on my face I heard the two spears whistle shrewdly over me.

At that game they were my masters; it would have been folly to have tried conclusions with them with their own weapons. As the spears clattered on the ground thirty feet away I sprang to my feet and ran to the farther side of the ledge, where I had before noticed some loose stones in a corner.

With two or three of these in my hands I ran back to the water's edge, meeting two more of the spears that came twisting at me through the air, one of which tore the skin from my left shoulder.

A quick glance at the crevice as I passed showed me Harry fighting at its entrance; they were at us there, too. I heard Desirée shout something at me, but didn't catch the words.

My first stone found its goal. The two rafts, side by side not forty feet away, were a fair mark. The stone was nearly the size of a man's head and very heavy; I had all I could do to get the distance.

It struck the raft on the right fairly; the thing turned turtle in a flash, precipitating its occupants onto the other raft. The added weight carried that, too, under the surface, and the six Incas were floundering about in the water.

I expected to see them turn and swim for the landing opposite; but, instead, they headed directly toward me!

The light from the urns was but faint, and it was not easy to distinguish their black heads against the black water; still, I could see their approach. Two of them held spears in their hands; I saw the copper heads flash on high.

I stood at the edge of the lake, wondering at their folly as I waited; they were now scarcely ten feet away. Another few strokes and the foremost stretched out his hand to grasp the slippery ledge; my spear came down crushingly on his head and he fell back into the water.

By that time another had crawled half onto the ledge, and another; a blow and a quick thrust, and they, too, slipped back beneath the surface, pawing in agony, not to rise again.

Just in time I saw that one of the remaining three had lifted himself in the water not five feet away, with his spear aimed at my breast. But the poor devil had no purchase for his feet and the thing went wide.

The next instant he had received a ten-pound stone full in the face and went down with a gurgle. At that the remaining two, seeming to acquire a glimmering of intelligence, turned and swam hastily away. I let them go.

Turning to Harry, I saw that the crevice also was clear. He had left his post and started toward me, but I waved him back.

"All right here, Hal: have they given it up?"

There was an expression of the most profound disgust on his face.

"Paul, it's rank butchery. I'm wading in blood. Will this thing never stop?"

I looked at him and said merely: "Yes."

No need to ask when; he understood me; he sent me the glance of a man who has become too familiar with death to fear it, and answered:

"Another hour of this, and—I'm ready."

I told him to keep an eye on both points of attack and went across to where Desirée sat crouched on the ground. I hadn't many words.

"How is your foot?"

"Oh, it is better; well. But your leg—"

"Never mind that. Could you sleep?"

Bon Dieu—no!"

"We have only raw fish. Can you eat?"

"I'll try," she answered, with a grimace.

I went to the edge of the ledge where we had the fish

stowed away near the water and took some of it both to her and Harry. We ate, but with little relish. The stuff did not seem very fresh.

I remained on guard at the mouth of the crevice while Harry went to the lake for a drink, having first helped Desirée to the water and back to her seat. Her foot gave her a great deal of pain, but instead of a sprain it appeared that there had been merely a straining of the ligaments. After bathing it in the cold water she was considerably relieved.

I remained on watch at the mouth of the crevice, from where I could also obtain a pretty fair view of the lake, and commanded Harry to rest. He demurred, but I insisted. Within two minutes he was sleeping like a log, completely exhausted.

Several hundred of the Incas remained huddled together on the ledge without, but they made no effort to attack us. I had been watching perhaps three hours when they began to melt away into the passage. Soon but a scant dozen or so remained. These squatted along the wall just under the lighted urns, evidently in the capacity of sentinels.

Soon I became drowsy—intolerably so; I was scarcely able to stand. I dozed off once or twice on my feet; and, realizing the danger, I called Harry to take my place.

Desirée also had been asleep, lying on the raft which Harry and I had concealed along with our fish. At sound of my voice she awoke and sat up, rubbing her eyes; then, as I assured her that all was quiet, she fell back again on her rude bed.

I have never understood the delay of the Incas at this juncture; possibly they took time to consult the great Pachacamas and found his advice difficult to understand. At the time I thought they had given up the attack and intended to starve us out, but they were incapable of a decision so sensible.

Many hours had passed, and we had alternated on four watches. We had plenty of rest and were really quite fit. The gash on my leg had proven a mere trifle; I was a little stiff, but there was no pain.

Desirée's foot was almost entirely well; she was able to walk with ease, and had insisted on taking a turn at watch, making such a point of it that we had humored her.

Something had to happen, and I suppose it was as well that the Incas should start it. For we had met with a misfortune that made us see the beginning of the end. Our fish was no longer fit to eat, and we had been forced to throw the remainder of it in the lake.

Then we held a council of war. The words we uttered, standing together at the mouth of the crevice, come to me now as in a dream; if my memory of them were not so vivid I should doubt their reality. We discussed death with a calmness that spoke eloquently of our experience.

Desirée's position may be given in a word—she was ready for the end, and invited it.

I was but little behind her, but advised waiting for one more watch—a sop to Harry. And there was one other circumstance that moved me to delay—the hope for a sight of the Inca king and a chance at him.

Desirée had refused to tell us her experiences between the time of our dive from the column and our rescue of her; but she had said enough to cause me to guess at its nature. There was a suppressed but ever present horror in her eyes that made me long to stand once more before the Child of the Sun; then to go, but not alone.

Harry advised retreat. I have mentioned that when he and I had started on our search for Desirée we had found two exits from the cabin—the one which we had taken and another which led through the maze of boulders and chasms back of us to a passage full of twists and turns and choked with massive rocks, almost impassable.

Through this he advised making our way to whatever might await us beyond.

The question was still undecided when our argument was brought to a halt and the decision was taken away from us. Through the crevice I saw a band of Incas emerge from the passage opposite and advance to the water's edge. At their head was the Inca king.

Soon the landing was completely covered with them—probably three hundred or more—and others could be seen in the mouth of the passage. Each one carried a spear; their heads of copper, upraised in a veritable forest, shone dully in the light of the urns on the wall above.

Harry and Desirée stood close behind me, looking through at the fantastic sight. I turned to him:

"This time they mean business."

He nodded.

"But what can they do? Except get knocked on the head, and I'm sick of it. If we had only left an hour ago!"

"For my part," I retorted, "I'm glad we didn't. Desirée, I'm going to put you in my debt, if fortune will only show me one last kindness and let me get within reach of him."

I pointed to where the Inca king stood in the forefront, at the very edge of the lake.

She shuddered and grew pale.

"He is a monster," she said in a voice so low that I scarcely heard, "and—I thank you, Paul."

Harry seemed not to have heard.

"But what can they do?" he repeated.

They did not leave us long in doubt. As he spoke there was a sudden sharp movement in the ranks of the Incas. Those in front leaped in the water, and others after them, until, almost before we had time to realize their purpose, hundreds of the hairy brutes were swimming with long, powerful strokes directly toward the ledge on which we stood. Between his teeth each man carried his spear.

I left Harry to guard the crevice, and ran to repel the attack at the water. Desirée stood just behind me. I called to her to go back, but she did not move. I grasped her by the arm and led her forcibly to a break in the rock at our rear, and pointed out a narrow ascending lane in the direction of the other exit.

When I returned to the ledge of the water the foremost of the Incas were but a few feet away. But I looked in vain for the one face I wanted to see and could recognize; the king was not among them. A hasty glance across the landing opposite discovered him standing motionless with folded arms.

The entire surface of the lake before me was one mass of heads and arms and spears as far as I could see. There were hundreds of them. I saw at once that the thing was hopeless, but I grasped my spear firmly and stood ready.

The first two or three reached the ledge. At the same instant I heard Harry call:

"They're coming through, Paul! It's you alone!"

I did not turn my head, for I was busy. My spear was whirling about my head like a circle of flame. Black, dusky forms swam to the ledge and grasped its slippery surface, but they got no farther. The shaft of the spear bent in my hand; I picked up another, barely losing a second.

A wild and savage delight surged through me at the sight of those struggling, writhing, slipping forms. I swung the spear in vicious fury. Not one had found footing on the ledge.

Something suddenly struck me in the left arm and stuck there; I shook it loose impatiently and it felt as though my arm went with it.

I did not care to glance up even for an instant; they were pressing me closer and closer; but I knew that they had begun to hurl their spears at me from the water, and that the game was up. Another struck me on the leg; soon they were falling thick about me.

Calling to Harry to follow, I turned and ran for the opening in the rock to which I had led Desirée. In an instant he had joined me.

By that time scores of the Incas had scrambled out of the water onto the ledge and started toward us, and as many more came rushing through the crevice, finding their way no longer contested.

Harry carried three spears. I had four. We sprang up a lane encircling the rock to the rear and at its top found Desirée.

A projecting bit of rock gave us some protection from the spears that were being hurled at us from below, but they came uncomfortably close, and black forms began to appear in the lane through which we had come.

Harry shouted something which I didn't hear, and, taking Desirée in his arms, sprang from the rock to another ledge some ten feet below.

I followed. At the bottom he stumbled and fell, but I helped him to his feet and then turned barely in time to beat back three or four of the Incas who had tumbled down almost on our very heads.

Immediately in front of us was a chasm several feet across. Harry cried to Desirée, "Can you make it?" and she shook her head, pointing to her injured foot.

"To me!" I shouted desperately; they were coming down from above despite my efforts to hold them back.

Then, in answer to a call from Harry, I turned and leaped across the chasm, throwing the spears ahead of me. Harry took Desirée in his arms and swung her far out; I braced myself for the shock and caught her on my feet.

I set her down unhurt, and a minute later Harry had joined us and we were scrambling up the face of a boulder nearly perpendicular, while the spears fell thick around us.

Desirée lost her footing and fell against Harry, who rolled to the bottom, pawing for a hold. I turned, but he shouted: "Go on; I'll make it!" Soon he was again at my side, and in another minute we had gained the top of the boulder, quite flat and some twenty feet square. We commanded Desirée to lie flat on the ground to avoid the spears from below, and paused for a breath and a survey of the situation.

It can be described only with the word chaotic.

The light of the urns were now hidden from us, and we were in comparative darkness, though we could see with a fair amount of clearness. Nothing could be made of the mass of boulders, but we knew that somewhere beyond them was the passage from the cavern which we sought.

The Incas came leaping across the chasm to the foot of the rock. Several of them scrambled up the steep surface, but with our spears we pushed them back and they tumbled onto the heads of their fellows below.

But we were too exposed for a stand there, and I shouted to Harry to take Desirée down the other side of the rock while I stayed behind to hold them off. He left me, and in a moment later I heard his voice crying to me to follow. I did so, sliding down the face of the rock feet first.

Then began a wild and desperate scramble for safety, with the Incas ever at our heels. Without Desirée we would have made our goal with little difficulty, but half of the time we had to carry her.

Several times Harry hurled her bodily across a chasm or a crevice, while I received her on the other side.

Often I covered the retreat, holding the Incas at bay while Harry assisted Desirée up the steep face of a boulder or across a narrow ledge. There was less danger now from their spears, protected as we were by the maze of rocks, but I was already bleeding in a dozen places on my legs and arms and body, and Harry was in no better case.

Suddenly I saw ahead of us an opening which I thought I recognized. I pointed it out to Harry.

"The exit!" he cried out, and made for it with Desirée. But they were brought to a halt by a cliff at their very feet, no less than twenty feet high.

I started to join them, but hearing a clatter behind, turned just in time to see a score of Incas rush at us from the left, through a narrow lane that led to the edge of the cliff.

I sprang toward them, calling to Harry for assistance. He was at my side in an instant, and together we held them back.

In five minutes the mouth of the lane was choked with their bodies; some behind attempted to scramble over the pile to get at us, but we made them sick of their job. I saw that Harry could hold it alone then, and calling to him to stand firm till I called, I ran to Desirée.

I let myself over the edge of the cliff and hung by my hands, then dropped to the ground below. It was even further than I had thought; my legs doubled up under me and I toppled over, half fainting.

I gritted my teeth and struggled to my feet, calling to Desirée. She was already hanging to the edge of the cliff, many feet above me. But there was nothing else for it, and I shouted: "All right, come on!"

She came, and knocked me flat on my back. I had tried to catch her, and did succeed in breaking her fall, at no little cost to myself. I was one mass of bruises and wounds. But again I struggled to my feet and shouted at the top of my voice:

"Harry! Come!"

He did not come alone. I suppose the instant he left the lane unguarded the Incas poured in after him. They followed him over the edge of the cliff, tumbling on top of each other in an indistinguishable mass.

Some rose to their feet; their comrades, descending from above, promptly knocked them flat on their backs.

Harry and Desirée and I were making for the exit, which was not but a few feet away. As I have said, the thing was choked up till it was almost impassable. We squeezed in between two rocks, with Desirée between us. Harry was in front, and I brought up the rear.

Once through that lane and we might hold our own.

"In Heaven's name, come on!" Harry shouted suddenly; for I had turned and halted, gazing back at the Incas tumbling over the cliff and rushing toward the mouth of the exit.

But I did not heed him, for, standing on the top of the cliff, waving his arms wildly at those below, I had seen the form of the Inca king. He was less than thirty feet away.

With cries from Harry and Desirée ringing in my ears, I braced my feet as firmly as possible on the uneven rock and poised my spear above my head. The Incas saw my purpose and stopped short.

The king must also have seen me, but he stood absolutely motionless. I lunged forward; the spear left my hand and flew straight for his breast.

But it failed to reach the mark. A shout of triumph was on my lips, but was suddenly cut short when an Inca standing near the king sprang forward and hurled himself in the path of the spear just as its point was ready to take our revenge. The Inca fell to the foot of the cliff with the spear buried deep in his side. The king stood as he had before, without moving.

Then there was wild rush into the mouth of the exit, and I turned to follow Harry and Desirée. With extreme difficulty we scrambled forward over the rocks and around them.

Desirée's breath was coming in painful gasps, and we had to support her on either side. The Incas approached closer at our rear; I felt one of them grasp me from behind, and in an excess of fury I shook him off and dashed him backward against the rocks. We were able to make little headway, or none; by taking to the exit we appeared to have set our own death-trap.

Harry went on with Desirée, and I stayed behind in the attempt to check the attack. They came at me from both sides. I was faint and bleeding, and barely able to wield my spear—my last one. I gave way by inches, retreating backward step by step, fighting with the very end of my strength.

Suddenly Harry's voice came, shouting that they had reached the end of the passage. I turned then and sprang desperately from rock to rock after them, with the Incas crowding close after me.

I stumbled and nearly fell, but recovered my footing and staggered on. And suddenly the mass of rocks ended abruptly, and I fell forward onto flat, level ground by the side of Desirée and Harry.

"Your spear!" I gasped. "Quick—they are upon us!"

But they grasped my arms and dragged me away from the passage to one side. I was half fainting from exhaustion and loss of blood, and scarcely knew what they did. They laid me on the ground and bent over me.

"The Incas!" I gasped.

"They are gone," Harry answered.

At that I struggled to rise and rested my body on my elbows, gazing at the mouth of the passage. It was so; the Incas were not to be seen! Not one had issued from the passage.

It was incomprehensible to us then; later we understood. And we had not long to wait.

Harry and Desirée were bending over me, attempting to stop the flow of blood from a cut on my shoulder.

"We must have water," said Desirée. Harry straightened up to look about the cavern, which was so dark that we could barely see one another's faces but a few feet away.

Suddenly an exclamation of wonder came from his lips.

Desirée and I followed the direction of his gaze, and saw the huge, black, indistinct form of some animal suddenly detach itself from the wall of the cavern and move slowly toward us through the darkness.

Chapter XVII.

THE EYES IN THE DARK.

The thing was at a considerable distance; we could barely see that it was there and that it was moving. It was of an immense size; so large that it appeared as though the very side of the cavern itself had moved noiselessly from its bed in the mountain.

At the same moment I became aware of a penetrating, disagreeable odor, nauseating and horrible. I had risen to my knees and remained so, while Harry and Desirée stood on either side of me.

The thing continued to move toward us, very slowly. There was not a sound. The strength of the odor increased until it was almost suffocating.

Still we did not move. I could not, and Harry and Desirée seemed rooted to the spot with wonder. The thing came closer, and we could see the outlines of its huge form looming up indistinctly against the black background of the cavern.

I saw, or thought I saw, a grotesque and monstrous slimy head stretched toward us from about the middle of its bulk.

That doubt became a certainty when suddenly, as though they had been lit by a fire from within, two luminous, glowing spots appeared about three feet apart. The creature's eyes—if eyes they were—were turned full on us, growing more brilliant as the thing came closer. It was now less than fifty feet away. The massive form blocked our view of the entire cavern.

I pinched my nostrils to exclude the horrible odor which, like the fumes of some deadly poison, choked and smothered me. It came now in puffs, like a draft of a fetid wind, and I realized that it was the creature's breath. I could feel it against my body, my neck and face, and knew that if I breathed it full into my lungs I should be overcome.

But still more terrifying were the eyes. There was something compelling, supernaturally compelling, about their steadfast and brilliant gaze. A mysterious power seemed to emanate from them; a power that hypnotized the mind and deadened the senses. I closed my eyes to avoid it, but was unable to keep them closed. They opened despite my extreme effort, and again I met that gaze of fire.

There was a movement at my side. I turned and saw that it came from Desirée. Her hands were raised to her face; she was holding them before her as though in a futile attempt to cover her eyes.

The thing came closer and closer; it was but a few feet away, and still we did not move, as though rooted to the spot by some power beyond our control.

Suddenly there came a cry from Desirée's lips—a scream of terror and wild fear. Her entire form trembled violently.

She extended her arms toward the thing, now almost upon us, and took a step forward. Her feet dragged unwilling along the ground, as though she were being drawn forward by some irresistible force.

I tried to put out my hand to pull her back, but was absolutely unable to move. Harry stood like a man of rock, immovable.

She took another step forward, with arms outstretched in front of her. A low moan of terror and piteous appeal came from between her slightly parted lips.

Suddenly the eyes disappeared. The huge form ceased to advance and stood perfectly still. Then it began to recede, so slowly that I was barely conscious of the movement.

I was gasping and choking for air; my chest seemed swelling with the poisonous breath. Still slowly the thing receded into the dimness of the cavern; the eyes were no longer to be seen—merely the huge, formless bulk. Desirée had stopped short with one foot advanced, as though hesitating and struggling with the desire to go forward.

The thing now could barely be seen at a distance; it would have been impossible if we had not known it was there. Finally it disappeared, melting away into the semi-darkness; no slightest movement was discernible. I breathed more freely and stepped forward.

As I did so Desirée threw her hands gropingly above her head and fell fainting to the ground.

Harry sprang forward in time to keep her head from striking on the rock and knelt with his arms round her shoulders. We had nothing, not even water, with which to revive her; he called her name aloud appealingly. Soon her eyes opened; she raised her hand and passed it across her brow wonderingly.

"God help me!" she murmured in a low voice, eloquent of distress and pain.

Then she pushed Harry aside and rose slowly to her feet, refusing his assistance.

"In the name of Heaven, what is it?" Harry demanded, turning to me.

"We have found the devil at last," I answered, with an attempt to laugh, which sounded hollow in my own ears.

Desirée could tell us nothing, except that she had felt herself drawn forward by some strange power that had seemed to come from the baneful, glittering eyes. She was bewildered and stunned and unable to talk coherently. We assisted her to the wall, and she sat there with her back propped against it, breathing heavily from the exhaustion of terror.

"We must find water," I said, and Harry nodded, hesitating.

I understood him. Danger could not have stayed him nor fear; but the horror of the thing which roamed about the cavern, dark as darkness itself and possessed of some strange power that could not be withstood, was enough to make him pause. For myself it was impossible; I was barely able to stand. So Harry went off alone in search of water and I stayed with Desirée.

It was perhaps half an hour before he returned, and we were shaken with fear for him long before he appeared. When he did so it was with a white face and trembling limbs, in spite of his evident effort at steadiness.

"There is water over there," said he, pointing across the cavern. "A stream runs across the corner and disappears beneath the wall. There is nothing to carry it in. You must come with me."

"What has happened?" I asked, for even his voice was unsteady.

"I saw it," he replied simply, but expressing enough in those three words to cause a shudder to run through me.

Then, speaking in a low tone that Desirée might not hear, he told me that the thing had confronted him suddenly as he was following the opposite wall, and that he, too, had been drawn forward, as it were, by a spell impossible to shake off. He had tried to cry aloud, but had been unable to utter a sound. And suddenly, as before, the eyes had disappeared, leaving him barely able to stand.

"No wonder the Incas wouldn't follow us in here," he finished. "We must get out of this. I'm not a coward, but I wouldn't go through that again for my life."

"You take Desirée," said I. "I want that water."

He led us around the wall several hundred feet. The ground was level and clear of obstruction; but we went slowly, for I could scarcely move. Harry kept his eyes strained intently on all sides; his experience had left him more profoundly impressed even than he had been willing to admit to me.

Soon we heard the low music of running water, and a minute later we reached the stream Harry had found.

The fact that there was something to be done seemed to infuse a new spirit into Desirée, and soon her deft fingers were bathing my wounds and bandaging them as well as her poor material would allow.

The cold water took the heat from my pumping veins and left me almost comfortable. Harry had come off much easier than I, since I had so often sent him ahead with Desirée, and myself brought up the rear and withstood the brunt of the attack.

As Harry had said, the stream cut across a corner of the cavern, disappearing beneath the opposite wall, forming a triangle bound by two sides of the cavern and the stream itself. I saw plainly that it would be impossible for me to move any distance for at least a few days, and that triangle appeared to offer the safest and most comfortable retreat.

I spoke to Harry, and he waded across the stream to try its depth. From the other side he called that the water was at no point more than waist-high, and Desirée and I started to cross; but about the middle I felt the current about to sweep me off my feet. Harry waded in and helped me ashore.

On that hard rock we lay for many weary hours. We had no food; but for that I would soon have been myself again, for, though my wounds were numerous, they were little more than scratches, with the exception of the gash on my shoulder. Weakened as I was by loss of blood, and lacking nourishment, I improved but slowly, and only the cold water kept the fever from me.

Twice Harry went out in search of food and of an exit from the cavern. The first time he was away for several hours, and returned exhausted and empty-handed and without having found any exit other than the one by which we had entered.

He had ventured through that far enough to see a group of Incas on watch at the other end. They had seen him and sprung after him, but he had returned without injury, and at the entrance into the cavern where we lay they had halted abruptly.

The second time he was gone out more than half an hour, and the instant I saw his face when he returned I knew what had happened.

But I was not in the best of humor; his terror appeared to me to be ridiculously childish, and I said so in no uncertain terms.

But he was too profoundly agitated to show any anger.

"You don't know, you don't know," was all he said in answer to me; then he added; "I can't stand this any longer. I tell you we've got to get out of here. You don't know how awful—"

"Yes," said Desirée, looking at me.

"But I can scarcely walk," I objected.

"True," said Harry. "I know. But we can help you. There must be another exit, and we'll start now."

"Very well," I said quite calmly; and I picked up one of the spears which we had carried with us, and, rising to my knees, placed the butt of the shaft against the wall near which I lay.

But Harry saw my purpose, and was too quick for me. He sprang across and snatched the spear from my hand and threw it on the ground a dozen feet away.

"Are you crazy?" he shouted angrily.

"No," I answered; "but I am little better, and I doubt if I shall be. Come—why not? I hinder you and become bored with myself."

"You blame me," he said bitterly; "but I tell you you don't know. Very well—we stay. You must give me your promise not to act the fool."

"In any event, you must go soon," I answered, "or starve to death. Perhaps in another twenty-four hours I shall be stronger. Come, Desirée; will that satisfy you?"

She did not answer; her back was turned to us as she stood gazing across the stream into the depths of the carvern. There was a curious tenseness in her attitude that made me follow her gaze, and what I saw left me with no wonder at it—a huge, black, indistinct form that moved slowly toward us through the darkness.

Harry caught sight of it at the same moment as myself; and on the instant he turned about, covering his face with his hands, and called to Desirée and me to do likewise.

Desirée obeyed; I had risen to my knees and remained so, gazing straight ahead, ready for a combat if it were not a physical one. I will not say that a certain feeling of dread did not rise in my heart, but I intended to show Desirée and Harry the childishness of their terror.

Nothing could be seen but the uncertain outline of the immense bulk; but the same penetrating, sickening odor that had before all but suffocated me came faintly across the surface of the stream, growing stronger with each second that passed. Suddenly the eyes appeared—two glowing orbs of fire that caught my gaze and held it as with a chain.

I did not attempt to avoid it, but returned the gaze with another as steadfast. I was telling myself: "Let us see this trick and play one stronger." My nerves centered throbbingly back of my eyes, and I gave them the whole force of my will.

The thing came closer and the eyes seemed to burn into my very brain. With a great effort I brought myself back to control, dropping to my hands and knees and gripping the ground for strength.

"This is nothing, this is nothing," I kept saying to myself aloud—until I realized suddenly that my voice had risen almost to a scream, and I locked my teeth tight on my lip.

I no longer returned the gaze from my own power; it held me of itself. I felt my brain grow curiously numb and every muscle in my body contracted with a pain almost unbearable. Still the thing came closer and closer, and it seemed to me, half dazed as I was, that it advanced much faster than before.

Then suddenly I felt a sensation of cold and moisture on my arms and legs and a pressure against my body, and I realized, as in a dream, that I had entered the stream of water!

I was crawling toward the thing on my hands and knees, without having even been conscious that I had moved.

That brought despair and a last supreme struggle to resist whatever mysterious power it was that dragged me forward.

Cold beads of sweat rolled from my forehead. Beneath the surface of the water my hands gripped the rocks as in a vise. My teeth had sunk deep into my lower lip and covered my chin with blood, though I did not know that till afterward.

But I was pulled loose from my hold, and forward. I bent the whole force of my will to the effort not to move, but my hand left the rock and crept forward. I was fully conscious of what I was doing. I knew that if I could once draw my eyes away from that compelling gaze the spell would be broken, but the power to do so was not in me.

The thing had halted on the farther bank of the stream. Still I moved forward. The water now lapped against my chest; soon it was about my shoulders.

I was fully conscious of the fact that in another ten feet the surface would close over my head, and that I had not the strength to swim or fight the current; but still I went forward. I tried to cry out, but could force no sound through my lips.

Then suddenly the eyes began to disappear. But that at least was comprehensible, for I could distinctly see the black and heavy lids closing over them, like the curtain on a stage. They fell slowly.

The eyes became half moons, then narrowed to a thin slit. I rose, panting like a man exhausted with extreme and prolonged physical exertion.

The eyes were gone.

A mad impulse rushed into my brain to dash forward and touch the monster, to see if that dim, black form were really a thing of flesh and blood or some contrivance of the devil. I smile at that phrase as I write it now in my study, but I did not smile then. I was standing above my knees in the water, trembling from head to foot, divided between the impulse to go forward and the inclination to flee in terror.

I did neither; I stood still. I could see the thing with a fair amount of distinctness and forced my brain to take the record of my eyes. But I could make nothing of it.

I guessed at rather than saw a hideous head rolling from side to side at the end of a long and sinuous neck, and writhing, reptilian coils lashing the rock at the edge of the water, like the tentacles of an octopus, only many times larger. The body itself was larger than that of any animal I had ever seen, and blacker even than the darkness.

Suddenly the huge mass began to move slowly backward. The sharpness of the odor had ceased with the opening of the eyes, which did not reappear. I could dimly see its huge legs slowly rise and recede and again meet the ground. Soon the thing was barely discernible.

I took a step forward as though to follow; but the strength of the current warned me of the danger of proceeding farther, and, besides, I feared every moment to see the lids again raised from the terrible eyes. The thought attacked my brain with horror, and I turned and fled in a sudden panic to the rear, calling to Harry and Desirée.

They met me at the edge of the stream, and their eyes told me that they read in my face what had happened, though they had seen nothing.

"You—you saw it—" Harry stammered.

I nodded, scarcely able to speak.

"Then—perhaps now—"

"Yes," I interposed. "Let's get out of here. It's horrible. And yet how can we go? I can hardly stand."

But Harry was now the one who argued for delay, saying that our retreat was the safest place we could find, and that we should wait at least until I had had time to recover from the strain of the last half-hour. Realizing that in my weakened condition I would be a hindrance to them rather than a help, I consented. Besides, if the thing reappeared I could avoid it as Harry and Desirée had done.

"What is it?" Harry asked presently.

We were sitting side by side, well up against the wall. It was an abrupt question, with no apparent pertinence, but I understood.

"Heaven knows!" I answered shortly. I was none too pleased with myself.

"But it must be something. Is it an animal?"

"Do you remember," I asked by way of answer, "a treatise of Aristotle concerning which we had a discussion one day? Its subject was the hypnotic power possessed by the eyes of certain reptiles. I laughed the idea to scorn; you maintained that it was possible. Well, I agree with you; and I'd like to have about a dozen of our modern skeptical scientists in this cave with me for about five minutes."

"But what is it? A reptile!" Harry exclaimed. "The thing is as big as a house!"

"Well, and why not? I should guess that it is about thirty feet in height and forty or fifty in length. There have been species, now extinct, several times as large."

"Then you think it is just—just an animal?" put in Desirée.

"What did you think it was?" I nearly smiled. "An infernal machine?"

"I don't know. Only I have never before known what it was to fear."

A discussion which led us nowhere, but at least gave us the sound of one another's voices.

We passed many hours in that manner. Utterly blank and wearisome, and all but hopeless. I have often wondered at the strange tenacity with which we clung to life in conditions that made of it a burden almost insupportable; and with what chance of relief?

The instinct of self-perservation, it is called by the learned, but it needs a stronger name. It is more than an instinct. It is the very essence of life itself.

But soon we were impelled to action by something besides the desire to escape from the cavern: the pangs of hunger. It had been many hours since we had eaten; I think we had fasted not less than three or dour days.

Desirée began to complain of a dizziness in her temples, and to weaken with every hour that passed. My own strength did not increase, and I saw that it would not unless I could obtain nourishment. Harry did not complain, but only because he would not.

"It is useless to wait longer," I declared finally. "I grow weaker instead of stronger."

We had little enough with which to burden ourselves. There were three spears, two of which Harry had brought, and myself the other. Harry and I wore only our woolen undergarments, so ragged and torn that they were but sorry covering.

Desirée's single garment, made from some soft hide, was held about her waist by a girdle of the same material. The upper half of her body was bare. Her hair hung in a tangled mass over her shoulders and down her back. None of us had any covering for our feet.

We crossed the stream, using the spears as staffs; but instead of advancing across the middle of the cavern we turned to the left, hugging the wall. Harry urged us on, saying that he had already searched carefully for an exit on that side, but we went slowly, feeling for a break in the wall. It was absolutely smooth, which led me to believe that the cavern had at one time been filled with water.

We reached the farther wall and, turning to the right, were about to follow it.

"This is senseless," said Harry impatiently. "I tell you I have examined this side, too; every inch of it."

"And the one ahead of us, at right angles to this?" I asked.

"That too," he answered.

"And the other—the one to the right of the stream?"

"No. I—I didn't go there."

"Why didn't you say so?" I demanded.

"Because I didn't want to," he returned sullenly. "You can go there if you care to; I don't. It was from there that—it came."

I did not answer, but pushed forward, not, however, leaving the wall. Perhaps it was cowardly; you are welcome to the word if you care to use it. Myself, I know.

Another half-hour and we reached the end of the lane by which we had first entered the cavern. We stood gazing at it with eyes of desire, but we knew how little chance there was of the thing being unguarded at the farther end. We knew then, of course, and only too well, why the Incas had not followed us into the cavern.

"Perhaps they are gone," said Harry. "They can't stay there forever. I'm going to find out."

He sprang on the edge of a boulder at the mouth of the passage and disappeared on the other side. In fifteen minutes he returned, and I saw by the expression on his face that there was no chance of escape in that direction.

"They're at the other end," he said gloomily; "a dozen of 'em. I looked from behind a rock; they didn't see me. But we could never get through."

We turned then, and proceeded to the third wall and followed it. But we really had no hope of finding an exit since Harry had said that he had previously explored it. We were possessed, I know, by the same thought: should we venture to follow the fourth wall? Alone, none of us would have dared; but the presence of the others lessened the fear of each.

Finally we reached it. The corner was a sharp right angle, and there were rifts and crevices in the rock.

"This is limestone," I said, "and if we find an exit anywhere it will be here."

I turned to the right and proceeded slowly along the wall, feeling its surface with my hand.

We had advanced in this manner several hundred yards when Desirée suddenly sprang forward to my side.

"See!" she cried, pointing ahead with her spear.

I followed the direction with my eye, and saw what appeared to be a sharp break in the wall.

It was some fifty feet away. We reached it in another moment, and I think none of us would have been able to express the immeasurable relief we felt when we saw before us a broad and clear passage leading directly away from the cavern. It was very dark, but we entered it almost at a run.

I think we had not known the extent of our fear of that thing in the cavern until we found the means of escape from it.

We had gone about a hundred feet when we came to a turn to the left. Harry stumbled against the corner, and we halted for an instant to wait for him.

Then we made the turn, side by side—and then we came to a sudden and abrupt stop, and a simultaneous gasp of terror burst from our lips.

Not three feet in front of us, blocking the passage completely, stood the thing we thought we had escaped!

The terrible, fiery eyes rolled from side to side as they stared straight into our own.

Chapter XVIII.

A VICTORY AND A CONVERSATION.

We stood for a long moment rooted to the spot, unable to move. Then, calling to Harry and grasping Desirée by the arm, I started to turn.

But too late. For Desirée, inspired by a boundless terror, suddenly raised her spear high above her head and hurled it straight at the glowing, flashing eyes.

The point struck squarely between then with such force that it must have sunk clear to the shaft. The head of the monster rolled for an instant from side to side, and then, before I was aware of what had happened, so rapid was the movement, a long, snakelike coil had reached out through the air and twisted itself about Desirée's body.

As she felt the thing tighten about her waist and legs she gave a scream of terror and twisted her face round toward me. The next instant the snaky tentacle had dragged her along the ground and lifted her to the head of the monster, where her white body could be seen in sharp outline sprawling over its black form, between the terrible eyes.

Harry and I sprang forward.

As we did so the eyes closed and the reptile began to move backward with incredible swiftness, lashing about on the ground before us with other tentacles similar to the one that had captured Desirée.

I cried out to Harry to avoid them. He did not answer, but rushed blindly forward.

Desirée's agonized shrieks rose to the pitch of madness.

The eyes were closed, leaving but a vague mark for our spears, and besides, there was the danger of striking Desirée. We were barely able to keep pace with the thing as it receded swiftly down the broad passage. Desirée had twisted her body half round, and her face was turned toward us, shadowy as a ghost. Then her head fell forward and hung loosely and her lips were silent. She had fainted.

The thing moved swifter than ever; we were barely able to keep up with it. Harry made a desperate leap forward.

I cried out a warning, but one of the writhing tentacles swept against him and knocked him to the ground. He was up again on the instant and came rushing up from behind.

Suddenly the passage broadened until the walls were no longer visible; we had entered another cavern. I heard the sound of running water somewhere ahead of us. The pace of the reptile had not slackened for an instant.

Harry had again caught up with us, and as he ran at my side I saw him raise his spear aloft; but I caught his arm and held it.

"Desirée!" I panted.

Her body covered the only part of the thing that presented a fair mark. Harry swore, but his arm fell.

"To the side!" he gasped. "We can't get at it here!"

I saw his meaning and followed at his heels as he swerved suddenly to the right and sprang forward in an attempt to get past the reptile's head.

But in our eagerness we forgot caution and went too close. I felt one of the snaky tentacles wrap itself round my legs and body, and raised my voice in a warning to Harry, but too late. He, too, was ensnared, and a moment later we had both been lifted bodily from the ground and swung through the air to the side of Desirée. She was still unconscious.

I writhed and twisted desperately, but that muscular coil held me firmly as a band of steel, tight against the huge and hideous head.

Harry was on the other side of Desirée, not three feet from me. I could see his muscles strain and pull in his violent efforts to tear himself free. I had given it up.

But suddenly, quite near my shoulder, I saw the lid suddenly begin to raise itself from one of the terrible eyes. I was almost on top of the thing and a little above it. I turned my head aside and called to Harry.

"The eye!" I gasped. "To your right! The spear! Are your arms free?"

Then as I saw he understood, I turned a quarter of the way round—as far as I could get—and raised my spear the full extent of my arm, and brought it down with every ounce of my strength into the very center of the glowing eye beneath me.

At the same moment I saw Harry's arm descend and the flash of his spear. The point of my own had sunk until the copper head was completely buried.

I grasped the shaft and pulled and twisted it about until it finally was jerked forth. From the opening it had made there issued a black stream.

Suddenly the body of the reptile quivered convulsively. The head rolled from side to side. There was a quick tightening of the tentacle round my body until my bones felt as though they were being crushed into shapelessness; and as suddenly it loosened.

Other tentacles lashed and beat on the ground furiously. The reptile's swift backward movement halted jerkily. I made a desperate effort to tear myself free. The tentacle quivered and throbbed violently, and suddenly flew apart like a released spring, and I fell to the ground.

In an instant Harry was at my side, and we both leaped forward with our spears, slashing at the tentacle which still held Desirée in its grasp. Others writhed on the ground about our feet, but feebly. There came a sudden cry from Harry, and his spear clattered on the ground as he opened his arms to receive Desirée's unconscious body, which came tumbling down with the severed coil still wrapped about it.

But there was life in the reptile's immense body. It staggered and swayed from side to side in drunken agony. Its monstrous head rolled about, sweeping the air in a prodigious circle. The poison of its breath came to us in great puffs. There was something supremely horrible about the thing in its very helplessness, and I was shuddering violently as I stooped to help Harry lift Desirée from the ground and carry her away.

We did not go far, for we were barely able to carry her. We

laid her on the hard rock with her head in Harry's lap. Her body was limp as a rag.

For many minutes we worked over her, rubbing her temples and wrists, and pressing the nerve centers at the back of the neck, but without effect.

"She is dead," said Harry with a curious calm.

I shook my head.

"She has a pulse—see! But we must find that water. I think she isn't injured; it is her weakened condition from the lack of food that keeps her so. Wait for me."

I started out across the cavern in the direction from which the sound of the water appeared to come, bearing off to the right from the huge, quivering form of the monster whose gigantic body rose and fell on the ground with a force that seemed to shake the very walls of the cavern.

I found the stream with little difficulty, not far away, and returned to Harry. Together we carried Desirée to its edge. The blood was stubborn, and for a long time refused to move, but the cold water at length revived her; her eyes slowly opened, and she raised her hand to her head with a faltering gesture.

But she was extremely weak, and we saw that the end was near unless nourishment could be found for her.

I stayed by her side, with my arms round her shoulders, and Harry set out with one of the spears. He bore off to the left, toward the spot where the body of the immense reptile lay; I was too far away to see it in the darkness.

"It isn't possible that the thing is fit to eat," I had objected, and he had answered me with a look which I understood, and was silenced.

Soon a sound as of a scuffle on the rocks came through the darkness from the direction he had taken. I called out to ask if he needed me, but there was no answer. Ten minutes longer I waited, while the sound continued unabated. Once I heard the clatter of his spear on the rock.

I was just rising to my feet to run to the scene when suddenly he appeared in the semidarkness. He was coming slowly, and was dragging along the ground what appeared to be the form of some animal. Another minute and he stood at my side as I sat holding Desirée.

"A peccary!" I cried, bending over the body of the four-footed creature that lay at his feet. "How the deuce did it ever get down here?"

"Peccary—my aunt!" observed Harry, bending down to look at Desirée. "Do peccaries live in the water? Do they have snouts like catfish? This animal is my own invention. There's about ten million more of 'em over there making a gorgeous banquet off our late lamented friend. And now, let's see."

He knelt down by the still warm body and with the point of his spear ripped it open from neck to rump. Desirée stirred about in my arms.

"Gad, that smells good!" cried Harry.

I shuddered.

He dragged the thing a few feet away, and I heard him slashing away at it with his spear. A minute later he came running over to us with his hands full of something.

That was not exactly a pretty meal. How Desirée, in her frightfully weakened condition, ever managed to get the stuff down and keep it there is beyond me. But she did, and I was not behind her. And, after all, it was fresh. Harry said it was "sweet." Well, perhaps it was.

We bathed Desirée's hands and face and gave her water to drink, and soon after she passed into a seemingly healthy sleep. There was about ten pounds of meat left. Harry washed it in the stream and stowed it away on a rock beneath the surface of the water. Then he announced his intention of going back for more.

"I'm going with you," I declared. "Here—help me fix Desirée."

"Hardly," said Harry. "Didn't I say there are millions of those things over there? Anyway, there are hundreds. If they should happen to scatter in this direction and find her, she wouldn't stand a chance. You take the other spear and stay here."

So I sat still, with Desirée's body in my arms, and waited

for him. My sensations were not unpleasant. I could actually feel the blood quicken in my veins.

Civilization places the temple of life in the soul or the heart, as she speaks through the mouth of the preacher or the poet; but let civilization go for four or five days without anything to eat and see what happens. The organ is vulgar, but its voice is loud. I need not name it.

In five minutes Harry returned, dragging two more of the creatures at his heels. In half an hour there were a dozen of them lying in a heap at the edge of the water.

"That's all," he announced, panting heavily from his exertions. "The rest have taken to the woods, which, I imagine, is quite a journey from here. You ought to see our friend—the one who couldn't make his eyes behave. They've eaten him full of holes. He's the most awful mess—sickening beast. He didn't have a bone in him—all crumpled up like an accordion. Utterly spineless."

"And who, in the name of goodness, do you think is going to eat all that?" I demanded, pointing to the heap of bodies.

Harry grinned.

"I don't know. I was so excited at the very idea of a square meal that I didn't know when to stop. I'd give five fingers for a fire and some salt. Just a nickel's worth of salt. Now, you lie down and sleep while I cut these things up, and then I'll take a turn at it myself?"

He brought me one of the hides for a pillow, and I lay back as gently as possible that I might not awaken Desirée. Her head and shoulders rested against my body as she lay peacefully sleeping.

I was awakened by Harry's hand tugging at my arm. Rising on my elbows, I demanded to know how long I had slept.

"Six or seven hours," said Harry. "I waited as long as I could. Keep a lookout."

Desirée stirred uneasily, but seemed to be still asleep. I sat up, rubbing my eyes. The heap of bodies had disappeared; no wonder Harry was tired! I reproached myself for having slept so long.

Harry had arranged himself a bed that was really comfortable with the skins of his kill.

"That is great stuff," I heard him murmur wearily; then all was still.

I sat motionless, stiff and numb, but afraid to move for fear of disturbing Desirée.

Presently she stirred again, and, bending over her, I saw her eyes slowly open. They met my own with a curious, steadfast gaze—she was still half asleep.

"Is that you, Paul?" she murmured.

"Yes."

"I am glad. I seem to feel—what is it?"

"I don't know, Desirée. What do you mean?"

"Nothing—nothing. Oh, it feels so good—good—to have you hold me like this."

"Yes?" I smiled.

"But, yes. Where is Harry?"

"Asleep. Are you hungry?"

"Yes—no. Not now. I don't know why. I want to talk. What has happened?"

I told her of everything that had occurred since she had swooned; she shuddered as memory returned, but forgot herself in my attempt at a humorous description of Harry's valor as a hunter of food.

"You don't need to turn up your nose," I retorted to her expressive grimace; "you ate some of the stuff yourself."

There was a silence; then suddenly Desirée's voice came:

"Paul—" She hesitated and stopped.

"Yes."

"What do you think of me?"

"Do you want a lengthy review?" I smiled.

What a woman she was! Under those circumstances, and amid those surroundings, she was still Desirée Le Mire.

"Don't laugh at me," she said. "I want to know. I have never spoken of what I did that time in the cavern—you know what I mean. I am sorry now. I suppose you despise me."

"But you did nothing," I objected. "And you wouldn't. You were merely amusing yourself."

She turned on my quickly with a flash of her old fire.

"Don't play with me!" she burst out. "My friend, you have never yet given me a serious word."

"Nor any one else," I answered. "My dear Desirée, do you not know that I am incapable of seriousness? Nothing in the world is worth it."

"At least, you need not pretend," she retorted. "I meant once for you to die. You know it. And since you pretend not to understand me, I ask you—these are strange words from my lips—will you forgive me?"

"There is nothing to forgive."

"My friend, you are becoming dull. An evasive answer should always be a witty one. Must I ask you again?"

"That—depends," I answered, hardly knowing what to say.

"On—"

"On whether or not you were serious, once upon a time, when you made a—shall we call it a confession? If you were, I offended you in my own conceit; but let us be frank. I thought you were acting, and I played my rôle. I do not yet believe that you were; I am not conceited enough to think it possible."

"I do not say," Desirée began; then she stopped and added hastily: "But that is past. I shall not tell you that again. Perhaps I forgot myself. Perhaps it was a pretty play. You have not answered me."

I looked at her. Strange and terrible as her experiences and sufferings had been, she had lost little of her beauty. Her face was rendered only the more delicate by its pallor. Her white and perfect body, only half seen in the half-darkness, conveyed a sense of the purest beauty with no hint of immodesty.

But I was moved not by what I saw, but by what I knew. I had admired her always as Le Mire; but her bravery, her hardihood, her sympathy for others under circumstances when any other woman would have been thinking only of herself—had these awakened in my breast a feeling stronger than admiration?

I did not know. But my voice trembled a little as I said: "I need not answer you, Desirée. I repeat that there is nothing to forgive. You sought revenge, then sacrificed it; but still revenge is yours."

She looked at me for a moment in silence, then said slowly: "I do not understand you."

For reply I took her hand in my own from where it lay idly on my knee, and, carrying it to my lips, pressed a long kiss on the top of each of the slender white fingers. Then I held the hand tight between both of mine as I aked simply, looking into her eyes:

"Do you understand me now?"

Another silence.

"My revenge," she breathed.

I nodded and again pressed her hand to my lips.

"Yes, Desirée. We are not children. I think we know what we mean. But you have not told me. Did you mean what you said that day on the mountain?"

"Ah, I thought that was a play!" she murmured.

"Tell me! Did you mean it?"

"I never confess the same sin twice, my friend."

"Desirée, did you mean it?"

Then suddenly, with the rapidity of lightning, her manner changed. She bent toward me with parted lips and looked straight into my eyes. There was passion in the gaze; but when she spoke her voice was quite even and so low I scarcely heard.

"Paul," she said, "I shall not again say I love you. Such words should not be wasted. Not now, perhaps; but that is because we are where we are. And if we should return?

"You have said that nothing is worth a serious word to you; and you are right. You are too cynical; things are bitter in your mouth, and doubly so when they leave it. Just now you are amusing yourself by pretending to care for me. Perhaps you do not know it, but you are. Search your heart, my friend, and tell me—do you want my love?"

Well, there was no need to search my heart; she had laid it open. I hated myself then; and I turned away, unable to meet her eyes, as I said:

"*Bon Dieu!*" she cried. "That is an ugly speech, *monsieur!*" And she laughed aloud.

"But we must not awaken Harry," she continued with sudden softness. "What a boy he is—and what a man! Ah, he knows what it is to love!"

That topic suited me little better, but I followed her. We talked of Harry, Le Mire with an amount of enthusiasm that surprised me. Suddenly she stopped abruptly and announced that she was hungry.

I found Harry's pantry after a few minutes' search and took some of its contents to Desirée. Then I retuned to the edge of the water and ate my portion alone. That meal was one scarcely calculated for the pleasures of companionship or conviviality.

It was several hours after that before Harry awoke, the greater part of which Desirée and I were silent.

I would have given something to have known her thoughts; my own were not very pleasant. It is always a disagreeable thing to discover that some one else knows you better than you know yourself. And Desirée had cut deep. At the time I thought her unjust; time alone could have told which of us was right. If she were here with me now—but she is not.

Finally Harry awoke. He was delighted to find Desirée awake and comparatively well, and demonstrated the fact with a degree of effusion that prompted me to leave them alone together. But I did not go far; a hundred paces made me sit down to rest before returning, so weak was I from wounds and fasting.

Harry's spirits were high, for no apparent reason other than that we were still alive, for that was the best that could be said for us. So I told him; he retorted with a hearty clap on the back that sent me sprawling to the ground.

"What the deuce!" he exclaimed, stooping to help me up. "Are you as weak as that? Gad, I'm sorry!"

"That is the second fall he has had," said Desirée, with a meaning smile.

Indeed, she was having her revenge!

But my strength was not long in returning. Over a long stretch our diet would hardly have been conducive to health, but it was exactly what I needed to put blood and strength in me. And Harry and Desirée, too, for that matter.

Again I had to withstand Harry's eager demands for action. He began within two hours to insist on exploring the cave, and would hardly take a refusal.

"I won't stir a foot until I am able to knock you down," I declared finally and flatly. "Never again will I attempt to perform the feats of a Hercules when I am fit only for an invalid's chair." And he was forced to wait.

As I say, however, my strength was not long in returning, and when it started it came with a rush. My wounds were healing perfectly; only one remained open. Harry, with his usual phenomenal luck, had got nothing but the merest scratches.

Desirée improved very slowly. The strain of those four days in the cavern had been severe, and her nerves required more pleasant surroundings than a dark and damp cavern and more agreeable diet than raw meat, to adjust themselves.

Thus it was that when Harry and I found ourselves ready to start out to explore the cavern and, if possible, find an exit on the opposite said from the one where we had entered, we left Desirée behind, seated on a pile of skins, with a spear on the ground at her side.

"We'll be back in an hour," said Harry, stooping to kiss her; and the phrase, which might have come from the lips of a worthy Harlem husband leaving for a little sojourn with friends on the corner, brought a smile to my face.

We went first toward the spot where lay the remains of "our friend with the eyes," as Harry called him, and we were guided straight by our noses, for the odor of the thing was beginning to be—to use another phrase of Harry's—"most awful vile."

There was little to see except a massive pile of crumpled hide and sinking flesh. As we approached, several hundred of the animals with which Harry had filled our larder scampered away toward the water.

"They're not fighters," I observed, turning to watch them disappear in the darkness.

"No," Harry agreed. "See here," he added suddenly, holding up a piece of the hide of the reptile; "this stuff is an inch thick and touch as rats. It ought to be good for something."

But by that time I was pinching my nostrils with my fingers, and I pulled him away.

Several hundred yards farther on we came to the wall of the cavern. We followed it, turning to the right; but though it was uneven and marked by projecting boulders and deep crevices, we found no exit. We had gone at least half a mile, I think, when we came to the end. There it turned in a wide circle to the right, and we took the new direction, which was toward the spot where we had left Desirée, only considerably to the left.

Another five minutes found us at the edge of the stream, which at that point was much swifter than it was farther up. We waded in and discovered that the cause was its extreme narrowness.

"But where does the thing go to?" asked Harry, taking the words from my mouth.

We soon found out. Proceeding along the bank to the left, within fifty feet we came to the wall. There the stream entered and disappeared. But, unlike the others we had seen, above this there was a wide and high arch, which made it appear as though the stream were passing under a massive bridge. The current was swift but not turbulent, and there was something about the surface of that stream flowing straight through the mountain ahead of us—

Harry and I glanced at each other quickly, moved by the same thought. There was an electric thrill in that glance.

But we did not speak—then.

For suddenly, startlingly, a voice sounded throughout the cavern—Desirée's voice, raised in a shrill cry of terror.

It was repeated twice before our startled senses found themselves; then we turned with one impulse and raced into the darkness toward her.

Chapter XIX.

AFLOAT.

As we ran swiftly, following the edge of the stream, the cries continued, filling the cavern with racing echoes. They could not quicken our step; we were already straining every muscle as we bounded over the rock. Luckily, the way was clear, for in the darkness we could see but a few feet ahead. Desirée's voice was sufficient guide for us.

Finally we reached her. I don't know what I expected to see, but certainly not that which met our eyes.

"Your spear!" cried Harry, dashing off to the right, away from the stream.

My spear was ready. I followed.

Desirée was standing exactly in the spot where we had left her, screaming at the top of her voice.

Around her, on every side, was a struggling, pushing mass of the animals we had frightened away from the carcass of the reptile. There were hundreds of them packed tightly together, crowding toward her, some leaping on the backs of others, some trampled to the ground beneath the feet of their fellows. They did not appear to be actually attacking her, but we could not see distinctly.

This we saw in a flash and an instant later had dashed forward into the mass with whirling spears. It was a farce, rather than a fight.

We brought our spears down on the swarm of heads and backs without even troubling to take aim. They pressed against our legs; we waded through as though it were a current of water. Those we hit either fell or ran; they waited for no second blow.

Desirée had ceased her cries.

"They won't hurt you!" Harry had shouted. "Where's your spear?"

"Gone. They came on me before I had time to get it."

"Then kick 'em, push 'em—anything. They're nothing but pigs."

They had the senseless stubbornness of pigs, at least. They seemed absolutely unable to realize that their presence was not desired till they actually felt the spear—utterly devoid even of instinct.

"So this is what you captured for us at the risk of your life!" I shouted to Harry in disgust. "They haven't even sense enough to squeal."

We finally reached Desirée's side and cleared a space round her. But it took us another fifteen minutes of pushing and thrusting and indiscriminate massacre before we routed the brutes. When they did decide to go they lost no time, but scampered away toward the water with a sliding, tumbling rush.

"Gad!" exclaimed Harry, resting on his spear. "And here's a pretty job. Look at that! I wish they'd carry off the dead ones."

"Ugh! The nasty brutes! I was never so frightened in my life," said Desirée.

"You frightened us, all right," Harry retorted. "Utterly fungoed. I never ran so fast in my life. And all you had to do was shake your spear at 'em and say boo! I thought it was the roommate of our friend with the eyes."

"Have I been eating those things?" Desirée demanded. Harry grinned.

"Yes, and that isn't all. You'll continue to eat 'em as long as I'm the cook. Come on, Paul; it's a day's work."

We dragged the bodies down to the edge of the stream and tossed them into the current, saving three or four for the replenishment of the larder.

I then first tried my hand at the task of skinning and cleaning them, and by the time I had finished was thoroughly disgusted with it and myself. Harry had become hardened to it; he whistled over the job as though he had been born in a butcher's shop.

"I'd rather go hungry," I declared, washing my hands and arms in the cool water.

"Oh, sure," said Harry; "my efforts are never appreciated. I've fed you up till you've finally graduated from the skeleton class, and you immediately begin to criticize the table. I know now what it means to run a boarding-house. Why don't you change your hotel?"

By the time we had finished we were pretty well tired out, but Harry wouldn't hear of rest. I was eager myself for another look at the exit of that stream. So, again taking up our spears, we set out across the cavern, this time with Desirée between us. She swallowed Harry's ridicule of her fear and refused to stay behind.

Again we stood at the point where the stream left the cavern through the broad arch of a tunnel.

"There's a chance there," said Harry, turning to me. "It looks good."

"Yes, if we had a boat," I agreed. "But that's a ten-mile current, and probably deep."

I waded out some twenty feet and was nearly swept beneath the surface as the water circled about my shoulders.

"We couldn't follow that on our feet," I declared, returning to the shore. "But it does look promising. At ten miles an hour we'd reach the western slope in four hours. Four hours to sunshine—but it might as well be four hundred. It's impossible."

We turned then and retraced our steps to our camp, if I may give it so dignified a title. I hated to give up the idea of following the bed of the stream, for it was certain that somewhere it found the surface of the earth, and I revolved in my brain every conceivable means to do so. The same thought was in Harry's mind, for he turned to me suddenly:

"If we only had something for stringers, I could make a raft that would carry us to the Pacific and across it. The hide of that thing over yonder would be just the stuff, and we could get a piece as big as we wanted."

I shook my head.

"I thought of that. But we have absolutely nothing to hold it. There wasn't a bone in his body; you know that."

But the idea was peculiarly tempting, and we spent an hour discussing it. Desirée was asleep on her pile of skins.

We sat side by side on the ground some distance away, talking in low tones.

Suddenly there was a loud splash in the stream, which was quite close to us.

"By gad!" exclaimed Harry, springing to his feet. "Did you hear that? It sounded like—remember the fish we pulled in from the Inca's raft?"

"Which has nothing to do with this," I answered. "It's nothing but the water-pigs. I've heard 'em a thousand times in the last few days. And the Lord knows we have enough of *them.*"

But Harry protested that the splash was much too loud to have been caused by any water-pig and waded into the stream to investigate. I rose to my feet and followed him leisurely, for no reason in particular, but was suddenly startled by an excited cry from his lips:

"Paul—the spear! Quick! It's a whale!"

I ran as swiftly as I could to the shore and returned with our spears, but when I reached Harry he greeted me with an oath of disappointment and the information that the "whale" had disappeared. He was greatly excited.

"I tell you he was twenty feet long! A big black devil, with a head like a cow."

"You're sure it wasn't like a pig?" I asked skeptically.

Harry looked at me.

"I have drunk nothing but water for a month," he said dryly. "It was a fish, and *some* fish."

"Well, there's probably more like him," I observed. "But they can wait. Come on and get some sleep, and then—we'll see."

Some hours afterward, having filled ourselves with sleep and food (I had decided, after mature deliberation, not to change my hotel), we started out, armed with our spears. Desirée accompanied us. Harry told her bluntly that she would be in the way, but she refused to stay behind.

We turned up-stream, thinking our chances better in that direction than toward the swifter current, and were surprised to find that the cavern was much larger than any we had before seen. In something over a mile we had not yet reached the farther wall, for we walked at a brisk pace for a quarter of an hour or more.

At this point the stream was considerably wider than it was below, and there was very little current. Desirée stood on the bank while Harry and I waded out above our waists.

There was a long and weary wait before anything occurred. The water was cold, and my limbs became stiff and numb; I called to Harry that it was useless to wait longer, and was turning toward the shore when there was a sudden commotion in the water not far from where he stood.

I turned and saw Harry plunge forward with his spear.

"I've got him!" he yelled. "Come on!"

I went. But I soon saw that Harry didn't have him. He had Harry. They were all of ten yards away from me, and by the time I reached the spot there was nothing to be seen but flying water thrashed into foam and fury.

I caught a glimpse of Harry being jerked through the air; he was holding on for dear life with both hands to the shaft of his spear. The water was over my head there; I was swimming with all the strength I had.

"I've got him—through the belly," Harry gasped as I fought my way through the spray to his side. "His head! Find his head!"

I finally succeeded in getting my hand on Harry's spear-shaft near where it entered the body of the fish; but the next instant it was jerked from me, dragging me beneath the surface. I came up puffing and made another try, but missed it by several feet.

Harry kept shouting: "His head! Get him in the head!"

For that I was saving my spear. But I could make nothing of either head or tail as the immense fish leaped furiously about in the water, first this way, then that.

Once he came down exactly on top of me and carried me far under; I felt his slippery, smooth body glide over me, and the tail struck me a heavy blow in the face as it passed. Blinded and half choked, I fought my way back to the surface and saw that they had got fifty feet away.

I swam to them, breathing hard and nearly exhausted. The water foamed less furiously about them now. As I came near the fish leaped half out of the water and came down flat on his side; I saw his ugly black head pointed directly toward me.

"He's about gone!" Harry gasped.

He was still clinging to the spear.

I set myself firmly against the water and waited. Soon it parted violently not ten feet in front of me, and again the head appeared; he was coming straight for me. I could see the dull beady eyes on either side, and I let him have the spear right between them.

There was little force to the blow, but the fish himself furnished that; he was coming like lightning. I hurled my body aside with a great effort and felt him sweep past me.

I turned to swim after them and heard Harry's great shout: "You got him!"

By the time I reached him the fish had turned over on his back and was floating on the surface, motionless.

We had still to get him ashore, and, exhausted as we were, it was no easy task. But there was very little current, and after half an hour of pulling and shoving we got him into shallow water, where we could find the bottom with our feet. Then it was easier. Desirée waded out to us and lent a hand, and in another ten minutes we had him high and dry on the rock.

He was even larger than I had thought. No wonder Harry had called him—or one like him—a whale. It was all of fifteen feet from his snout to the tip of his tail. The skin was dead black on top and mottled irregularly on the belly.

As we sat sharpening the points of our spears on the rock, preparatory to skinning him, Desirée stood regarding the fish with unqualified approval. She turned to us:

"Well, I'd rather eat that than those other nasty things."

"Oh, that isn't what we want him for," said Harry, rubbing his finger against the edge of his spear-point. "He's probably not fit to eat."

"Then why all this trouble?" asked Desirée.

"Dear lady, we expect to ride him home," said Harry, rising to his feet.

Then he explained our purpose, and you may believe that Desirée was the most excited of the lot as we ripped down the body of the fish from tail to snout and began to peel off the tough skin.

"If you succeed you may choose the new hangings for my boudoir," she said, with an attempt at lightness not altogether successful.

"As for me," I declared, "I shall eat fish every day of my life out of pure gratitude."

"You'll do it out of pure necessity," Harry put in, "if you don't get busy."

It took us three hours of whacking and slashing and tearing to pull the fish to pieces, but we worked with a purpose and a will. When we had finished, this is what we had to show: A long strip of bone, four inches thick and twelve feet long, and tough as hickory, from either side of which the smaller bones projected at right angles. They were about an inch in thickness and two inches apart. The lower end of the backbone, near the tail, we had broken off.

We examined it and lifted it and bent it half double.

"Absolutely perfect!" Harry cried in jubilation. "Three more like this and we'll sail down the coast to Callao."

"If we can get 'em," I observed. "But two would do. We could make it a triangle."

Harry looked at me.

"Paul, you're an absolute genius. But would it be big enough to hold us?"

We discussed that question on our way back to camp, whither we carried the backbone of our fish, together with some of the meat. Then, after a hearty meal, we slept. After seven hours of the hardest kind of work we were ready for it.

That was our program for the time that followed—time that stretched into many weary hours, for, once started, we worked feverishly, so impatient had we become by dint of that faint glimmer of hope. We were going to try to build a raft, on which we were going to try to embark on the stream, by which we were going to try to find our way out of the mountain. The prospect made us positively hilarious, so slender is the thread by which hope jerks us about.

The first part of our task was the most strenuous. We waited and waded round many hours before another fish appeared, and then he got away from us. Another attempt was crowned with success after a hard fight. The second one was even larger than the first.

The next two were too small to be of use in the raft, but we saved them for another purpose. Then, after another long search, lasting many hours, we ran into half a dozen of them at once.

By that time we were fairly expert with our spears, besides having discovered their vulnerable spot—the throat, just forward from the gills. To this day I don't know whether or not they were man-eaters. Their jaws were roomy and strong as those of any shark; but they never closed on us.

Thus we had four of the large backbones and two smaller ones. Next we wanted a covering, and for that purpose we visited the remains of the reptile which had first led us into the cavern.

Its hide was half an inch thick and tough as the toughest leather. There was no difficulty in loosening it, for by that time the flesh was so decayed and sunken that it literally fell off. That job was the worst of all.

Time and again, after cutting away with the points of our spears—our only tools—until we could stand it no longer, we staggered off to the stream like drunken men, sick and faint with the sight and smell of the mess.

But that, too, came to an end, and finally we marched off to the camp, which we had removed a half-mile upstream, dragging after us a piece of the hide about thirty feet long and half as wide. It was not as heavy as we had thought, which made it all the better for our purpose.

The remainder of our task, though tedious, was not unpleasant.

We first made the larger bones, which were to serve as the beams of our raft, exactly the same length by filing off the ends of the longer ones with rough bits of granite. I have said it was tedious. Then we filed off each of the smaller bones projecting from the neural arch until they were of equal length.

They extended on either side about ten inches, which, allowing four inches for the width of the larger bone and one inch for the covering, would make our raft slightly over a foot in depth.

To make the cylindrical column rigid, we bound each of the vertebræ to the one in direct juxtaposition on either side firmly with strips of hide, several hundred feet of which we had prepared.

This gave us four beams held straight and true, without any play in either direction, with only a slight flexibility resulting from the cartilages within the center cord.

With these four beams we formed a square, placing them on their edges, end to end. At each corner of the square we lashed the ends together firmly with strips of hide. It was both firm and flexible after we had lashed the corners over and over with the strips, that there might be no play under the strain of the current.

Over this framework we stretched the large piece of hide so that the ends met on top, near the middle. The bottom was thus absolutely water-tight. We folded the corners in and caught them up with strips over the top. Then, with longer strips, we fastened up the sides, passing the strips back and forth across the top, from side to side, having first similarly secured the two ends. As a final precaution, we passed broader strips around both top and bottom, lashing them together in the center of the top. And there was our raft, twelve feet square, over a foot deep, water-tight as a town drunkard, and weighing not more than a hundred pounds. It has taken me two minutes to tell it; it took us two weeks to do it.

But we discovered immediately that the four beams on the sides and ends were not enough, for Desirée's weight alone caused the skin to sag clear through in the center, though we had stretched it as tightly as possible. We were forced to unlash all the strips running from side to side and insert supports, made of smaller bones, across the middle each way. These we reinforced on their ends with the thickest hide we could find, that they might not puncture the bottom. After that it was fairly firm; though its sea-worthiness was not improved, it was much easier to navigate than it would have been before.

For oars we took the lower ends of the backbones of the two smaller fish and covered them with hide. They were about five feet long and quite heavy; but we intended to use them more for the purpose of steering than for propulsion. The current of the stream would attend to that for us.

Near the center of the raft we arranged a pile of the skins of the water-pigs for Desirée; a seat by no means uncomfortable. The strips which ran back and forth across the top afforded a hold as security against the tossing of the craft; but for her feet we arranged two other strips to pass over her ankles what time she rested. This was an extreme precaution, for we did not expect the journey to be a long one.

Finally we loaded on our provisions—about thirty pounds of the meat of the fish and water-pigs, wrapping it securely in two or three of the skins and strapping them firmly to the top.

"And now," said I, testing the strips on the corners for the last time, "all we need is a name for her and a bottle of wine."

"And a homeward-bound pennant," put in Harry.

"The name is easy enough," said Desirée. "I hereby christen her Clarté du Soliel."

"Which means?" asked Harry, whose French came only in spots.

"Sunshine," I told him. "Presumably after the glorious King of the Incas, who calls himself the Child of the Sun. But it's a good name. May Heaven grant that it takes us there!"

"I think we ought to take more grub," said Harry—an observation which he had made not less than fifty times in the preceding fifty minutes. He received no support and grumbled to himself something about the horrible waste of leaving so much behind.

Why it was I don't know, but we were fully persuaded that we were about to say good-by forever to this underground world and its dangers. Somehow, we had coaxed ourselves into the belief that success was certain; it was as though we had seen the sunlight streaming in from the farther end of the arched tunnel into which the stream disappeared. There was an assurance about the words of each that strengthened this feeling in the others, and hope had shut out all thought of failure as we prepared to launch our craft.

It took us some time to get it to the edge of the water, though it was close by, for we handled it with extreme care, that it might not be torn on the rocks. Altogether, with the provisions, it weighed close to one hundred and fifty pounds.

We were by no means sure that the thing would carry us, and when once we had reached the water we forgot caution in our haste to try it. We held it at the edge while Desirée arranged herself on the pile of skins. The spears lay across at her feet, strapped down for security.

Harry stepped across to the farther edge of the raft.

"Ready!" he called, and I shoved off, wading behind. When the water was up to my knees I climbed aboard and picked up my oar.

"By all the nine gods, look at her!" cried Harry in huge delight. "She takes about three inches! Man, she'd carry an army!"

"*Allons!*" cried Desirée, with gay laughter. "*C'est perfection!*"

"Couldn't be better," I agreed; "but watch yourself, Hal. When we get into the current things are going to begin to happen. If it weren't for the beastly darkness 'twould be easy enough. As it is, one little rock the size of your head could send us to the bottom."

We were still near the bank, working our way out slowly. Harry and I had to maintain positions equidistant from the center in order to keep the raft balanced; hence I had to push her out alone.

Considering her bulk, she answered to the oar very well.

Another five minutes and we were near the middle of the stream. At that point there was but little current and we drifted slowly. Harry went to the bow, while I took up a position on the stern—if I may use such terms for such a craft—directly behind Desirée. We figured that we were then about a mile from the point where the stream left the cavern.

Gradually, as the stream narrowed, the strength of the current increased. Still it was smooth, and the raft sailed along without a tremor. Once or twice, caught by some trick of the current, she turned half round, poking her nose ahead, but she soon righted herself.

The water began to curl up on the sides as we were carried more and more swiftly onward, with a low murmur that was music to us. The stream became so narrow that we could see the bank on either side, though dimly, and I knew we were aproaching the exit.

I called to Harry: "Keep her off to the right as we make the turn!" and he answered: "Aye, aye, sir!" with a wave of the hand. This, at least, was action with a purpose.

Another minute and we saw the arch directly ahead of us, round a bend in the stream. The strength of the current carried us toward the off bank, but we plied our oars desperately and well, and managed to keep fairly well in to the end of the curve.

We missed the wall of the tunnel—black, grim rock that would have dashed out our brains—by about ten feet, and were swept forward under the arch, on our way—so we thought—to the land of sunshine.

Chapter XX.

AN INCA SPEAR.

Here I might most appropriately insert a paragraph on the vanity of human wishes and endeavor. But events, they say, speak for themselves; and still, for my own part, I prefer the philosopher to the historian. Mental digestion is a wearisome task; you are welcome to it.

To the story. As I have said, we missed the wall of the tunnel by a scant ten feet, and we kept on missing it. Once under the arch, our raft developed a most stubborn inclination to bump up against the rocky banks instead of staying properly in the middle of the current, as it should.

First to one side, then to the other, it swung, while Harry and I kept it off with our oars, often missing a collision by inches. But at least the banks were smooth and level, and as long as the stream itself remained clear of obstruction there was but little real danger.

The current was not nearly so swift as I had expected it would be. In the semidarkness it was difficult to calculate our rate of speed, but I judged that we were moving at about six or seven miles an hour.

We had gone perhaps three miles when we came to a sharp bend in the stream, to the left, almost at a right angle. Harry, at the bow, was supposed to be on the lookout, but he failed to see it until we were already caught in its whirl.

Then he gave a cry of alarm, and together we swung the raft to the left, avoiding the right bank of the curve by less than a foot. Once safely past, I sent Harry to the stern and took the bow myself, which brought down upon him a deal of keen banter from Desirée.

There the tunnel widened, and the raft began to glide easily onward, without any of its sudden dashes to right or left. I rested on my oar, gazing intently ahead; at the best I could make out the walls a hundred yards ahead, and but dimly. All was silence, save the gentle swish of the water

227

against the sides of the raft and the patter of Harry's oar dipping idly on one side or the other.

Suddenly Desirée's voice came through the silence, soft and very low:

> *"Pendant une anne' toute entiere,*
> *Le regiment n'a pas r'paru.*
> *Au Ministere de la Guerre*
> *On le r'porta comme perdu.*

> *"On se r'noncait a r'trouver sa trace,*
> *Quand un matin subitement,*
> *On le vit r'paraitre sur la place,*
> *L'Colonel toujours en avant."*

I waited until the last note had died away in the darkness.

"Are those your thoughts?" I asked then, half turning.

"No," said Desirée, "but I want to kill my thoughts. As for them—"

She hesitated, and after a short pause her voice again broke into melody:

> "Fresh as the first beam glittering on a sail
> That brings our friends up from the underworld;
> Sad as the last which reddens over one
> That sinks with all we love below the verge;
> So sad, so fresh, the days that are no more."

Her voice, subdued and low, breathed a sweetness that seemed almost to be of another world. My ear quivered with the vibrations, and long after she was silent the last mellow note floated through my brain.

Suddenly I became conscious of another sound, scarcely less musical. It, too, was low; so low and faint that at first I thought my ear deceived me, or that some distant echo was returning Desirée's song down the dark tunnel.

Gradually, very gradually, it became louder and clearer,

until at length I recognized it. It was the rush of water, unbroken, still low and at a great distance. I turned to remark on it to Harry, but Desirée took the words from my mouth.

"I seem to hear something—like the surf," she said. "That isn't possible, is it?"

I could have smiled but for the deep note of hope in her voice.

"Hardly," I answered. "I have heard it for several minutes. It is probably some shallows. We must look sharp."

Another fifteen minutes, and I began to notice that the speed of the current was increasing. The sound of the rushing water, too, was quite distinct. Still the raft moved more and more swiftly, till I began to feel alarmed. I turned to Harry:

"That begins to sound like rapids. See that the spears are fastened securely, and stand ready with your oar. Sit tight, Desirée."

One thing was certain: there was nothing to do but go ahead. On both sides the walls of the tunnel rose straight up from the surface of the water; there was nowhere room for a landing-place—not even a foot for a purchase to stay our flight. To go back was impossible; at the rate the current was now carrying us we could not have held the raft even for a moment without oars.

Soon we were gliding forward so swiftly that the raft trembled under us; from the darkness ahead came the sound of the rapids, now increased to a roar that filled the tunnel and deafened us. I heard Harry shouting something, but could not make out the words; we were shooting forward with the speed of an express train and the air about us was full of flying water.

The roar of the rapids became louder and louder. I turned for an instant, shouting at the top of my voice: "Flat on your faces, and hold on for dear life!" Then I dropped down with my oar under me, passing my feet under two of the straps and clinging to two others with my hands.

Another few seconds passed that seemed an hour. The

raft was swaying and lurching with the mad force of the current. I called out again to Harry and Desirée, but my words were completely drowned by the deafening, stunning roar of the water. All was darkness and confusion. I kept asking myself: "Why doesn't it come?" It seemed an age since I had thrown myself on my face.

Suddenly the raft leaped up under me and away. It seemed as though some giant hand had grasped it from beneath and jerked it down with tremendous force. The air was filled with water, lashing my face and body furiously. The raft whirled about like a cork. I gripped the straps with all the strength that was in me. Down, down we went into the darkness; my breath was gone and my brain whirled dizzily.

There was a sudden sharp lurch, a jerk upward, and I felt the surface of the water close over me. Blinded and dazed, I clung to my hold desperately, struggling with the instinct to free myself. For several seconds the roar of the cataract sounded in my ears with a furious faintness, as though it were at a great distance; then I felt the air again and a sudden cessation of motion.

I opened my eyes, choking and sputtering. For a time I could see nothing; then I made out Desirée's form, and Harry's, stretched behind me on the raft. At the same instant Harry's voice came:

"Paul! Ah, Desirée!"

In another moment we were at her side. Her hands held to the straps on each side with a grip as of death; we had to pry off each of her fingers separately to loosen them. Then we bent her over Harry's knee and worked her arms up and down, and soon her chest heaved convulsively and her lungs freed themselves of the water they had taken. Presently she turned about; her eyes opened and she pressed her hands to her head.

"Don't say 'Where am I?'" said Harry, "because we don't know. How do you feel?"

"I don't know," she answered, still gasping for breath. "What was it? What did we do?"

I left them then, turning to survey the extent of our damage. There was absolutely none; we were as intact as when we started. The provisions and spears remained under their straps; my oar lay where I had fallen on it. The raft appeared to be floating easily as before, without a scratch.

The water about us was churned into foam, though we had already been carried so far from the cataract that it was lost behind us in the darkness; only its roar reached our ears. To this day I haven't the faintest idea of its height; it may have been ten feet or two hundred. Harry says a thousand.

We were moving slowly along on the surface of what appeared to be a lake, still carried forward by the force of the falls behind us. For my part, I found its roar bewildering and confusing, and I picked up my oar and commenced to paddle away from it; at least, so I judged.

Harry's voice came from behind:

"In the name of goodness, where did you get that oar?"

I turned.

"Young man, a good sailor never loses an oar. How do you feel, Desirée?"

"Like a drowned rat," she answered, but with a laugh in her voice. "I'm faint and sick and wet, and my throat is ready to burst, but I wouldn't have missed that for anything. It was glorious! I'd like to do it again."

"Yes, you would," said Harry skeptically. "You're welcome, thank you. But what I want to know is, where did that oar come from?"

I explained that I had taken the precaution to fall on it.

"Do you never lose your head?" asked Desirée.

"No, merely my heart."

"Oh, as for that," she retorted, with a lightness that still had a sting, "my good friend, you never had any."

Whereupon I returned to my paddling in haste.

Soon I discovered that though, as I have said, we appeared to be in a lake—for I could see no bank on either side—there was still a current. We drifted slowly, but our movement was plainly perceptible, and I rested on my oar.

Presently a wall loomed up ahead of us and I saw that the stream again narrowed down as it entered the tunnel, much lower than the one above the cataract. The current became swifter as we were carried toward its mouth, and I called to Harry to get his spear to keep us off from the walls if it should prove necessary. But we entered exactly in the center and were swept forward with a rush.

The ceiling of the tunnel was so low that we could not stand upright on the raft, and the stream was not more than forty feet wide. That was anything but promising; if the stream really ran through to the western slope, its volume of water should have been increasing instead of diminishing. I said nothing of that to Harry or Desirée.

We had sailed along thus without incident for upward of half an hour, when my carelessness, or the darkness, nearly brought us to grief. Suddenly, without warning, there was a violent jar and the raft rebounded with a force that all but threw us into the water. Coming to a bend in the stream, the current had dashed us against the other bank.

But, owing to the flexibility of its sides, the raft escaped damage. I had my oar against the wall instantly, shoving off, and we swung round and caught the current again round the curve.

But that bend was to the left, as the other had been, which meant that we were now going in exactly the opposite direction of that in which we had started! Which, in turn, meant the death of hope; we were merely winding in and out in a circle and getting nowhere. Harry and Desirée had apparently not noticed the fact, and I said nothing of it. Time enough when they should find out for themselves; and besides, there was still a chance, though a slim one.

Soon the bed of the stream became nearly level, for we barely moved. The roof of the tunnel was very low—but a scant foot above our heads as we sat or crouched on the raft. It was necessary to keep a sharp lookout ahead; a rock projecting from above would have swept us into the water.

The air, too, was close and foul; our breath became labored and difficult; and Desirée, half stifled and drowsy, passed into a fitful and broken sleep, stirring restlessly and panting for air. Harry had taken the bow and I lay across the stern. Suddenly his voice came, announcing that we had left the tunnel.

I sat up quickly and looked round. The walls were no longer to be seen; we had evidently entered a cavern similar to the one in which we had embarked.

"Shall we lay off?" I asked, stepping across to Harry's side.

He assented, and I took the oar and worked the raft over to the left. There was but little current and she went well in. In a few minutes we were in shallow water, and Harry and I jumped off and shoved her to the bank.

Desirée sat up, rubbing her eyes.

"Where are we?" she asked.

Harry explained while we beached the raft. Then we broke out our provisions and partook of them.

"But why do we stop?" asked Desirée.

The words "Because we are not getting anywhere" rose to my lips, but I kept them back.

"For a rest and some air," I answered.

Desirée exclaimed: "But I want to go on!"

So as soon as we had eaten our fill we loaded the stuff again and prepared to shove off. By that time I think Harry, too, had realized the hopelessness of our expedition, for he had lost all his enthusiasm; but he said nothing, nor did I. We secured Desirée on her pile of skins and again pushed out into the current.

The cavern was not large, for we had been under way but a few minutes when its wall loomed up ahead and the stream again entered a tunnel, so low and narrow that I hesitated about entering at all. I consulted Harry.

"Take a chance," he advised. "Why not? As well that as anything."

We slipped through the entrance.

The current was extremely sluggish, and we barely seemed to move. Still we went forward.

"If we only had a little speed we could stand it," Harry grumbled.

Which shows that a man does not always appreciate a blessing. It was not long before we were offering up thanks that our speed had been so slight.

To be exact, about an hour, as well as I could measure time, which passed slowly; for not only were the minutes tedious, but the foulness of the air made them also extremely uncomfortable. Desirée was again lying down, half-unconscious but not asleep, for now and then she spoke drowsily. Harry complained of a dizziness in the head, and my own seemed ready to burst through my temples. The *soroche* of the mountains was agreeable compared to that.

Suddenly the swiftness of the current increased appreciably on the instant; there was a swift jerk as we were carried forward. I rose to my knees—the tunnel was too low to permit of standing—and gazed intently ahead. I could see nothing save that the stream had narrowed to half its former width, and was still becoming narrower.

We went faster and faster, and the stream narrowed until the bank was but a few feet away on either side.

"Watch the stern!" I called to Harry. "Keep her off with your spear!"

Then a wall loomed up directly ahead. I thought it meant another bend in the stream, and I strained my eyes intently in the effort to discover its direction, but I could see nothing save the black wall. We approached closer; I shouted to Harry and Desirée to brace themselves for a shock, praying that the raft would meet the rock squarely and not on a corner.

I had barely had time to set myself and grasp the straps behind when we struck with terrific force. The raft rebounded several feet, trembling and shaking violently. The water was rushing past us with noisy impetuosity.

There was a cry from Desirée, and from Harry, "All

right!" I crawled to the bow. Along the top the hide covering had been split open for several feet, but the water did not quite reach the opening.

And we had reached the end of our ambitious journey. For that black wall marked the finish of the tunnel; the stream entered it through a narrow hole, which accounted for the sudden, swift rush of the current. Above the upper rim of the hole the surface of the water whirled about in a widening circle; to this had we been led by the stream that was to have carried us to the land of sunshine.

When I told Desirée she stared at me in silence! I had not realized before the strength of her hope. Speechless with disappointment, she merely sat and stared straight ahead at the black, unyielding rock. Harry knelt beside her with his arm across her shoulders.

I roused him with a jerk of the arm.

"Come—get busy! A few hours in this hole and we'd suffocate. Do you realize that we've got to pull this raft back against the current?"

First it was necessary to repair the rent in the hide covering. This we did with strips of hide; and barely in time, for it was becoming wider every minute, and the water was beginning to creep in over the edge. But we soon had the ends sewed firmly together and turned our hands to the main task.

It appeared to be not only difficult, but actually impossible to force the raft back up-stream against the swift current. We were jammed against the rock with all the force of many tons of water. The oar was useless.

Getting a purchase on the wall with our hands, we shoved the raft to one side; but as soon as we got to the wall on the left the whirling stream turned us around again, and we found ourselves back in our original position, only with a different side of the raft against the rock. That happened three times.

Then we tried working to the right instead of the left, but with no better success. The force of the current, coming with all its speed against the unwieldy raft, was irresisti-

ble. Time and again we shoved round and started up-
stream, after incredible labor, only to be dashed back again
against the rock.

We tried our spears, but their shafts were so slender that
they were useless. We took the oar and, placing its end
against the wall, shoved with all our strength. The oar
snapped in two and we fell forward against the wall. We
tore off some of the strips of hide from the raft and tried to
fasten them to the wall on either side, but there was no
protuberance that would hold them. Nothing remained to
be done.

Harry and I held a consultation then and agreed on the
only possible means of escape. I turned to Desirée:

"Can you swim?"

"Parfaitement," she replied. "But against that"—pointing
to the whirling water—"I do not know. I can try."

I, who remember the black fury of that stream as it swept
past us, can appreciate the courage of her.

We lost no time, for the foulness of the air was weakening
us with every breath we took. Our preparations were few.

The two spears and about half of the provisions we
strapped to our backs—an inconsiderable load which
would hamper us but little. We discarded all our clothing,
which was very little. I took the heavy skin which Desirée
had worn and began to strap it also on top of my bundle, but
she refused to allow it.

"I will not permit you to be handicapped with my
modesty," she observed.

Then, with Desirée between us, we stepped to the edge
of the raft and dived off together.

Driven as we were by necessity, we would have hesitated
longer if we had known the full force of the undercurrent
that seized us from beneath. Desirée would have disappeared without a struggle if it had not been for the support
which Harry and I rendered her on either side.

But we kept on top—most of the time—and fought our
way forward by inches. The black walls frowning at us from
either side appeared to me to remain exactly the same,

stationary, after a long and desperate struggle; but when I gave a quick glance behind I saw that we had pulled so far away from the raft that it was no longer in sight. That gave me renewed strength, and, shouting assurance to Harry and Desirée, I redoubled my efforts. Desirée was by now almost able to hold her own, but we still supported her.

Every stroke made the next one easier, carrying us away from the whirlpool, and soon we swam smoothly. Less and less strong became the resistance of the current, until finally it was possible to float easily on our backs and rest.

"How far is it to the cavern?" Harry panted.

"Somewhere between one and ten miles," was my answer. "How the deuce should I know? But we'll make it now, I think. Can you hold out, Desirée?"

"Easily," she answered. "If only I could get some air! Just one good, long breath."

There was the danger, and on that account no time was to be lost. Again we struck out into the blackness ahead. I felt myself no longer fresh, and began to doubt seriously if we should reach out goal.

But we reached it. No need to recount our struggles, which toward the end were inspired by suffering amounting to agony as we choked and gasped for sufficient air to keep us up.

Another hundred yards would have been too much for us; but it is enough that finally we staggered onto the bank at the entrance to the cavern in which we had previously rested, panting, dizzy, and completely exhausted.

But an hour in the cavern, with its supply of air, revived us; and then we sat up and asked ourselves: "What for?"

"And all that brings us—to this," said Harry, with a sweeping gesture round the cavern.

"At least, it is a better tomb," I retorted. "And it was a good fight. We still have something in us. Desirée, a good man was lost in you."

Harry rose to his feet.

"I'm going to look round," he announced. "We've got to do something. Gad, and it took us a month to build that raft!"

"The vanity of human endeavor," said I, loosening the strap round my shoulders and dropping my bundle to the ground. "Wait a minute; I'm going with you. Are you coming, Desirée?"

But she was too tired to rise to her feet, and we left her behind, arranging what few skins we had as well as possible to protect her from the hard rock.

"Rest your weary bones," said Harry, stooping to kiss her. "There's meat here if you want it. We'll be back soon."

So we left her, with her white body stretched out at its full length on the rude mat.

Bearing off to the left, we soon discovered that we would have no difficulty to leave the cavern; we had only to choose our way. There was scarcely any wall at all, so broken was it by lanes and passages leading in all directions.

We followed some of them for a distance, but found none that gave any particular promise. Most of them were choked with rocks and boulders through which it was difficult to force a passage. We spent an hour or more in these futile explorations, then followed the wall some distance to the right.

Gradually the exits became less numerous. High on a boulder near the entrance of one we saw the head of some animal peering down at us. We hurled our spears at it, but missed; then were forced to climb up the steep side of the boulder to recover our weapons.

"We'd better go back to Desirée," said Harry when we reached the ground again. "She'll wonder what's become of us. We've been gone nearly two hours."

After fifteen minutes' search we found the stream, and followed it to the left. We had gone farther than we thought, and we were looking for the end, where we had left Desirée, long before we reached it. Several times we called her name, but there was no answer.

"She's probably asleep," said Harry. And a minute later: "There's the wall at last! But where is she?"

My foot struck something on the ground, and I stooped over to examine it.

It was the pile of skins on which Desirée had lain!

I called to Harry, and at the same instant heard his shout of consternation as he came running toward me, holding something in his hand.

"They've got her! Look! Look at this! I found it on the ground over there."

He held the thing in his hand out before me.

It was an Inca spear.

Chapter XXI.

THE MIDST OF THE ENEMY.

Harry and I stood gazing at each other blankly in the semidarkness of the cavern.

"But it isn't possible," I objected finally to my own thoughts. "She would have cried out and we would have heard her. The spear may have been there before."

Then I raised my voice, calling her name many times at the top of my lungs. There was no answer.

"They've got her," said Harry, "and that's all there is to it. The cursed brutes crept up on her in the dark—much chance she had of crying out when they got their hands on her. I know it. Why did we leave her?"

"Where did you find the spear?" I asked.

Harry pointed toward the wall, away from the stream.

"On the ground?"

"Yes."

"Is there an exit from the cavern on that side?"

"I don't know."

"Well, that's our only chance. Come on!"

We found the exit, and another, and a third. Which to take? They were very similar to one another, except that the one in the middle sloped upward at a gentle incline, while the others were level.

"One is as good as another," I observed, and entered the one on the left.

Once started, we advanced with a rush. The passage was straight and narrow, clear of obstruction, and we kept at a steady run.

"They may have an hour's start of us," came Harry's voice at my side.

"Or five minutes," I returned. "We have no way of knowing. But I'm afraid we're on the wrong trail."

Still as I had said, one chance was as good as another, and we did not slacken our pace. The passage went straight forward, without a bend. The roof was low, just allowing us

241

to pass without stooping, and the walls were rough and rugged.

It was not long before we found that we had taken the wrong chance, having covered, I think, some two or three miles when a wall loomed up directly in our path.

"At last, a turn!" panted Harry.

But it was not a turn. It was the end of the passage. We had been following a blind alley.

Harry let out a string of oaths, and I seconded him. Twenty minutes wasted, and another twenty to return!

There was nothing else for it. We shouldered our spears and started to retrace our steps.

"No use running now," I declared. "We can't keep it up forever, and we may as well save our strength. We'll never catch up with 'em, but we may find 'em."

Harry, striding ahead two or three paces in front, did not answer.

Finally we reached the cavern from which we had started.

"And now what?" asked Harry in a tone of the most utter dejection.

I pointed to the exit in the middle. "That! We should have taken it in the first place. On the raft we probably descended altogether something like five hundred feet from the level where we started—possibly twice that distance. And this passage which slopes upward will probably take us back."

"At least, it's as good as the other," Harry agreed; and we entered it.

We had not proceeded far before we found ourselves in difficulties. The gentle slope became a steep incline. Great rocks loomed up in our path.

In spots the passage was so narrow that two men could hardly have walked abreast through it, and its walls were rough and irregular, with sharp points projecting unexpectedly into our very faces.

Still we went forward and upward, scrambling over, under, round, between. At one point, when Harry was a few yards in front of me, he suddenly disappeared from sight as though swallowed by the mountain.

Rushing forward, I saw him scrambling to his feet at the bottom of a chasm some ten feet below. Luckily he had escaped serius injury, and climbed up on the other side, while I leaped across—a distance of about six feet.

"They could never have brought her through this," he declared, rubbing a bruised knee.

"Do you want to go back?' I asked.

But he said that would be useless, and I agreed with him. So we struggled onward, painfully and laboriously. The sharp corners of the rocks cut our feet and hands, and I had an ugly bruise on my left shoulder, besides many lesser ones. Harry's injured knee caused him to limp and thus further retarded our progress.

At times the passage broadened out until the wall on either side was barely visible, only to narrow down again till it was scarcely more than a crevice between the giant boulders. The variation of the incline was no less, being at times very nearly level, and at others mounting upward at an angle whose ascent was all but impossible. Somehow we crawled up, like flies on a wall.

When we came to a stream of water rushing directly across our path at the foot of a towering rock Harry gave a cry of joy and ran forward. I had not known until then how badly his knee was hurt, and when I came up to where he was bathing it in the stream and saw how black and swollen it was, I insisted that he give it a rest. But he absolutely refused, and after we had quenched our thirst and gotten an easy breath or two we struggled to our feet and on.

After another hour of scrambling and falling and hanging on by our finger nails, the way began to be easier. We came to level, clear stretches with only an occasional boulder or ravine, and the rock became less cruel to our bleeding feet. The relief came almost too late, for by that time every movement was painful, and we made but slow progress.

Soon we faced another difficulty when we came to a point

where a split in the passage showed a lane on either side. One led straight ahead; the other branched off to the right. They were very similar, but somehow the one on the right looked more promising to us, and we took it.

We had followed this but a short distance when it broadened out to such an extent that the walls on either side could be seen but dimly. It still sloped upward, but at a very slight angle, and we had little difficulty in making our way. Another half-hour and it narrowed down again to a mere lane.

We were proceeding at a fairly rapid gait, keeping our eyes strained ahead, when there appeared an opening in the right wall at a distance of a hundred feet or so. Not having seen or heard anything to recommend caution, we advanced without slackening our pace until we had reached it.

I said aloud to Harry, "Probably a cross-passage," and then jerked him back quickly against the opposite wall as I saw the real nature of the opening.

It led to a small room, with a low ceiling and rough walls, dark as the passage in which we stood, for it contained no light.

We could see its interior dimly, but well enough to discover the form of an Inca standing just within the doorway. His back was toward us, and he appeared to be fastening something to the ceiling with strips of hide.

It was evident that we had not been seen, and I started to move on, grasping Harry's arm. It was then that I became aware of the fact that the wall leading away in front of us—that is, the one on the right—was marked as far as the eye could reach with a succession of similar openings.

They were quite close together; from where we stood I could see thirty or forty of them. I guessed that they, too, led to rooms similar to the one in front of us, probably likewise occupied; but it was necessary to go on in spite of the danger, and I pulled again at Harry's arm.

Then, seeing by his face that something had happened, I turned my eyes again on the Inca in the room. He had turned about, squarely facing us. As we stood motionless he took a hasty step forward; we had been discovered.

There was but one thing to do, and we didn't hesitate about doing it. We leaped forward together, crossing the intervening space in a single bound, and bore the Inca to the floor under us.

My fingers were round his throat, Harry sat on him. In a trice we had him securely bound and gagged, using some strips of hide which we found suspended from the ceiling.

"By gad!" exclaimed Harry in a whisper. "Look at him! He's a woman!"

It was quite evident—disgustingly so. Her eyes, dull and sunken, appeared as two large, black holes set back in her skull. Her hair, matted about her forehead and shoulders, was thick and coarse, and blacker than night. Her body was innocent of any attempt at covering.

Altogether, not a very pleasant sight; and we bundled her into a corner and proceeded to look round the room, being careful to remain out of the range of view from the corridor as far as possible.

The room was not luxuriously furnished. There were two seats of stone, and a couch of the same material covered with thick hides. In one corner was a pile of copper vessels; in another two or three of stone, rudely carved. Some torn hides lay in a heap near the center of the room. From the ceiling were suspended other hides and some strips of dried fish.

Some of the latter we cut down with the points of our spears and retired with it to a corner.

"Ought we to ask our hostess to join us?" Harry grinned.

"This tastes good, after the other," I remarked.

Hungry as we were, we made sad havoc with the lady's pantry. Then we found some water in a basin in the corner and drank—not without misgivings. But we were too thirsty to be particular.

Then Harry became impatient to go on, and though I had no liking for the appearance of that long row of open doorways, I did not demur. Taking up our spears, we stepped out into the corridor and turned to the right.

We found ourselves running a gantlet wherein discovery seemed certain. The right wall was one unbroken series of open doorways, and in each of the rooms, whose interiors we could plainly see, were one or more of the Inca Women; and sometimes children rolled about on the stony floor.

In one of them a man stood; I could have sworn that he was gazing straight at us, and I gathered myself together for a spring; but he made no movement of any kind and we passed swiftly by.

Once a little black ball of flesh—a boy it was, perhaps five or six years old—tumbled out into the corridor under our very feet. We strode over him and went swiftly on.

We had passed about a hundred of the open doorways, and were beginning to entertain the hope that we might, after all, get through without being discovered, when Harry suddenly stopped short, pulling at my arm. At the same instant I saw, far down the corridor, a crowd of black forms moving toward us.

Even at that distance something about their appearance and gait told us that they were not women. Their number was so great that as they advanced they filled the passage from wall to wall.

There was but one way to escape certain discovery; and distasteful as it was, we did not hesitate to employ it. In a glance I saw that we were directly opposite an open doorway; with a whispered word to Harry I sprang across the corridor and within the room. He followed.

Inside were a woman and two children. As we entered they looked up, startled, and stood gazing at us in terror. For an instant we held back, but there was nothing else for it; and in another minute we had overpowered and bound and gagged them and carried them to a corner.

The children were ugly little devils and the woman very little above a brute; still we handled them as tenderly as possible. Then we crouched against the wall where we could not be seen from the corridor, and waited.

Soon the patter of many footsteps reached our ears. They passed; others came, and still others. For many minutes the sound continued steadily, unbroken, while we sat huddled up against the wall, scarcely daring to breathe.

Immediately in front of me lay the forms of the woman and the children; I could see their dull eyes, unblinking, looking up at me in abject terror. Still the patter of footsteps sounded from without, with now and then an interval of quiet.

Struck by a sudden thought, I signaled to Harry; and when he had moved further back into his corner I sprang across the room in one bound to his side. A word or two of whispering, and he nodded to show that he understood. We crouched together flat against the wall.

My thought had come just in time, for scarcely another minute had passed when there suddenly appeared in the doorway the form of an Inca. He moved a step inside, and I saw that there was another behind him. I had not counted on two of them! In the arms of each was a great copper vessel, evidently very heavy, for their effort was apparent as they stooped to place the vessels on the ground just within the doorway.

As they straightened up and saw that the room before them was empty, their faces filled with surprise. At the same moment a movement came from the woman in the corner; the two men glanced at them with a start of wonder; and as I had foreseen, they ran across and bent over the prostrate forms.

They next instant they, too, were prone on the floor, with Harry and me on top of them. They did not succumb without a struggle, and the one I had chosen proved nearly too much for me.

The great muscles of his chest and legs strained under me with a power that made me doubtful for a moment of the outcome; but the Incas themselves had taught us how to conquer a man when you attack him from behind, and I grasped his throat with all the strength there was in my fingers.

With a desperate effort he got to his knees and grasped my wrists in his powerful black hands and tore my own grip loose. He was half-way to his feet, and far more powerful than I; I changed my tactics. Wrenching myself loose, I fell back a step; then, as he twisted round to get at me, I lunged forward and let him have my fist squarely between the eyes.

The blow nearly broke my hand, but he dropped to the floor. The next instant I was joined by Harry, who had overcome the other Inca with little difficulty, and in a trice we had them both bound and gagged along with the remainder of the family in the corner.

Owing to my strategy in withholding our attack until the Incas had got well within the room and to one side, we had not been seen by those constantly passing up and down in the corridor without; at least, none of them had entered. We seemed by this stroke to have assured our safety so long as we remained in the room.

But it was still necessary to remain against the wall, for the soft patter of footsteps could still be heard in the corridor.

They now came at irregular intervals, and there were not many of them. Otherwise the silence was unbroken.

"What does it all mean?" Harry whispered.

"The Incas are coming home to their women," I guessed. "Though, after seeing the women, it is little wonder if they spend most of their time away from them. He is welcome to his repose in the bosom of his family."

There passed an uneventful hour. Long before it ended the sound of footsteps had entirely ceased; but we thought it best to take no chances, and waited for the last minute our impatience would allow us. Then, uncomfortable and stiff from the long period of immobility and silence, we rose to our feet and made ready to start.

Harry was for appropriating some of the strips of dried fish we saw suspended from the ceiling, but I objected that our danger lay in any direction other than that of hunger, and we set out with only our spears.

The corridor was deserted. One quick glance in either direction assured us of that; then we turned to the right and set out at a rapid pace, down the long passage past a succession of rooms exactly similar to the one we had just left—scores, hundreds of them.

Each one was occupied by from one to ten of the Incas lying on the couch which each contained, or stretched on hides on the floor. No one was stirring. Everywhere was silence save the patter of our own feet, which we let fall as noiselessly as possible.

"Will it never end?" whispered Harry at length, after we had traversed upward of a mile without any sign of a cross-passage or a termination.

"Forward, and silence!" I breathed for a reply.

The end—at least, of the silence—came sooner than we had expected. Hardly were the last words out of my mouth when a whirring noise sounded behind us. We glanced over our shoulders as we ran, and at the same instant an Inca spear flew by not two inches from my head and struck the ground in front.

Not a hundred feet to the rear we saw a group of Incas rushing along the passage toward us. Harry wheeled about, raising his spear, but I grasped him by the arm, crying, "Run; it's our only chance!" The next moment we were leaping forward side by side down the passage.

It would have fared ill with any who appeared to block our way in that mad dash; but it remained clear. The corridor led straight ahead, with never a turn. We were running as we had never run before; the black walls flashed past us an indistinguishable blur, and the open doorways were blended into one.

Glancing back over my shoulder, I saw that the small group of Incas was no longer small. Away to the rear the corridor was filled with rushing black forms. But I saw plainly that we were gaining on them; the distance that separated us was twice as great as when we had first started to run.

"How about it?" I panted. "Can you hold out?"

"If it weren't for this knee," Harry returned between breaths and through clenched teeth. "But—I'm with you." He was limping painfully, and I slackened my pace a little, but he urged me forward with an oath, and himself sprang to the front. His knee must have been causing him the keenest agony; his face was white as death.

Then I uttered a cry of joy as I saw a bend in the passage ahead. We reached it, and wheeled to the right. There was solid wall on either side; the series of doors was ended.

"We'll shake 'em off now," I panted.

Harry nodded.

A short distance ahead we came to another cross-passage, and turned to the left. Glancing over my shoulder, I saw that our pursuers had not yet reached the first turn. Harry kept in the lead, and was giving me all I could do to keep up with him.

We found ourselves now in a veritable maze of lanes and cross-passages, and we turned to one side or the other at every opportunity. At length I grasped Harry by the arm and stopped him. We stood for two full minutes listening intently. There was absolutely no sound of any kind.

"Thank Heaven!" Harry breathed, and would have fallen to the ground if I had not supported him.

We started out then in search of water, moving slowly and cautiously. But we found none, and soon Harry declared that he could go no further. We sat down with our backs against the wall of the passage, still breathing heavily and all but exhausted.

In that darkness and silence the minutes passed into hours. We talked but little, and then only in whispers. Finally Harry fell into a restless sleep, if it may be called that, and several times I dozed off and was awakened by my head nodding against the stone wall.

At length, finding Harry awake, I urged him to his feet. His knee barely supported his weight, but he gritted his teeth and told me to lead on.

"We can wait—" I began; but he broke in savagely:

"No! I want to find her, that's all—and end it. Just one more chance!"

We searched for an hour before we found the stream of water we sought. After Harry had bathed his knee and drunk his fill he felt more fit, and we pushed on more rapidly, but still quite at random.

We turned first one way, then another, in the never-ending labyrinth, always in darkness and silence. We seemed to get nowhere; and I for one was about to give up the disheartening task when suddenly a sound smote our ears that caused us first to start violently, then stop and gaze at each other in comprehension and eager surprise.

"The bell!" cried Harry. "They are being summoned to the great cavern!"

It was the same sound we had heard twice before; a sound as of a great, deep-toned bell ringing sonorously throughout the passages and caverns with a roar that was deafening, And it seemed to be close—quite close.

"It came from the left," said Harry; but I disagreed with him and was so sure of myself that we started off to the right. The echoes of the bell were still floating from wall to wall as we went rapidly forward. I do not know what we expected to find, and the Lord knows what we intended to do after we found it.

A short distance ahead we came to another passage, crossing at right angles, broad and straight, and somehow familiar. As with one impulse we took it, turning to the left, and then flattened ourselves back against the wall as we saw a group of Incas passing at its farther end, some two hundred yards away.

There we stood, motionless and scarcely breathing, while group after group of the savages passed in the corridor ahead. Their number swelled to a continuous stream, which in turn gradually became thinner and thinner until only a few stragglers were seen trotting behind. Finally they, too, ceased to appear; the corridor was deserted.

We waited a while longer, then as no more appeared we

started forward and soon had reached the corridor down which they had passed. We followed in the direction they had taken, turning to the right.

We had no sooner turned than we saw that which caused us to glance quickly at each other and hasten our step, while I smothered the ejaculation that rose to my lips. The corridor in which we now found ourselves stretched straight ahead for a distance, then turned to one side; and the corner thus formed was flooded with a brilliant blaze of light!

There was no longer any doubt of it: we were on our way to the great cavern. For a moment I hesitated, asking myself for what purpose we hastened on thus into the very arms of our enemies; then, propelled by instinct or premonition—I know not what—I took a firmer grasp on my spear and followed Harry without word, throwing caution to the winds.

Yet we avoided foolhardiness, for as we approached the last turn we proceeded slowly, keeping an eye on the rear. But all the Incas appeared to have assembled within, for the corridor remained deserted.

We crept silently to the corner, avoiding the circle of light as far as possible, and, crouching side by side on the rock, looked out together on a scene none the less striking because we had seen it twice before.

It was the great cavern. We saw it from a different viewpoint than before; the alcove which held the golden throne was far off to our left, nearly half-way round the vast circumference. On the throne was seated the king, surrounded by guards and attendants.

As before, the stone seats which surrounded the amphitheater on every side were filled with the Incas, crouching motionless and silent. The flames in the massive urns mounted in steady tongues, casting their blinding glare in every direction.

All this I saw in a flash, when suddenly Harry's fingers sank into the flesh of my arm with such force that I all but cried out in actual pain. And then, glancing at him and following the direction of his gaze, I saw Desirée.

She was standing on the top of the lofty column in the center of the lake.

Her white body, uncovered, was outlined sharply against the black background of the cavern above.

Chapter XXII.

Neither Harry nor I spoke; our eyes were concentrated on the scene before us, trying to comprehend its meaning.

It was something indefinable in Desirée's attitude that told me the truth—what, I cannot tell. Her profile was toward us; it could not have been her eyes or any expression of her face; but there was a tenseness about her pose, a stiffening of the muscles of her body, an air of lofty scorn and supreme triumph coming somehow from every line of her motionless figure, that flashed certainty into my brain.

And on the instant I turned to Harry.

"Follow me," I whispered; and he must have read the force of my knowledge in my eyes, for he obeyed without a word. Back down the passage we ran, halting at its end. Harry opened his lips to speak, but I took the words from his mouth; seconds were precious.

"They have fired the column—you remember. Follow me; keep your spear ready; not a sound, if you love her."

I saw that he understood, and saw too, by the expression that shot into his face, that it would go ill with any Incas who tried to stop us then.

We rushed forward side by side, guessing at our way, seeking the entrance to the tunnel that led to the foot of the column. A prayer was on my lips that we might not be too late; Harry's lips were compressed together tightly as a vise. Death we did not fear, even for Desirée; but we remembered the horror of our own experience on the top of that column, and shuddered as we ran.

As I have said, we had entered the great cavern at a point almost directly opposite the alcove, and therefore at a distance from the entrance we sought. It was necessary to half encircle the cavern, and the passages were so often crossed by other passages that many times we had to guess at the proper road.

But not for an instant did we hesitate; we flew rather

than ran. I felt within me the strength and resolve of ten men, and I knew then that there was something I must do and would do before I died, though a thousand devils stood in my way.

I do not know what led us; whether a remorseful Providence, who suddenly decided that we had been played with long enough, or the mere animal instinct of direction, or blind luck. But so fast did we go that it seemed to me we had left the great cavern scarcely a minute behind us when I suddenly saw the steps of a steep stairway leading down from an opening on our right.

How my heart leaped then! Harry uttered a hoarse cry of exultation. The next instant we were dashing headlong down the steps, avoiding a fall by I know not what miracle. And there before us was the entrance to the tunnel.

I held Harry back, almost shouting: "You stay here; guard the entrance. I'll get her."

"No," he cried, pushing forward. "I can't stay."

"Fool!" I cried, dashing him back. "We would be caught like rats in a trap. Defend that entrance—with your life!"

I saw him hesitate, and, knowing that he would obey, I dashed forward into the tunnel. When nearly to its end I made a misstep on the uneven ground and precipitated myself against the wall. A sharp pain shot through my left shoulder, but at the time I was scarcely conscious of it as I picked myself up and leaped forward. The end was in sight.

Just as I reached the foot of the spiral stairway I saw a black form descending from it. That Inca never knew what hit him. I did not use my spear; time was too precious. He disappeared in the whirlpool beneath the base of the column through which Harry and I had once miraculously escaped.

But despair filled my heart as, with my feet on the first step of the spiral stairway, I cast a quick glance upward. The upper half of the inside of the column was a raging furnace of fire. How or from what it came I did not stop to inquire; I bounded up the stairway in desperate fury.

I did not know then that the stone steps were baking and

blistering my feet; I did not know, as I came level with the base of the flames, that every hair was being singed from my head and body—I only knew that I must reach the top of the column.

Then I saw the source of the flames as I reached them. Huge vats of oil—six, a dozen, twenty—I know not how many—were ranged in a circle on a ledge of stone encircling the column, and from their tops the fire leaped upward to a great height. I saw what must be done; how I did it God only knows; I shut my eyes now as I remember it.

Hooking the rim of the vat nearest me with the point of my spear, I sent it tumbling down the length of the column into the whirlpool, many feet below. Then another, and another, and another, until the ledge was empty.

Some of the burning oil, flying from the overturned vats, alighted on the stairway, casting weird patches of light up and down the whole length of the column. Some of it landed on my body, my face, my hands. It was a very hell of heat; my lungs, all the inside of me, was on fire.

My brain sang and whirled. My eyes felt as though they were being burned from their sockets with red-hot irons. I bounded upward.

A few more steps—I could not see, I could hardly feel—and my head bumped against the stone at the top of the column. I put out my hand, groping around half crazily, and by some wild chance it came in contact with the slide that moved the stone slab. I pushed, hardly knowing what I did, and the stone flew to one side. I stuck my head through the opening and saw Desirée.

Her back was toward me. As I emerged from the opening the Incas seated round the vast amphitheater and the king, seated on the golden throne in the alcove, rose involuntarily from their seats in astonished wonder.

Desirée saw the movement and, turning, caught sight of me. A sudden cry of amazement burst from her lips; she made a hasty step forward and fell fainting into my arms.

I shook her violently, but she remained unconscious, and this added catastrophe all but unnerved me. For a moment

I stood on the upper step with the upper half of my body, swaying from side to side, extending beyond the top of the column; then I turned and began to descend with Desirée in my arms.

Every step of that descent was unspeakable agony. Feeling was hardly in me; my whole body was an engine of pain. Somehow, I staggered and stumbled downward; at every step I expected to fall headlong to the bottom with my burden. Desirée's form remained limp and lifeless in my arms.

I reached the ledge on which the vats had been placed and passed it; air entered my burning lungs like a breeze from the mountains. Every step now made the next one easier. I began to think that I might, after all, reach the bottom in safety. Another twenty steps and I could see the beginning of the tunnel below.

Desirée's form stirred slightly in my arms. A glance showed me her eyes looking up into mine as her head lay back on my shoulder.

"Why?" she moaned. "In the name of Heaven above us, why?" I had no time for answer; my lips were locked tightly together as I sought the step below with a foot that had no feeling even for the stone. We were nearly to the bottom; we reached it.

I placed Desirée on her feet.

"Can you stand?" I gasped; and the words were torn from my throat with a great effort.

"But you!' she cried, and I saw that her eyes were filled with horror. No doubt I was a pitiful thing to look at.

But there was no time to be lost, and, seeing that her feet supported her, I grasped her arm and started down the tunnel just as Harry's voice, raised in a great shout, came to us from its farther end.

"No!" cried Desirée, shrinking back in terror. "Paul—" I dragged her forward.

Then, as Harry's cry was repeated, she seemed to understand and sprang forward beside me.

Another second wasted and we would have been too late.

Just as we reached Harry's side, at the end of the tunnel, the Incas, warned by my appearance at the top of the column, appeared above on the stairway, at the foot of which Harry had made his stand.

At the sight of Desirée Harry uttered a cry of joy, then gazed in astonishment as I appeared behind her.

"Run for your lives!" he shouted, pointing down the passage leading to the apartments beyond. As he spoke a shower of spears descended from above, rattling on the steps and on the ground beside us. I stooped to pick up two of them, and as Desirée and I darted forward into the passage, with Harry bringing up the rear, the Incas dashed down the stairway after us.

We found ourselves at once in the maze of lanes and passages leading to the royal apartments. That, I thought, was as good a goal as any; and, besides, the way led to the cavern where we had once before successfully withstood our enemies. But the way was not so easy to find.

Turn and twist about as we would, we could not shake off our pursuers. Harry kept urging me forward, but I was using every ounce of strength that was left to me. Desirée, too, was becoming weaker at every step, and I could hear Harry's cry of despair as she peceptibly faltered and slackened her pace.

I soon realized that we were no longer in the passage or group of passages that led to the royal apartments and the cavern beyond. But there was no time to seek our way; well enough if we went forward. We found ourselves in a narrow lane, strewn with rocks, crooked and winding.

Desirée stumbled and would have fallen but for my outstretched arm. A spear from behind whistled past my ear as we again bounded forward. Harry was shouting to us that the Incas were upon us.

I caught Desirée's arm and pulled her on with a last great effort. The lane became narrower still; we brushed the wall on either side, and I pushed Desirée ahead of me and followed behind. Suddenly she stopped short, turning to face me so suddenly that I was thrown against her, nearly knocking her down.

"Your spear!" she cried desperately. "I can go no farther," and she sank to the ground.

At the same moment there came a cry from Harry in the rear—a cry that held joy and wonder—and I turned to see him standing some distance away, gazing down the lane through which we had come.

"They've given up!" he called. "They're gone!"

And I saw that it was true. No sound came, and no Inca was to be seen.

Then, seeing Desirée on the ground, Harry ran to us and sprang to her side. "Desirée!" he cried, lifting her in his arms. She opened her eyes and smiled at him, and he kissed her many times—her hair, her lips, her eyes. Then he placed her gently on her feet, and, supporting her with his arm, moved forward slowly. I led the way.

The lane ahead of us was scarcely more than a crevice between the rocks; I squeezed my way through with difficulty. Then the walls ended abruptly, just when I had begun to think we could go no farther, and we found ourselves at the entrance to a cavern so large that no wall was to be seen on any side save the one behind us.

On the instant I guessed at the reason why the Incas had ceased their pursuit so abruptly, and I turned to Harry:

"I'm afraid we've jumped from the frying-pan into the fire. If this cavern holds anything like that other—you remember—"

"If it does, we shall see," he replied.

Supporting Desirée on either side, we struck out directly across the cavern, halting every few steps to listen for a sound, either of the Incas, which we feared, or of running water, which we desired. We heard neither. All was blackness and the most complete silence.

Then I became aware, for the first time, of intolerable pains shooting up through my legs into my body. The danger past, reason returned and feeling. I could not suppress a low cry, wrung inexorably from my chest, and I halted, leaning my whole weight on Desirée's shoulder.

"What is it?" she cried, and for answer—though I strained every atom of my will and strength to prevent it—I toppled to the ground, dragging her with me.

What followed came to me as in a dream, though I was not wholly unconscious. I was aware that Harry and Desirée were bending over me; then I felt my head and shoulders being lifted from the ground, and a soft, warm arm supporting me.

A minute passed, or an hour—I did not know—and I felt hot drops of moisture fall on my cheek. I struggled to open my eyes, and saw Desirée's face quite near my own; my head was resting on her shoulder. She was weeping silently, and great tears rolled down her cheeks unrestrained.

To have seen the sun or stars shining down upon me would not have astonished me more. I gazed at her a long moment in silence; she saw that I did so, but made no effort to turn her head or avoid my gaze. Finally I found my tongue.

"Where is Harry?" I asked.

"He is gone to look for water," she replied; and, curiously enough, her voice was quite steady.

I smiled.

"It is useless. I am done for!"

"That isn't true," she denied, in a voice almost of anger. "You will get well. You are—injured badly—" After a short pause she added, "for me."

There was a long silence—I thought it hardly worth while to contradict her—and then I said simply, "Why are you crying, Desirée?"

She looked at me as though she had not heard; then, after another silence, her voice came, so low that it barely reached my ears:

"For this—and for what might have been, my friend."

"But you have said—"

"I know! Would you make me doubt again? Do not! Ah"—

she passed her hand gently over my forehead and touched the tips of her fingers to my burning eyes—"you must have cared for me in that other world. I will not doubt it; unless you speak, and you must not. Nothing would have been too high for us. We could have opened any door—even the door to happiness."

"But you said once—forgive me if I remind you of it now—you said that you are—you called yourself 'La Marana.'"

She shrank back, exclaiming: "Paul! Indeed, I need to forgive you!"

"Still, it is true," I persisted, turning to look at her. The movement caused me to halt, closing my eyes, while a great wave of pain swept over me from head to foot. Then I went on: "Could you expect to confine your heart? You say we could have opened any door—well, tell me, what could we have done, you and I?"

"But that is what I do not think of!" cried Desirée impatiently. "I would perhaps have placed my hand on your heart, as I do now; you would perhaps have fought for me, as you have done. I might even—" She hesitated, while the ghost of a smile that had died before it reached the light appeared on her lips, as her head was lowered close, quite close, to mine.

A long moment, and then, "Must I ask for it?" I breathed.

She jerked her head up sharply.

"You do not want it," she said dryly.

I raised my hand, groping for her fingers, but could not find them. She saw, and slowly, very slowly, her hand crept to mine and was caught and held there.

"Desirée—I want it," I said half fiercely, and I forgot my pain and our danger—forgot everything but her white face in dim outline above me, and her eyes, glowing and tender against her wish, and her hand that nestled in my hand. "Be merciful to me—I want it as I have never wanted anything in my life. Desirée, I love you."

At that I felt her hand move quickly, as for freedom, but I held it fast. And then slowly her head was lowered. I waited breathlessly. I felt her quick breath on my face, and the next moment her lips had found my lips, hot and dry, and remained there.

Then she raised her head, saying tremulously:

"That was my soul, and it is the first time it has ever escaped me."

At the same instant we were startled by the sound of Harry's voice in the darkness:

"Desirée! Where are you?"

I waited for her to answer, but she was silent, and I called out to him our direction. A moment later his form appeared at a distance, and soon he had joined us.

"How about it, old man?" he asked, bending over me.

Then he told us that he had found no water. He had explored two sides of the cavern, one at a distance of half a mile or more, and was crossing to find the third when he had called to us.

"But there is little use," he finished gloomily. "The place is silent as the grave. If there were water we would hear it. I can't even find an exit except the crevice that let us in."

Desirée's hand was still in mine.

"It may be—perhaps I can go with you," I suggested. But he would not hear of it, and set out again alone in the opposite direction to that which he had taken previously.

In a few minutes he returned, reporting no better success than before. On that side, he said, the wall of the cavern was quite close. There was no sign anywhere of water; but to the left there were several narrow lanes leading at angles whose sides were nearly parallel to each other, and some distance to the right there was a broad and clear passage sloping downward directly away from the cavern.

"Is the passage straight?" I asked, struck with a sudden idea. "Could you see far within?"

"A hundred feet or so," was the answer. "Why? Shall we follow it? Can you walk?"

"I think so," I answered. "At any rate, I must find some water soon or quit the game. But that isn't why I asked. Perhaps it explains the sudden disappearance of the Incas."

They knew they couldn't follow us through that narrow crevice; what if they have made for the passage?"

Harry grumbled that we had enough trouble without trying to borrow more.

We decided to wait a little longer before starting out from the cavern; Harry helped me to my feet to give them a trial, and though I was able to stand it was only by a tremendous effort and exertion of the will.

"Not yet," I murmured between clenched teeth, and again Desirée sat on the hard rock and supported my head and shoulders in her arms, despite my earnest remonstrances. Harry stood before us, leaning on his spear.

Soon he left us again, departing in the direction of the crevice by which we had entered; I detected his uneasiness in the tone with which he directed us to keep a lookout around in every direction.

"We could move to the wall," I had suggested; but he shook his head, saying that where we were we at least had room to turn.

When he had gone Desirée and I sat silent for many minutes. Then I tried to rise, insisting that she must be exhausted with the long strain she had undergone, but she denied it vehemently, and refused to allow me to move.

"It is little enough," she said; and though I but half understood her, I made no answer.

I myself was convinced that we were at last near the end. It was certain that the Incas had merely delayed, not abandoned, the pursuit, and our powers and means of resistance had been worn to nothing.

Our curious apathy and half indifference spoke for itself; it was as though we had at length recognized the hand of fate and seen the futility of further struggle. For, weak and injured as I was, I still had strength in me; it was a listlessness of the brain and hopelessness of the heart that made me content to lie and wait for whatever might come.

The state of my feelings toward Desirée were even then elusive; they are more so now. I had told her I loved her; well, I had told many women that. But Desirée had moved me; with her it was not the same—that I felt. I had never so admired a woman, and the thrill of that kiss is in me yet; I can recall it and tremble under its power by merely closing my eyes.

Her warm hand, pressed tightly in my own, seemed to send an electric communication to every nerve in my body and eased my suffering and stilled my pain. That, I know, is not love; and perhaps I was mistaken when I imagined that it was there.

"Are you asleep?" she asked presently, after I had lain perfectly quiet for many minutes. Her voice was so low that it entered my ear as the faintest breath.

"Hardly," I answered. "To tell the truth, I expect never to sleep again—I suppose you understand me. I can't say why—I feel it."

Desirée nodded.

"Do you remember, Paul, what I said that evening on the mountain?" Then—I suppose my face must have betrayed my thought—she added quickly: "Oh, I didn't mean that—other thing. I said this mountain would be my grave, do you remember? You see, I knew."

I started to reply, but was interrupted by Harry, calling to ask where we were. I answered, and soon he had joined us and seated himself beside Desirée on the ground.

"I found nothing," was all he said, wearily, and he lay back and closed his eyes, resting his head on his hands.

The minutes passed slowly. Desirée and I talked in low tones; Harry moved about uneasily on his hard bed, saying nothing. Finally, despite Desirée's energetic protests, I rose to my knees and insisted that she rest herself. We seemed none of us to be scarcely aware of what we were doing; our movements had a curious purposelessness about them that gave the thing an appearance of unreality—I know not what; it comes to my memory as some indistinct and haunting nightmare.

Suddenly, as I sat gazing dully into the semidarkness of the cavern, I saw that which drove the apathy from my brain with a sudden shock, at the same time paralyzing my senses. I strained my eyes ahead; there could be no doubt of it; that black, slowly moving line was a band of Incas creeping toward us silently, on their knees, through the darkness. Glancing to either side I saw that the line extended completely around us, to the right and left.

The sight seemed to paralyze me. I tried to call to Harry—no sound came from my eager lips. I tried to put out my hand to rouse him and to pick up my spear; my arms remained motionless at my side.

Desirée lay close beside me; I could not even turn my head to see if she, too, saw, but kept my eyes, as though fascinated, on that silent black line approaching through the darkness.

"Will they leap now—now—now?" I asked myself with every beat of my pulse.

It could not be much longer—they were now so close that each black, tense form was in clear outline not fifty feet away.

Chapter XXIII.

WE ARE TWO.

Whether I would have been able to rouse myself to action before the shock of the assault was actually upon us, I shall never know.

It was not fear that held me, for I felt none; I think that dimly and half unconsciously I saw in that black line, silently creeping upon us, the final and inexorable approach of the remorseless fate that had pursued us ever since we had dashed after Desirée into the cave of the devil, rendering our every effort futile, our most desperate struggles the laughing-stock of the gods.

I was not even conscious of danger. I sat as in a stupor.

But action came, though not from me, so suddenly that I scarcely knew what had happened. There was a cry from Desirée. Harry sprang to his feet. The Incas leaped forward.

I felt myself jerked violently from the ground, and a spear was thrust into my hand. Harry's form flashed past me, shouting to me to follow. Desirée was at his heels; but I saw her halt and turn to me, and I, too, sprang forward.

Harry's spear whirled about his head, leaving a gap in the black line that was now upon us. Through it we plunged. The Incas turned and came at us from behind; one whose hands were upon Desirée got my spear in his throat and sank to the ground.

"Cross to the left!" Harry yelled. He was fighting them off from every direction at once.

I turned, calling to Desirée to follow, and dashed across the cavern. We saw the wall just ahead, broken and rugged. Again turning I called to Harry, but could not see him for the black forms on every side, and I was starting to his rescue when I saw him plunge toward us, cutting his way through the solid mass of Incas as though they had been stalks of corn. He was not a man, but a demon possessed.

"Go on," he shouted. "I'll make it!"

Then I turned and ran with Desirée to the wall. We followed it a short distance before we reached one of the lanes of which Harry had spoken; at its entrance he joined us, still bidding us to leave him to cover our retreat.

Once within the narrow lane his task was easier. Boulders and projecting rocks obstructed our progress, but they were even greater obstacles to those who pursued us. Still they rushed forward, only to be hurled back by the point of Harry's spear. Once, turning, I saw him pick one of them up bodily and toss him whirling through the air into the very faces of his comrades.

I had all I could do with Desirée and myself. Many times I scrambled up the steep face of some boulder and, after pulling her up safely after me, let her down again on the other side. Then I returned to see that Harry got over safely, and often he made it barely by inches, while flying spears struck the rock on every side.

It is a wonder to me now that I was able even to stand, after my experience on the spiral stairway in the column. The soles of my feet and the palms of my hands were baked black as the Incas themselves. Blisters covered my body from head to foot, swelling, indescribably painful.

Every step I took made me clench my teeth to keep from sinking in a faint to the ground; I expected always that the next would be my last—but somehow I struggled onward. It was the thought of Desirée, I think, that held me up, and Harry.

Suddenly a shout came from Harry that the Incas had abandoned the pursuit. It struck me almost as a matter of indifference; nor was I affected when almost immediately afterward he called that he had been mistaken and that they had rushed forward with renewed fury and in greater numbers.

"It is only a matter of time now," I said to Desirée, and she nodded.

Still we went forward. The land had carried us straight away from the cavern, without a turn. Its walls were the roughest I had seen, and often a boulder which lay across our path presented a serrated face that looked as though it had but just been broken from the wall above. Still the stone was comparatively soft—time had not yet worked its leveling finger on the surfaces that surrounded us.

We were standing on one of these boulders when Harry came running toward us.

"They're stopped," he cried gleefully, "at least for a little. A piece of rock as big as a house gently slid from above onto their precious heads. It may have blocked them off completely."

We hurried forward then; Harry helped Desirée, while I painfully brought up the rear. At every few steps they were forced to halt and wait for me, though I did my utmost to keep us with them. Harry had taken my spear that I might have both hands to help me over the rocks.

Climbing, sliding, jumping, we left the Incas behind; no sound came from the rear. I began to think that they had really been completely shut off, and several times opened my mouth to call to Harry to ask him if it would not be safe to halt; for every movement I made was torture. But each time I choked back the cry; he thought it was necessary to go on and I followed.

This lasted I know not how long; I was staggering and reeling forward like a drunken man, so little aware of what I was doing that when Harry and Desirée finally stopped at the beginning of a level, unbroken stretch in the lane, I stumbled directly against them before I knew they had halted.

"Go on!" I gasped, struggling to my feet in a mania.

Harry stooped over to assist me and set me with my back resting against the wall. Desirée supported herself near by, scarcely able to stand.

"We can go no farther," said Harry. "If they come—"

As he spoke I became aware of a curious movement in the wall opposite—a movement as of the wall itself. At first I thought it a delusion produced by my disordered brain, but when I saw Desirée's astonished gaze following mine, and heard Harry's cry of wonder as he turned and saw it also, I knew the thing was real.

A great portion of the wall, the entire side of the passage for a length of a hundred feet or more, was sliding slowly downward. Glancing above I saw a space of several feet where the rock had departed from its bed. The only noise audible was a low, grating sound like the slow grinding of a gigantic millstone.

None of us moved—if there were danger we would seem to have welcomed it. Suddenly the great mass of rock appeared to halt in its downward movement and hang as though suspended; then with a sudden jerk it seemed to free itself, swaying ponderously toward us; and the next moment it had fallen straight down into some abyss below, thundering, tumbling, sliding with terrific velocity.

There was a deafening roar under our feet, the ground rocked as from an earthquake, and it seemed as though the wall against which we stood was about to fall in upon us. Dust and fragments of rock filled the air on every side, and one huge boulder, detached from the roof above, came tumbling at our feet, missing us by inches.

We were completely stunned by the cataclysm, but in a moment Harry had recovered and run to the edge of the chasm opposite thus suddenly formed. Desirée and I followed.

There was nothing to be seen save the blackness of space. Immediately before us was an apparently bottomless abyss, black and terrifying; the side descended straight down from our feet. Looking across we could see dimly a wall some distance away, smooth and with a faint whiteness. On either side of us other walls extended to meet the farther wall, smooth and polished as glass.

"The Incas didn't do that, I hope," said Harry, turning to me.

"Hardly," I answered; and in my absorbing interest in the phenomenon before me I half forgot my pain.

I moved to the edge of one of the walls extending at right angles to the passage, but there was little to be made of it.

It was of soft limestone, and most probably the portion that had disappeared was granite, carried away by the force of its own weight.

"We are like to be buried," I observed, returning to Harry and Desirée. "Though for that matter, even that can hardly frighten us now."

"For my part," said Harry, with a curious gravity beneath the apparent lightness of his words, "I have always admired the death of Porthos. Let it come, and welcome."

"Are we to go further?" put in Desirée.

Just as Harry opened his mouth to reply a more decisive answer came from another source. The rock that had fallen, obstructing the path of the Incas, must have left an opening that Harry had missed; or they had removed it—what matter?

In some way they had forced a passage, for as Desirée spoke a dozen spears whistled through the air past our heads and we looked up to see a swarm of Incas climbing and tumbling down the face of a boulder over which we had passed to reach our resting-place.

I have said that we had halted in a level, unbroken stretch that still led some distance ahead of us. At its farther end could be seen a group of rocks and boulders completely choking the lane, Beyond, other rocks arose to a still greater height—the way appeared to be impassable.

But there was no time for deliberation or the weighing of chances, and we turned and made for the pile of rocks, with the Incas rushing after us.

There Desirée and I halted in despair, but with a great oath Harry brushed us aside and leaped upon a rock higher than his head with incredible agility. Then, lying flat on his face and extending his arms downward over the edge, he pulled first Desirée, then myself, up after him. The whole performance had occupied a scant two seconds, and, waiting only to pick up the three spears he had thrown up the sloping surface of the rock to another yet higher and steeper.

"Why don't we hold them here?" I demanded. "They could never come up that rock with us on top."

Harry looked at me.

"Spears," he said briefly; and, of course, he was right. They would have picked us off like birds on a limb.

We scaled the second rock with extreme difficulty, Harry assisting both Desirée and me; and as we stood upright on its top I saw the Incas scrambling over the edge of the one below. Two or three of them had already started to cross; many more were coming up from behind; and one, as he made the top and arose to his feet, braced himself on the sloping rock and raised a spear high above his head.

At sight of him I started, crying to Harry and Desirée. They turned.

"The king!" I shouted; and I saw a shudder of terror run over Desirée's face as she, too, recognized the black form below. At the same instant the spear darted forward from the hand of the Child of the Sun, but it landed harmlessly against the rock several feet away.

The next moment the Inca king had bounded across the rock toward us, followed by a score of others.

I was minded to try my luck with his own weapon, but we had no spears to waste, and Harry was dragging Desirée forward and shouting to me to follow. I turned and ran after them, and just as we let ourselves down into a narrow crevice below the Incas appeared over the edge of the rock behind.

Somehow we scrambled forward, with the Incas at our heels. Sharp corners of projecting rocks bruised our faces and bodies; once my leg bent double under me as I fell from a ledge onto a boulder below, and I thought it was broken; but Harry jerked me to my feet and I struggled on.

Harry seemed possessed of the strength of ten men and the heart of a thousand. He pulled Desirée and me up and over boulders and rocks as though we had been feathers; the Lord knows how he got there himself! Half of the time he carried Desirée; the other half he supported me. His energy and exertions were titanic; even in the desperate excitement of our retreat I found time to marvel at it.

We did not gain an inch; our pursuers kept close behind us; but we held our own. Now and then a stray spear came hurtling through the air or struck the rock near us, but they were infrequent and we were not hit.

One, flying past my head, stuck in a crevice of the rock and I grasped the shaft to pull it out, but abandoned my effort when I heard Harry shouting to me from the front to come to his aid.

He and Desirée were standing on the rim of a ledge that stood high above the ground of the passage. At its foot began a level stretch leading straight ahead as far as we could see.

"We must lift her down," Harry was saying.

He let himself over the ledge, hung by his hands, and dropped. "All right!" he called from below; and I lay flat on the rock while Desirée scrambled over the edge, holding to my hands. For a moment I held her suspended in my outstretched arms; then, at a word from Harry, I let her drop. Another moment and I was over myself, knocking Harry to the ground and tumbling on top of him as he stood beneath to break my fall.

By then the Incas had reached the top of the ledge above us, and we turned and raced down the long stretch ahead. I was in front; Harry came behind with Desirée.

Suddenly, as I ran, I felt a curious trembling of the ground beneath my feet, similar to the vibrations of a bridge at the passing of a heavy load.

Then the ground actually swayed beneath me; and, realizing the danger, I sent a desperate shout to Harry over my shoulder and bounded forward. He was at my side on the instant, with Desirée in his arms.

The ground rocked beneath our feet like a ship in a storm; and, just as I thought we were gone, my foot touched firm rock as I passed a yawning crevice a foot wide under me.

One more leap to safety, and we turned just in time to see

the floor of the passage which we had traversed disappear into some abyss beneath with a shattering roar.

We stood at the very edge of the chasm thus suddenly formed, gazing at each other in silent wonder and awe.

"The beggars are stopped now," said Harry finally. "That break in the game is ours."

Looking back across the chasm, we saw the Incas tumbling by twos and threes over the boulder on the other side. As they saw the yawning abyss that separated them from their prey they stopped short and gazed across in profound astonishment.

Others came to join them, until there were several hundred of the black, ugly forms huddled together on the opposite rim of the chasm, a hundred feet away.

I ran over the group with a keen eye, seeking the figure of the Inca king, and soon my search was successful. He stood a step in front of the others, a little to the right. I pointed him out to Harry and Desirée.

"It's up to him to walk right out again," said Harry.

Desirée shivered, and proceeded to send her last invitation to the devil.

Turning suddenly, she grasped Harry's spear and tore it from his hand. Before we realized her purpose, she stepped forward until her foot rested on the very edge of the chasm, and had hurled the spear across straight at the Inca king.

It missed him, but struck another Inca standing near full in the breast. Quick as lightning the king turned, grasped the shaft of the spear, and pulled it forth, and with his white teeth gleaming in a snarl of furious hate, sent it whistling through the air straight at Desirée.

Harry and I sprang forward with a shout of warning; Desirée stood motionless as a statue. We grasped her frantically and pulled her back, but too late.

She came, but only to fall lifeless into our arms with the spear buried deep in her white throat.

We laid her on the ground and knelt beside her for a moment, then Harry arose to his feet with a face white as death; and I uttered a silent and vengeful prayer as I saw him level a spear at the Inca king across the chasm. But it went wide of its mark, striking the ground at his feet.

"There was another!" cried Harry, and soon he had found it where it lay on the ground and sent it, too, hurtling across.

This time he missed by inches. The spear flew just past the shoulder of the king and caught one who stood behind him full in the face. The stricken savage threw his arms spasmodically above his head, reeling forward against the king.

There was a startled movement along the black line; hands were outstretched in a vain effort at rescue; a savage cry burst from Harry's lips, and the next instant the king had toppled over the edge of the chasm and fallen into the bottomless pit below.

Harry turned, quivering from head to foot.

"Little enough," he said between his teeth, and again he knelt beside the body of Desirée and took her in his arms.

But her fate spoke eloquently of our own danger, and I roused him to action. Together we picked up the form of our dead comrade and carried it to the rear. I hesitated to pull forth the barbed head of the spear, and instead broke off the shaft, leaving the point buried in the soft throat, from which a crimson line extended over the white shoulder.

A short distance ahead we came to a projecting boulder, and behind that we gently laid her on the hard rock. Neither of us had spoken a word. Harry's lips were locked tightly together; a lump rose in my throat, choking all utterance and filling my eyes with tears.

Harry knelt beside the white form and, gathering it gently in his arms, held it against his breast. I stood at his side, gazing down at him in mute sympathy and sorrow.

For a long minute there was silence—a most intense silence throughout the cavern, during which the painful throbbing of my heart was plainly audible; then Harry murmured, in a voice of the utmost tenderness: "Desirée!" And again, "Desirée! Desirée!" until I half expected the very strength and sweetness of his emotion to bring our comrade back to life.

Suddenly, with a quick, impulsive movement, he raised his head to glance at me.

"She loved you," he said; and though there was neither jealousy nor anger in his voice, somehow I could not meet his gaze.

"She loved you," he repeated in a tone half of wonder. "And you—you—"

I answered his eyes.

"She was yours," I said, with a touch of bitterness that persuaded him of the truth. "All her beauty, all her loveliness, all her charm, to be buried—Ah! God help us—"

My voice broke, and I knelt on the ground beside Harry and pressed my lips to the white forehead and golden hair of what had been Le Mire.

Thus we remained for a long time.

It was hard to believe that death had in reality taken possession of the still form stretched as in repose before us. Her body, still warm, seemed quivering with the instinct of life; but the eyes were not the eyes of Desirée. I closed them, and arranged the tangled mass of hair as well as possible over her shoulders. As I did so the air, set in motion by my hand, caused some of the golden strands to tremble gently across her lips; and Harry bent forward with a painful eagerness, thinking that she had breathed.

"Dearest," he murmured, "dearest, speak to me!"

His hand sought her swelling bosom gropingly; and his eyes, as they looked pleadingly even into mine, shot into my heart and unnerved me.

I rose to my feet, scarcely able to stand, and moved away.

But the fate that had finally intervened for us—too late, alas! for one—did not leave us long with our dead. Even now I do not know what happened; at the time I knew even less. Harry told me afterward that the first shock came at the instant he had taken Desirée in his arms and pressed his lips to hers.

I had crossed to the other side of the passage and was

gazing back toward the chasm at the Incas on the other side, when again I felt the ground, absolutely without warning, tremble violently under my feet. At the same moment there was a low, curious rumble as of the thundering of distant cannon.

I sprang toward Harry with a cry of alarm, and had crossed about to the middle of the passage, when a deafening roar smote my ear, and the entire wall of the cavern appeared to be falling in upon us. At the same time the ground seemed to sink directly away beneath my feet with an easy, rocking motion as of a wave of the ocean. Then I felt myself plunging downward with a velocity that stunned my senses and took away my breath; and then all was confusion and chaos—and oblivion.

When I awoke I was lying flat on my back, and Harry was kneeling at my side. I opened my eyes, and felt that it would be impossible to make a greater exertion.

"Paul!" cried Harry. "Speak to me! Not you, too—I shall go mad!"

He told me afterward that I had lain unconscious for many hours, but that appeared to be all that he knew. How far we had fallen, or how he had found me, or how he himself had escaped being crushed to pieces by the falling rock, he was unable to say; and I concluded that he, too, had been rendered unconscious by the fall, and for some time dazed and bewildered by the shock.

Well! We were alive—that was all.

For we were weak and faint from hunger and fatigue, and one mass of bruises and blisters from head to foot. And we had had no water for something like twenty-four hours. Heaven only knows where we found the energy to rise and go in search of it; it is incredible that any creatures in such a pitiable and miserable condition as we were could have been propelled by hope, unless it is indeed immortal.

Half walking, half crawling, we went forward.

The place where we had found ourselves was a jumbled mass of boulders and broken rock, but we soon discovered a passage, level and straight as any tunnel built by man.

Down this we made our way. Every few feet we stopped to rest. Neither of us spoke a word. I really had no sense of any purpose in our progress; I crept on exactly as some animals, wounded to death, move on and on until there is no longer strength for another step, when they lie down for the final breath.

We saw no water nor promise of any; nothing save the long stretch of dim vista ahead and the grim, black walls on either side. That, I think, for hours; it seemed to me then for years.

I dragged one leg after the other with infinite effort and pain; Harry was ahead, and sometimes, glancing back over his shoulder to find me at some distance behind, he would turn over and lie on his back till I approached. Then again to his knees and again forward. Neither of us spoke.

Suddenly, at a great distance down the passage, much further than I had been able to see before, I saw what appeared to be a white wall extending directly across our path.

I called to Harry and pointed it out to him. He nodded vaguely, as though in wonder that I should have troubled him about so slight an object of interest, and crawled on.

But the white wall became whiter still, and soon I saw that it was not a wall. A wild hope surged through me; I felt the blood mount dizzily to my head, and I stilled the clamor that beat at my temples by an extreme effort of the will. "It can't be," I said to myself aloud, over and over; "it can't be, it can't be."

Harry turned, and his face was as white as when he had knelt by the body of Desirée, and his eye was wild.

"You fool," he roared, "it is!"

We went faster then. Another hundred yards, and the thing was certain; there it was before us. We scrambled to our feet and tried to run; I reeled and fell, then picked myself up again and followed Harry, who had not even halted as I had fallen. The mouth of the passage was now but a few feet away; I reached Harry's side, blinking and stunned with amazement and the incredible wonder of it.

I tried to shout, to cry aloud to the heavens, but a great lump in my throat choked me and my head was singing dizzily.

Harry, at my side, was crying like a child, with great tears streaming down his face, as together we staggered forth from the mouth of the passage into the bright and dazzling sunshine of the Andes.

Chapter XXIV.

CONCLUSION.

Never, I believe, were misery and joy so curiously mingled in the human breast as when Harry and I stood— barely able to stand—gazing speechlessly at the world that had so long been hidden from us.

We had found the light, but had lost Desirée. We were alive, but so near to death that our first breath of the mountain air was like to be our last.

The details of our painful journey down the mountain, over the rocks and crags, and through rushing torrents that more than once swept us from our feet, cannot be written, for I do not know them.

The memory of the thing is but an indistinct nightmare of suffering. But the blind luck that seemed to have fallen over our shoulders as a protecting mantle at the death of Desirée stayed with us; and after endless hours of incredible toil and labor, we came to a narrow pass leading at right angles to our course.

Night was ready to fall over the bleak and barren mountain as we entered it. Darkness had long since overtaken us, when we saw at a distance a large clearing, in the middle of which lights shone from the windows of a large house whose dim and shadowy outline appeared to us surrounded by a halo of peace.

But we were nearly forced to fight for it. The proprietor of the *hacienda* himself answered our none too gentle knock at the door, and he had no sooner caught sight of us than he let out a yell as though he had seen the devil in person, and slammed the door violently in our faces. Indeed, we were hardly recognizable as men.

Naked, black, bruised, and bleeding, covered with hair on our faces and parts of our bodies—mine, of recent growth, stubby and stiff—our appearance would have justified almost any suspicion.

But we hammered again on the door, and I set forth our

pedigree and plight in as few words as possible. Reassured, perhaps, by my excellent Spanish—which could not, of course, be the tongue of the devil—and convinced by our pitiable condition of our inability to do him any harm, he at length reopened the door and gave us admittance.

When we had succeeded in allaying his suspicions concerning our identity—though I was careful not to alarm his superstitions by mentioning the cave of the devil, which, I thought, was probably well known to him—he lost no time in displaying his humanity.

Calling in some *hombres* from the rear of the *hacienda*, he gave them ample instructions, with medicine and food, and an hour later Harry and I were lying side by side in his own bed—a rude affair, but infinitely better than granite—refreshed, bandaged, and as comfortable as their kindly ministrations could make us.

The old Spaniard was a direct descendant of the good Samaritan—despite the slight difference in nationality. For many weeks he nursed us and fed us and coaxed back the spark of life in our exhausted and wounded bodies.

Our last ounce of strength seemed to have been used up in our desperate struggle down the side of the mountain; for many days we lay on our backs absolutely unable to move a muscle and barely conscious of life.

But the spark revived and fluttered. The day came when we could hobble, with his assistance, to the door of the *hacienda* and sit for hours in the invigorating sunshine; and thenceforward our convalescence proceeded rapidly. Color came to our cheeks and light to our eyes; and one sunny afternoon it was decided that we should set out for Cerro de Pasco on the following day.

Harry proposed a postponement of our departure for two days, saying that he wished to make an excursion up the mountain. I understood him at once.

"It would be useless," I declared. "You would find nothing."

"But she was with us when we fell," he persisted, not

bothering to pretend that he did not understand me. "She came—it must be near where we landed."

"That isn't it," I explained. "Have you forgotten that we have been here for over a month? You would find nothing."

As he grasped my thought his face went white and he was silent. So on the following morning we departed.

Our host furnished us with food, clothing, mules, and an *arriero,* not to mention a sorrowful farewell and a hearty blessing. From the door of the *hacienda* he waved his sombrero as we disappeared around a bend in the mountain-pass; we had, perhaps, been a welcome interruption in the monotony of his lonely existence.

We were led upward for many miles until we found ourselves again in the region of perpetual snow. There we set our faces to the south. From the *arriero* we tried to learn how far we then were from the cave of the devil, but to our surprise were informed that he had never heard of the thing.

We could see that the question made him more than a little suspicious of us; often, when he thought himself unobserved, I caught him eyeing us askance with something nearly approaching terror.

We journeyed southward for eleven days; on the morning of the twelfth we saw below us our goal. Six hours later we had entered the same street of Cerro de Pasco through which we had passed formerly with light hearts; and the heart which had been gayest of all we had left behind us, stilled forever, somewhere beneath the mountain of stone which she had herself chosen for her tomb.

Almost the first person we saw was none other than Felipe, the *arriero.* He sat on the steps of the hotel portico as we rode up on our mules. Dismounting, I caught sight of his white face and staring eyes as he rose slowly to his feet, gazing at us as though fascinated.

I opened my mouth to call to him, but before the words left my lips he had let out an ear-splitting yell of terror and bounded down the steps and past us, with arms flying in every direction, running like one possessed. Nor did he return during the few hours that we remained at the hotel.

Two days later found us boarding the yacht at Callao. When I had discovered, to my profound astonishment, at the *hacienda,* that another year had taken us as far as the tenth day of March, I had greatly doubted if we should find Captain Harris still waiting for us. But there he was; and he had not even put himself to the trouble of becoming uneasy about us.

As he himself put it that night in the cabin, over a bottle of wine, he "didn't know but what the *señora* had decided to take the Andes home for a mantel ornament, and was engaged in the little matter of transportation."

But when I informed him that "the *señora"* was no more, his face grew sober with genuine regret and sorrow. He had many good things to say of her then; it appeared that she had really touched his salty old heart.

"She was a gentle lady," said the worthy captain; and I smiled to think how Desirée herself would have smiled at such a characterization of the great Le Mire.

We at once made for San Francisco. There, at a loss, I disposed of the remainder of the term of the lease on the yacht, and we took the first train for the East.

Four days later we were in New York, after a journey saddened by thoughts of the one who had left us to return alone.

It was, in fact, many months before the shadow of Desirée ceased to hover about the dark old mansion on lower Fifth Avenue, incongruous enough among the ancient halls and portraits of Lamars dead and gone in a day when La Marana herself had darted like a meteor into the hearts of their contemporaries.

That is, I suppose, properly the end of the story; but I cannot refrain from the opportunity to record a curious incident that has just befallen me. Some twenty minutes ago, as I was writing the last paragraph—I am seated in the library before a massive mahogany table, close to a window through which the September sun sends its golden rays—twenty minutes ago, as I say, Harry sauntered into the room and threw himself lazily into a large armchair on the other side of the table.

I looked up with a nod of greeting, while he sat and eyed me impatiently for some seconds.

"Aren't you coming with me down to Southampton?" he asked finally.

"What time do you leave?" I inquired, without looking up."

"Eleven-thirty."

"What's on?"

"Freddie Marston's Crocodiles and the Blues. It's going to be *some* polo."

I considered a moment. "Why, I guess I'll run down with you. I'm about through here."

"Good enough!" Harry arose to his feet and began idly fingering some of the sheets on the table before me. "What is all this silly rot, anyway?"

"My dear boy," I smiled, "you'll be sorry you called it silly rot when I tell you that it is a plain and honest tale of our own experiences."

"Must be deuced interesting," he observed. "More silly rot than ever."

"Others may not think so," I retorted, a little exasperated by his manner. "It surely will be sufficiently exciting to read of how we were buried with Desirée Le Mire under the Andes, and our encounters with the Incas, and our final escape, and—"

"Desirée *what?*" Harry interrupted.

"Desirée Le Mire," I replied very distinctly. "The great French dancer."

"Never heard of her," said Harry, looking at me as if he doubted my sanity.

"Never heard of Desirée, the woman you loved?" I almost shouted at him.

"The woman I—piffle! I say I never heard of her."

I gazed at him, trembling with high indignation. "I

suppose," I observed with infinite sarcasm, "that you will tell me next that you have never been in Peru?"

"Guilty," said Harry. "I never have."

"And that you never climbed Pike's Peak to see the sunrise?"

"Rahway, New Jersey, is my farthest west."

"And that you never dived with me from the top of a column one hundred feet high?"

"Not I. I retain a smattering of common sense."

"And that you did not avenge the death of Desirée by causing that of the Inca king?"

"So far as that Desirée woman is concerned," said Harry, and his tone began to show impatience, "I can only repeat that I have never heard of the creature. And"—he continued—"if you're trying to bamboozle a gullible world by concocting a tale as silly as your remarks to me would seem to indicate, I will say that as a cheap author you are taking undue liberties with your family, meaning myself. And what is more, if you dare to print the stuff I'll let the world know it's a rank fake."

This threat, delivered with the most awful resolution and sincerity, unnerved me completely, and I fell back in my chair in a swoon.

When I recovered Harry had gone to his polo game, leaving me behind, whereupon I seized my pen and hastened to set down in black and white that most remarkable conversation, that the reader may judge for himself between us.

For my part, I do swear that the story is true, on my word of honor as a cynic and a philosopher.

MORE MYSTERIOUS PLEASURES

HAROLD ADAMS
THE NAKED LIAR
When a sexy young widow is framed for the murder of her husband, Carl Wilcox comes through to help her fight off cops and big-city goons.
#420 $3.95

EARL DERR BIGGERS
THE HOUSE WITHOUT A KEY
Charlie Chan debuts in the Honolulu investigation of an expatriate Bostonian's murder.
#421 $3.95

JAMES M. CAIN
THE ENCHANTED ISLE
A beautiful runaway is involved in a deadly bank robbery in this posthumously published novel.
#415 $3.95

WILLIAM DeANDREA
THE LUNATIC FRINGE
Police Commissioner Teddy Roosevelt and Officer Dennis Muldoon comb 1896 New York for a missing exotic dancer who holds the key to the murder of a prominent political cartoonist.
#306 $3.95

DICK FRANCIS
THE SPORT OF QUEENS
The autobiography of the celebrated race jockey/crime novelist.
#410 $3.95

JOHN GARDNER
THE GARDEN OF WEAPONS
Big Herbie Kruger returns to East Berlin to uncover a double agent. He confronts his own past and life's only certainty—death.
#103 $4.50

JOE GORES
A TIME OF PREDATORS
When Paula Halstead kills herself after witnessing a horrid crime, her husband vows to avenge her death. Winner of the Edgar Allan Poe Award.
#215 $3.95

BRIAN GARFIELD

DEATH WISH
Paul Benjamin is a modern-day New York vigilante, stalking the rapist-killers who victimized his wife and daughter. The basis for the Charles Bronson movie.   #301 $3.95

DEATH SENTENCE
A riveting sequel to DEATH WISH. The action moves to Chicago as Paul Benjamin continues his heroic (or is it psychotic?) mission to make city streets safe.   #302 $3.95

TRIPWIRE
A crime novel set in the American West of the late 1800s. Boag, a black outlaw, seeks revenge on the white cohorts who crossed him and left him for dead. "One of the most compelling characters in recent fiction"—Robert Ludlum.   #303 $3.95

FEAR IN A HANDFUL OF DUST
Four psychiatrists, three men and a woman, struggle across the blazing Arizona desert—pursued by a fanatic killer they themselves have judged insane. "Unique and disturbing"—Alfred Coppel.   #304 $3.95

NAT HENTOFF

BLUES FOR CHARLIE DARWIN
Gritty, colorful Greenwich Village sets the scene for Noah Green and Sam MacKibbon, two street-wise New York cops who are as at home in the Village's jazz clubs as they are at a homicide scene.
#208 $3.95

THE MAN FROM INTERNAL AFFAIRS
Detective Noah Green wants to know who's stuffing corpses into East Village garbage cans . . . and who's lying about him to the Internal Affairs Division.   #409 $3.95

PATRICIA HIGHSMITH

THE BLUNDERER
An unhappy husband attempts to kill his wife by applying the murderous methods of another man. When things go wrong, he pays a visit to the more successful killer—a dreadful error.   #305 $3.95

ELMORE LEONARD

THE HUNTED
Long out of print, this 1974 novel by the author of *Glitz* details the attempts of a man to escape killers from his past.   #401 $3.95

MR. MAJESTYK
Sometimes bad guys can push a good man too far, and when that good guy is a Special Forces veteran, everyone had better duck.
#402 $3.95

THE BIG BOUNCE
Suspense and black comedy are cleverly combined in this tale of a dangerous drifter's affair with a beautiful woman out for kicks.
#403 $3.95

STUART KAMINSKY'S "TOBY PETERS" SERIES
NEVER CROSS A VAMPIRE
When Bela Lugosi receives a dead bat in the mail, Toby tries to catch the prankster. But Toby's time is at a premium because he's also trying to clear William Faulkner of a murder charge! #107 $3.95

HIGH MIDNIGHT
When Gary Cooper and Ernest Hemingway come to Toby for protection, he tries to save them from vicious blackmailers. #106 $3.95

HE DONE HER WRONG
Someone has stolen Mae West's autobiography, and when she asks Toby to come up and see her sometime, he doesn't know how deadly a visit it could be. #105 $3.95

BULLET FOR A STAR
Warner Brothers hires Toby Peters to clear the name of Errol Flynn, a blackmail victim with a penchant for young girls. The first novel in the acclaimed Hollywood-based private eye series. #308 $3.95

THE FALA FACTOR
Toby comes to the rescue of lady-in-distress Eleanor Roosevelt, and must match wits with a right-wing fanatic who is scheming to overthrow the U.S. Government. #309 $3.95

ED MCBAIN
SNOW WHITE AND ROSE RED
A beautiful heiress confined to a sanitarium engages Matthew Hope to free her—and her $650,000. #414 $3.95

PETER O'DONNELL
MODESTY BLAISE
Modesty and Willie Garvin must protect a shipment of diamonds from a gentleman about to murder his lover and an *un*civilized sheik. #216 $3.95

SABRE TOOTH
Modesty faces Willie's apparent betrayal and a modern-day Genghis Khan who wants her for his mercenary army. #217 $3.95

A TASTE FOR DEATH
Modesty and Willie are pitted against a giant enemy in the Sahara, where their only hope of escape is a blind girl whose time is running out. #218 $3.95

I, LUCIFER
Some people carry a nickname too far . . . like the maniac calling himself Lucifer. He's targeted 120 souls, and Modesty and Willie find they have a personal stake in stopping him. #219 $3.95

THE IMPOSSIBLE VIRGIN
Modesty fights for her soul when she and Willie attempt to rescue an albino girl from the evil Brunel, who lusts after the secret power of an idol called the Impossible Virgin. #220 $3.95

DAVID WILLIAMS' "MARK TREASURE" SERIES

UNHOLY WRIT

London financier Mark Treasure helps a friend reacquire some property. He stays to unravel the mystery when a Shakespeare manuscript is discovered and foul murder done.   #112 $3.95

TREASURE BY DEGREES

Mark Treasure discovers there's nothing funny about a board game called "Funny Farms." When he becomes involved in the takeover struggle for a small university, he also finds there's nothing funny about murder.   #113 $3.95